BOOMER'S GOLD

BOOMER'S GOLD

Jack Walker

Thorp Springs Press

Library of Congress Cataloging in Publication Data

Walker, Jack, 1915–
   Boomers' gold.

   I. Title.
PZ4.W178370i [PS3573.A425333] 813'.5'4 77-16196
ISBN 0-914476-74-2

THORP SPRINGS PRESS

3414 Robinson Ave.   1218 S. Austin
Austin, Texas   Amarillo, Texas
78722   79102

*To Jo N. and B.K.W. and all the other highrollers of this world who
get things done, when others say they can't be done.*

PREFACE

A cold winter wind blew across the plains of the Texas Panhandle that winter morning of January 11, 1926. The grama and buffalo grass along the Canadian river bent to its constant push. Across the endless acres, cattle grazed, intent only on a full belly.

Cowmen glanced anxiously at the blue north and hurried their chores. On the north bank of the Canadian, where the headquarters of the Beatenbow ranch sat in rugged splendor among the giant cottonwoods, old Granny Beatenbow, matriarch of the Beatenbow family hobbled to the gallery of the house and squinted weather-wise eyes into the cold wind. She tapped her cane impatiently, for her bones felt a storm brewing. Then she summoned her foreman and instructed him to lay in extra feed for the cattle and horses.

On the banks of Dixon creek, just south of the river, and a thirty minute horseback ride from the Beatenbow ranch, stood an alien thing in that windswept land. An oil derrick!

In a small tar paper shack by the derrick a crew of oil drillers cursed as they blew on cold hands and waited for the night shift to come on. The cables raised and lowered monotonously as the drill bit of *Dixon Creek No. 2* pounded its way relentlessly downward.

No living man could have known that less than one foot from its greedy tongue lay one of the great pools of oil in the earth!

For millions of years the huge mass of petroleum had lain unmolested, a slumbering, massive giant needing only the prick of a drill bit to awaken it to a swelling fury.

Then it happened!

Oil blew over the derrick! It began as an angry roar of a sleeping bear suddenly awakened, as escaping gas pushed thousands of pounds of drill tools up into the spiderwork of the wooden derrick, and tangled cables whipped and lashed as the entire structure tumbled to the earth.

Men scampered to safety and watched fearfully for the spark that could make the well an inferno. But the spark didn't come, and the men suddenly began to yell and laugh and curse. They slapped each other on the back, and forgot that they were cold and hungry and tired.

Five miles to the north the Beatenbow ranch foreman, a gaunt and weather-beaten old man, almost as old as Granny herself, saw the black tower rise from the earth as he rode in response to Granny's summons. He showed no surprise other than a slight narrowing of his eyes, but the cat-footed sorrel gelding he rode pointed his little fox ears inquisitively.

A cowboy carried the news of the gusher to the small cattle town of Panhandle, twenty-eight miles to the south. His horse was foaming with sweat when he arrived. The telegrapher at the Santa Fe station gave the cowboy a drink of whiskey and rubbed his horse down with a gunny sack.

Then he flashed the news to the farthest corners of the country!

CHAPTER I

Deafy Jones heard news of the oil strike just as he was finishing a shallow well for a wildcat driller in south Texas. Blake Terrell was in New Orleans when the news reached him, and he was immediately confronted with the problem of persuading a new and lovely young wife to forsake the gay night life of the town to accompany him to the strike before the lure of it drew him away without her.

But Blake Terrell was not a man to doubt himself, and he sent a wire to his superintendent in Granger, Texas, ordering men and equipment to the new site. Then he telephoned his daughter, Wendy, in New York and instructed her to meet him at the oil camp in two weeks.

In a small town some forty miles to the south of Oklahoma City, Kim Wingate, the only son of the late Kimball Z. Wingate, Sr., sat and glumly surveyed the room in which, except for three years of sporadic attendance and vague direction at the University of Oklahoma, he had spent most of his twenty-two years.

It was almost time to go. He looked at the one bag that remained in the room and a lump rose in his throat. In the bag was an envelope that contained a thousand dollars in bills of various denominations. Kim knew that the money had come from skimping on groceries, returning expensive gifts that his father had lavished on his mother over the years, and other sundry and surreptitious sources.

Kim protested vehemently when his mother had pressed the money on him. His share of the estate left by his father was more than adequate to finance any college career that he might choose, for his flamboyant father had left both him and his mother in far better circumstances than anyone could have expected, considering his affinity for anything involving chance—including betting on anything from a terrapin race to a prize fight. But evidently his career in law, which consisted mainly of defending the errant citizens of the small town of charges ranging from stealing chickens to murder, had been much more lucrative than anyone had suspected.

But his mother had been adamant about his taking the money. "It is terrible to be without money, Kimball," she had insisted. "Believe me, I know! Your father was one of the first in the land rush of 'eighty-nine' and I met him soon after. We had so little to begin with—. I was always frightened and—banks *do* fail—anyway please take this and keep it until you need it badly—if you ever do—." She didn't finish the sentence, but great tears welled in her eyes, and Kim took the envelope containing the money.

He wished for the thousandth time that he had not succumbed to his mother's constant harassment since his father's death to enter Stanford University Law School in California.

Law had absolutely no appeal for him; although many of the town people, including his mother, considered him the "spittin' image"of his father, Kim did not. In fact, Kim had no idea what he wanted to do with his life.

With a long sigh he lifted his tall, but slender, frame from the chair and picked up his bag. His two trunks had been sent ahead two days before, and the bag contained only a minimum amount of clothing, his toilet articles, and—his mother's money.

He had deliberately delayed in his room in order to avoid a lengthy farewell. As he descended the stairs he, with considerable effort, erased the glum look from his face and assumed the gay smile and fun-loving twinkle in his grey-blue eyes that was characteristic of him.

He gave "Old Kate," the enormously fat black woman who had been their cook since he could remember, a mighty hug. Then he turned to his mother who was waiting at the door. He started to say something, but found that he simply could not speak. He hugged her tightly, and kissed her on the cheek. Then, without a word, he strode out the door and down the walk where Caleb, Kate's husband and the Wingate handy-man, waited beside the Dodge touring car to drive him to Oklahoma City.

"All set, Mr. Kim?" Caleb grinned his toothless grin.

Kim nodded silently. As they drove away, he didn't look back at the imposing house, nor the well-kept lawn and hedge of which Caleb was so proud.

It was dark when they arrived at the depot in Oklahoma City. Kim had not spoken since he had left home. Caleb stopped the Dodge, and Kim got out and reached to shake Caleb's hand. Then he hugged the old Negro very hard and strode toward the depot.

At approximately the time Kim and Caleb left for Oklahoma City, the harassed stationmaster there was putting in frantic telephone calls to the local police. Since the discovery of oil in the Texas

Panhandle, two weeks before, trains going west had been crowded with rough, boisterous oil field workers on their way to the strike. Today, because of schedule difficulties, most of them had had to lay over for several hours, and the incoming trains kept bringing more until the station was overrun. They all seemed to have whiskey, and when the food ran out in the station cafe,the mob grew profane and unruly to the extent that regular passengers in the depot were protesting.

The arrival of the police only aggravated the mob. The most unruly were carted off to jail until it was full, but still the mob raged. Finally the police took the passengers who were not headed to the oil strike to a downtown hotel and left them there. Then they set up guards to confine the rest to the depot while the stationmaster hurriedly made plans to send a special train west in order to take the oil men to their destination.

Kim had arrived at the depot just as the sentries posted outside the doors were drawn away by a furor a hundred yards down the track.

He glanced briefly at the poster on the depot wall, noting that Charlie Chaplin in *Gold Rush* was playing at a local theatre.

He had heard that they were making movies in which you could hear the actors talking, but he hadn't seen one. Maybe in California he would.

Kim shifted his bag to his left hand and pushed open the depot door to be met by a tide of warm, stale air and a loud rabble of voices.

The waiting room was filled with men. Raucous laughter and obscenities boomed everywhere.

"Shut the door, you damned Arkansawyer!" someone yelled.

Kim quickly complied and then stepped hesitantly forward. He set his bag on the floor and looked for the ticket window. There was no one behind it. Kim stood indecisively for a moment. The temperature change was extremely noticeable. Outside, it was cold even for February. In the warm air of the depot, his wool topcoat was too much, and he removed it and folded it under his arm.

A red cap hurried by, and, because of the din that would have made it necessary to shout at the man, Kim stopped him by the simple method of taking his arm. At once the red cap cringed and attempted to pull free. Kim was surprised but held firmly. The Negro finally quit struggling. There was fear in his white rimmed eyes.

"Yassuh! Yassuh!" he babbled. "I ain't doin' nobody no harm, mister. Just gonna load some bags, suh!"

The man's body trembled, and Kim felt sorry for him. "I'm not going to hurt you," he said soothingly. "What's wrong with you?"

"Ain't nothin' the matter, suh!" the Negro said apologetically. "Just busy. That's all, suh. Just busy! Please let me go, suh! Don't mean no harm to nobody!"

"Of course, you don't!" Kim said soothingly. "And neither do I. I simply want to ask you a question."

For the first time the Negro looked at Kim and evidently was reassured by what he saw. He took a deep breath, and his trembling ceased. "Yas *suh!*" he said with relief in his voice. "Be *glad* to answer your questions, suh! Scuse me! Thought for a minute yo was one of dem oil boomers."

"What's an oil boomer?" Kim was puzzled.

"Dey's oil boomers," the Negro nodded at the men milling about the depot, and his eyes walled. "Dey drills oil wells—or somethin', and dey is sure *mean!*" He felt gingerly of a skinned cheek from which blood was oozing.

Kim looked again at the milling mob. They *were* talking in loud, excited voices. "Why are they here?" Kim asked.

"They done struck oil over in Texas," the Negro said. "These men is going there—up close to Amarillo. Dey been flockin' in dat direction for mos' a month now, and den today we had some train mixups, and dey been pilin' up here in de depot. We gettin' together a special now to haul em out, I *sho* will be glad when it leaves."

Kim smiled and the Negro grinned ruefully. "What was de question you wanted to ask me, suh?" the Negro asked.

"Never mind," Kim said kindly as he reached into his pocket. "You have already answered it."

Kim flipped a coin in the air, and the Negro grinned as he reached for it. But the black, pink-palmed hand never closed around the coin—a brown, hairy one snaked it out of the air before the Negro reached it.

A jeering laugh beside them startled both Kim and the Negro. Kim looked quickly at the man who had grabbed the coin. He was much taller and heavier than Kim and was dressed in heavy boots, greasy trousers, and sheepskin coat. Long, white teeth shone brilliantly in the dark, unshaven face. The deep, black eyes glittered evilly. Kim's glance swept back to the frightened Negro who tried to slip away, but the man grabbed him by the collar and twisted it brutally.

"Well, well! If it ain't my old friend, Rastus, again!" The man laughed, and it was an ugly sound.

"I was just leavin' suh." The Negro tried to wriggle free. There was stark terror in his eyes.

"Just leaving, he says!" the man jeered as he twisted the collar tighter, and his face darkened with fury. "I thought I told you once to get out of town, you black bastard!" he shouted.

The room suddenly quieted, and the stale tobacco smoke drifted toward the unshaded bulbs in the ceiling. Kim, whom the episode had caught totally unprepared, stood in dumbfounded silence.

"Know what I'm going to do to you, Rastus?" the man sneered. "I'm going to trim them big ears of yours so's maybe you can hear better the next time a white man talks to you." A white handled knife came out of the heavy coat pocket; there was the click of a snap-open blade, and the collar was twisted tighter.

"Please suh!" the Negro moaned. "I'm leavin' suh. Honest I is. This gentleman here," he nodded awkwardly toward Kim, "he just stopped me to ask a question. Honest! I'm leavin'."

"You damned right you're leaving, just after I trim them black ears of yours." He twisted the collar tighter. "Maybe I ought to cut your balls off too. Then we wouldn't have so many little nigger bastards running around bothering white folks."

"Just a minute," Kim's voice sounded weak and far off. He simply couldn't believe what he was seeing, but the blazing eyes of the man, so filled with malicious intent, told him that this was no macabre joke. Kim looked about helplessly. Not a man in the room moved. One old fellow, sitting on a long bench, squirted a stream of tobacco juice on the floor just as the Negro screamed. Kim jerked his gaze back just in time to see one black ear held between the thumb of the big man and the blade of his knife. Without thinking or hesitating, Kim grabbed the man's arms and pulled with all his might. The big arm swung, and Kim was hurled half way across the room, scattering men as he went. The action stimulated whispers of excitement among the crowd and focused the man's attention on Kim for the first time. Kim got quickly to his feet.

The man stared at Kim for a moment with a look of disbelief. Then an evil grin split his face. He shoved the Negro away and slowly closed the knife and returned it to his pocket. His eyes never left Kim's face.

"Well, well! Now look what jumped up. Ain't it pretty." He threw back his head and laughed. Kim shivered. "Mister, you just matched up with the best damn tool dresser that ever come out of Smackover, and you're gonna wish to hell you hadn't done it."

Instantly there was a roar from the men in the depot.

"Bust his gut, Joe!"

"Trim *his* ears!"

"Kill the damned jellybean!"

The man was unbuttoning his coat, and a space was quickly cleared around them. The old fellow sitting on the bench did not move. He spat tobacco juice on the floor again. Kim heard the squish distinctly.

Kim looked about helplessly. Surely someone would stop this! But there was neither sympathy nor concern on the face of any man he could see. "Wait a minute," Kim said desperately.

"Wait, hell!" the man yelled and rushed.

Kim braced himself as best he could, but his hundred and sixty pounds were like a ball before a bat. The man didn't attempt to strike Kim with his fists. Instead, he buried his shoulder in Kim's ribs. There was a dull, tearing sound and Kim fell and skidded several feet before an obstacle stopped him.

Kim shook his head dazedly. His vision was blurred, and he was very sick. Something was coming from his mouth, and he thought he was vomiting. In a second his eyes cleared, and he saw that it was blood.

"Stomp him, Joe!"

"Give him hell!"

Kim heard the advice of the human mob as he rolled over and attempted to rise. He saw that the obstacle that had stopped his skid was the legs of the weatherbeaten old man who had been sitting on the bench. He had not moved, and now Kim was lying at his feet, and again Kim heard the squish of tobacco juice.

Everything had happened in split second, and before Kim could rise, Joe was standing over him. Kim struggled to gain his feet, but there was no breath left in him. Joe bent down and grabbed him by the collar to pull him up, and for the first time Kim felt anger rise in him. He balled his fist and with a weak and pitifully inadequate gesture struck at the evil face just as he heard a dull thud, somewhat like an axe sinking into a wet log and Kim felt Joe's heavy body slowly crumple on top of him.

Kim lay still, thankful for a moment to recover some strength, and totally unaware of what had happened. He heard the old man spit again and looked up into the face that had been partially hidden under a pulled down hat. The man was one-eyed, and the glare from the overhead light furnished enough illumination for Kim to see a steel-dust gleam in it. In one gnarled hand the man gripped a long, strange looking pistol.

The old man spoke. It was a heavy, comfortable sound. "If any of the rest of you sons-of-bitches want some of the same thing, just come and get it." The voice was flat and hard, and the pistol was moving in a small arc. "This here little old shotgun of mine is sure going to blow somebody's guts out if you do, though."

Then Kim knew why the pistol looked so strange. It wasn't a pistol, but a small shotgun with a pistol grip. The room was very quiet.

"Hell, Deafy," a man volunteered. "We don't want no trouble."

"Joe was just having some fun with the jellybean!"

Others quickly joined in the assertion that they meant no harm. There was a general babble, and Kim took advantage of it to squirm from under Joe and regain his feet.

"All right." Deafy lowered his gun. "Take Joe away and pour some water on him—or some whiskey down him."

Two or three men moved forward.

"And," Deafy stopped the men, "you tell Joe that the next time he knocks a feller down to be damned sure he don't knock him down on one of my corns."

Someone laughed. Deafy grinned a brown stained grin, and immediately the tension in the room vanished. The loud talk and laughter resumed. Two men dragged Joe away, and Kim sat beside his rescuer. He coughed and spat blood again.

"You had better just set a spell, son," Deafy said kindly. "Joe hits pretty hard."

Kim nodded. Deafy didn't say anything else for a few minutes.

"Thanks." Kim finally felt he could talk.

Deafy simply nodded absently.

"Do you know the man that hit me?" Kim asked.

Deafy nodded again.

"I suppose I was foolish," Kim said as he wiped blood from his mouth. "He probably was just having fun with that Negro. But for a minute I thought he actually meant to harm him."

"Harm, Hell!" Deafy spat disgustedly. "He'd have trimmed his ears if you hadn't stopped him. He's just plain damned mean. And he'd have killed you, young feller."

Suddenly Kim was a very frightened. He hoped that Deafy didn't notice his hands shaking when he wiped his face again with his blood soaked handkerchief.

"You got some busted ribs, young feller," Deafy said. "You ought to see a doc."

Kim nodded. "I'll get a taxi to take me downtown," he said weakly. Then he proferred his hand to Deafy. "I—I—thank you." He knew that the words were terribly inadequate but could think of nothing else to say.

Deafy merely nodded and shook hands. Kim made his way unsteadily toward the door. Just as he reached it, the door burst open, and a man was shoved in ahead of two others who were wearing badges and guns.

"You ain't leavin' this depot, mister," one of the officers said to Kim. "You ain't going nowhere."

"But," Kim protested, "I'm no oil man. And I need a doctor."

"The last bastard that got out of here wasn't no oil man neither—so he said. Now you git back! You damned boomers ain't spreading out over Oke City no more. The next man that sticks his head out of this door before the special leaves gets it knocked off. You damned boomers have done all the hell-raising you're going to for one night." With that the officer jabbed Kim in the ribs with his night stick.

The blow, though not severe, hit Kim where his ribs were hurting most, and he was almost sick again. He stared at the man and hesitated until the threatening stick was raised. Then he walked slowly and uncertainly back toward the old man on the bench. He supposed he *did look* like a boomer. His face was bloody; his suit was stained with tobacco juice and dirt from the floor.

"Might as well do what they say, young feller," Deafy said solicitiously. "Them law men can be tough."

Kim nodded and sat down heavily. Deafy's one good eye looked at Kim appraisingly for a moment and then seemed to soften.

"You go back and wash up," he said and rose. "I'll buy us a cup of coffee." He didn't wait for an answer.

Kim found the washroom and was almost afraid to enter lest Joe be in it. But it was empty, and he felt much better after he washed his face. He went back to the bench where Deafy was waiting with two cups of hot coffee. Kim nodded his thanks and sipped the coffee gingerly. Deafy blew on his a couple of times and drained the cup.

Just then a train threshed and groaned to the front of the depot. The boomer special!

The men yelled and whistled as the train stopped. There was a general scampering for bedrolls and suitcases. One man started out the door but was met by the officers who had stopped Kim. He came back in again, and the rabble of sound continued.

Finally the door opened, and the officers came in.

"All right, boomers," the smaller of the two yelled. "This is your train. Get on it. I don't want a man left in this depot when it pulls out." He patted the gun on his hip significantly.

The men rushed from the depot, yelling and cursing. Kim sat. Deafy got to his feet and picked up a small bag.

"Let's go, young feller," he said.

"I'm not going," Kim said. "My train doesn't leave for another half hour."

"Your train leaves right now," Deafy said flatly. "Them law men says it does, and you ain't in no shape to argue with them."

"But—"

"You can hop off at the next town, young feller," Deafy said firmly. "Right now the best thing to do is get out of Oke City. Come on."

Kim didn't feel like arguing. He didn't think there was any use anyway. Besides, the train was going west!

"All right," he said with resignation. "Let me get my bag." He looked to the spot where he had left it. Only the barren, dirty floor was there.

"My bag is gone, Deafy!" he exclaimed.

"It'll be on the train," Deafy said. "But you probably won't ever get it back."

"But—but," Kim gulped in desperation, "That bag had money in it."

"You get on that train and get stretched out," Deafy said, "or one of them busted ribs is going to puncture a lung, and you ain't never going' to need no money."

"But that money belonged to my mother!" Kim said desperately.

"I don't know why in hell I'm takin' all this trouble with you," Deafy said grumpily. "Anyway, there's always plenty of money in a boom town."

Kim nodded grimly, and a hard glint came into his eyes. He'd ride that train to the oil field, or to the end of the track if necessary to get his bag back. He had no intention of letting someone steal that money! He followed Deafy out the depot door.

The air was clean and cold. Kim took a deep breath and felt better. It seemed a year since he had arrived in Oklahoma City.

The cars immediately in front of the depot were filled, so Kim and Deafy started walking toward empty cars down the track. As they passed a lighted car, Deafy stopped suddenly and looked through the car window. Kim's glance followed Deafy's.

Seated at a table, which was covered with a white linen cloth and laden with steaming food, were a man and a woman. The man was big and handsome, grey of hair and commanding of bearing. Seated opposite him was a woman with a faintly foreign look. Her brown eyes strayed to the window as she sensed Kim's gaze upon her, but she could not see out, for it was light inside and dark outside. Kim continued to stare until Deafy nudged him. They moved on down to the dark car beyond.

They found seats in the next car down, and Kim sat gratefully. His ribs still ached, but the pain was beginning to ease a bit. Deafy threw his small bag on the rack above and sat down with a grunt.

"Who was that?" Kim asked.

"If you mean that son-of-a-bitch up there in that fancy, special car," Deafy said, "That was Blake Terrell. The biggest damned oil pirate in Oklahoma."

"Was that his daughter with him?"

Deafy looked at Kim, his one good eye showing surprise. Then he grinned crookedly.

"I didn't notice nobody with him," Deafy said grimly. "Wasn't looking at anybody else. But I doubt if it was Wendy, though. She usually ain't with Blake. It might have been. What did she look like?"

Kim thought for a moment. "She had real dark hair, and her eyes were—"

"That wasn't Wendy. Her hair is sort of brown, and her eyes are real blue, and—"

"Who is Wendy?"

"Blake's daughter. Though I'm damned if I know how he ever sired her."

Kim smiled warmly. This old man was surprising and interesting.

"I get the impression that you don't like Blake, Deafy."

"You get the right impression, young feller," Deafy said flatly. "I ought to have killed the bastard a long time ago."

"Why?"

"Why? Hell! I got a thousand reasons," Deafy said with conviction. "But I guess the best one is this bad lamp of mine. I owe that to Blake Terrell. He gouged it out in a fight one time."

"Oh!" Kim was sorry he had pursued the subject.

"But," Deafy continued, "I'll give him his due. He has the finest daughter a man could have. They don't come no better than Wendy. She's like her mother. Now that bitch you saw up there with Blake, eatin' off that fancy table, is just his latest whore—though he's probably married to her. He's got a new one all the time. Plenty of money to buy them with. I heard that he was in South America. I was hopin' he wouldn't come to Hutchison County."

"Hutchison County?"

"Hutchison County, Texas," Deafy explained. "That's up north of Amarillo on the Canadian river. Big oil strike there. Some say it's bigger than Spindletop. They always sound big at first. Most of 'em ain't."

"Is that where you are going?"

"Yep," Deafy said. "That's where I'm going, young feller." He turned and laid his head back on the seat. He closed his one good eye.

Kim didn't want him to quit talking. He still was a bit afraid, and his chest hurt.

"What will you do there, Deafy?"

"What will I do?" Deafy's voice was a little incredulous. He raised his head from the seat.

"Yes. Are you an oil man?"

"I'm an oil man," Deafy admitted as he sat up in the straight backed seat. "I'm a driller. And you sure do talk a mighty lot, young feller," he added testily, but there was no anger in his voice, and Kim was glad he had prodded the old man to continue.

"Now, as to what I'm goin' to do up in Hutchison County—I'm goin' to steal myself a string of tools from Blake Terrell and drill myself a million dollar oil well." Deafy laughed aloud.

"You're what!!" Deafy actually sounded serious.

"Don't be so damned finicky, young feller," Deafy said. "Blake got his start by stealin' a string of tools from me."

"But—the law—"

"Law, hell! There ain't no law in a boom town. It's every man for hisself."

"That's a funny way to live," Kim said uncertainly.

"Maybe so," Deafy agreed as he laid his head back on the seat again.

Kim figured that Deafy had done all the talking he was going to. "I'm going to look through the train to see if I can find my bag, Deafy," he said as he rose.

"Best bet is to wait till they unload," Deafy said without opening his eye. "You start traipsin' around through this train and you're gonna find more trouble."

Kim considered the logic of Deafy's statement and sat back down. He was going to get his bag back though. He'd fully decided that. But Deafy's way was probably best. In the meantime he would get some rest. Deafy began to snore gently.

The night seemed endless. The special boomer train stopped countless times—for water, to let regularly scheduled trains pass, and for a thousand other things that Kim did not know or care about.

Kim's injury was causing fever, and he grew terribly thirsty, but there was no service on the train. The Negro attendants, if such there were, dared not venture into the cars. Undoubtedly they had heard of the incident in the depot at Oklahoma City.

Kim turned and tossed. Sleep was impossible. The right angle back of the seat hurt his ribs. And there was an incessant babble of profanity and bickering in the car. Several fights broke out, though no one bothered Kim and Deafy. Kim knew that the men had real respect for Deafy.

Joy Shay passed their seat once and stopped briefly. Kim glanced uneasily at Deafy, and to his surprise there was a dull gleam of one good eye squinting from under the pulled down hat brim. One of Deafy's hands moved almost imperceptibly toward the inside of his coat. Joe grinned evilly, and moved on.

"I thought you were asleep, Deafy," Kim said with relief.

"Have been."

"How did you know when Joe came by?"

"The smell of Joe is enough to wake up anybody," Deafy said in disgust. "I don't hear too good, and I don't see too good—but I sure as hell can smell."

Kim laughed aloud. Deafy hadn't been asleep! He wondered why the old fellow took such an interest in him. Certainly violence was not new to him, and Kim suspected that Deafy wouldn't go very far out of his way just to keep a dude from getting mauled. Deafy glared when Kim laughed.

"You don't seem very damned scared, young feller," Deafy growled. "You must think that Joe just wants to play patty cake."

Kim sobered instantly.

"The truth is, Deafy," Kim said candidly, "I have never been as scared before in my life as I was tonight when Joe bent over me—just before you cracked his skull with that shot-gun pistol of yours. And I was scared to death when he stopped here a minute ago. In fact, that was the first fight I ever had."

"Wasn't no hell of a fight, but then, that's all right," Deafy was mollified. "I just don't want to be traipsing around with no damned fools. I like a man that can laugh when he's scared—but a man that don't scare ain't got no sense. How's the ribs feel?"

"They hurt."

"Don't doubt it a bit," Deafy said. Then he reached inside his coat and pulled out his big gun. He handed it to Kim. "You keep this, and I'll be back in a few minutes. If Joe comes by and stops—you *shoot* him, young feller. Shoot him right in the gut. And don't wait too long to do it."

Deafy didn't wait for an answer, and Kim slid over to the window and cradled the gun in his lap. He had never shot a pistol in his life, and he was immensely relieved when Deafy returned.

"Now, young feller," he said firmly "You stand up here in this aisle and pull your coat and shirt off."

Kim stood up, and Deafy pulled from beneath his coat a small linen tablecloth which he began to tear into two-inch strips. Kim stripped to the waist, and Deafy wound the strips about him, binding his ribs rigidly. The throbbing reduced appreciably.

"Well," Deafy looked approvingly at the job. "Blake Terrell's fancy tablecloth worked real good." Then he added with mock sympathy, "Sure is goin' to be terrible for him and that woman of his to have to eat breakfast without that in the mornin'."

Kim grinned his appreciation. "Feels good, Deafy."

"All a doc would do for you, son," Deafy said. "But he would charge you ten dollars for it. You can buy me a drink of good whiskey your first payday."

Kim grinned again.

"Now you get some sleep, young feller. Ain't nobody going to bother us. We will be gettin' close to the jumpin off place by sunup."

"My name is Kim Wingate." Kim suddenly remembered that Deafy didn't even know his name.

"Pleased to meet you, Kim," Deafy said, showing tobacco-stained teeth. "They call me Deafy Jones."

Kim didn't think he could possibly sleep, but he closed his eyes, and when he opened them again, the first light of the east was visible. He looked out the window of the train, and as far as he could see there was nothing but flat farm and grass land. At first, he thought he had been dreaming, and he looked quickly at Deafy who was sitting, patiently chewing a cud of tobacco. It hadn't been a dream.

"Where are we, Deafy?"

"About two hours west of Shamrock, Texas. We'll be in Panhandle by sunup."

"What is Panhandle?"

"A little railroad town. Jumpin' off place. Closest railroad to the oil strike."

"Good!" Kim said feelingly. "I'll find my bag when they unload and catch the next train on west."

"You headin' on west?" Kim realized that it was the first question that Deafy had asked him.

"California," Kim said. "But I'm going to find my bag first."

"Suit yourself," Deafy said noncommittally.

Suddenly Kim found himself telling Deafy of the money in the bag and why it was there. Deafy nodded solemnly. "Doubt like hell if the money's worth what you're gonna have to go through to get it," he said thoughtfully. "But I reckon I'd try for it too, if I was you."

The men yelled as the train began to stop, and there was a wild rush toward the doors. Bags were being thrown from one end of the car to the other. Kim watched carefully. They waited until the bedlam had died down, and then Deafy took his small bag from the rack above and walked to the end of the car. Kim followed.

A north wind was blowing, and it hit them full in the face as they stepped down. It was dry and sharp.

Panhandle, Texas! Kim looked about in wonder. The sun was just coming up. He had never seen it look so big and so red.

The small town consisted of a general store, a livery stable, the depot, and a few other assorted buildings. He wondered why it was named Panhandle. The activity was furious. Down the track, on a siding, was a string of flatcars loaded with long, square-cut derrick timbers, huge boilers and great pieces of machinery. Around the depot and on the rutty streets were every kind of truck and wagon imaginable. All were loaded with equipment of one kind or another.

Throughout the night, campfires had burned at the tiny embarkation point, for there were no accommodations for the hundreds who passed through. The fires still burned, and the men who had come in on the last train were greeted hilariously by others who had been waiting. Some of the men were eating, and others were drinking coffee. A few were drinking whiskey, and all were talking—or shouting.

"She's a vinagaroon!" someone shouted.

"Bigger than Spindle and Smackover put together!"

"They're damming up the creeks to hold the oil!"

"Ten thousand barrels a day!"

"She's a son-of-abitch with the hair on!"

"Arkansas Sal is already there!"

"Money, whiskey, women and gambling!"

"Little Oklahoma!"

Kim looked and listened. It was unreal. Unbelievable.

Deafy walked toward one of the campfires. He didn't look back, and for a moment Kim was tempted to follow, but he didn't. A cup of coffee would taste wonderful, but he had to find his bag.

He looked through the pile that had been tossed pell-mell beside the depot, but it was not to be found. He went through the pile again, almost frantically, to no avail.

Moving the luggage caused his chest to hurt again, and he began to feel very weak. A dirty bedroll lay beside the depot, and he sat upon it. He removed his hat and pulled at his ear.

He could, of course, go on without the bag. But the money in that bag represented much more than its value, and if he had to stay at the depot all day and check every bag going through, he would do it. But in the meantime, he might as well go ahead and get his ticket to California.

With that thought in mind, he put his hat firmly on his head and strode purposefully toward the depot door. Inside, a sleepy, harassed telegrapher was bent over the key. Kim waited. The man didn't turn.

"When can I get a train to California?" Kim asked.

"How the hell should I know," the man said crossly as he turned. "Seems like the whole damned Santa Fe is running trains to Panhandle and no place else! But you can catch a truck to the oil camp every hour on the hour."

"I don't want to go to the oil camp," Kim protested. "I want to go to California."

"Then *go* to California," the man bellowed. "Go anywhere! Go to hell! Just get out of here and leave me alone."

Kim turned and stomped disgustedly out of the depot. He walked determinedly toward the campfire where Deafy had gone. Train or no train, he wanted a cup of coffee.

Deafy was squatting on his haunches drinking from a smoking tin cup. He didn't look up as Kim approached. No one paid the slightest bit of attention to him. A big pot of coffee was on the live coals, and several tin cups were on the flat bed of a truck parked near the fire. Kim walked over and selected one. He knew that it had been used, but he judged that the coffee was hot enough and strong enough to sterilize the cup. Maybe even melt it! He dipped into the pot. Then he blew carefully and sipped gingerly. He was right about the coffee.

Before he finished, a man in greasy overalls came stalking up to the fire.

"The boomer special is now leaving for the damndest oil country in the world," the man yelled. "One way fare is ten bucks—and there ain't no round trip tickets. If you ain't got the price, you can walk or crawl. It's money on the barrel head, and you pay when you get on!"

The announcement was followed by yelling and wild scramble to get on the flat bed of the truck. Luggage flew like hailstones. Kim was instantly alert, but it was impossible for him to see each piece of luggage as it was thrown on. He saw Deafy pick up his small bag and hop on the side of the truck. But Deafy didn't look Kim's way. The driver quickly collected his fares, counting heads and the money in his hand. Kim hurriedly made his way around the truck, craning his neck to see if his brown leather bag was aboard but he had not finished his search when the driver climbed into the cab. There was a roar as the truck motor caught, and the men yelled again.

"Here we come!"

"Boomer's Gold!"

The truck gained speed, and the men jockeyed for positions on it as Kim spied the corner of his bag protruding from the pile on which a dozen men were seated. Grimly, he gave chase and felt as if his ribs must surely break as he did so. He was going full tilt when he almost reached the truck, and Deafy Jones held out his hand. Kim grabbed the outstretched hand and was yanked aboard. Deafy crowded over and made room beside him.

"I saw it, Deafy," Kim gasped.

"You sure want that bag mighty bad, young feller," Deafy said almost harshly.

"I'm going to get it, too," Kim replied with all the conviction he could muster at the moment.

"Then I reckon I'll help," Deafy grinned and spat tobacco juice.

CHAPTER II

Blake Terrell had not missed the table cloth that Deafy Jones had appropriated the night before until his wife mentioned that it was gone.

"Doesn't your special car supply a cloth for the breakfast table, Blake?" she asked icily.

Blake was embarrassed that he had not noticed. He had eaten far more meals from a rough wooden table than he ever had from a white cloth, but unlike so many men who had risen from humble beginnings, he was not at all proud of the fact. He didn't even like to remember that part of his life.

Blake yelled for the waiter. The Negro was visibly uneasy when he appeared.

"Waiter, where is our tablecloth?" Blake wanted to know.

"I'se sorry, Mr. Terrell, but it's gone."

"Any fool can see that! Where is it?"

"I don't know suh!"

"Well what *do* you mean?" Blake shouted at the confused Negro.

"I means, *no suh!*" the Negro said imploringly.

"What!"

"There just *ain't* another one suh. I'se looked high and low."

"You mean to tell me," Blake said ominously, "that the railroad can't furnish a tablecloth for special cars? I'm paying you enough to buy the damned railroad, and you can't even furnish a tablecloth!"

"Let it go Blake. It isn't important," Maria said placatingly.

"Let it go, hell! These guys all want to take your money, but they don't give you anything in return."

"Must be suh, that they forgot to lay in a fresh supply when our car left the other train over in Houston. I'se awful sorry, suh!"

"All right! All right!" Blake said disgustedly. "Just bring the one we used last night. It's clean."

"It's gone too, suh."

"Gone!" Blood rose in Blake's face for he had a feeling that the Negro was baiting him. "Now you look here, you damned nigger! I've had about all the back talk I want from you. Where is that tablecloth?"

"It was gone when I came in this morning, Mr. Terrell. Honest! Looks like somebody done stole it during the night."

Blake slammed his fist on the table, spilling most of his coffee.

"God dammit!" he yelled, "I'm telling you just one more time, nigger. You get me a tablecloth—now and don't you come back without one."

"Yassuh!" the waiter exited hurriedly.

"Must you use such harsh language, Blake?" Maria said petulantly.

Blake simply glowered at her. She had heard worse in the night clubs where she danced before he married her. At the moment Blake was almost sorry he had stopped off in New Orleans on his way back from South America.

They ate in silence which Blake welcomed. He was busy with his own thoughts. Damn South America anyway! People without guts enough to kick a dictator out didn't deserve any better. Gomez could take half your oil—or all of it, if he wanted it. There was nobody to stop him. And there was oil there. A lot of it. But a man would be a fool to sink a lot of capital in a place where one man told everybody what to do. It wasn't for Blake Terrell!

But now he was back. On his way to oil again! In a country where a man could do anything he was big enough to do. He had a feeling about this Texas oil strike. It was going to be a big one. Maybe the biggest. And maybe the *last* big one!

I would take only a few days to move drilling tools from Smackover and Ranger. He was glad he had wired Kincaid to move as much equipment as possible to the camp and to build him a house immediately. He didn't want a fretting woman bothering him in a new field. It was comforting to know that Maria would have the best house in camp. Trust Kincaid for that. Kincaid was a good super! And the house would have a bathroom. Blake had specifically ordered it. He didn't intend his new wife to live in an oil field shack. He seriously doubted if Maria would stay under such conditions. She hadn't been raised like Wendy—even if Wendy had gone college.

Thinking of Wendy erased some of the scowl from Blake's face. She would be in Panhandle, and Blake was looking forward to seeing her more than he would have admitted to anyone.

They had finished breakfast when the train pulled into the bleak station. Blake looked out the window and had to restrain himself to keep from rushing out to join the boomers who seemed to erupt from every car on the train. He would have loved getting out and talking to them and drinking a cup of the hot coffee that he could see boiling on the camp fires. Those men would have a lot of information! They knew more about oil and where to find it than half a dozen of those high-priced geologists he employed.

Maria sat quietly when the train stopped. She was aware of her husband's excitement and was taking simple delight in holding him in the car as long as possible. He would have much preferred, she knew, to join the ruffians that she could see from the train window. As a matter of fact, Maria too was enjoying the melee immensely, though she would not have wanted her husband to suspect that. She looked as far down the tracks as she could see from the train window. She half expected to see a long-legged freckle-faced girl in overalls waiting for them. Blake had talked very little of his daughter except to say that she was attending school in the east. That was strange, thought Maria. For Blake took great pleasure in boasting of his possessions.

But, boastful or not, her husband was a very wealthy man. She had made very sure of that before she married him. Wealth had been her prime requirement.

Maria sighed delicately and looked at the men again through the train window. Men interested her and she liked them. But these were a greasy, unkempt lot. She wondered if her husband would look like them when he was in his oil field.

Then her wandering glance passed two men and immediately came back to rest on one of them. He was a tall, slender young man with short-cropped hair that was rumpled by the wind. He wore a brown suit and white shirt. He was following an unkempt old man who slouched as he walked. Maria's interest quickened. If her new husband was going to be as busy as she suspected, then she would need some diversion. She started to ask him if he knew the pair, but as she turned, she heard him shout excitedly.

"There's the car. It's a Stutz," he was shouting through the window. "Wendy is here!"

With that remark, he started hurrying toward the exit. Maria sat quietly waiting.

Five minutes later, Blake stormed back into the coach. His face was flushed and gray moustache bristled.

"Are you ready?" Maria questioned.

"No." Blake said shortly.

"What's the delay?"

"Wendy wasn't with that damned driver." Blake almost shouted.

"She was supposed to be?"

"She certainly was," Blake affirmed. "That idiotic driver said that Kincaid told him to pick us up and not to worry about Wendy. She's driving her own car. A Marmon. That's what I get for letting her write her own checks. The damned fools! I ought to fire them both!"

"Wouldn't it be difficult to fire your own daughter," Maria said sarcastically.

"I mean Kincaid and that damned fool driver, and you know it, Maria." Blake said irritably.

Maria said nothing more but a tiny gleam had lighted her dark eyes. What manner of person was this daughter of her husband? A child who, doubtlessly, was more boy than girl! And Blake was foolish to let her have so much money!

Maria watched as Blake paced restlessly up and down the aisle of the coach. His eyes were squinted and he repeatedly stroked his moustache with a bent forefinger.

"What are your plans now, Blake?" Maria finally asked.

He hesitated a moment, then pulled a big watch from his vest pocket.

"We will give that young lady just one hour to show up," he said testily. "If she doesn't, then we will go on to camp without her."

"But, Blake," Maria protested. "Surely you wouldn't leave without her."

"If she's big enough to buy her own car, then she's big enough to take care of herself," Blake rejoined harshly.

"Just how old is Wendy, Blake?" Maria asked pointedly.

Blake didn't answer. He simply growled and strode to the end of the coach and stood at the door just in time to see a truck piled high with men and baggage pull away and head north.

Kim Wingate wished a thousand times during the first ten miles of his journey toward the oil camp that he had never even heard of that money in the suitcase.

The truck bounced over the buffalo and grama grass tufts that served as endless implements of shock, transmitted through the solid rubber tires and heavy overload springs into his pain-wracked body. He had never known real pain before. And, worst of all, he had an uneasy, almost premonitory, feeling about the oil camp. He wished that he could rescue his bag and be on his way without going to the place. But he knew that it would be impossible to move the men and baggage now. He would simply have to wait until they unloaded at camp. Then he faced the likely, and most unpleasant, prospect of someone else claiming the bag.

Kim sighed wistfully and tried to make himself more comfortable on the jolting truck. There was no regular road from Panhandle to the oil camp, for the flat country made a specific trail unnecessary. One way was as good as another. It had rained recently, and tracks made by trucks and wagons were cut deep into the prairie. The grass furnished a certain amount of protection from bogging. Consequently each vehicle made its own road in order to prevent sinking into the tracks of another. But all roads converged as they got farther north.

The sun had risen higher and the wind had quieted. It was getting warm and there was a sober atmosphere amon g the men on the truck. The boisterous, sleepless night was beginning to take its toll, for almost all of the boomers sprawled on the luggage and bedrolls and slept. Perhaps the excitement of the new field and the preposterous lure of riches was growing dimmer as they drew closer.

Kim tried to sleep too, but the bouncing truck made him wince with pain, and his ribs continued to ache. Deafy remained calm, inscrutable and tireless.,

The broad, flat prairies crept past the lumbering truck in stark, majestic beauty. A great slab of flat land. Kim had read something about the staked Plains in a history book once and now he visualized the transient, lonely Indian tribes as they scoured the vast country in search of the buffalo.

Now, in February, the grass was brown, but it was abundant. Near the horizon, which was visible in every direction, the sky seemed lighter. It seemed to Kim that he was in the very center of a gigantic flat saucer, and beyond the edge there was only blue sky and nothingness.

So absorbed had Kim become in the passing countryside that he almost forgot his aching chest and did not notice the decline until they were lumbering down it. At the bottom there was a narrow, sandy creek. There was no water in it, and the driver who, Kim was firmly convinced, derived a fiendish pleasure from making the ride as uncomfortable as possible, gunned his engine as the back wheels of the truck hit the dry sand. There was a roar as the power grabbed, and then came the breaking and grinding sound of cracking metal.

The truck shuddered a second as the transmission gears shredded. Then the engine roared as it was suddenly freed from the restraining load. But the truck did not move farther. It settled like a tired horse when the driver cut the ignition.

For a moment there was complete silence. Then, as of one accord, the men began to curse the truck driver. Kim had never heard such blasphemy. He was still a little shocked by it.

"What the hell's wrong now?" one sleepy man wanted to know as he rose from a bedroll.

"Nothing you couldn't expect from a cut-throat bastard that'd charge a man ten dollars to ride this damned torture rack to camp!"

"We ought to make him carry every damned one of us piggyback the rest of the way."

So it went. Almost every man aboard heaped abuse on the driver of the truck. Deafy said nothing. He simply squirted a stream of tobacco juice and hopped off the truck.

Kim's first reaction had been one of relief that the incessant bouncing had stopped. He could think of nothing more pleasant than stretching his body full length on the warm sand of the creek bottom. He immediately hopped off the truck and proceeded to do just that. Deafy walked over and sat by him.

"Ribs still hurt?"

Kim only nodded.

"Be a truck or wagon by in a few minutes and we'll grab us a ride on in. Ten or twelve miles at most."

Kim nodded again. He felt very weak and tired. And he was thirsty. Deafy said nothing more, for which Kim was grateful. He didn't feel like talking. He propped himself up on one elbow so that he could watch the truck as the men removed baggage to sit on while the driver crawled under the truck to find the trouble. One man lifted a bedroll, and Kim spied his bag. He jumped up and ran to the truck. Almost frantically, he dug the bag out. It was his all right.

Quickly Kim dragged the bag from the truck and hurried back to Deafy. He waited grimly for the man who would claim it, but none did, and he breathed a sigh of relief.

"It's my bag, Deafy," Kim said excitedly as he unbuckled the straps, loosened the catch and felt inside. There, tucked inside the suitcase pocket was the envelope. It had not been disturbed.

"The money's still in it," Kim whispered to Deafy. "It hasn't even been touched!"

"You're lucky!" Deafy said without interest as he spat on the ground.

Kim used his bag for a pillow as he lay back on the sand again. He was almost comfortable when the driver crawled from beneath the truck. There was a big, fresh spot of black oil on his already greasy clothing. The transmission housing had broken, and the grease was leaking out. Everyone knew that the truck would go no farther until it had been repaired.

"Ought to stick his damned face in that grease," one burly man declared.

The truck driver glared but said nothing. He went to the cab of the truck and removed a small bag, then came to face the men.

"All right," he said defiantly. "So we got a little trouble. What do you expect for ten bucks! I'll grab a ride on the first truck that comes by and go get a team to drag us in."

"The hell, you will!" the men shouted almost in unison. "You're going to walk to camp. We'll take the rides!"

The truck driver started to say something else, but the angry faces of the men changed his mind. Without another word, he turned and started walking to the north. Almost immediately a big truck lumbered to the top of the incline to the south and came slowly down the hill to the creek. It was loaded with derrick timbers and pipe. The men began to wave coats and hats.

"Get out of the way!" the driver yelled as the loaded truck approached. "Ain't got room for no riders."

"You got 'em whether you want 'em or not," one man yelled.

The truck had to slow for the creek, and as the driver shifted his gears to take the sand and hill ahead, the men swarmed aboard like flies.

"Can you make it, Kim?" Deafy asked. He had a peculiar way of asking a question without looking at the person he was addressing.

"I'm not even going to try, Deafy," Kim said tiredly. "You go ahead. I'll catch the next one by, regardless of the direction it's going."

Deafy merely nodded and squirted a stream of tobacco juice as he settled in a more comfortable position. Then Kim heard the men who had clambered aboard the truck shouting obscenities and laughing. He knew that they were passing the hapless driver of the broken-down truck. That driver had about as much chance of boarding the truck as he would have of whipping Jack Dempsey, Kim thought. He was pleased at the prospect of the surly driver walking all the way to the oil camp.

After the shouts of the men and the noise of the departing truck had subsided, a welcome silence descended. It was a wonderful thing, and Kim felt that he would like just to lie and listen to the silence of the years. The only break came from the periodic squish of Deafy's squirting tobacco juice.

Almost an hour passed. Neither man spoke. Kim began to feel much better. In fact, he was beginning to think that he might like to see the monstrous thing called an oil camp. He wasn't at all sure that it was worth it, but it would make good conversation when he got to California.

"Are we going to have to walk, Deafy?" Kim firmly asked.

"Maybe so," Deafy said sourly. "I figured there would be a truck or a wagon by here before now."

"Well, walking would be better than another truck like that one," Kim said feelingly as he nodded toward the abandoned truck.

Deafy merely showed his brown-toothed grin and said nothing.

Another fifteen minutes passed, and Deafy began to walk about. It was the first time Kim had seen the old man show any signs of restlessness.

"What's the matter with you, Deafy?" Kim inquired.

"Damned if I know." Deafy shook his head in a puzzled way. "But something ain't quite right. Something has changed in the last few minutes. Haven't you noticed?"

Kim hadn't, but he rose from the warm sand and looked about. Something *had* changed. It was subtle, but definite. Atmospheric conditions were not the same as they had been an hour before. He scanned the horizon. To the north, the sky seemed to be a bit bluer than in other directions. He pointed toward it and Deafy nodded. They began to walk toward the crest of the hill.

Just as they came to the top, there was a faint puff of cool wind. Low in the north lay a deep blue color. It wasn't a cloud, but it seemed to be moving. They stood for a few moments watching the mass move closer. At first it seemed to move slowly but as it got nearer it increased its pace. As Kim and Deafy stood looking into the north, a wave of sharp, cold air hit them full in the face. In a matter of minutes, the temperature dropped from a very comfortable degree almost to freezing. It was an eerie, unreal thing.

They looked at each other. Deafy grinned.

"Heard about 'em," he said. "But this is the first one I ever saw. They call 'em northers. Dinger, ain't it!"

It was a dinger, all right! Kim agreed. It was like nothing he had ever seen or felt before. He was freezing. They started walking back toward the truck. When they arrived, Kim immediately took additional clothing from his bag and quickly donned it. Then he noticed Deafy was simply standing, looking at the north. Immediately Kim searched for something suitable to offer Deafy. The only thing he could find was a coat of one of his most expensive and stylishly cut suits.

"Here, Deafy," he said, tossing the coat to the old man as he turned around. "Put this on."

"Hell, I ain't cold," Deafy said.

"Put it on anyway." Kim was surprised that he sounded so bossy. He was even more surprised when Deafy complied without argument. The coat looked a bit strange on Deafy, not at all like the well cut garment it was.

They climbed inside the cab of the truck. There were no curtains, but the windshield kept the wind from hitting them with such force.

"Now ain't this hell!" Deafy growled a few minutes later. "You'd think they would be a truck by here before now. You suppose they shut the damned field down before we get there!"

Kim was trying to think of a reply when a Stutz touring car pulled up beside the truck and honked. The wind had kept them from hearing it approach, and Kim was startled. He looked at the car. The curtains were up, and he was unable to see anyone through the small celluloid windows. The curtain on the driver's side, which was next to Kim, was pulled back and someone shouted.

"You fellows in trouble?"

"We sure are!" Kim shouted back. "Thanks for stopping." He hadn't seen anything that looked so wonderful as that big comfortable car in a long time.

"Come on. Hop in, and we'll take you on in to camp."

Kim complied quickly and grunted in pain as he jumped to the ground. He kept forgetting his sore ribs. Deafy followed more slowly. Kim grabbed his bag and opened the front door of the car. He hadn't quite realized how hard the wind was blowing until he felt the comparatively warm and still interior of the car.

Kim scooted over beside the driver and turned to help Deafy in with his bag. Deafy had one foot on the running board when he glanced into the back of the car. He stopped dead still. He stared for a moment then deliberately set his foot back on the ground. He reached for the bag that Kim had taken. Kim turned and looked behind him. There sat Blake Terrell and the darkly beautiful woman that they had seen in the special car at the Oklahoma City depot.

"Get in, Deafy," Blake Terrell growled. "I wouldn't leave a dog out in this weather."

Deafy didn't indicate that he had heard. He simply stood and stared as the cold north wind whipped his eyes and made the bad one water.

Kim wasn't sure what was going on but he decided suddenly that he wasn't going to ride with anyone that Deafy wouldn't ride with. He started to get out.

"Aren't we all being very foolish!" Blake's wife spoke for the first time. Her voice was low and husky but carried well.

"Get in, please. And close the door. I'm freezing."

Kim hesitated a moment and when Deafy made no move to get in, he reached for his bag. Deafy, seeing Kim's move hesitated a moment longer then pushed him back inside the car. Without a word he slid in beside Kim and slammed the door. Kim knew that Deafy wouldn't have ridden if he had not been along.

The powerful motor of the Stutz roared, as it moved up the hill.

No one spoke for a few minutes. Kim heard a whispered conversation in the back seat, and the driver looked uneasy.

"Since my husband will not introduce you gentlemen, and you will not introduce yourselves, perhaps you won't mind if I do that for us." The voice was musical, and it was very close to Kim's ear.

"I am Mrs. Terrell," the voice continued. "Mrs. Blake Terrell."

Still no one else spoke. Kim knew that Deafy didn't intend to. He didn't even look around.

"This is my husband, Mr. Terrell." There was a hint of laughter in the voice and Kim heard something like a snort come from the back seat as she spoke. "My husband has had a very bad trip from New Orleans and really isn't feeling very well. Do you gentlemen have names? My name is Maria."

Kim grinned. Blake Terrell might have Deafy angry, and his driver scared, but he certainly didn't have his own wife intimidated. Kim turned. Maria's face was very close to his own, and a misty, tantalizing odor touched his nostrils.

"My name is Kimball Z. Wingate, from Oklahoma," he said formally. "And this is my friend Mr. Deafy Jones." Maria matched Kim's formal tone. Then she continued in a lilting voice. "I think my husband hasn't told me everything about his oil field. He said it would be very dreary. I think it may be very exciting. And I shall want to hear all about Oklahoma."

Kim saw the gay twinkle in Maria's dark eyes and the infuriated gleam in Blake's at one glance. There was no doubt that Maria was needling her husband. Kim turned and stared ahead again, .

The rest of the trip was made in silence. Blake was disgusted with himself for having let Maria coax him into stopping in the first place. He hadn't wanted to. The sight of Kim, young and presentable, had perturbed him, for his wife was almost thirty years younger than he. And Blake was a jealous man. Then, when he had seen Deafy Jones, he had been outraged.

Finally they came to the top of the long rise, and below them, sprawled in disorderly fashion across the prairie, lay the oil camp. The driver stopped the car. Kim stared. It was incredible that the monstrosity before him could excite anyone. It was simply a mass of canvas tents and building frames covered with tar paper. There were a few frame buildings with false fronts facing an open space, resembling a street, which ran through the sordid structures.

They sat for a moment, and then Kim heard a faint feminine sigh from the back seat of the car.

"Let's go, driver!" Terrell's harsh voice interrupted the silence. The driver, in his rush to comply, grabbed Kim's knee instead of the gear-shift bar protruding from the floor board. The gears ground harshly as they started.

They drove down the open space among the structures which proclaimed themselves to be hardware stores, groceries, drug stores, and home furnishings. There was even an auto shop.

The street was rutted and rough. The driver was forced to proceed in low gear to avoid bouncing the occupants. Kim sat forward in the seat, fascinated by the scene. People were hurrying to and fro and seemingly not paying the least bit of attention to anyone. There were stalled cars and trucks in the muddy street, and the road simply veered around them.

Finally the driver pulled in front of an odd looking structure. "This here is the *Double-Six,*" he said.

It was not a building, but an enclosure almost a block square, separated from the flimsy board sidewalk by a high, wooden fence. An opening served as a doorway, and into, and out of it, poured men and women of every description. All the women were heavily rouged and wore the fashionable, curveless clothing.

Deafy, without a word, opened the door of the Stutz and got out. Kim took his own bag and followed. Then he turned and looked into the back seat.

"We do appreciate the ride, Mr. and Mrs. Terrell," he said pleasantly. "Perhaps we can someday repay you."

Blake only grunted. Maria scooted forward on the seat.

"Perhaps you can, Mr. Wingate," she said purringly. "You won't forget, will you, that I shall want to hear all about the oil camp."

"I won't forget," Kim said. Then as an afterthought, "And I do appreciate the use of your tablecloth. It made a wonderful bandage."

Maria's big eyes opened even wider. Blake started rising in his seat, and the last thing Kim heard was Blake's oath and Maria's delighted laugh.

Deafy was waiting on the sidewalk, and Kim set his bag beside him. Deafy looked up and down the street.

"What do we do now, Deafy?"

Deafy didn't answer immediately. He squirted tobacco juice.

"Better find us a room, I reckon," he finally said. "You need to get a little rest and let them ribs settle down."

The prospect of finding a suitable room in the place looked rather dim to Kim at the moment. He supposed that Deafy was thinking the same thing. Across the street there was an unpainted frame building with ROOMS painted in black, irregular letters across the false front.

"Let's go inside the *Double-Six* a minute," Deafy said. "Maybe I'll find somebody I know."

As they stepped through the opening, Kim stopped and stared in dumbfounded amazement. The enclosure was nothing more than a high board fence around the huge wooden floor that covered almost an entire block. It was filled with people. Roulette wheels, black jack tables, dice games, and poker games were everywhere. There was a small open space in the center where several couples were dancing to the squeaky tones of a gramaphone playing "Gimme a Little Kiss, Will Ya, Huh?"

Kim stared. It was difficult to believe that here, at two o'clock in the afternoon, on the high plains of Texas, surrounded by a six foot wooden fence, people were dancing and gambling as though completely oblivious of time and place. Above was the blue sky, and the wind of the norther whipped around the wooden fence.

Deafy surveyed the crowd with his one good eye, apparently unsurprised by the incongruous scene. Kim felt that he must be in another world. But he knew, unless his reason was completely gone, that Amarillo, Texas, was only about sixty miles to the southwest. He could be there in two hours if he could catch a ride on a truck. And that he fully intended to do as soon as he was rested.

With that comforting thought Kim looked at the scene with more interest and less awe. Some of the dancing women were almost pretty, though they wore more rouge and lipstick than he liked. The men were intent on their games, and huge stacks of bills were under almost every whiskey bottle on the tables. Kim was fascinated by the faces of the men. Every expression that he had ever seen was present. Some were sad, bitter and malevolent. Others were greedy, cruel and vicious. A few were honest and wholesome. And all were intense.

Then Kim's heart lurched. There, seated at one of the blackjack tables was Joe Shay, the man who had broken his ribs! He had two whiskey bottles beside him and another holding down a huge stack of bills in front of him. A woman stood beside him and occasionally he reached over to rub her thigh. She seemed not to mind.

Kim stared. And suddenly Joe's eyes raised and looked squarely into his. Kim felt a cold chill steal along his neck and was irritated with himself for having stared at the man so long as to draw his attention. Joe recognized him all right! He looked a moment and then, to Kim's surprise, he laughed and waved.

"Hi, Jelly-bean!" Joe's voice was loud and raucous, but his laugh seemed genuine. Kim nodded dumbly.

Deafy had been watching the interchange between Joe and Kim closely. When Joe spoke and waved, he nodded his head in satisfaction.

"Be back in a minute," Deafy said and left.

Kim sat on his bag as he watched Deafy make his way through the tables. Occasionally he stopped to speak to someone and then moved on. Finally Kim lost sight of him.

Kim sat and shivered. It was getting colder, and he was thirsty. He hadn't had a drink since the coffee this morning. Kim had about decided to try to find a drink when Deafy returned. He beckoned Kim with a nod of his head, and Kim followed him back to the street.

"Rooms is scarce," Deafy said. "Let's try across the street." He started toward the building with the sign on the false front.

They picked their way across. Puddles of water were still standing, and the ruts were deep. They entered the rooming house. The front room was very small, and a cot was placed beside a coal-burning stove. The warmth was welcome. A man sat reading a paper and did not even look up as they entered.

"You got sleeping rooms for rent?" Deafy questioned.

The man nodded and put down his paper. Then he pulled a big, silver watch from his pocket and looked at it. He frowned at the watch and then consulted a dirty sheet of paper on a small counter.

"Have one at three o'clock. Rent 'em for eight hours at a stretch," he finally said. "You'll have to be out by eleven tonight." He sat down again and started reading the paper.

Deafy nodded and spat out the front door.

"Business good, huh?" Deafy asked.

"Good enough," the man's voice was irritable. "You want the room, or don't you? Thirty dollars for eight hours. Woman and whiskey throwed in."

Kim gasped and Deafy raised his head sharply.

"We don't want nothing but a bed," Deafy said flatly.

"All the same to me," the clerk said complacently. "You don't have to use the woman or the whiskey either. But you pay for 'em, mister."

"The hell we do!" Deafy said. "I ain't paying for no woman that I don't want, nor no whiskey that I ain't going to drink."

"Suit yourself," the man shrugged.

Deafy spat disgustedly. He half turned to leave and then addressed the man again.

"Where's Arkansas Sal's place?"

The man moved his paper a bit but did not otherwise indicate that he had heard. Kim saw Deafy's good eye blaze. Then, with a minimum of effort and a maximum of efficiency, Deafy kicked the man in the face as hard as he could. Kim simply stood and stared. Before the man had hit the floor, Deafy grabbed the chair he had been sitting in and held it poised.

"All right, you hold-up son of a bitch!" Deafy said harshly. "You lay right there on the floor till you've answered my question."

The man lay still for a second and then slowly raised his hand to wipe away the blood that was beginning to ooze down his face. He looked in astonishment at Deafy and Kim; then his hand started to move inside his coat. Deafy raised the chair threateningly.

"Go ahead," he invited. "I'd as lief knock you in the head with this chair as sit in it."

The man withdrew his hand.

"Now?" Deafy asked again. "Where is Arkansas Sal's place?"

"Down the street south," the man murmured, "nearly a quarter of a mile. On the left."

Deafy set the chair down and stalked out the door. Kim followed as Deafy strode ahead, his back stiff.

"You shouldn't have done that, Deafy," Kim panted as he came abreast.

"I oughta killed the bastard!" Deafy grated.

"No, you shouldn't," Kim maintained stoutly. He had abhorred violence all his life.

"Kim, Deafy explained, "You find all kinds of people in the oil fields. Most of 'em are honest and hard working, even if you may not believe that at this present time. But you've met the worst of 'em. Now that feller there—you won't find 'em any meaner than him. He just happens to have something that a lot of people need. A place to rest. And he's hijackin' everybody that comes along. Can't hold with a feller like him. He's robbin' people, but he ain't takin' no risk—or didn't think he was. I got more respect for Blake Terrell than somebody like that. At least Blake ain't afraid to risk something for what he wants. That little pip-squeak back there would rob his granny if he thought nobody would find it out."

Kim was glad that Deafy explained though he still considered him a bit barbaric.

"Besides," Deafy continued, "I didn't hurt that feller much back there. Didn't want to, otherwise I'd a kicked him with the point of my shoe instead of the side of it."

"Where are we going now, Deafy," Kim sighed.

"Arkansas Sal's place."

"What's that?" Kim wanted to know.

"It ain't a *that.*" Deafy said gruffly. "Sal's a friend of mine."

"Isn't she the one that the men were talking about back in

Panhandle?"

"She is, Kimmy, me boy!" There was a bit of gaiety in Deafy's voice as he used the phrase Kim had heard his father use a thousand time. "She runs the very best whore house in the camps."

"Well," Kim protested, "I sure don't need a place like that now. What I need is a drink of water and a bed."

"There's the drink of water you need." Deafy nodded in the direction of a two-wheeled cart being drawn by a mule. On it was a sign: *Water Five Cents a Cup.* Deafy headed toward the cart.

The water was muddy and vile tasting, but Kim enjoyed it. He thought perhaps he still had fever. The water vendor explained that he had to haul the water all the way from Dixon Creek, but the spring he got it from was pretty clean. Besides it was the only drinking water around. Everyone had to get their drinking water there. And his was only five cents a cup. Other vendors sold theirs for ten cents a cup.

"Mighty big hearted of you," was Deafy's comment as he took another cup. Kim did likewise.

"Where's Arkansas Sal's place?"

"Right on down the street, Mister. You can't miss it."

They continued on their way and eventually came to a frame building. There was a sign on the front of it that simply said *Sal's.* Deafy looked at the sign a moment, smiled slightly and went in. Kim followed reluctantly.

Inside it was warm, and the place was clean. The room in which they found themselves was much like a living room of a modest home. Drapes were on the windows, and there was a rug on the floor. The stove was burning, and there was even a rocking chair. Kim glanced at it longingly, and Deafy nodded toward it. Kim sank in it gratefully. He hadn't realized how tired he was. Deafy opened the stove door with the triangular windows in it and spat into the flames. Kim luxuriated in the heat from the stove and in a moment was almost asleep. He had no idea what was coming and didn't care.

The door in the back of the room was opened and a huge, blond woman entered. She stopped and looked at them for a moment; then a wide smile, that showed big white teeth, broke as she saw Deafy.

"Why it's Deafy Jones!" she cried as she rushed to him. "I haven't seen you since I left Smackover."

"Hello, Sal!" Deafy grinned his brown-toothed grin. "Long time no see!"

"You old goat!" Sal said affectionately as she took Deafy's hand. "Am I glad to see you! Got just what you need, too! Little Chink girl! You'll like her, Deafy!"

"Thanks, just the same, Sal," Deafy said. "Ain't lookin' for no woman. Me and my friend here need a place to sleep."

"You don't need a woman!" Sal said in mock disbelief. "I guess both of us are getting old, Deafy."

"Well not right this minute anyway, Sal." Deafy grinned again. "My friend here," he nodded toward Kim, "had a sort of run in with Joe Shay. He's a bit tuckered. So am I. What we need is a bed—just to sleep in."

"Never thought I'd see the day when Deafy Jones wanted a bed just for sleeping purposes," Sal said. "But I got one for you, Deafy. You knew I would have, didn't you? You can have anything Sal's got, and you know it. Besides, one of the girls got married and left yesterday. Probably be a couple of weeks before she's back. You can have her room."

"That's fine, Sal. Where's the room? I got a notion we're going to want it for about twenty-four hours!"

"Third room back on the left. Let your friend go on back, Deafy. You stay and talk to Sal for a while."

"All right, Sal." Deafy agreed. "You ready to go to bed, Kim?"

His acceptance was too quick and Kim knew it. But his chest was hurting, and he could think of nothing nicer than a place to lie down. He stood up and looked about for his bag. The money was still in it. He wondered if he should leave it there. Deafy seemed to read his thoughts.

"If you want a place to leave your money, Kim," he said, "I expect Sal will take care of it for you."

Kim looked at Deafy in surprise, but Deafy was not looking at him. Neither was Sal. Some quick thinking made Kim realize that if he kept the money someone could certainly take it while he slept. He might as well let Sal have it. At least he would know where it went. With a sigh he opened the bag and took from it the envelope containing the thousand dollars. He withdrew it and handed it to Deafy.

"How much is there, Kim?"

"A thousand dollars!"

Neither Sal nor Deafy seemed impressed. In fact they seemed not to hear at all; they were busy talking to each other. Deafy handed the envelope to Sal.

"How much did you say, young man?" Sal asked.

"A thousand dollars, Kim said sharply. He was a bit irked at being ignored.

"I'll put your name on it," Sal said as she wetted the lead of a short pencil between her painted lips. Then she added. "What *is* your name?"

"Kimball Z. Wingate," Kim said resignedly.

Sal frowned in thought a moment, then smiled.

"I'll just put *Deafy's friend* on it," she said. "Then when you want it, you ask for it."

"That will be fine," Kim said crossly, "as long as Deafy doesn't have more than one friend."

Sal looked at him sharply. "Deafy Jones has more friends than you're likely to ever have, young man!"

"I'm sorry." Kim said apologetically. He was ashamed of himself. "I'm awfully tired. And my chest hurts."

"Never mind," Sal said. "I'll remember you. Just ask for it when you want it."

Deafy seemingly had paid no attention to the exchange between Sal and Kim, but Sal was looking at Kim for the first time.

"You know, Deafy," she said, squinting her eyes as she looked at Kim from head to foot, taking in his slender build, his well cut clothing, his grey eyes and tousled hair. "Some of the girls would be mighty put out with Sal if they saw your friend and found out he was sleeping by himself."

"Won't always be this way, Sal," Deafy said pleasantly. "Kim needs to get some ribs healed up. Then, maybe he'll be back again."

"I'll *bet* he will," Sal said.

Sal and Deafy were exchanging reminiscences when Kim left. He found his way to the third door on the left and opened it with some misgivings. It was the first time he had ever been in a whore house. He was pleasantly surprised to find a double bed that exhibited clean, white sheets. It was a wonderful sight. He eagerly undressed, leaving his clothing lying on the floor. He stretched his full length on the bed and in less than two minutes was asleep.

CHAPTER III

Blake was relieved when they dropped Deafy Jones and his friend at the Double-Six. And he curtly directed the driver to take him to his house.

Seeing Deafy had shaken Blake badly. He had many enemies in the oil fields. A man couldn't get rich without making enemies. But in the past few years he had become big enough to at least command respect from them. All but Deafy.

Blake had been a tooldresser when he first started working for Deafy. Almost immediately he realized that Deafy was a master driller. And Deafy had been willing to teach Blake the trade. Their association finally grew into a partnership, and they bought their own drilling rig. Deafy, who hated any sort of paper work, asked Blake to take care of the bill of sale for the equipment. Blake had done so, and, though each had put up an equal amount of money, Blake simply had the bill of sale made out in his own name, rather than to both.

Deafy hadn't suspected. Nor would he have cared had he known. Blake fully intended to tell Deafy and rib him about it, but the fact that he held the whip had begun to give Blake a sense of power. He became irritable and bossy with Deafy. And, even then, Deafy Jones was not a man that anyone could boss. He and Blake quarreled, and the quarrel ended in a bloody and brutal fight. Blake won. He left Deafy senseless and bloody and blind in one eye.

Blake claimed the rig then. It was legally his, and he had proof of it. Deafy didn't even go to court. He knew it was useless.

That rig, and a lot of good luck in the next few years made Blake Terrell a rich man. But thoughts of Deafy tormented him though he tried desperately to rationalize an escape from his conscience. After all it had been perfectly legal.

They were often in the same camp after that, and Blake knew that Wendy visited Deafy when he was away on a job. It rankled him that

Deafy and Wendy were still friends. He had fervently hoped that Deafy would not show up at the Panhandle oil strike.

Blake shook the thoughts of Deafy from his mind as the Stutz started down a steep incline. Across a small creek, set on top of a low hill was a house. Blake noted with satisfaction that it was painted. And, though he was irritated with Maria at the moment, he wanted her to be pleased.

They alighted from the car, and Maria looked about with a slight frown. She was a long way from the gay night life of New Orleans that she loved, and the barren hills and the oblong, frame structure did not appeal to her.

Blake curtly dismissed the driver after ordering him to have the car serviced and return it to the house as soon as possible. They went inside.

"Well, now!" Blake exclaimed as he looked about. "Kincaid really did a job on this, didn't he? How do you like it, Maria? Pretty nice, isn't it?"

"Very nice," Maria agreed orally as she took in the new, but ill-chosen furniture and the loud, floral rug clashing with the equally brilliant papered walls.

"Yes, sir! *Very* nice!" Blake continued enthusiastically. "Let's look at the bath room."

They inspected the house thoroughly. Wendy's luggage was in the closet of the smallest of the three bedrooms. The kitchen was adequate; the living room was spacious, and the bathroom had a tub and hot water.

Blake's exclamations of delight caused Maria to surmise, correctly, that luxury in the oil fields must indeed be scarce if her husband could be so pleased with such a very ordinary house. The stoves were coal burning, the bedrooms small, and the decor atrocious.

But these things did not particularly bother Maria. She had no intention of remaining long in the dismal place. She had not married a wealthy older man in order to spend her life on a barren prairie. Soon she could lure him away and they would see all the wonderful places of the world as he had promised.

But Maria could not know the powerful and mysterious lure of black gold that was so deeply imbedded in the man she had married. Already it was dimming the lustre of her dark eyes and dulling his desire for her beautiful body.

Maria was not aware of this, nor troubled by it. It was the daughter that she awaited with apprehension. She had been barely able to suppress her desire to look in Wendy's closet. She knew that she could tell a great deal about the girl simply by looking at her clothes. Blake's reticence concerning his daughter was disturbing. He had been surprisingly obstinate when Maria had suggested that the child not live with them. Well, Blake would soon tire of the girl and send her back to school. Maria would see to that.

Perhaps her thoughts of Blake's daughter were, in the mysterious manner humans sometimes use unknowingly, transmitted to her husband. He suddenly stopped exclaiming over the white porcelain bathtub and frowned.

"Now where do you suppose Wendy is?" he asked crossly.

Maria offered no comment, and Blake was about to pursue the subject further when a knock sounded on the front door. Blake hurried to answer. As he pulled the door open, there was a smile on his face that softened his countenance and sent a chill of apprehension through Maria. This daughter might be more formidable than she had suspected. Then she relaxed as she saw her husband's face show disappointment.

"Oh. It's you, Kincaid. Come on in." Blake's voice was neither friendly nor unfriendly. He didn't offer to shake hands.

Kincaid was a man of medium height, but powerfully built. His eyes were very blue and his hair very red. Maria guessed his age to be near that of her husband. His hands were calloused and work worn, and his face was peeling from wind and sun. His clothing was rough and greasy. He was not at all attractive, Maria decided.

"Hello, Blake." Kincaid's voice was very quiet. He stood, ill at ease, holding his greasy hat in his hands.

"Maria, this is my superintendent, Kincaid." Blake introduced the man without looking at Maria. "You did a good job on the house, Kincaid. Knew you would though. You get paid for doing a good job."

"Had to haul the whole thing from Amarillo," Kincaid replied. "You can't get any material here in camp. This house cost you a lot of money, Blake."

"I'll bet it did," Blake said with satisfaction. "But it is worth it." He looked at Maria with pride.

"Glad you like it, Blake." Then Kincaid glanced at Maria. "Hope you like it too, Mrs. Terrell."

"I like it very much, Mr. Kincaid," Maria said graciously. She was beginning to like Kincaid. At least he was more courteous than her husband. He hadn't even asked Kincaid to sit down.

"Got a bathroom and everything!" Kincaid seemed inordinately glad that Maria was pleased. "Have to haul the water from the river and put it in the tank, but it works real good even if the water is a little muddy. I built a fire in the water heater this morning. I expect it is still hot."

"That sounds wonderful, Mr. Kincaid," Maria said pleasantly and shuddered delicately at the thought of bathing in muddy water.

"You did a good job, Kincaid." Blake's tone told Kincaid that the subject was closed.

"You need anything else, Blake?"

"Where is Wendy?"

Kincaid twisted his hat in his hands. He didn't look at Blake as he answered. "She's in Amarillo."

"She's what?" Blake almost shouted in angry surprise.

Kincaid simply nodded.

"Why, that damned fool driver told us she was already here. I'll fire that—"

"She was here, Blake. Been here a couple of days. But she left early this morning for Amarillo. Said tell you she'd be back before night, if she didn't meet you in Panhandle."

"And you let her go!" Blake was angry. "Kincaid, I thought you had more sense than that. Amarillo is sixty miles away. You know what an oil field is like! There's no telling what will happen to her. She might get hi-jacked, or—anything." Blake was breathing heavily. "Who drove her over?"

"Nobody."

"What!" Blake yelled again, "Kincaid, you damned fool! I ought to fire you."

Kincaid's face flushed and his red hair seemed to bristle. "I know what oil fields are like, Blake," he said in a tight voice. "And this one is worse than most. I tried to talk Wendy out of going."

"You certainly didn't do much of a job of that." Blake's voice was sarcastic.

"I notice she didn't stay in Amarillo and drive out to meet you either, like you told her to," Kincaid said hotly. He was obviously becoming angry. "And if she won't mind you, she sure as hell don't have any reason to pay me any mind."

Maria had been watching with interest and was delighted with Kincaid's strong rejoinder. Blake would push Kincaid just so far, Maria decided. Her husband's red-headed superintendent just might be helpful to her in persuading Blake to leave the field.

"All right, Kincaid," Blake said resignedly. "I guess you did your best, but I still think you should have stopped her. What did she want to go to Amarillo for anyway?"

"She went to get some wall paper," Kincaid said uncomfortably.

"Now why in hell would she go all the way to Amarillo for wall paper?" Blake asked in disbelief.

"She didn't like this blue rug and that green paper." Kincaid gulped as he indicated his decorative effort with a nod of his head.

Maria's gleeful laugh caused both men to look at her in astonishment.

"What's wrong with you, Maria?" Blake scowled.

"I think your daughter may be quite wonderful, Blake," Maria said gaily. "I really don't blame her for driving all the way to Amarillo."

"Is it really that bad, Mrs. Terrell?" Kincaid asked tragically.

"Yes, Mr. Kincaid," Maria said, but her voice told Kincaid that she didn't mind at all. "I think I have never seen worse colors. But I also think you have done a very wonderful job to make us comfortable. I know my husband is very fortunate to have such a fine man as his superintendent."

"Well, *I* don't see anything wrong with the colors," Blake growled sourly.

"Anyway, Blake," Kincaid said stoutly, "I wouldn't worry about Wendy if I was you. Nobody could catch her in that Marmon of hers. She sure can drive."

"Well, she ought to be able to drive," Blake said, pleased by Kincaid's compliment of Wendy, "I taught her how. She could drive a *White* truck when she was ten years old."

Maria's interest in the conversation was considerably heightened when the two men had begun to talk of her husband's daughter. Wendy was almost certainly older than Blake had led her to believe. Maria had gained the impression that she was perhaps in her early teens. She must be older, however, or she would not have dared to drive sixty miles across the prairies alone. And she must have taste of sorts. At least she recognized clashing colors. She was anxious for the discussion of Wendy to continue.

"Won't you sit down, Mr. Kincaid?" she asked, "I will serve us a drink—provided there is liquor."

"We will talk outside, Maria," Blake said hastily.

Kincaid hesitated, "There is whiskey in the kitchen cabinet, Mrs. Terrell," he said quietly as he put on his hat. Without another word he left the house.

"You were very rude, Blake," Maria said angrily. She had liked Kincaid.

"Rude or not," Blake said calmly, "Kincaid works for me and I pay him for it. His duties don't extend to social mixing."

"But, you could at least have asked him to sit, and offered him a drink."

"I could," Blake agreed as he jammed on his hat, "But I didn't, and I won't."

With that he stamped out of the house. Kincaid was waiting in a small truck. Blake got in and sat beside him. Neither spoke for a moment.

"Well, Kincaid—what does it look like?"

"There is oil here. Plenty of it, and they are piling in from all over. I've seen crews from Desdemona and Ranger and Smackover coming in today."

"What about leases?"

"Hard to get. You have to find a man broke before he will sell. And that ain't easy. They brought in a ten thousand barrel well on January 11, and now they are popping up all over. Looks like it might be a real boom."

"Think it will last?"

"Hard to tell, Blake," Kincaid said after a moment of consideration. "Phillips, Magnolia, Gulf and some other big companies are moving in fast. That is what makes leases so hard to get. They have already hit wells in Carson, Gray and Potter counties. All of them adjoin this county. Nobody knows how big it is, yet."

Blake was silent a moment as he considered the news. He knew Kincaid to be conservative, and the report simply intensified the feeling that he had when he first received the news of the strike in New Orleans.

"How many rigs have we got here?"

"Two," Kincaid said. "I think I might have got some leases if you would have let me buy a couple of weeks ago."

"I will buy my own leases, Kincaid," Blake said sharply. He didn't like suggestions from his hired help. He expected them to follow orders.

"All right, Blake," Kincaid said grimly. "But you're going to have a hell of a time finding leases now—and you are going to have a harder time getting crews for your rigs."

Blake looked at Kincaid in astonishment, "We've *got* crews, Kincaid."

"We *had* crews, Blake. I am the only man in camp now that is on your payroll. The crews that came in with the rigs quit before sundown the day they got in."

"Quit!" Blake was incredulous. "Now why in hell did you let them do that?"

"Because," Kincaid said shortly, "You put a ceiling on your wages. You wouldn't let me pay a driller more than twenty-five dollars a tower and a tool dresser fifteen, remember?"

"I don't give a damn what I said," blustered Terrell. "You got no right to let my men quit!"

"Have it your own way, Blake. But a tool dresser can get fifty dollars a tower here, and a good driller can just about name his own price."

"Bad as that, huh?" Blake said thoughtfully. He wondered quickly how much Deafy could make. It would be a lot.

"Bad as that," Kincaid said. "I had to pay as much as three dollars an hour for labor on your house. Figured you'd raise hell—but you never put a ceiling on what I could pay carpenters."

Blake nodded absently. He wasn't thinking of wages right then. This strike must big. He was anxious to get started.

"What about the rest of the layout?"

"Well," Kincaid began deliberately. "They're putting up stores in camp. I hear they may even build a regular town. Some think it may last as long as five years. Everything has to be hauled by truck and wagon from Panhandle, and it's slow. The whores are already here. Sal's place is open. Hijacking is getting bad, and eastern money is moving in—gamblers and such. Bootleggers operate openly."

He paused and considered again. Then he continued. "There's been some trouble between the drillers and the cowmen here, but it hasn't amounted to much. I guess that's about it," he continued.

"Who owns the leases?"

"The big companies got most of them. A few wildcatters picked up some, and a few of the ranchers still haven't sold."

Figure their land will be worth more, huh?"

"Not their land," Kincaid said. "Just their leases. Hell! You could have leased this whole country for a dollar an acre a year ago."

"The law giving anybody trouble?"

"Not much. The camp is a regular hell, but there isn't any law. They only got a county sheriff and a couple of deputies here."

"Where's the court house?"

"At a little place called Plemons, about ten miles northeast. Across the river, and there isn't a bridge."

"Well," Blake said, drawing a deep breath. "Looks like I'd better get us some land leased. Let some of the wildcatters hit a couple of dusters, and they ought to be easy bought."

"Hell!" snorted Kincaid. ' You couldn't hit a duster in Hutchinson County if you tried!"

"Anyway, you just don't worry about a place to drill. I'll find it," Blake said crossly. "You just have those rigs ready to go—and bring some more in."

"We got a couple down at Spindle that we could pull in and three or four at Ranger. I figure we might get ten rigs in here in a month."

"In two weeks!" Blake said. "And I want them here sooner if possible."

"All right, Blake," Kincaid said resignedly. "I'll do my best, but you're going to have trouble finding men and leases."

"I told you once to let me worry about that," Blake said angrily. "I pay you to follow orders—not worry about my business."

Kincaid's face flushed again. "I ain't worrying, Blake. Fact is, I could have gone to work a dozen times since I've been here for more than you're paying me."

The gazes of the two men locked and held for several seconds. It was Blake who gave way.

"All right, Kincaid," he said finally. "As of now, your wages are raised to whatever you can get here."

"All right."

"One more thing—have you seen anyone here that we know?"

"Several," Kincaid affirmed. "Most of them are tool dressers and roustabouts and gamblers. And I saw Joe Shay."

"Any drillers?"

"Only one that I know of. Oschner. He's a new driller. Been in the fields only a couple of years. Got one rig here. You may know him."

"I know Oschner," Blake said, and there was contempt in his voice. "I bought some leases from him a couple of years ago. He'd have made a lot of money if he'd kept them, but I offered him a profit, and he didn't have the guts to gamble on keeping them. He's a jack-leg operator and always will be."

"Maybe," agreed Kincaid. "But he's got a rig going on a hundred and sixty acre lease, and said he had another rig coming in. But he lost his men. Somebody hired them out from under him. I got the idea that he was running short on money. They don't give these leases away."

"Hmmmm—" Blake said softly. "You say he's in camp?"

"Was this morning."

"Know where I could find him now?"

"If he's in camp, he'll probably be at the Double-Six waiting for a crew to lose their money at the card tables so he can pick them up!"

"All right, Kincaid," Blake said by way of dismissal. "Where are you staying?"

"I got a bunk under a truck over by the rigs. Have to watch them like a hawk. They'll steal a whole string of tools if you bat an eye."

"All right. Report here at seven o'clock tomorrow."

Kincaid nodded agreement. "You might tell your wife that there's a nigger woman washing dishes down at the Whiteway Cafe that she

could get for a cook. There's a shack out behind the water tank
platform that she could stay in. There's groceries in the kitchen."

A retort was almost out before Blake checked it. As a matter of
fact, he didn't know whether Maria could cook or not.—Oh well,
Wendy could.

"I'll tell her."

"One other thing, Blake."

"What now?"

"If you're going into camp, you'd better take a gun—and leave
your money home. Tell your wife to lock the doors. I've seen 'em
rough—but never like this. Everybody has gone crazy."

Blake watched as Kincaid drove away, the truck bouncing on the
small white rocks and grass tufts. Then he looked at the sun. It was
still about two hours high. He wished Wendy would come.

He turned and walked back to the house. Maria was not in the
living room, and Blake paused to look at the rug and wall paper. He
still couldn't see anything wrong with it. Then he heard Maria's voice
from the bathroom.

"There's a drink on the kitchen table, Blake. Get it and come on
in. I'm bathing."

"Blake grinned and walked to the kitchen. There was his drink, all
right. He sipped it and walked toward the bath. He knocked.

"Come in, my husband," Maria's voice was musical.

He entered to see Maria lying in the tub that was almost filled with
warm water. She looked at him provocatively.

"How's the water, Maria?" Blake smiled appreciatively.

"A little muddy, my husband, but warm and nice." She rubbed
her slim legs gently with soapy hands, and Blake looked longingly at
her firm breasts and slender waist. Maria smiled; she liked men to
look at her body with desire.

"You are a beautiful woman, Maria."

"Am I, Blake?"

"You know you are," Blake sat on the side of the tub.

"Am I as pretty as Wendy?"

"As Wendy?" Blake's eyes opened in surprise.

"Yes."

"Hell, Maria. I don't know. I don't even know whether Wendy is
pretty or not."

"How old is she?"

Blake didn't answer immediately. He would have liked Maria to
think him younger than he was. He knew, though, that she would
find out. There was little she could do anyway. She was married to
him now.

"Wendy was twenty-one in December," he said.

"But, Blake," Maria said reprovingly, "You said that she was in school back east."

"She was. Up until six months ago—she was in college."

"You didn't tell me that. I thought she was just a child."

"She is."

"*I'm* only twenty-five."

"That's different, Maria, and you know it."

"Why is it different?"

"Well, it just *is*," Blake said defensively.

"I don't think it is different at all," Maria said poutingly. "And I am not pleased that you did not tell me."

"There are lots of things I didn't tell you, Maria," Blake said angrily.

"I'm beginning to suspect that, Blake," Maria said cooly. "Will you please bring in my small bag."

"All right," Blake slammed the door as he left. A moment later he opened the door and set the small bag just inside, without looking at her. "I have to go down to camp for a while. I'll be back."

"Blake!"

"What do you want?"

"Not just any man would go away and leave me as I am now." Maria's voice was tantalizing.

"Well, *I'm* not just *any* man," Blake said shortly and shut the door.

A touch of uncertainty clouded Maria's eyes as she heard the front door close.

The car was waiting, and Blake got in the Stutz and gunned the motor as he drove down the hill. He was disturbed. Kincaid's report was encouraging, but Maria's attitude was not to his liking. He wanted to keep Maria. Blake was no fool and he knew that she had married him for his money but, in his way, he loved her. She was young and beautiful and she provided diversion from too much business. But she was tempestuous and head-strong. So was Wendy. It was too much to expect the two of them to get along well.

The rough street claimed most of Blake's attention as he drove, but from the corner of his eyes he was aware of the feverish activity. People streamed down the hastily constructed wooden sidewalks. Ahead, he could see several tents and tar-paper shacks from which people entered and exited. Probably cafes or gambling halls and liquor joints, he decided.

When he came abreast of the large wooden fence in front of which he had left Deafy and Kim, he parked the car and got out. He stamped his feet and looked with distaste at the spoiled shine on his patent leather shoes.

He stood for a moment and was the object of stares by the passing people. He *was* a possessing figure, tall and strongly built. His well-tailored suit was of the finest material, and a huge diamond stickpin adorned the expensive cravat. A big diamond flashed on his hand. Blake was sensitive about his hands. They were large and muscular. Hard work when he was a young man had left its indelible stamp that Blake did his best to erase. His nails were polished, and his hands were now white. He was proud of his greying hair, for he felt that it lent him distinction.

He frowned slightly as he looked about. Then he flicked his well-cropped moustache three times with a bent forefinger. Wendy would have known by the gesture that her father was impatient and undecided. And Blake did not enjoy indecision. Finally he adjusted his hat and headed toward the wooden enclosure bearing the hastily painted *Double-Six*. Inside he stopped and looked about. He drew a short breath in surprise. Even after Kincaid's report he had expected nothing like this. It was wide open all right! But Blake didn't tarry long looking at the gaming tables or the dancing couples. He wanted to find Oschner, or anyone else that was broke and had land under lease.

Nobody paid the slightest attention to him as he walked about the gaming tables and slot machines. A woman, gaudily dressed in a pencil slim skirt that ended at her hose tops, walked from the dance floor toward him. Her face was decorated with rouge and her eyes ringed with pale grey. Her eyebrows were arched and greased, and she wore heavy mascara on her lashes.

"You wanna buy me a drink, hamdsome?" she asked as she emitted a smoke ring through painted lips.

Blake looked at the woman with contempt. Then he spat.

"You bastard!" she said softly and vehemently as she walked away. Blake didn't look after her. A commotion at one of the tables claimed Blake's attention. A man was cursing as he rose from the nail keg that had served as his chair. It was Joe Shay!

Blake silently nodded satisfaction. Everyone in the fields knew that Joe was a killer, but he had never been caught. Once, at Ranger, a Negro roustabout had been found wandering naked, castrated, and dying from loss of blood. He lived only long enough to babble Joe Shay's name.

That, of course, was not enough evidence for a white jury to convict Joe, but everyone knew that he had done the deed. The oil field hands had considered it a macabre joke. They called him "Cutting Joe" for a while after that. But never to his face.

Blake looked at Joe a moment and then he brushed his mustache with a bent forefinger and walked toward the table. His gait was smooth and calm. Violence never troubled Blake.

"You're a hi-jacking bunch of sons-of-bitches!" Joe was yelling.

Blake smiled sardonically. Joe had lost his money and it served him right. Any fool that thought he could win at cards in an oil camp didn't deserve to keep his money.

"I'll be back," Joe promised as he put on his hat with a violent jerk.

Blake eased between Joe and the doorway.

"Joe!" he said softly as Shay walked past him.

"Yeah?" snarled Joe. His eyes were dark and flashing and he was obviously very drunk.

"I want to talk to you, Joe," Blake said quietly.

"Get the hell out of my way," Joe snarled.

"I think, Joe," Blake continued calmly, "that you and I should have a little talk."

Joe glared at Blake a bit wildly. Then his eyes focused and he recognized Blake. "What about?" he wanted to know.

"I just landed in camp, Joe," Blake's voice was soothing. "I need a crew."

"You ain't looking for me, Terrell," Joe said nastily. "I done my last tool dressing. There is more money to be had other ways. Look around you!" he nodded knowingly toward the gambling tables.

"I'm not looking for a tool dresser," Blake said. "I'm looking for a good, tough man to help me find a crew."

"Are you now!" Joe leered at Blake.

"I pay good wages—for a good man," Blake said. "You know that."

Joe became cagey. He looked at Blake suspiciously. "You and me might do business and we might not."

"I want to find a man named Oschner. Know him?"

"Yeah. I know Oschner," Joe admitted. "Seen him just a few minutes ago."

"Think you could help me find him?"

"What's in it for me?"

"How much does a good tool dresser draw here?"

"Fifty dollars a tower," Joe said. "And they ain't begging for work."

"You find Oschner for me, and you make a hundred dollars before sundown."

"Come on, Terrell," Joe said. "I'll make that hundred before sundown."

Joe lurched through the doorway and Blake followed. They stepped out on the street, and Joe bumped roughly into a man entering the *Double-Six.*

"Watch where you're going!" the man yelled and pushed against Joe.

Joe didn't hesitate a second. He swung with his long, powerful arm and there was a dull thud. The man fell into the muddy street and, with a yell, Joe landed on top of him. Taken completely by surprise the man didn't have a chance. In less than ten seconds he was lying semi-conscious and bleeding in the mud. Joe stood up and then mashed the man's face into the mud with a big boot. He looked at his hapless victim with a gleam of satisfaction in his dark eyes. Then he turned to Blake.

"You ready, Terrell?" Joe wasn't even breathing heavily.

"When you are, Joe," Blake said conversationally. "No hurry."

A small group had gathered, but neither Blake nor Joe paid the least attention. They turned and walked down the board sidewalk.

From the back, Blake and Joe looked strangely alike. Both were big men and carried themselves with an air of confidence. But there was something more to their resemblance. Perhaps it was their complete unconcern for anything about them.

"Oschner was playing at the same table with me," Joe volunteered as they walked along. "He won some money. Said he was going to get something to eat and then pick up a crew for a rig he's got."

Blake felt a pang of disappointment. He had hoped that Oschner would be broke.

"Do you know where he eats?"

"Not many eating joints," Joe said. "We can look through all of them in an hour."

In the third cafe they found Oschner. It was a sordid place in an oblong canvas tent with a wooden floor. It reeked of burned grease and stale cooking odors. Oschner was sitting with a smallish man of swarthy complexion and venomous eye.

"Hello, Oschner," Blake's greeting was hearty.

Oschner looked up and gazed steadily at Blake for two or three seconds. His face showed no surprise or emotion. He was a man of medium size with unusually large and slightly protruding dark eyes.

"Hello, Terrell," he said. "Heard you were in town."

"What else do you hear?"

Oschner did not answer but gestured toward a chair and continued eating. He made no pretense of introducing his companion, nor did

Blake introduce Joe Shay. They pulled up chairs and seated themselves. Joe and the small man with Oschner eyed each other warily.

"What's on your mind, Terrell?"

"Leases."

"Figured as much," Oschner nodded as he sipped his coffee.

"Know where I can get some?"

Oschner blew his coffee and sipped again. "Hard to find."

"They can be found," Blake said with conviction.

"Maybe," admitted Oschner. "And maybe not. Oh, you can find unleased land all right. But getting it is something else. I know where there are twelve thousand acres that are not leased."

"Where?" Blake asked eagerly.

"Close to camp. Maybe three or four miles out. Right in the middle of the play."

"Why aren't they leased?"

"Don't know for sure." Oschner wiped his mouth with his handkerchief, "It isn't money. The land belongs to one of the oldest ranch families in Hutchinson county. They just aren't ready to lease. The old lady is nearly ninety years old. Says she doesn't know what she would do with so much money. Her daughter, a widow, lives with her in the big ranch house that is the headquarters of the outfit. There is a grand-daughter and her husband that live on another part of the ranch. They just run cattle and make a living. The old lady has three or four sons, but they all have ranches of their own—up and down the river."

"Any men live at the ranch headquarters?"

"One," Oschner said. "He's an old baldheaded man who looks older than the old lady. Sort of a handy man, I guess. Used to work for the old lady's husband before he died."

"Can you deal with her sons?"

"Some of the drillers went to see the boys. I did too. They just say that the old lady can do what she pleases. It isn't any of their business."

"That old woman must be crazy," Blake said in disgust.

"I don't know about that," Oschner said dubiously. "She could buy half of Amarillo with the lease money, but she just says that she hasn't decided yet. I've been out there three or four times. She's hard to deal with."

"Anybody has a price," Blake said with conviction. "Somebody will get those leases. Nobody is going to just let cattle eat the grass off of land with a million dollars worth of oil under it."

"I'm not so sure about that, Blake." Oschner shook his head. "These folks out here seem to be sort of different."

"Different, hell!" snorted Blake. "That old lady is just smarter than the others. She will get her price if she waits. And she knows it."

"You may be right about that," Oschner admitted, "But you are wrong about there being a million dollars under that land—there's closer to ten million!"

"Her land clear?" Blake asked. "Does she owe anything on it?"

"Thought of that before you did, Blake," Oschner grinned knowingly. "There isn't a chance to buy up a mortgage and close her out."

Blake merely grunted and brushed at his moustache.

"I'm not sure it would be worth it, even if you could buy a mortgage on her place," Oschner continued. "I have talked to two of the old lady's sons. They live down close to Mobeetie. They don't talk much, but they sure do look at you close. I think either one of them would shoot a man that even spoke rough to that old woman."

"Think they are tough, do they?" Joe Shay sneered. The man with Oschner sat up a bit straighter.

"I don't know what *they* think," Oschner said quietly, "But *I* think they are tough."

"I can take care of them, Mr. Oschner," the small man said in a soft voice. It was the first time he had spoken.

"Shut up, Ralph," Oschner didn't even look at the man.

Joe Shay laughed, and Blake looked at Oschner with something like respect. It was the first time he had recognized Oschner's companion as a bodyguard. He was even more impressed that the man had called Oschner *Mister.* But Blake's attention was not to be diverted long.

"That land can be had," he started the conversation again. "May take a while, but someone will get it. Do you know of any more land around that a man can lease?"

"Not right off."

"I heard that you might have some extra leases."

"Heard I was broke, huh?" Oschner smiled bleakly. "It doesn't hurt to have people in this camp think that, Blake. Besides, I even won a little in a black-jack game with your friend tonight. I got no leases to sell."

"You sure as hell won some money all right," Joe said nastily, "enough to drill a well with."

Oschner laughed and then sobered. "Wait a minute Blake! I did hear about a little eighty acre lease about two miles out of camp that a man might buy. Driller went broke in a poker game. Wildcatter anyway. Tried to borrow some money off of me today. Fact is, I would have tried to buy his lease myself but most of my ready cash is tied up right now. I'll have plenty to spare when my first well comes in."

"*If* it comes in!"

Oschner laughed. "You haven't been in camp long, Blake, or you would know that nobody hits a duster in Hutchinson County."

Blake looked keenly at Oschner. "Big is it?"

"Big. Maybe the biggest yet," Oschner said in a tense voice. "I have never seen anything like it. The first well was a ten thousand barrel gusher. It's a boom, Terrell. Maybe the last big one. And maybe the last chance for me to get rich."

Blake felt the tension in the man. And the desire. Here was the opportunity. He could feel it. Blake leaned back and pulled a cigar out of a vest pocket. He didn't like to smoke, but he occasionally did, for he felt that it made him look even more impressive.

"You know, Oschner," he said slowly as he carefully trimmed the end of the cigar and lit it, "Getting rich isn't too difficult. It just takes brains and a few connections." He paused to let the effect of his statement sink in. "I have been thinking that I might like to have a partner in some of my operations. You just might be that man."

Oschner stared at Terrell, but said nothing. He was remembering the leases that he had sold Blake two years ago. Blake had made a lot of money out of those leases. It still rankled Oschner to think about that. But Terrell was no fool. He was a very shrewd business man. Oschner would like to be associated with him.

"I might be able to find the man," Oschner finally said. "What is the proposition?"

"Let's wait and see," Blake said complacently.

Oschner considered a moment and then shrugged his shoulders. "Might as well. *Somebody* is going to get that lease."

On the sidewalk in front of the cafe tent they stopped momentarily and were pressed by the stream of men hurrying along. Trucks and wagons clawed down the rutted street.

"I'll be leaving you here, Blake," Joe said. His voice was strained. His liquor was wearing off.

Blake reached into his pocket and brought forth a fold of bills. He was immediately aware of the hungry stare of the man with Oschner. He glanced up and down the street at the seething mass of rough looking men. He put the fold back in his pocket.

"Step inside a minute Joe," he said brusquely. "Wait Oschner, I will be right back."

Inside the cafe again, Blake pulled the roll from his pocket and peeled off two bills and handed them to Joe, "You know, Joe, I think you had better stay with me the rest of the night. Maybe for lots of nights."

"Like hell!" Joe was in no mood for innuendoes, "I done the job you hired me to do and you paid up. That is all of it as far as I am concerned."

"There is lots more money where that came from Joe," Blake said significantly.

"What are you driving at, Terrell?"

"I mean, Joe," Blake said patiently, "That there is a lot of money to be made here in camp. I'm going to make it. I need a good man to see that someone doesn't take it off of me. You report to my house at sunup, and every night when I get home I will give you a nice, new hundred dollar bill—provided nobody else gets my money first."

Joe grinned evilly. "I know what you mean. You got yourself a man, Blake."

"You got yourself a man—*Mr. Terrell,*" Blake said significantly.

Joe frowned a second and then comprehension dawned. "All right—*Mr. Terrell.* Let's go."

Blake nodded his satisfaction, and they rejoined Oschner and his henchman. Blake was immensely pleased. He was back in operation!

But they were not able to locate the driller with the lease for sale. They made their way from one filthy dive to another. Gambling and drinking were flourishing at every stop. Dozens of times they were offered whiskey. The girls in the dance halls plied their wiles openly. They even tried the rooming houses, to no avail.

It was near midnight when Blake reluctantly decided to abandon the search. He would have liked to continue, but he was still uneasy about Wendy. He wondered whether she had returned safely from Amarillo.

Arrangements were made to meet Oschner in the same cafe early the next morning. Joe accompanied Blake home.

A big Marmon coupe was parked in front of the house when they arrived. Blake noted it with relief and a surge of pride. The best was not too good for Wendy!

Blake dismissed Joe curtly and instructed him to report at sunup. Joe grinned and sauntered back toward camp.

Blake let himself in quietly. No one was in the living room. He was making his way eagerly toward Wendy's room when he heard the tinkle of girlish laughter and excited talk. His first reaction was one of immense relief that Maria and Wendy were even speaking. They weren't even missing him!

Blake considered this a moment and then tiptoed past the door of Wendy's room to the bigger room that Maria had chosen for them. He took a pair of pajamas and started to undress. Then he changed his mind and flung the pajamas in a corner. He hated sleeping in the things. They were Maria's idea.

Blake lay across the bed and contemplated the situation. The hurdle that he had dreaded most seemed to be made, for obviously Maria and Wendy were getting along well. If this happy circumstance continued, there was little he couldn't do in this camp. It was tailor made for him. The strike was big. There was little law enforcement, and it was a rough, raw country. Just the way he liked it. In a few years he would be one of the biggest oil men in the business. A million people would know his name!

If only it weren't for that damned Deafy Jones! Blake would have given the best rig he owned to have him half way around the world. He wished he had a driller like Deafy!

Suddenly Blake sat on the side of the bed. He slapped his leg with his hand and a smile broke over his face. Maybe, just *maybe*, he had the answer to Deafy Jones—and a proposition for Oschner. He lay back and smiled his satisfaction.

Blake napped, and it was daylight when he awoke. He looked with distaste at his wrinkled suit. There was no sign that Maria had even come to the room while he slept. Blake made his way toward Wendy's room and paused outside the door. Everything was quiet. He opened the door gently and peeped inside. Maria and Wendy were both sound asleep. Blake looked at them with pride. They were so different. Maria, dark and exciting. Wendy, fair and wholesome. They made a beautiful picture as they lay sleeping, oblivious of everything. Blake reached down and put his hand on the covers until he felt Wendy's even breathing, as he had done a thousand times when she was little. He smiled and tiptoed from the room.

He washed and shaved in the new bathroom and was pleased that the water was still a little warm. The sun was beginning to show as he left the house. Joe was waiting.

The sound of the two men greeting each other came through the open bedroom window and awakened Wendy. She immediately recognized her father's voice and started to call him when she heard Joe Shay. His was not a voice easily forgotten. Wendy shivered slightly, lay back, and pulled the covers about her. There was something sinister and evil about Joe Shay. Wendy wished that her father would have nothing to do with him. She wondered why he did.

"Did you and Oschner find our man?" Wendy heard Blake ask Joe.

"*I* found him!" Joe said meaningfully. "Oschner had nothing to do with it. His name is Webb."

"Where is Oschner?"

"He's waiting at the cafe."

"Then let's go," Blake said crisply.

Wendy lay listening to the Stutz as it roared down the hill. A small frown creased her brow. Who was Oschner? It seemed she could vaguely remember the name, but she could attach no significance to it. With a slight shrug, Wendy snuggled deeper in the warm covers and went to sleep again.

Oschner was at the cafe. He and Ralph were drinking coffee. Blake ordered breakfast, and Oschner opened the conversation.

"Well, Blake," he said importantly. "We got our man located. And I think he will sell. In fact he had a little more hard luck last night."

"How's that?" Blake inquired.

"He got beat up last night. Happened out behind the *Double-Six*. Nobody seems to know who did it." Oschner glanced significantly at Joe Shay.

Joe was studiously clipping his dirty fingernails with a long, sharp bladed knife. "Mr. Terrell pays good wages for a good man," he said smugly.

"Too bad about him getting beat up," Blake laughed. "But maybe he will be easier to deal with."

Joe was going to be very useful to him, Blake decided.

They finished breakfast and then went to the place where the bankrupt driller was staying. It was a tent in which there were several cots. Webb was surly and hard to deal with. He asked more than Blake thought the lease could possibly be worth. His well was already down to a thousand feet, and he wanted five dollars per foot for the drilling. And he wouldn't sell the lease unless his rig was bought too.

Ordinarily, Blake Terrell would not have made such a deal. He never bought anything sight unseen, and that drilling rig certainly couldn't be worth much. But Blake wanted a Terrell rig in operation. They haggled for half an hour.

"All right," Blake finally agreed. "I'll pay, but I know damned well it isn't worth it. Let's find a lawyer to fix up the contract."

"We don't need no lawyer," Webb said surlily. "You just pay up, and that's all there is to it."

"Not me," Blake said firmly. "I don't do business that way."

Both Oschner and Webb argued with Blake. They maintained that they could fix up the agreement themselves. But Blake was adamant.

"There probably isn't a lawyer in camp anyway, Blake," Oschner said persuasively.

"The hell there isn't," Blake said. "Money draws them like flies. There's some here all right, and I want one. If I'm going to pay twice what a lease is worth, I want it to be legal."

They set about finding the lawyer by the simple method of

stopping at every establishment open and asking if the proprietor knew one. It was a half hour before they had any luck.

"Feller in here just a few minutes ago," the proprietor of a gambling hall told them. "Said he was a lawyer. Looking for a place to set up operations."

"Where did he go?" Blake asked eagerly.

"Across the street to eat," the man nodded to a cafe across the street. "Won't be hard to spot. Wearing real fancy clothes and a loud vest."

They made their way across the street to the cafe. Inside, they immediately spied their man. He was sitting alone. He was of slender build and swarthy complexion. His dark, straight hair was combed back and parted in the middle. His clothing was well tailored and expensive.

Blake motioned for his party to stay behind, and he walked toward the man with long, purposeful strides. The lawyer did not look up as he stopped beside the table. For a moment Blake stood, looming over the man. Still the lawyer did not indicate the he was aware of Blake's presence. Blake felt the irritation rise in him as he watched the man roll a gold topped fountain pen between long, tapering fingers.

"You a lawyer?" Blake finally asked brusquely.

For a moment the lawyer continued to roll the fountain pen, and it seemed that all his attention was concentrated on it. Then he leisurely leaned back and looked at Blake with black, expressionless eyes.

"I am a lawyer," he admitted in a low, well modulated voice.

"Then I got need of you," Blake said without further preliminaries.

"Fortunately," the man replied calmly, "A great many people have need of lawyers, Mr. ———" He lifted an eyebrow daintily.

"Terrell," Blake answered the implied question gruffly. "Blake Terrell. And I got no time for fancy talk. I want a contract fixed up legal."

"Ah yes, Mr. Terrell," the lawyer said suavely. "I think that it is very commendable of you to conduct your business in a legal fashion. Unfortunately, however, I arrived in camp only a few hours and, as yet, have not secured office space. As soon as I do, I shall be glad to talk with prospective clients."

"I got no time to wait for you to find an office," Blake said impatiently. He had the uncomfortable feeling that the man was baiting him. "I just bought an oil lease, and we're ready to sign. I want the papers fixed up so they're legal. I'm willing to pay."

When Blake mentioned oil leases, the lawyer's bland expression changed to interest. He replaced the fountain pen in his pocket, and one, small, almost delicate hand strayed to a gold coin suspended from a watch chain across his vest front. He caressed the coin gently.

"Mr. Terrell," he said quietly. "You impress me as a man who gets things done. If we can persuade the proprietor of this establishment to let us use one of his tables, perhaps we could design a legal document suitable to your needs."

"We can use the table," Blake said with conviction. Then he turned and motioned to Oschner and Webb. They started making their way toward Blake and the lawyer. Joe and Ralph followed them.

"If you are sure, Mr. Terrell, that we will not inconvenience the proprietor," the lawyer said with a hint of amusement in his voice, "my—er—secretary will bring the required equipment from the car."

"Then bring it."

"Terrence," the lawyer said without removing his eyes from Blake, "Will you please bring a typewriter from the car."

One of the two men seated at the table directly behind the lawyer rose and walked quickly from the cafe. He was a young man of medium size and build. His movements were fluid and graceful. Blake frowned. Those two men were hoodlums if he had ever seen one!

Two minutes later the secretary inserted a sheet of paper into a typewriter.

The lawyer asked names, locations, price and other pertinent questions. Then he began dictating in legal terms. Terrence started typing. His fingers flew rapidly, though he had to stop several times to ask how to spell a word.

Finally the contract was completed, and the lawyer offered it to Blake for him to read. A look of pleased surprise crossed Blake's face as he scrutinized the document carefully.

"Looks legal enough to me," Blake admitted as he handed it back.

"It is a legal and binding document," the lawyer said as he handed it to Webb.

Webb gave the contract a cursory glace and returned it. All he wanted was his money.

"Now," the lawyer said, "If you are ready to make payment, Mr. Terrell, we are ready to sign the contract."

"I've got my check book," Blake said bluntly.

"Oh, no you don't!" Webb shouted. "I ain't taking no damn piece of paper for my lease and rig. You pay cash, mister, or you don't get anything from me."

Blake protested violently, to no avail. Oschner joined in to help, but the man was adamant. Cash money—or no sale. The lawyer listened with wry amusement. Finally Blake gave up in disgust and stamped out of the cafe toward Sal's place.

A half block from Sal's, he stopped in mid-stride. Coming out the door was the young man that had been with Deafy Jones yesterday.

Kim did not see Blake. And Blake was just as pleased that he didn't. He wanted absolutely nothing to do with him.

Blake had to wake Sal to get the money. A few minutes later, he was back in the cafe. He slapped the currency down in front of the lawyer.

"Now," the lawyer said with a hint of contempt in his voice. "If everyone is satisfied, I think we are ready to close the transaction."

He slid the contract across the table toward Blake. Blake signed. Then the lawyer handed his gold topped pen to Webb. He signed his name to the paper and then reached for the stack of bills.

"Just a moment!" The lawyer's hand snaked toward the bills before the man could take them.

"What the hell!" the man growled belligerently. "You give me the money or—"

"You will get your money," the lawyer said calmly, "After I have deducted my fee."

Then the lawyer very deliberately withdrew several bills from the bundle of currency and tucked them into his vest pocket. "Why you damned shyster!" Webb started toward the lawyer threateningly. "You're not stealing my money!"

"You certainly are right, sir!" The lawyer was unperturbed. "I'm not stealing your money. This is my money. That contract that you just signed stipulates that party of the first part agrees to pay all legal fees involved. My fee is five hundred dollars—and you are the party of the first part."

"Like hell!" Webb snarled as he rose and stood threateningly over the lawyer. Instantly the bigger of the two men with the lawyer grabbed him by the coat collar from the rear.

"What you want me to do with him, Mr. Butler?" the man said almost indifferently.

"Why nothing, I think, Martin," the lawyer said in mock surprise. "I'm sure that Mr. Webb, after thinking a moment, will want to pay his legal debts."

Blake Terrell's laugh rang out, and Webb looked at the faces of the men about him. There was no sympathy in any of them, only amusement. He started to say something further but changed his mind. Then he jammed the money the lawyer had handed him in his pocket and rushed from the cafe.

"Well," Blake said with approval, "You certainly handled that piece of business all right."

"I always handle business all right," the lawyer said quietly.

"I saw that clause in the contract about him paying when I read it, myself," Blake said with a bit of pride in his voice. "I didn't figure the damn fool would read it close enough to notice it. Why did you put it in there, anyway?"

"Mr. Terrell," the lawyer said suavely. "It has been my experience that the men who *buy* are the men who stay in business. I plan to be in this camp for some time. I want clients. My clients receive the very best legal service available."

"Well," Blake laughed his approval of the lawyer. "You will get plenty of clients. In fact, I'll have enough business myself to keep you busy. I operate big, and I need a smart lawyer to keep my business legally in the clear."

"Then perhaps I'd better introduce myself," the lawyer smiled thinly. "I am Claude Butler. These two gentlemen are my—assistants, Terrence and Martin."

"Where can I get in touch when I want you?" Blake asked.

"You will see my shingle on main street within the next few days, Mr. Terrell," Butler said as he rose from his chair. "And now, if you gentlemen will excuse us, we must be going."

With that, Butler and his two men left the cafe.

"There's a damn smart lawyer," Blake laughed as the door closed behind them.

"If somebody doesn't kill him—" Oschner added.

"They won't," Blake said complacently. "Those two hoodlums with him will take care of their boss."

"They didn't look so tough to me," Ralph put in.

Blake had forgotten about Ralph and Joe, but Ralph's statement suddenly brought his mind back to the business at hand.

"Joe," he said. "You put in some overtime last night. Why don't you and Ralph go and buy yourselves a drink while Oschner and I talk business. Be gone an hour, then report back here."

Blake peeled a bill from a fold he took from his pocket and pitched it on the table in front of Joe. Joe grinned and reached for it.

"I don't go anywhere unless Mr. Oschner tells me to," Ralph said menacingly. His hand had flashed to his pocket when Blake reached for his money.

"You go ahead, Ralph," Oschner said without looking at him.

"Come on, little man!" Joe said contemptuously. "We got an hour off."

An hour later Joe and Ralph returned. Their bosses were evidently in high spirits.

"Joe," Blake said. "I have a job for you—you know Deafy Jones."

Joe's face darkened. "I know him. I saw that jelly bean friend of his in a cafe up the street just a few minutes ago."

"Good," Blake replied quickly. "You are going to be a good man, Joe. Here is what I want you to do. Go with Oschner, here, and point Deafy Jones out to him. He doesn't know Deafy. Don't let Deafy see you together. Got it?"

"I got it," Joe said sourly. Obviously he had no taste for Deafy Jones. "When do you want me to report back, and where?"

"At my house. As soon as you have pointed Deafy out to Oschner."

They prepared to leave. Blake paid for the coffee, and they stepped out on the street together.

"By the way, Oschner," Blake said casually. "What was the old lady's name that owned that twelve thousand acres?"

"Beatenbow," Oschner said shortly. "But you'll never get that lease, Terrell."

CHAPTER IV

That first night in the oil camp as Kim Wingate slept snug and warm in Sal's place, the range cattle along the Canadian river humped their backs to the violent turbulence of the Texas norther. Crews of the oil drilling rigs squatted in the engine rooms, away from the biting cold, and watched their cable tools pound toward the vast pool of oil which lay less than a mile underground.

Throughout that night, the norther blew unabated. And as it blew a steady caravan of Model T's, trucks, wagons, and other nondescript vehicles plowed their way over the rolling grasslands north of the small town of Panhandle toward the Canadian river breaks and the new oil strike. Those nearing camp toward morning saw a great shaft of flame shoot skyward when a pebble, pushed by the tremendous force of gas suddenly released from its underground prison by a driller's bit, struck the metal casing and caused the spark to ignite the roaring gas.

The flame bent to the push of the wind and fired the long grass about the well. Those who saw the flame as they neared camp simply increased their pace. To them the golden spiral was a beacon of light promising riches untold. They had no thought of the wild things that perished in the grass fire that raced before the norther.

It was after the sun had risen that the wind, like an unruly child that had rollicked itself into exhaustion, subsided. In the wake of the wind came a gentle breeze.

The gentle breeze was blowing when Kim Wingate awakened. He felt the soft sting of it on his face and opened his eyes. For a moment he could not remember where he was. Then he took a deep breath of the clean, cold air, and the sharp pain that accompanied the expansion of his chest muscles recalled, very vividly, the events of the day before.

Kim lay a moment and then started moving his body experimentally. Deafy's bandage was still tight around his chest. He sat up in the bed and bent forward. His ribs were still sore, but he didn't believe they were broken. He hoped Joe Shay's head was just as sore as his ribs. It probably was, for Deafy had certainly whacked him with that big pistol.

The floor was cold to his feet, and the breeze coming through the open window was sharp. He closed the window and wondered idly who had opened it. He hadn't. The wind had been like ice the day before.

Kim looked about the room with interest. It was rather bare. There were two chairs, straight backed and cane bottomed. The dresser had a wash basin and a pitcher. The bed was of iron and painted a light blue. Kim wondered where Deafy had slept. Not with him, for he had sprawled in the very middle of the bed. Deafy must have found another bed. Maybe Sal's.

Kim glumly surveyed his clothing that he had left piled on the floor beside the bed. They were wrinkled and stained. He brushed futilely for a few minutes. Finally he decided the task was impossible and took a fresh shirt and trousers from his bag. The trousers matched the coat he had given Deafy the day before, and Kim felt a moment of regret for having done so. Then he shrugged his shoulders slightly. He would bet that old Deafy had never worn such a stylish coat before. On second thought, he wasn't so sure. Deafy was a very surprising man.

Kim dressed hurriedly and wondered where he could find breakfast. He was hungry. Sal's place didn't serve food. Deafy would know. But where was Deafy? The door of Kim's room opened into a long hallway, and he looked up and down before he stepped out. He debated whether to knock on a door and ask where he could find Sal. He decided against that. He would find breakfast by himself. Surely food wasn't as hard to come by as sleep.

The main street was still teeming with humanity. Kim looked at the sun and judged it to be about an hour high. That meant that he had slept almost eighteen hours. No wonder he was hungry!

Along the narrow, rutted main street of the camp, the various business establishments were thriving. The wooden shacks and tents swarmed with people and the smell of liquor and beer was pungent, and the reek of unclean human bodies seemed to cling in the air.

The wind had dried most of the water along the street. Chuck holes, covered with oil slick, still remained, but Kim was able to cross without getting his shoes muddy. Then, sandwiched between a saloon and a gambling den, Kim spied a small, oblong building bear-in a cafe sign. He walked eagerly toward it.

There were several tables covered with checked oil cloths. Kerosene lamps, set in wire racks, were on the walls above the tables. The place was full of men, but eventually a place at the counter was vacated, and Kim sat. A tired looking waiter with thin hair and stooped shoulders wiped unenthusiastically at the counter.

"What'll it be, mister? We got bacon an', or pancakes."

"Bacon an'," Kim said. "And may I have some coffee now, please."

"You can have coffee when I get around to it," the waiter said tiredly. "And there ain't no use to be so damned polite about it. You won't get it no quicker."

Kim said nothing more. As he waited scraps of conversation among the men floated about. Most of them had just come in from work—or were going to work. Their conversation meant little to Kim. Words such as *crown block, dog house, drill stem,* and *gathering line,* were tossed back and forth. It sounded like a foreign language.

Finally his order was set before him. The bacon was greasy and the eggs a dark yellow, but they looked delicious. And they were. The coffee was strong and black. He had finished one egg and started on the other when the tired waiter came back to refill his cup.

"That'll be two dollars, mister."

Kim wouldn't have been surprised if the man had said twenty. He reached into his pocket for the money and felt nothing. He realized, to his consternation, that he had neglected to transfer his money from the soiled trousers that he had left at Sal's place. But he continued to search.

The waiter was at first impatient. Then he grew suspicious and finally beligerent.

"All right, mister," he growled. "Cough up the two dollars and don't give me no trouble. I ain't got all day."

"I'm very sorry," Kim said apologetically. "But it seems that I left my money in—."

"Oh, no you don't, mister," the waiter said levelly. "I don't go for that stuff. Now you fetch out my two dollars—and be quick about it."

"Honest, mister," he said. "I've got money. I'll go and get it right now."

"You ain't going no place right now," the waiter rejoined quickly, then yelled at the top of his thin voice, "Hey cookie!"

Immediately a huge, bald headed man wearing a greasy white apron appeared. He held a big meat cleaver in his hand.

"What's the trouble up here, Clyde?" he asked gloweringly.

"This feller says he left his money in his other pants," Clyde reported.

"He does, eh!" The cook leered menacingly at Kim. "Dude too, ain't he? White shirt and all!"

Kim sat in embarassed silence.

"Bash his damned head in with that cleaver, Cookie," Clyde encouraged. "Either that, or make him give me that two dollars."

"You're going to give Clyde his two dollars, ain't you, dude?" Cookie's voice was conversational.

"If you will just give me a few minutes to go and get it out of my other trousers," Kim said pleadingly, "I'll pay you *five* dollars. I'll—"

The meat cleaver came, flat side down, with explosive force. Kim's coffee spilled, and there was a sudden silence in the cafe.

"In the first place, Dude," the cook's voice was no longer conversational. "There ain't no son-of-a-bitch in camp that owns two pairs of pants. And in the second place, you either fork over Clyde's two dollars, or I'm going to take that fancy pair of pants you're wearing and keep them in place of the money." He grabbed Kim's shoulder.

Just at that second, a big man strode into the cafe. He saw Kim immediately. "Well, well, if it ain't my jelly-bean friend." Joe Shay yelled with relish. "Take you hand off him, cookie. He's mine."

Kim had thought he could not have been in a worse situation, but he changed his mind when he saw Joe. Joe was accompanied by a small, weasel faced man dressed in a blue suit. Kim eyed the cleaver in the cook's hand and wondered if he could snatch it before Joe got to him.

"If he's yourn," the cook growled, "then you can pay for his breakfast."

"Sure. Sure," Joe said soothingly. "How much does he owe you?"

"Two dollars."

Joe pulled a roll of bills from his pocket and tossed a five on the counter.

"Now, cookie," Joe said. "You go back to your little old kitchen there and cook up the rest of that for my friend here. He's had a little accident, and I want him to get well real fast. Then him and me has some unfinished business to take care of."

Kim felt a fluttering chill as Joe talked. The tired waiter grabbed the bill and stuffed it into a bulging pocket, and the cook started back to the kitchen.

"Oh Cookie!" Joe's voice halted the bald headed man in stride. "The next time you come out of that kitchen, you leave your meat chopper in there. Otherwise I'll make you eat it—handle and all."

The cook started to reply and changed his mind. Joe and the small man sat on the stools that had been vacated during the confusion. Almost immediately the waiter set a cup of coffee in front of Joe and his companion. Joe took a pint bottle from his pocket and poured whiskey in his coffee. He paid not the slightest bit of attention to the man with him.

"Yes sir! Jelly-bean, you eat hearty cause you and me has got some unfinished business to tend to," Joe said jovially. Then he added in a voice designed to make him sound like a reasonable man, "You just go ahead and get real good and well, and then we'll finish it."

Kim couldn't think of anything to say and was grateful when the waiter set another platter of bacon and eggs in front of him. He hesitated a moment and then started eating. If Joe was going to pay for them, then he was certainly going to eat them. Besides, he was still hungry.

"You know, jelly-bean," Joe said between gulps of coffee. "Me and you may have to make special arrangements to finish our business because I'm going to be awful busy here in this camp. Fact is, I'm working right now. Some men wouldn't call it actual work, but I ain't a toolie no more. Money is easier to get than that."

Kim decided to be conversational. "What sort of work are you doing, Joe?"

"Keeping my boss from getting his pretty clothes dirty," Joe laughed heartily. "Supposed to watch him all the time to see that nothing happens to him. He and another man are down at the Whiteway Cafe right now. Talking big money. Yes sir! This is going to be a mighty fine job. The boss has got a mighty pretty wife."

Kim felt a tinge of sympathy for Joe's employer. If he weren't careful, Joe's boss would find something other than his clothes soiled.

Joe gulped his coffee and rose. "Got to go, right now, Jelly-bean, but I'll sure be seeing you. Don't forget that." The small man followed him out.

Kim wished he *could* forget Joe Shay! Well, he probably wouldn't see him again, anyway. What a ridiculous situation! Less than four blocks away he had more than a thousand dollars—at least he hoped he did have—and the anemic waiter and fat cook had threatened to bash his head in because of a two dollar breakfast. At the moment he was not very well impressed with oil camps.

The wind seemed less chilly when he walked from the cafe. He supposed he should find Deafy, though he wasn't quite sure why. If he were going to leave the oil camp, then the logical thing for him to do was pick up his money at Sal's place and find some sort of transportation.

Men bumped into him as he stood looking up and down the street. It was surprising that so much had been accomplished in such a short time. Deafy said that the oil had been discovered only about a month and a half before. A long banner was strung completely across the street proclaiming the attractions of a dance hall. Model T's, Dodges, Marmons, and various other makes of cars lined the streets.

There was nothing attractive about the place. But there was a feeling of excitement and adventure. Kim realized that he had subconciously been toying with the idea of seeking his fortune in the dismal place. Once the thought was recognized, Kim rejected it wholeheartedly.

Nevertheless, he decided to explore the camp a bit before he got a ride back to the railroad. He had always enjoyed seeing new places and new sights. He headed north along main street. Three times he was offered liquor. As he neared the edge of camp, the tents and shacks became thinner. He kept on walking and soon was away from all the buildings.

On a little rise just out of camp, he stopped and looked back. It was the first time he had been aware of the sound. There came from the cluster of shacks a muffled roar that was like the hum of millions of bees. Around him, on the grassy slopes were sage, mesquite and yucca. White, cumulous clouds floated against an azure sky. They changed shape, shifting from one entrancing configuration to another, forming strange patterns in their lazy gyrations.

Kim continued his walk. It felt good to stretch his muscles. At the top of a grassy slope, he stopped. To the north was a small creek, and beyond the creek he could see what seemed to be a wide ribbon of sand. It was lined on either side with trees and smaller growth.

The Canadian River! Treacherous, wild, romantic. Its quicksands held a thousand secrets. Kim felt a tiny thrill as he looked at it, for Oklahomans heard many stories about the Canadian. As his eyes adjusted to the distance he could see the tiny stream of water threading down the broad, sandy river bed.

So engrossed was he in the scene before him that he did not at first notice the sound of a car motor nearby. As the sound impressed itself on his consciousness, he looked about. The motor roared again, but the sound did not move. Evidently it was coming from the bottom of the small creek just ahead, and from a point where the slight trace of a road dipped down to the creek. Kim listened and the roar came again. The car was stalled.

He walked toward the sound. Fifty yards farther on he came to the creek. In the dry sand of the creek bed was a new Marmon coupe. The back wheels were buried almost to the axles in sand.

Standing beside the car, hands on hips, was a girl. Her hair was light brown; she was, he guessed, about five feet five and very trim. She was wearing snug fitting trousers and was, to Kim's appreciative eye, a most pleasant view. He walked toward her. He was within twenty feet before he spoke.

"May I help you?" he asked.

Like a startled deer, the girl whirled. Kim had only the briefest glance of blue and gold. Then with two long strides, she moved to the side of the car. Quickly she reached inside and, to Kim's utter amazement, he found himself looking at the business end of a small pearl handled pistol.

So swift had been her movements that Kim had not moved since he had spoken. But when the pistol was suddenly pointed at him, he gasped and inadvertently stepped backward. His heel caught on a white gypsum rock and he sat heavily on the ground. The girl stood poised above him, gold flecked and graceful. She pointed the gun unwaveringly. Her eyes were almost the same color as the sky against which he was outlined. The wind blew gently at her soft brown hair and pushed her clothing against her supple body. Kim could even see the freckles dotting the smoothly tanned face.

"I'm sorry." Kim said apologetically, "But I thought you were a woman—I mean—I thought—."

A twinkle appeared in the eyes of the girl as she saw Kim's discomfiture and listened to his stammered apologies. Then she laughed. Kim thought he had never heard anything so lovely. It was as though a bubbly, mountain brook had suddenly burst forth in the dry creek bed.

"Do I look like a man?" the girl asked impishly.

"Sort of a silly thing to say wasn't it?" Kim grinned, "You scared me when you pointed that gun."

The girl's blue eyes twinkled, but she did not put the gun away.

"I saw you from the top of the hill," Kim continued, "I thought you were in trouble. I came down to see if I could be of assistance."

The girl looked at him speculatively. Finally she said, "If you will be kind enough to walk back to camp and send help I will appreciate it very much."

"I'll be glad to," Kim answered. "Do you mind if I get up?"

She laughed again. "No. But please don't come any closer. You look like a very nice person, but this is an oil camp. I have lived in them most of my life, and I have learned not to trust strangers."

"I don't blame you," Kim said feelingly as he rose and brushed at his clothing. "Whom shall I ask to come out here?"

"If you can find a man named Kincaid, he will send someone. Or you may be able to find Blake Terrell. He is my father."

"Blake Terrell?" Kim asked in open-mouthed astonishment. Was it possible that this was the girl of whom Deafy had spoken so highly? Kim really hadn't given it much thought, but somehow he had expected her to be as mannish and preemptory as Blake himself.

"Is something wrong?" the girl asked curiously.

"Yes." Kim stammered. "I mean no. I think perhaps I met your father."

A faint shadow, like a thin stratus cloud over the sun, passed her lovely face.

"He and your—I mean—well, he gave me and a friend of mine a lift into camp yesterday after the truck on which we were riding broke down."

Instantly the cloud lifted from her face and the sparkle of her smile was like the sun shining again. Her white teeth gleamed.

"Then you must be Deafy's friend!" she cried and lowered the gun.

There was so much pleasure and delight in her voice that Kim knew instantly that he had been unwittingly recommended to her. This was the second time he had been called Deafy's friend. Once by a whore house madam—and now by the loveliest girl he had ever seen. Each time the results had been most gratifying.

Swiftly the girl transferred the small pistol to her left hand and extended her right. Her hand was soft and her grip firm.

"I'm Wendy Terrell," she said.

"I am Kim Wingate."

"I know—Mr. Kimball Z. Wingate." Wendy laughed, "Maria told me that you and Deafy rode into camp with them yesterday."

"That was the most welcome ride I ever had," Kim grinned. "Deafy and I were cold."

"How is he, Kim?" she asked eagerly. "Where can I find him?"

Kim was somehow very pleased that she had called him by his first name and he would gladly have sworn lifelong friendship with Deafy rather than rob her of the pleasure she seemed to be deriving from hearing of the old man.

"He's fine, Wendy. He will be glad to see you. He has told me about you."

"Oh, he has, has he?" she said in mock severity. "Wait until I see that crotchety, lovable old darling!"

Kim couldn't think of a more inappropriate term to apply to Deafy than "Darling," but when Wendy said it, he had to agree that it fitted pretty well.

"Where is he?"

"I don't know. I haven't seen him this morning."

"Where did you spend the night? He must still be sleeping."

"We stayed in a—a rooming house last night," Kim said haltingly, "but he was gone when I got up this morning."

"Let's go find him," Wendy said enthusiastically.

"All right," Kim agreed. "Shall we try to get your car out of the creek?"

"Yes." Wendy turned and put the small gun back in the car. "You pull some sage brush to put under the back wheels. I'll be digging the sand out from in front of them."

Kim pulled the sage brush. Wendy got down on her knees and dug the sand from around the wheels. Her movements were fluid and smooth, but she worked effectively. She finished digging the sand before Kim had enough sage branches to furnish footing for the tires. Wendy helped him, and Kim was surprised to note that she broke the tough sage branches as easily as he.

But, Kim assured himself, that was the only masculine thing about her. And he could not help but agree with Deafy that it was a near miracle that a man like Blake Terrell had sired such a daughter. Kim had seen very little of Terrell, of course, but he had gained the very definite impression that the man was an egotistical boor. And a bully. Perhaps his conclusion had been unfair. He had been more than ready to hate the man on Deafy's recommendation alone. But a man who had such a lovely daughter and such a pretty wife could hardly be completely without merit.

It took almost half an hour for them to get the car to the grassy bank where the tires would not sink in the soft sand. They accomplished the feat by repeatedly making a bed of sage branches in front of the rear tires. Wendy drove and Kim pushed. When the car passed over some of the branches, Kim took them from behind the wheels and put them in front again.

Kim was puffing and his sore ribs hurt when they finally had the car out. He got in beside Wendy, and they drove toward camp. She parked the car expertly beside the board sidewalk. They got out and walked down the long street.

The sidewalk was crowded. People hurried about. Most of them were men, and they stopped, or turned to stare, as Wendy and Kim passed. Kim almost strutted. He knew many attractive girls, but this one seemed rather special in some way he could not quite describe.

They walked almost the entire length of the street without seeing Deafy. Kim was secretly hoping that they would not find him until the last possible minute. He kept trying to think of reasons to prolong his meeting with Wendy.

"Which rooming house did you spend the night in, Kim?" she finally asked.

Kim was embarassed. He certainly couldn't tell a girl like Wendy that he had spent the night in a whore house. But what could he tell her?

"I'm—I'm not sure. It must be along here somewhere." He nodded vaguely down the street. "But I am sure Deafy has already left. We will find him."

"Maybe he is eating breakfast. It's still early." She nodded toward the cafe in which Kim had eaten earlier that morning, "Will you buy me a cup of coffee?"

For a moment Kim stood motionless. He still didn't have any money. He was at a loss as to what to do until, to his complete surprise, he found himself telling Wendy of the entire embarassing episode. He didn't leave out any of it.

Wendy's laugh pealed up and down the street. Several people stopped and looked. Then they grinned and moved on.

"Then I'll buy *you* a cup," Wendy said.

Kim grinned sheepishly and agreed. The cafe was still filled with men, and they all stared as Kim and Wendy entered. The same waiter, with the thin hair and the stopped shoulders, waited on He glared at Kim.

The coffee was strong and black as it had been at breakfast, but Kim could have been drinking creosote and not known it. The men who were in the cafe were very quiet, and all of them were looking at Wendy. She was not in the least perturbed or self-conscious. Kim suspected that she was accustomed to such situations.

A tiny frown caused Wendy's blue eyes to narrow slightly and the long lashes to curve a bit. She sipped her coffee thoughtfully.

"Did he have any money?"

"Who?" Kim asked in surprise.

"Deafy."

"Oh." Kim had not been thinking of Deafy, "I'm not sure."

"No one is ever sure about Deafy," Wendy grinned. "But if he is broke, he will be looking for a job. If he isn't, he will be drinking or gambling."

"I didn't know Deafy drank and gambled," Kim blurted.

"Well he does," Wendy grinned again. "He is a wicked old man. He likes whiskey and gambling and women."

There was so much tenderness in her voice that Kim knew Wendy was not condemning Deafy. The mischievous grin that made her eyes sparkle and crinkle at the corners led Kim to believe that she actually enjoyed knowing of Deafy's faults. It surprised him that Wendy said Deafy liked women. Such a statement from most girls would have sounded vulgar. Wendy made it sound as if Deafy were an errant child who liked candy.

"I suppose all men are alike," Kim said lightly. He wanted Wendy to continue talking.

She looked at him quizzically for a second. The light left her eyes, and Kim wished that he hadn't spoken at all.

"No," she said seriously, "I don't think all men are alike. In fact, I think they are very different." Then she added with conviction, "Deafy Jones has a thousand vices—but for every vice he has a thousand virtues."

Kim didn't say anything. He shouldn't have tried to be facetious, he decided.

"All men don't have virtues that outweigh their vices," Wendy continued, almost defiantly.

Kim nodded in agreement. He didn't want Wendy to remember her errand of finding Deafy. He wished she would talk of something else. Besides, in a moment of introspection, he wondered whether Kim Wingate had either vices or virtues worthy of comment. It was an uncomfortable thought.

"How long have you known Deafy?" Kim thought he detected just the slightest trace of suspicion in her voice.

Kim honestly intended to lie to her, but to his utter amazement he found himself telling Wendy the entire story. Her eyes showed concern when he told of his fight with Joe Shay and Deafy's rescue. But when he told of Deafy stealing the tablecloth to bind his chest and of spending the night in Sal's place, the twinkle came back to Wendy's eyes.

"That's just like Deafy!" she said. "He wouldn't hesitate for a moment to ask one friend to do a favor for another."

"I had that same feeling," Kim admitted candidly. "But somehow I don't think Deafy would have asked Sal for a bed if it hadn't been for me."

"He wouldn't," confirmed Wendy.

"Then why for *me?*"

"Because he liked you, I suppose." She looked at Kim appraisingly, thinking of a picture packed away in a box of childhood mementoes. "And he knew that Sal would take care of you."

"You know Sal?" he asked incredulously.

"Yes. I know Sal," she answered calmly. "I also know Joe Shay. You will find, Kim, that many of the same people travel from one field to another. They are a little like a band of gypsies, or artists, or thieves. The lure of oil draws them. Most of them are wonderful, hard working and generous people—like Deafy Jones. Then there are the Joe Shays."

"Who is Joe Shay?"

"Joe is a product of Spindletop," Wendy said almost grimly. "He has an insane hatred for Negroes. No one knows who his parents were. He just sort of grew up in the oil fields. When he was small, everyone called him 'Nig' because of his dark features. When he got older, he beat anyone who called him by the nickname, and he developed a terrible hatred for Negroes. He shows up in every camp. Father occasionally lends him money, and gives him jobs. Once he kept Joe from going to the penitentiary. I don't know why Father does it. He usually lets people take care of themselves. I have never seen anyone except Deafy Jones, and Father, who was not afraid of him."

A tiny variation in the pitch of Wendy's voice when she spoke Joe Shay's name stirred something in Kim.

"Are you afraid of him, Wendy?"

She hesitated for a fraction of a second, her face troubled and her eyes veiled, "Yes."

"Why?"

"It doesn't matter, Kim."

It mattered to Kim. He wanted to tell her so. But he heard a gasp from Wendy.

"Oh!" she said softly, and a gleam lit her eyes. "There he is now."

Deafy was coming in the door. Wendy jumped up and ran toward him. Deafy grinned broadly as he saw her.

"Hello, Wendy." Deafy extended his hand, and Wendy ignored it. She threw her arms around his neck and kissed him on his weather-beaten and bearded cheek. Deafy's hat was on the back of his head, and his one good eye was gleaming with delight. His flat, hard lips were parted in a tobacco-stained grin.

"You're the hardest man to find, Deafy Jones!" There was a tear in Wendy's voice.

"That damned Deafy!" a man in dirty overalls growled in awe.

"Deafy," Wendy said excitedly. "Where can we talk? I have a million things to ask you."

"Right here is as good a place as any," he said gesturing toward the table from which Wendy had risen. It was then that he spied Kim. "Now where in tarnation did you find Kim Wingate?" he asked Wendy in surprise.

"I fished him out of a creek," she said gaily. Kim grinned at

Deafy.

They sat at the table, and the tired waiter wiped half-heartedly at the red and white checked oil cloth.

"What'll it be?"

"Coffee, I reckon," Deafy said without looking at the waiter.

"That will be fine," Wendy echoed and Kim nodded.

"Four bits a cup if you set at a table and don't order nothing else," the waiter said sourly.

Deafy looked at the waiter for the first time. His good eye gleamed.

"It'll be fifteen cents, just like every place else," Deafy said flatly. "And don't you slosh it on the table."

"Hey Cookie!" the waiter yelled.

The big cook appeared in the kitchen doorway. He had the meat cleaver in his hand.

"What's the matter now, Clyde?"

"This gent says our coffee is only fifteen cents served to him and his girl griend at a table—and they ain't ordering nothing else."

The cook looked at Deafy, and recognition dawned in his small eyes. Deafy wasn't looking at the cook. He was glaring murderously at Clyde.

"That's Deafy Jones, Clyde," the cook said as if that explained everything. "And he can have his coffee *free* if he wants it. You quit calling me from my kitchen so damned much."

The cook turned and walked toward the kitchen. Clyde followed him.

"Now look, Cookie," Clyde whined his protest. "You said if I had any trouble just to call you. Now you won't back me up when some old devil tries to steal our coffee."

Cookie glared at Clyde.

"I don't give a damn what I said. You give Deafy Jones and that lady their coffee." Then he justified his stand. "You come from Amarillo, Clyde. I come from Smackover. You got a lot to learn about oil boomers. Now you do like I said."

"All right," Clyde said complainingly. "But don't blame me if—"

"Blame you, hell!" The big cook whirled on the hapless waiter. "You're going to be lucky if Deafy don't make you eat that fifteen cents for calling Blake Terrell's daughter his girl friend!"

Clyde served the coffee. Deafy didn't look at him as he did so. But Kim couldn't resist grinning at the man.

"Coffee ain't too good," Deafy said gruffly in a tone that the waiter could hear. "But I reckon it beats nothing."

"It's delicious," Wendy said as she sipped. "I haven't drunk such good coffee in—ages."

"You have grown up since I last seen you, Wendy." Deafy squinted his good eye at her. "You've put on a lot of chest and leg."

"I'm twenty-one years old, Deafy—had a birthday in December," she said softly. "Now, tell me. What have you been doing, and where have you been?"

"Same old thing," Deafy said. "I been drilling. Went over to Mexia from Ranger. Then back to Spindle for a while. Lately, things have been a little slack."

"I know."

"I thought about writing you Wendy, a few times. But never got around to it. Where you been? You didn't come in with Blake yesterday."

"I was already here. Have been for three days. Dad wired me to stay at the Herring Hotel in Amarillo until he arrived, but I came on into camp. The house was ready and I didn't see any reason to wait for him."

"I'll bet Blake raised hell." Deafy said gleefully.

"He probably will," Wendy grinned. "I haven't seen him yet."

"He stayed in camp, didn't he?" Deafy asked in surprise.

"Oh, he's in camp, all right," Wendy said. "But I had gone to Amarillo when he and Maria got in yesterday. And when I got back he had left Maria at the house and had come back to camp. Maria and I talked until after midnight. Father must have come home later. Maria slept with me, and I heard father leave about sunup this morning." Then she added a bit wistfully, "I haven't seen him in almost six months."

"What happened after I left Ranger?" Deafy asked gruffly.

"Well," Wendy said thoughtfully, "You remember, I was just starting to high school when you and father—." She stopped, and her face flushed.

"Hell!" Deafy growled consolingly, "men fall out once in a while. Don't mean nothing."

"It meant something to me!"

"Never mind, lass," Deafy said kindly. "What happened to you?"

"Well," Wendy brightened again and Kim listened intently, "I finally finished high school and then I persuaded Father to let me go to college in the east."

"I'll be damned!" Deafy said in awe.

"I did," Wendy grinned. "And then, last year, when I had a vacation, father was enthused about an oil strike in South America. He wanted to go there, but he couldn't very well take me. So before he quite knew what was happening, he had bought me a ticket to

New York for a wonderful vacation. I finished school at mid-term a few weeks ago. Then I came to Amarillo by train, bought a car and—here I am."

"Now don't that beat all!" Deafy said. "Blake must be getting soft, Wendy."

"You know better than that, Deafy," Wendy said matter-of-factly. "He would never have let me go to New York if he hadn't wanted so badly to go to South America. There just wasn't anything else to do with me. He was coming back east to see me, but on his way back from South America he stopped in New Orleans and got involved with a dancer. He married her. I think you already know that, though. I'm glad he did. She's very beautiful and very nice. I like her."

"What you got in mind to do now, Wendy?"

"I'm not sure, Deafy," she said seriously. "I don't intend to stay here long. Maybe I'll go to Europe. Maria says that Father thinks this strike is a big one, though. It may last a long time."

"Well, he was right about the strike."

"How big is it, Deafy?"

"Big. Maybe bigger than Spindletop. Nobody knows how big. But I can feel it."

"I can feel it too," Wendy said, and Kim wondered what they were talking about.

"Sure you can, Wendy," Deafy agreed. "You got oil in your veins, too."

"What are your plans, Deafy?"

"Don't know yet. I been offered a dozen jobs this morning. Gushers are coming in all over the prairie—and not half enough men to drill them. Blake will have a dozen rigs in here in thirty days. So will the big companies. Gulf and Twin Six and Huber and a lot more are moving in fast."

"Will you hire out to one of them?"

"I reckon," Deafy said. "Fact is, I may go out today if I can find a toolie."

"What's a toolie?" Kim wanted to know.

"Feller that keeps the bit sharp, fires the boiler and a thousand other damned things that don't take no sense to do," Deafy said. Wendy grinned at Kim.

"Deafy," Kim blurted involuntarily, "do you suppose I could do that?"

"Do what?" Deafy looked at Kim in surprise.

"Be a tooler—toolie, whatever you call it," Kim said eagerly.

"Thought you was on your way to California," Deafy said.

"I was," Kim said. "I am. But if you think I could learn to do the kind of work you want, I'd like to stay around a while." Kim was shocked at himself. He wondered why he was suddenly so eager to stay in this tawdry place.

"Any damn fool can do the kind of work I do," Deafy said crossly.

"Then let me help," Kim said hurriedly. "I'll try hard."

"What kind of work have you done?" Deafy asked as he looked sternly at Kim.

"I've never done a bit of work in my life, outside of mowing a few lawns," Kim answered truthfully. "But I'm not afraid to try."

"Guess you wouldn't be," Deafy admitted, "the way you was chasing that suitcase of yours all over hell and back."

"Give him a chance, Deafy," Wendy entered the conversation again.

"Being a tool dresser ain't what I'd call much of a chance," Deafy said gruffly. "But if you want to be a damn fool then I reckon it ain't any of my business. Anyway, you can make a hundred dollars a tower."

"A hundred dollars a tower!" Wendy exclaimed. "For a tool dresser? Who's paying that kind of money?"

"What's a tower?" Kim asked. It might mean a month for all he knew.

"One twelve hour shift," Wendy said without looking at him. "Who did you hire out to, Deafy?"

"Man named Oschner," Deafy said. Kim saw Wendy's eyes open a bit and then narrow at the mention of Oschner's name. He was certain that she knew the man though she said nothing more.

"I didn't aim to go out for a couple of days," Deafy continued. "But this feller is in a hurry."

"When are you going out?" Wendy asked.

"Right now," Deafy rose from his chair.

"Oh," Wendy's voice betrayed her disappointment. "Couldn't you wait until tomorrow?"

"Not this time, Wendy," Deafy's voice was gentle. "I'll get word to you next time I am in camp." Then to Kim: "You and Wendy pick up our gear at Sal's and meet me in front of that little grocery tent down the street as soon as you can. That is, if you still want to go."

"I still want to go, Deafy," Kim said. "If you think I can do the work."

Wendy smiled directly at him and Kim felt an inch taller.

"The work ain't hard to learn," Deafy said shortly and dropped a half dollar on the table. Without another word he walked from the cafe. Kim and Wendy sat for a moment in silence.

"Deafy doesn't waste time, does he?" Wendy smiled.

Kim merely shook his head. He was wondering if Wendy really would go to Sal's place with him to get their gear. At the moment he was having misgivings about the whole affair. He wished he hadn't been so impulsive.

"Let's go," Wendy said as she rose. "Deafy will be waiting."

Kim followed her from the cafe. Wendy walked into Sal's Place without the least hesitation. No one was in the front room and Wendy rapped sharply on the counter. Kim heard a stirring in the hallway, and the door opened. Sal opened it.

Her eyes were still blinded with sleep and she was grumbling.

"Ought to be a law against a man wanting a woman before noontime," she said heavily without looking at Kim and Wendy.

"Hello, Sal." Wendy's voice was friendly.

Sal stopped still, and then swiftly adjusted her slovenly robe. "Wendy Terrell!"

"How are you, Sal?" Wendy extended her hand.

"I'm fine, Wendy," she grasped Wendy's hand and pumped it several times. "Sal heard you was in New York. My, but you are a pretty thing. Sal is mighty glad to see you."

"I'm glad to see you, too, Sal," Wendy assured her. "We came to get Deafy's things."

"Deafy's gear is here," Sal said. "He was in yesterday with a—." She noticed Kim for the first time, "with this young fellow here." She pointed toward Kim.

"I know he was, Sal," Wendy said. "He is waiting for us now. He and Kim have a job."

"Now ain't that fine," Sal said approvingly. Then she squinted her large eyes at Kim. "Young man, you have been in good company both times I've seen you."

"That I have, Sal," Kim admitted.

"You want your money now?"

"Not now, Sal. I'll come back for it."

"You do that."

Kim and Wendy got the gear and walked out on the street again.

"Oh!" Kim exclaimed in consternation.

"What, Kim?" Wendy inquired anxiously.

"I'll have to let my mother know," Kim said. "She thinks I'm on my way to California."

"You could write her," Wendy said practically. "Sal would have paper and an envelope."

They returned to Sal's and she furnished the necessary materials. Kim worded the message as thoughtfully and as diplomatically as he possibly could. He explained only briefly that he had stopped off to visit a friend and would soon be on his way again. It took him fifteen minutes to compose the message.

"What return address can I put on it?" Kim asked Wendy querulously.

"Put Box 61, Amarillo, Texas, on it," Wendy said matter of factly. "I rented the box when I was there yesterday." Kim complied.

Deafy was waiting beside a *White* truck. He didn't pay any attention to them. He was busy tinkering with the hood.

"You drive, Kim," he finally said. Then he added, "That's our boss in that Stutz right behind us."

Kim saw two men sitting in the car. One was of medium size and the other was small and looked, Kim thought, something like a weasel.

The truck had no cab or windshield. Kim climbed into the seat and turned the ignition. Deafy spun the crank and the motor caught with a roar which was not reduced by any muffler. Kim looked at Wendy and she smiled.

It took Kim a few seconds to figure out the gear shift combination. Then he shoved the truck into low gear and they roared down the street. He turned to wave to Wendy. Deafy looked straight ahead.

Wendy stared after them as they moved down the street. She was glad Deafy had someone with him, for she knew he was often lonely. And Kim seemed like a nice young man. She knew he had been pleased with her company, and she expected that she would see him again. He was an unusual person to find in an oil field; she doubted that he would stay long.

She turned back to her car and sat a moment before starting it. The excitement of the place infected her, too. She was, after all, her father's daughter. She returned home in a happy mood. She had seen Deafy and Sal; Deafy had a job, and what's more he had someone to share it with him!

CHAPTER V

In the days following Deafy and Kim's departure for the drilling rig, news of the oil strike in the Texas Panhandle spread like a prairie fire blown by a hard wind. Every conceivable specimen of human being was drawn to the camp. From all sections of the country, and even from foreign lands, they converged, until in less than three months, where there had not been a hundred people in a ten mile radius, there was now a surging, seething mass of more than forty thousand.

In the boiling, turbulent cauldron of humanity there were honest workmen, drillers, riggers, tool dressers, roustabouts and casing men. And there were thieves, dope peddlers, bootleggers, pickpockets, bandits, prostitutes, murderers and fools.

The land of the Indian watched silently and brooded as those who had conquered it, seemingly sought to destroy themselves. For there *was* loosed upon its surface the naked and ugly *passions* of men and women who fought for the fabulous material treasures of the land like hungry animals over a bone.

The small railroad town of Panhandle, south of camp, where the stationmaster had loaded crates of eggs and an occasional shipment of cattle, was now handling tonnage second only to Chicago. From it there was a continuous stream of trucks and wagons loaded with equipment flowing toward the oil camp.

And crime was rampant. A harassed and exhausted county sheriff and his two deputies tried vainly to enforce the law. A man was found dead from a stab wound in the back, and another was hi-jacked in broad daylight on the one long main street of camp. Gambling flourished, and liquor was bought and sold in almost every building and tent. Prostitutes operated without molestation, and narcotics peddlers hawked their wares from alley entrances.

Echoes of the strike invaded the far eastern parts of the United States. A crime syndicate of a big city sent a representative to determine whether it would be profitable to move into the camp.

Farmers and ranchers in the area saw smoke from the fires and shook their heads dubiously.

The land throbbed, and the flood roared on.

Blake Terrell was intensely happy in the new camp. It was a raw, rough, roaring thing and he thrived on it. Day by day, he grew more feverish in his activity.

He ranged the fields, and when he heard that there might be land for lease, he was the first to arrive. Many of the ranches were involved in legal complications caused by heirs that had long forgotten their interests in the worthless land until oil had made it almost priceless. Blake put Claude Butler on retainer to handle his affairs exclusively. Butler was a man after Blake's own heart. He was a cold, heartless man and never showed emotion of any kind, but his knowledge of the law was extensive. Many times he was able to untangle legal webs which had held land of small ranchers and farmers. Invariably, Blake Terrell wound up with the land under lease.

Butler was earning his money! What was more, he always inserted the ingenious clauses which were advantageous to his client, and Blake never had to worry about the legality of his transactions. Besides, it gave Blake a feeling of importance to have a lawyer working exclusively for him. Life was good to Blake Terrell. The sky was the limit! Never again in his lifetime would he find a situation more to his liking.

But he had his difficulties too! Three times during the first two weeks, he went to the Beatenbow ranch. The first time, he took Wendy with him, for he knew that people were naturally attracted to his friendly daughter. That day he was his most expansive. He made no attempt to talk of leasing the Beatenbow land.

The next two times he went there, however, Wendy did not accompany him, and Blake tried every trick he knew to get the gnome-like old woman who owned the place to lease her twelve thousand acres to the Terrell Oil Company.

He did not succeed in leasing the Beatenbow land, but he hadn't given up. He would try again and again. And finally, he would get it. In the meantime, he was getting started! He made numerous trips to Amarillo to expedite, by telephone, the moving of more equipment to the camp. Blake came home irregularly and stayed only long enough to sleep a few hours and was off again.

He saw his new bride only briefly and occasionally. She was becoming morose, and, in Blake's presence, she pouted. Maria was beginning to doubt, for the first time in her life, her influence with men. Not once since they had arrived in camp had her husband asked her to dance for him. And Maria liked to be admired by men! And Blake would not even let her go into the camp alone! How foolish! Maria had no fear of men. What could they do to her that she had not experienced a hundred times!

But all was not bad for Maria. Strangely, the thing that she had feared most, now was her greatest ally. Maria knew that her husband still considered Wendy a child. He would be surprised, thought Maria, to know that she was actually a very lovely and desirable woman. Maria had been prepared to dislike her husband's daughter very much and was even more determined when she had found that Wendy was only a few years younger than she. But even Maria's instinctive suspicion of members of her own sex and her plans to alienate father and daughter were soon banished by Wendy's outgoing friendliness and winsome personality.

In a few short weeks, Wendy Terrell and her father's wife were good friends. To Maria, the experience was new and pleasant, for she had never had a friend of her own sex before. They found adventure in redecorating the house and rearranging the furniture. They had a piano hauled from Amarillo, and Maria taught Wendy new songs and dance steps. Wendy helped Maria learn to paint with oils.

When they had finished one project, Wendy always had another in the offing. There seemed to be no end of interesting things they could find to do.

"I learned to do a great many things when Father and I spent so much time alone in the camps," Wendy explained one day when Maria remarked about it. "You need things to do to keep from being lonely."

"You *are* lonely, aren't you, Wendy?" Maria said softly.

Wendy looked surprised at Maria's question. "No," she said seriously. "I don't think I am. I used to be lonely when I was small, and Father brought me from my grandparents to stay with him in camp. I was so lonely that I dreaded the nights and the mornings. But that was a long time ago."

"I *still* think you are lonely," Maria said. "There are no men in your life."

"Oh, but there are!" Wendy's light-hearted laugh caused Maria to smile in spite of herself. "There was an artist in New York who wanted to paint me in the nude, and there was a Frenchman who told me that I reminded him of the Champs Elysees in Spring, and there is Deafy Jones, and—"

"Has there ever really been a man in your life, Wendy?" Maria asked in all seriousness.

"I have never slept with a man, if that is what you mean. I have never wanted to," Wendy said candidly.

"Have you seen that young friend of Mr. Deafy Jones again?"

"No," Wendy answered, and Maria noted that there was just the slightest pause before her answer.

That was the end of their discussion of men and life. Maria liked to talk of men and she was disappointed that Wendy did not.

Perhaps that was why Maria was never jealous of Wendy's beauty. There were no men in their life whose favors they had to vie for. There was only Blake Terrell. And Joe Shay! Occasionally, Blake brought him by the house for a few minutes. But Joe Shay was more animal than human. Still, Maria liked to feel his eyes upon her. Strange that he never seemed to notice Wendy! He ignored her almost completely.

And, of course, there was Claude Butler. His expressionless eyes and face irritated Maria. He had been to their house twice, but he had never looked at either her or Wendy with desire or animation. Maria found his demeanor frustrating and uncomplimentary and said as much to Wendy. Wendy only laughed and shrugged.

Blake was vaguely aware that his new wife and his daughter were compatible and he was glad they were, for he had no time for trouble at home. He had to concentrate on his business. The bickering, trading, and incessant activities of the oil camp were Blake's element. He enjoyed every minute of the exciting, hectic days.

Not so with Kim Wingate!

He suffered through the most nightmarish days of his twenty-two year life. It all began the day he and Deafy Jones hired out to Oschner. The derrick was located about two miles from camp, near a small ravine. Just north of the rig was a barbed wire fence running east and west.

Kim and Deafy bumped along behind Oschner's car until they came to the derrick. Oschner got out and was immediately followed by the small man who accompanied him. Kim and Deafy dismounted from the truck.

None of the four men spoke for several minutes. Deafy busied himself looking over the equipment. Kim covertly studied the two men as they watched Deafy. Oschner was, decided Kim, easy to figure out. Money and ambition. But the little weasel-eyed man with him was different. Both were well dressed, but there was something sinister about the small man.

"This is it, huh?" Deafy spat tobacco juice as he walked back to the group.

"This is it, Oschner agreed. "Spudded in and down to a thousand feet."

"How come your crew to quit?" Deafy asked.

Oschner considered a moment. "They got drunk."

"They quit a good paying job," Deafy said. "Even a driller don't quit just to get drunk. What happened?"

"Now look, Jones," Oschner's face flushed a bit. "Do you want the job, or don't you? I didn't come all the way out here to answer questions. I made you an offer, and you took me up on it. Now if you're going to back out—"

"I never said anything about backing out," Deafy said flatly. "But I sure as hell can ask questions if I want to."

Kim had been watching the small man during the exchange. When Oschner raised his voice the man drew off a leather glove and put his right hand in his overcoat pocket. Kim wondered if Deafy had noticed.

"Well," Oschner said crossly. "You can ask all the questions you want. I don't have to answer them."

"You don't," agreed Deafy. "But that don't mean I can't ask them."

"All right. All right," Oschner said in exasperation. "There is your rig. You're in charge. I will send out some food before dark."

"Send some blankets and cots, too," Deafy instructed. "Me and Kim can run till tomorrow, but we will need a couple more men by then. A feller has got to get some sleep."

"All right. I will send out two more men tomorrow, or earlier if I can find them."

"You do that."

"And I want this rig running twenty-four hours a day until you hit oil."

"If there is oil down there, we will hit it," Deafy said.

"Then fire up," Oschner said, and he and his shadow left Kim and Deafy standing by the rig.

Deafy seemed not to hear. He walked about the rig for a few minutes after Oschner drove away. Kim followed Deafy about, having not the least idea what to do. Deafy was squatting beside a long belt when he finally spoke.

"Loosen that idler wheel, Kim," he said.

"The what?"

"That wheel that takes the slack out of this belt," Deafy said, pointing to the wheel to which he referred.

Kim grabbed the wheel, glad at last to be doing something. He tugged and pulled, but nothing happened.

"Loosen that dog-ear screw—there, just below your left hand."

Kim twisted the screw and felt the wheel give. Then he pulled, and the belt loosened. It gave him a feeling of intense satisfaction. It was his first effort and perhaps the beginning of something worthwhile and big! Then he felt a bit embarrassed at himself for having gained so much satisfaction out of a simple act. But the Chinese said that a journey of a thousand miles began with a single step, didn't they?

The air was sharp, and Kim took a deep breath of it as he walked down the belt to Deafy. "Now what, Deafy?"

Deafy spat and stopped working with the belt. Kim saw that he was putting new lacing in it.

"Tell you what, Kim," Deafy stopped and considered again. "Why don't you just take a little walk and get yourself a big chest full of fresh air? I got a lot of thinking to do, and when I got to think, I can't talk to nobody."

Kim started to protest, but Deafy continued. "No offense meant, Kim. I just can't talk and work and think at the same time. I can work and think all right, but I can't do all three. Might do you a lot of good to stretch a little anyway. Them ribs of yours ain't healed in twenty-four hours."

"All right, Deafy," Kim said a bit sullenly.

Deafy nodded and spat as Kim walked away. And as he walked, Kim felt his back stiffen as he had seen Deafy's do when he walked away from the man he had kicked in camp. At the thought of it, Kim grinned a bit and let his shoulder muscles loosen. He would have to watch himself or he would be another Deafy Jones!

A hundred yards from the rig, Kim came to the top of a small rise. To the north the land sloped toward the Canadian River. The country was fairly rough, and the several ravines visible were lined with brush and wild plum thickets. Beyond the ravines lay the river. It was a wide expanse of sand, lined on each side with cottonwood trees and some smaller growth that he could not distinguish. Perhaps they were small willow trees. Kim guessed the distance to the river to be a half mile.

Hanging over the river was a faint blue haze. It was the second time Kim had seen the river, and both times the haze had been present. He wondered if it always hung there. The river held a sort of fascination for Kim. Far out from the sandy banks he thought he could see the water flowing. It must be a fairly small stream, he thought.

From his vantage point, Kim turned slowly and looked about. Mile upon mile of the strange country was visible. To the north was the river. To the east were the breaks and rough country. To the south was the wide, flat prairie he had come over the day before. To the west, lay the oil field camp. And though the tents and frame structures were not visible, Kim fancied he could hear the rabble and see smoke rising from it.

He could see more than twenty oil derricks pointing from the tufted earth toward the blue sky. From those derricks, the oil driller's bit clawed at the earth. But with a deep satisfaction, Kim knew that those gouging holes were no more to the land than the irritating sting of summer flies to a grizzly bear. Men would never conquer this country! It was too big—too strong.

Suddenly, Kim was very glad he was where he happened to be at the moment, and college seemed far away. He was at the center of the world.

He walked back toward the rig and Deafy. Somehow he felt years older than he had when he left it a few minutes before. There was a sureness in his stride, and a purposefulness that had not been there when he left. He wondered what his mother would think when she got his letter. He hoped she wouldn't be too disappointed with him.

"I'm ready to go to work, Deafy," he said calmly.

Deafy looked up from his sitting position. He tossed the belt from his lap and reached for his pocket knife and a fresh chew of tobacco.

"All right, Kim. There's plenty of work to do." Deafy put the plug back in his pocket and ran the blade of his knife between his lips to wash away the tobacco stains. He snapped the blade and returned the knife to his pocket.

"You will have to show me what to do, Deafy."

"I can do that all right, Kim. It ain't hard to learn." Deafy was silent for a moment and made no move to rise. "Let's set a minute, Kim—and talk. Likely, this is the last chance we will get to set down for a long time, anyway."

There was a bit of uncertainty and puzzlement in Deafy's voice that Kim had not heard before. He sat down beside Deafy and lit a cigarette.

"I'll show you how this thing works in a minute. But there's a couple of things I'd like to talk about first."

Kim nodded.

"First off—this here strike is a big one. I got a feeling. Every real oil man gets it if he stays in the fields long enough. There's going to be a lot of money pulled up out of this ground." Deafy threw a stone and continued as Kim looked at him in mild surprise. "There's going to be a lot of money made, and it's going to be hard to keep. But I ain't exactly pleased about this job we're on. I can't help but think there's something about it we ought to know, and don't. A man like Oschner hadn't ought to be running a two-bit rig like this here. It's got a coal burning engine. Nearly all the new ones has got gas or oil. And they ain't a storage tank in a half a mile of here in case we hit oil. Course he's got plenty of time to build one.—And these tools— they're old and wore out. The man that's been running this rig didn't have money, or he would have had a lot of equipment that he ain't got."

Deafy shook his head again and spat a stream of tobacco juice. Kim was silent; he knew Deafy wasn't through talking.

"Just don't stand to reason," Deafy said with concern, "that a man like Oschner would own this kind of rig. Most likely he bought it offen some driller that's went broke. Now Kim, that don't make sense either—if this field is as good as they say it is. If a man had a rig, he could get backing. And another thing—Oschner is paying you and me a hundred dollars a tower to work for him. That's two hundred dollars a day if we work only twelve hours. I heard in town that drillers are drawing fifty dollars a tower and toolies thirty. Then why is he paying you and me that much? If he can't afford a better rig than this, he sure can't afford to pay his men double the going wage!"

Again, Deafy paused, and again Kim waited.

"Kim, I got a feeling, a sort of hunch, that Blake Terrell is mixed up in this some way or other!"

Kim pulled his ear thoughtfully and remembered the look that Wendy had given Deafy when he told her who they were going to work for. It was a strange situation.

"You think we ought to look into it more, Deafy? You certainly have plenty of reason not to want to work for Terrell. I don't think talking a thing out will hurt anybody."

"It ain't that," Deafy said with a frown. "I don't like Blake Terrell, and I won't work for him. But he's got guts. He wasn't afraid to cheat me—and it ain't every man that's got guts enough to do that. But Blake thinks too much of money, and he's mean." Deafy paused and continued. His voice was bitter. "He didn't have to punch my eye out! He's strong as a bull. I never was much to look at, and now I don't even like to see myself when I shave."

"Deafy!" Kim said. "Your face isn't that bad."

"Yes, it is, Kim. Wendy Terrell and Sal are the only two women I know who don't flinch when they look at me. I even put a patch over it when I go whoring."

Kim searched for something to say and could find nothing. Deafy's eye *was* unsightly.

Deafy continued. Kim knew that he was doing all his talking at one time, and he was content to listen.

"I never did hold it against Blake too much for beating me out of a rig. It was the *reason* he cheated me that made me mad. That, and gouging my eye out, though I reckon that's the only way he could of whipped me. But he could have made just as much money by staying with me. He just wanted it all to himself. And he got it. If he had wanted something for Wendy, I would have forgotten about it. I'd cheat *him* if it would help that girl of his. If it hadn't been for Wendy, I would have killed Blake. But I didn't—and I won't."

"Were you and Terrell partners, Deafy?" Kim asked hesitantly.

Deafy nodded and spat. "Yep. I reckon you'd call it that. We owned a rig together—and worked together."

"How did he cheat you?"

"One of them damned legal shenanigans of his," Deafy said bitterly. "It's no matter now."

"Wendy certainly doesn't take after him, does she?" Kim said almost timidly. He didn't want Deafy to think he was prying.

"She sure don't," Deafy said and a smile of pleasure crossed his face. "Wendy don't take after nobody."

"How long have you known her, Deafy?" Kim asked casually. He hoped Deafy didn't think him unduly inquisitive.

"Most all of her life." Deafy didn't mind in the least. "She was three years old when Blake started working for me as a toolie. Wendy's mother had been dead a year. Blake kept her. But he couldn't always do that so his wife's folks had to keep her a lot. That's how come Wendy has got good manners. They saw that she got proper schooling and treatment. It always galled Blake when he had to leave her with them and it's a damn shame that they didn't keep her all the time. But Blake wouldn't have that. When we got to a place that we was going to stay a while, Blake always sent for her and hired some woman to look after her. I'll give Blake his due, he done the best he could by her. He sent her to school, but it was the grandparents' teaching that caused Wendy to be a lady. After she was ten years old Blake kept her all the time. She learned to cook and take care of things. She's got spunk—Wendy has. I've seen her whip boys bigger than she was. Mostly she took after her mother I guess, but she's got that much of her daddy in her."

"Well, I'll be darned," Kim said in surprise, "I just sort of supposed that Blake Terrell was a coward. Most bullies are."

"Huh! snorted Deafy, "Don't ever think that. Blake Terrell would fight a circle saw to get something he wanted—or to keep something he has."

"The oil fields must have been a lonely place for a little girl," Kim said feelingly.

"I guess it was," Deafy admitted sadly. "But we had some good years, too. We had another—man with us at the time."

The touch of tenderness in Deafy's voice and his hesitation when he mentioned the other man caused Kim to look at him sharply. But Deafy did not elaborate, and Kim thought it best that he not question him further.

"Well," Kim finally offered. "She certainly did turn out to be a very self-sufficient young lady."

"Wendy can take care of herself," Deafy said.

"She sure can," Kim admitted sheepishly. "She pulled a gun on me the first time I saw her."

"Did she now?" There was surprise in Deafy's face.

"She sure did." Then Kim told Deafy how Wendy's car had been stuck in the sand, and he had walked up to be of assistance.

"Well, now!" Deafy grinned his appreciation of the story. "That sure is fine. I've seen her hit a tin can six shots out of six with that little pistol of hers. I gave it to her myself when she was twelve years old. Glad she hasn't forgot how to use it."

"I'm glad she *didn't* use it!" Kim said feelingly.

"Well," Deafy said belligerently, "she sure as hell would've."

"I don't doubt it," Kim laughed. "I don't think her father need worry about her safety."

Deafy suddenly chuckled. "I guess you're right, Kim. Anyway, Blake has got trouble enough as it is—right now."

"What do you mean?"

"That wife of his! A woman that pretty in a oil field is just like carrying a package of TNT around in your hip pocket. Oil men go after what they want, and they will be a lot of men after Blake's woman. From the looks of her, I doubt if she will discourage 'em much," Deafy said with satisfaction.

"She may not be so bad, Deafy." Kim felt vaguely that he should defend Terrell's wife, though he secretly agreed with Deafy.

"And—Blake ain't only got his wife and a whole field full of jar heads and gamblers to worry about, but he's going to have that woman of his and Wendy under the same roof." Deafy chuckled again.

"What's wrong with that?"

"Maybe nothing," Deafy admitted. "Depends on Blake's wife. Wendy's easy to get along with if she ain't pushed. But if that woman tries to push Wendy around, Blake might as well try to feed two wildcats out of the same saucer of milk."

Kim grinned. "Let's let Blake worry about that, Deafy," he said. "You and I have an oil well to drill."

"You let me set and talk till I'm through!" Deafy said touchily. "Talking is going to stop pretty soon, and you'll wish we *could* set down."

"I expect you are right, Deafy. I guess I'm just a little curious to see if this pile of junk will really work."

"Oh, it'll work all right," Deafy said calmly. "We'll make it work. For a hundred dollars a tower we could dig a well with post hole diggers. Just think, Kim, in sixty days we'll have six thousand dollars apiece. More probably, because we'll have to work extra shifts to keep this rig going. With six thousand, and what you got stashed at Sal's, you might be able to buy yourself some leases and get rich." There was a bantering quality in Deafy's voice.

"Quit kidding me, Deafy," Kim grinned. He had the un- comfortable feeling that Deafy had been reading his thoughts. "And how is it that I'm drawing the same wages as you, when I don't know the first thing about an oil well?"

"Well, now, that *is* right peculiar," Deafy said blandly. "But the feller said he'd pay it, so I guess we got no call to argue with him. Besides, you'll learn. You'll learn fast. And when you get enough money together, you ought to buy yourself some rigs, too. I'll help you."

"Let's do it together, Deafy!" Kim said earnestly.

"Nope," Deafy said emphatically. "They's two kinds of people, Kim. Them that get rich—and the work horses of the world. I just happen to be in the work horse class. I figure maybe you ain't."

Kim started to say something in protest. Deafy stayed him.

"Now me—I'll work here for a while, and then I'll go to camp and get drunk and gamble my money away, or give it away. I ain't got much sense."

"All right, Deafy," Kim laughed. I'll get drunk, too. I owe you a drink anyway, for bandaging my ribs."

"You do at that," Deafy said. "How is them ribs?"

"A little sore, but they don't hurt much."

"Good! Maybe they ain't broke after all."

Deafy rose to his feet and looked up at the derrick. "Well, let's get to work."

"I'm ready, Deafy," Kim said eagerly. "What do we do?"

"You know anything at *all* about a oil well, Kim?"

"Nothing," Kim said flatly.

"That's as good a place to start as any," Deafy said. "Since our derrick is already built and the engine set, and she's spudded in, we don't have to worry about that. That usually takes a couple of days. This well is already down to a thousand feet, so Oschner said. Usually we spud in with a 24 inch bit and go down to three or four hundred feet. Then we cut down to a 19 inch bit till we get to about a thousand feet. From there on we use the bit you see here." Deafy slapped his hand on a big piece of metal that looked a little like a wedge with a flared point.

"That's the bit?" Kim asked in surprise.

"That's it."

"I don't see how that does any digging," Kim said.

"It don't dig," Deafy said. "It's just a big weight with a sharp point, and this cable hooks to the band wheel arm. The engine turns the wheel, and that lifts the cable and bit. What it does is just pound a hole in the earth. This here is jerk-line drilling."

"Oh."

"The bull wheel is up there at the top of the derrick, and the cables run over it. The crown block is that little platform on top. That's where you stand when you are working up there. These belts run to the engine and turn the band wheel. That turns the beam, and the cable moves. When we drill a few inches, we loosen the sprocket chain and lower the bit and pound some more."

Deafy's explanation was sketchy, and Kim was certain that he would never understand it, but Deafy kept on talking of calf wheels, sand line, throw offs, drilling lines, bailers, and numerous other mechanical devices. Kim nodded as Deafy talked.

"We go through a lot of different kinds of earth," Deafy continued. "First is the top soil, then clay bed. Then comes the shale, and that's bad about caving. Lose a lot of tools in shale. Then there's a limestone and granite wash. Granite wash is hard. Dulls a bit fast. Then if we're lucky we hit oil."

Again, Deafy paused and seemed unsure of how to proceed. "Oil here in this field is supposed to be about three thousand or thirty-three hundred feet. We are already down to a thousand. We can drill from fifteen to twenty-five feet a day if everything goes good. We are two thousand feet from oil. At twenty feet a day that means we got to run for about a hundred days to hit it. And we can't stop. Now—is everything clear to you?"

"No it isn't, Deafy," Kim said truthfully. "But maybe if we fire up and start, I can see how it works."

"All right, Kim," Deafy said. Then he yelled, "Let's drill us a oil well."

Two hours later Kim had learned to fire the steam engine. His ribs hurt as he scooped the coal, but the pain gradually lessened as he worked. Then the forge was fired, and the bit was heated until it was red hot. Deafy patiently showed Kim how to beat the point and flanges with a heavy sledge until it was sharp. Kim was impressed with the thoroughness of the work Deafy did. No matter how small or trivial the adjustment, Deafy did not leave it until everything was to his satisfaction. And, though Kim was anxious to get started, he knew that Deafy was really saving time by being so meticulous.

Deafy rechecked everything once more. The engine was running well. Deafy instructed Kim in how to replenish the water from the tank beside the engine house and how to read the pressure gauge. When the gauge got to a certain point marked in red on the dial, a pop-off valve would open and let the overloaded boiler release some pressure.

"Everything looks like it might work," Deafy said sourly. "One other thing we got to check. Go up on the crown block and see for sure that the cables are riding all right and grease it while you are up there."

"You mean climb up to the top of the derrick?"

Deafy looked at Kim in surprise. "Climb, or fly; I don't give a damn. Just grease the crown block. Here's a oil can."

Kim took the proffered can and gazed dubiously at the ladder leading upward. He moved the can from one hand to the other and looked about vaguely. He would need both hands to hold with.

"Stick the spout of the oil can under your belt," Deafy advised.

Kim started to obey and then paused. His pants were already greasy, but he hated to soil them more. Then he shrugged and jammed the spout under his belt. He didn't have anything but wool clothing, anyway. He would have to buy some overalls when he went to town.

He was almost half way up when he paused to look down. His head began to swim, and he immediately held tighter and started climbing faster. On top of the derrick he lay for a moment on the platform and panted for breath. He heard Deafy yell but paid no attention. He was scared. High places had always bothered him. He wondered how often he would have to do this.

Finally he sat upright and then stood. There was a railing around the platform that offered some semblance of security, but it seemed that the derrick swayed a bit. He squirted oil at the pulley over which the cable ran and hoped that he had performed the task he was supposed to perform. The cable seemed to be fitting into the groove. Wasn't that what Deafy had said for him to examine? He hoped so.

Then, summoning his strength, Kim looked about him. From the top of the tower he could see the camp. Cars and trucks were still grinding through it, and the people, though small, were scurrying about like ants. From the south and from the east and southwest he could see vehicles converging on the camp. There were hundreds of them. To the north was the river, and even there, vehicles were crossing. It looked as if cars were being towed across by teams of mules and horses.

Closer to the derrick, Kim could see a barbed wire fence which ran east and west for some distance, and then north to the river's edge. In the enclosure, which Kim judged to be approximately a hundred acres, were several horses. A few small colts cavorted around the bigger horses. He surmised, correctly, that the pasture was for foaling mares.

Kim knew something about horses and he looked at the herd with interest. The colts were early. More would be coming in the spring. For the moment Kim forgot that he was perched atop an oil derrick.

It was Deafy's yell floating up to him that reminded Kim that he was a hundred and twenty feet above the ground and was supposed to be working. And he certainly wasn't looking forward to the trip back to the ground! But he gritted his teeth and secured the oil can under his belt again. Gently he eased himself over the side of the platform. He was grateful when his foot found the ladder rung.

Once more on the ground, Kim felt a sense of accomplishment and of immense relief.

"How often do I have to go up there, Deafy?"

"Often as necessary. You're the toolie, and that's your job—along with firing the boiler, and dressing the bit, and a thousand other damn things."

"What do you do?"

"I'm the jar head," Deafy said. "I don't do nothing."

"What's a jar head?"

"A jar head is a driller," Deafy said. "You will see why he's called that when that bit starts jarring up and down."

"Oh."

Deafy checked again and then moved over to a big lever that engaged the band wheel. Kim felt a thrill of anticipation as Deafy eased the lever down, and the belt took hold. Then the engine gathered its load, and the band wheel turned. The cable raised and then fell with a jar as the bit, far in the earth, drove another inch toward oil!

For a few minutes, Kim stood and stared, fascinated, as he watched the rhythmic up and down movements of the cable. Only forty-eight hours ago he had been on his way to California to go back to college. Now he was an oil man!

Then he heard Deafy yelling at him.

"Check your gauge, Kim. We ain't got as much steam as we ought to have."

Kim hurriedly shoveled in more coal—more than Deafy had told him to. Then he checked the water. Everything was fine.

Ten minutes later, as Kim was staring at the cable again, he heard a hissing, spewing sound. For a second he was sure that the well had blown in. Then he looked at the engine room, and white smoke was erupting from it. He rushed toward it, not knowing in the least what he expected to do. He yelled frantically to Deafy. Deafy walked unhurriedly toward him.

"Pop-off valve is working, all right," Deafy said calmly.

It was. The boiler had built up enough pressure so that the pop-off had opened and let some steam escape. The hot, moisture-laden air coming from the pop-off valve turned white in the cold air outside.

Kim breathed a sigh of relief.

Four hours later, Kim decided that Deafy's description of the tool dresser's job had not been adequate. He had performed a hundred tasks, and there was more to do. He hadn't stopped more than a few minutes at a time.

And Deafy worked too. He made adjustments and examinations constantly. Kim was tired, and he suddenly remembered that he was hungry. The sun was almost down. They had been working nearly five hours. He wondered when the men would get there with the food.

He was still wondering the same thing at midnight. Oschner had promised food and blankets and cots. But he had not shown up. The bedding wouldn't have been worthwhile anyway, for they would not have had time to use them. But the food would have been most welcome.

Kim was becoming irritable. He could never remember being so hungry. He had not even had lunch. If Oschner expected men to work, he had to feed them! If that was the reason his first crew had quit, Kim didn't blame them.

"They'll get here." Deafy was unperturbed. "Didn't much figure they'd get back today, anyway."

"Oschner *said* he would," Kim argued.

"Have a chew of tobacco," Deafy offered. "Keeps you from getting too hungry."

For a moment, Kim was tempted but refused. He lighted a cigarette instead.

"You'll have to be careful with them matches when we get close to pay dirt. If a flame was to set the gas that comes out, we would lose a string of tools and maybe our scalps."

Kim started to drop the cigarette.

"Not yet, Kim. Maybe another sixty or ninety days."

"Well, I hope we eat before then."

Deafy grinned.

"Is a well likely to catch fire, Deafy?"

"A lot of them do. A piece of gravel may hit the casing and cause a spark. That starts it, and all hell breaks loose when that happens."

"What do you do?"

"Run like hell. If you're lucky enough to get awway, then you find some man that ain't got much sense to pack a bunch of nitro-glycerine up to the well. He puts a weight on it and drops it into the hole. When the nitro goes off, the fire goes out."

"It seems to me that it would be too hot for a man to get close enough to it."

"They wear asbestos suits, and there is a truck with a water tank and a hose that shoots water on them as they get close to it. Dangerous work, though."

"What happens if the TNT goes off too soon?"

"Then," Deafy grinned, "you have to find another man to shoot it."

"I wouldn't want that job!" Kim said feelingly.

"Not many men do. I hear they got a good one though in Amarillo. Man named Tex Thornton."

"Well, he can have it!"

"Steam's getting low, Kim."

Kim shoveled in more coal. His back was getting sore, and he had blisters on his hands.

It was almost noon next day when a car approached the rig. Kim knew that he would never be as tired again. But his hunger had abated somewhat. A tall, slender man got out of the car and started walking toward them. Kim was watching the man when he heard Deafy's voice above the engine.

"That's close enough, mister. What you want?" The man stopped and for a moment seemed about to retrace his way to the car.

"Is this Oschner's rig?" he yelled.

"Yes."

"I got some grub for his crew."

"Come on in, then." Deafy removed his hand from his coat.

The man went back to the car and returned with a large cardboard box.

"Oschner sent this out and told me to tell you that he hasn't been able to find any men yet, but he will try to get some out before night."

"Did he send some bedding?"

"Yeah. It's in the car."

Kim was not as interested in the bedding as he was in the food. When the man set the box down to return for the bedding, he immediately started exploring the contents. There were several tins of sardines, boxes of crackers, some bologna, a loaf of bread, and a can of coffee. There were also several small cans of evaporated milk and some cheese.

Kim borrowed Deafy's pocket knife to slice the bread and make a sandwich. Deafy walked back to the car with the driver, and Kim was eating hungrily when he returned.

"Taste all right?" Deafy asked as he walked over.

"Sure does," Kim agreed. "I was hungry."

"Me too. But what I want most is a good cup of hot coffee."

Deafy started toward the engine room. Kim watched as he opened the boiler door and then laid his sandwich back in the box. He reached Deafy just as he picked up the shovel.

"This is my job, Deafy," he said. "I'll tend to it."

"The fire's hot enough, Kim," Deafy replied testily. "I just wanted to build up enough steam to catch some water from the pop-off."

"Get your bucket ready." Kim shoveled in the coal.

Five minutes later the pop-off blew, and Deafy caught a small bucket half full of water. Then he set the bucket over hot coals in the forge, and soon Kim smelled the aroma of boiling coffee. It smelled good.

The rig was running smoothly, and they sat and drank coffee after they had finished eating. Kim lighted a cigarette and offered Deafy one. Deafy took the cigarette and stuck it in his mouth. It looked strange, almost fragile, there. In a matter of seconds, Deafy had the end bitten off and a long, fiery ash on it. Finally he spat it out and took a chew.

"We'll set up our beds, and maybe we can get a wink of sleep now and then," Deafy said. "Oschner hasn't found any men yet, and from what that feller said, I doubt if he will for some time."

"We can't run this thing forever without sleep, Deafy."

"I know." Deafy sipped his coffee. "When Oschner comes out Saturday night, I'll talk to him about building us a shack out here and putting us a stove and stuff in it. Then we can do a little cooking. There ain't no use going to camp when we get a few hours off. If we can sleep and eat here at the rig, we can run better."

"How do you know he will be out here Saturday night, Deafy?"

"He'll be here," Deafy said complacently. "Saturday is payday. He knows that if he ain't here, I'll shut his rig down and come looking for him."

"You'd quit drilling!"

"I would," Deafy said soberly. "And Oschner knows it, too. But he'll show up."

Kim shook his head in wonder. He pulled his ear gently and grinned feebly. Maybe he would get more education here than in college anyway.

"Steam is getting low, Kim!"

During the first twenty-four hours, Kim was hungry and tired. The next twenty-four he was moving slowly, and with effort. His hunger had died. At the end of seventy-two hours, neither he nor Deafy had had a wink of sleep. It seemed that every time they thought they might get some sleep, something happened. Kim was astonished at the number of things that the relatively simple operation of drilling required.

Kim was performing his duties automatically and vaguely, wondering how much longer he would be able to stay on his feet. But the rig had not shut down since they started it. And they had drilled seventy-five feet!

Oschner finally returned, along with two men dressed in work clothing. Kim didn't even talk to Oschner. He didn't want to. The man's neat appearance and clean hands irritated him. Besides, he was much too tired to talk to anyone. Let Deafy do it.

Deafy did it. Oschner stayed almost half an hour. As soon as he left, Deafy gave instructions to the two surly-faced men. They wore soiled clothing and obviously had been on a job before this. When one walked close to Kim, he smelled the stale, fetid odor of whiskey that had soured the man's breath. But it was an old whiskey smell. The man wasn't drunk, but he had *been* drunk.

Kim shoveled in another batch of coal, and Deafy approached him.

"Put in an extra shovel or two, Kim," Deafy said tiredly. "And let's get some sleep. I'll tell you what Oschner said when we wake up."

Kim nodded and threw in two extra shovels.

They set their cots up on the south side of the engine room out of the wind, and to one side of the pop-off valve.

Kim sat on the side of his cot and thought whimsically and dully of the incongruity of going to bed in broad daylight on the open plains. He unlaced his low quarter shoes and was so tired that he didn't even notice that they were scuffed and oil soaked. It was the first time he had had them off in more than three days, and his socks were wet with sweat. The cool air felt good to his feet. He slowly unbuttoned his shirt. The pop-off valve opened, and Kim glanced dully at the white spout of steam.

Then his eyes opened in wide in surprise and horror.

"Stop, Deafy!" he yelled hoarsely and jumped to his feet.

But Deafy didn't hear for the hissing steam drowned out Kim's shout. Deafy was walking, stark naked, into the scalding steam of the pop-off valve. He must have gone raving mad, Kim thought, as he rushed toward him!

The grass tufts and small rocks hurt Kim's bare feet, but he was not aware of the pain. He tackled Deafy just in time to keep the steam from hitting him full on the body. Kim felt the hot breath of the pop-off as he dived through it. Then they were both rolling over the hard ground, Deafy completely naked and Kim barefooted and his shirt unbuttoned.

They rolled to a stop, and Kim felt a moment of sympathy for Deafy, knowing how the stones and sharp grass blades must have hurt his naked body. Nevertheless, he had saved Deafy from something worse.

Deafy lay for a moment and looked at Kim in utter disbelief. He made no effort to rise, and Kim knew he must be almost unconscious. The strain had just been too great!

Then, like a striking snake, Deafy launched himself at Kim. A second later Kim was flat on his back and Deafy astraddle of him. Deafy raised his fist and seemed about to strike. They he slowly lowered his arm.

"What did you do that for, Kim?" he asked querulously.

"You will be all right, Deafy," Kim said in a voice that he hoped would calm Deafy. "You're just tired. After you get some sleep and rest you will be all right."

"*I'll* be all right!" Deafy said in astonishment. "Hell, there ain't nothing wrong with me. What's the matter with *you?*"

"Let me up, Deafy."

"Not till I know what went wrong," Deafy said reasonably.

"You're all right now, Deafy," Kim said. "You just went out of your head for a minute—that's all."

"*I* did?"

"Yes. You were walking into the steam pop-off without your clothes. I tackled you to keep you from getting scalded. I guess it woke you up. You're all right now."

Slowly Deafy loosed his grip on Kim. Then he scooted off and sat on the ground. For a moment he seemed stunned, and then he started laughing. First it was only a chuckle, and then it grew until he was laughing uncontrollably. Kim became alarmed again and tried to calm him.

"You'll be all right, Deafy," Kim soothed.

"You damned—fool—" Deafy said between gasps for breath. "I thought *you* had gone crazy. That pop-off steam ain't hot. Looks hot, but it ain't. It's just right for a bath. It's the only bath tub an oil man knows."

It took a minute for Kim to convince himself that Deafy really was sane. When it did dawn on him, he grinned ruefully and pulled his ear. It was funny all right, but he just didn't have the energy to laugh.

"I'm sorry, Deafy," he said, shaking his head slowly. "I guess I have quite a bit to learn."

"Thanks anyway, Kim," Deafy said. "And I wasn't laughing at you. I'm just glad them two other fellers was on the other side of the engine room while I was rolling over across the prairie in my birthday suit."

Kim nodded again. He sat on the ground and watched as Deafy walked into the steam spout. He still wasn't convinced that Deafy's flesh wouldn't start falling from the bone when the steam hit him. But Deafy didn't even flinch when he walked into it. He rubbed vigorously, and Kim noticed the rope-like muscles of Deafy's body. His skin was almost milk white, except for his face and hands, but huge, knotty muscles spanned his chest and back. His biceps looked like a weight lifter's, and Kim was less surprised that Deafy had so easily flipped him. He wondered how old Deafy was.

Deafy walked out of the steam bath and stood, drying himself in the cold wind. Only then, did the significance of the discovery dawn on Kim. He'd been wanting a bath since he hit camp. And here it was! Hot and clean. What was he waiting for?

Fifteen minutes later, clean and warm between the blankets, Kim looked up at the sky. He pulled the blanket up a bit to shade his eyes from the sun, and with a long sigh, went to sleep.

The two new men turned out to be fairly good workmen. They worked twelve hour shifts, and Kim and Deafy worked twelve hours. Occasionally, Deafy had to help make repairs when he should have been resting, but they were able to keep the rig going.

Deafy and Kim slept through the first shift of the relief men. The next time the relief men took over, however, they took the White truck and drove into camp. Luckily, they were able to find Oschner fairly quickly. Deafy arranged with him to purchase some lumber and tar paper. They were also able to find a small, coal-burning cook stove and varied cooking utensils. They hauled their materials back to the lease, and during their next two off shifts, they fashioned a small shack near the rig. The stove was installed and their cots moved inside. That night, Kim and Deafy had their first hot meal in more than a week.

No longer would they have to depend on Oschner to bring them food, and the small stove would feel good on cold nights. It gave them a measure of independence.

It was a good arrangement. The relief men continued to sleep in the tool shed. Kim had no particular feeling about that for he assumed that as soon as they received their wages, they would be off to camp again.

Kim's assumption was correct. Oschner brought their money out on Saturday. Deafy collected their wages but did not pay the men until they came off their tower. As soon as they were paid, they headed for camp. Kim did not expect to see them again, and he was correct in that also.

It was Tuesday before Oschner finally brought two more men out. Kim and Deafy were able to get snatches of sleep in the shack and managed to keep the rig moving. Nevertheless, the two relief men were a welcome sight.

Soon after the two men arrived, Deafy went to the shack to prepare supper. Deafy was a good cook, and a bit to Kim's surprise, a meticulous housekeeper.

While Deafy was preparing the meal, Kim showed the men about the antiquated rig. The driller Kim did not like. He was fat and used obscene language almost incessantly. The tool dresser was a nondescript fellow given to loud laughing.

After checking the men out, Kim sat near the rig for a few minutes to observe their operation. They worked quietly for a few minutes and observed Kim surreptitiously. They had survivied the throes of a drunken hangover, and the routine work seemed to make them feel better. They began to banter with each other.

"Easy in—and out again," the toolie chanted as the cable moved up and down.

"Like a pretty woman on Saturday night!" the driller answered.

"The money is looking for oil. Let's give it to 'em jar head," the toolie yelled as he shoveled coals into the furnace.

"What a day!" the driller sighed in mock disgust. "Gig that balky donkey engine, toolie. It's forty-eight hours till Saturday night, and Sal's gals is waiting."

"There's more steam coming from you than there is from this engine, jar-head. Your gas is strong, but it won't burn. Just relieves the pressure."

"Oh, the whine of the line, as it sings through the shivs," chanted the driller.

"Shovel in the coal, and watch her roll!" answered the toolie. "Skid my rig and drill right by."

"Hurry up, toolie, that Swill seeder from the rotary has taken my floozy from the hash house. Let's finish this hole and make a hotel."

"What for? We can sleep in the dog house. When I go to bed I want it to be making plenty of circles so I have to catch it on the fly. When I lay down I want the ceiling to turn around like a fly wheel on that old donkey engine in reverse."

"Woo, woo!" yelled the driller. "How did we get here? Who brought us in? Up and down—and back to town!"

Kim listened to the banter between the two men with a tinge of disgust, but he was interested nevertheless. He knew the exchange was mostly for his benefit even though the men seemed to be ignoring his presence.

Thirty minutes passed, and Deafy had not called Kim to eat. It usually took him less time to prepare a meal, and Kim decided to investigate.

He walked to the shack and stepped inside. The stove was hot, and a pan of bacon was on it. But the bacon was burned to a crisp, and Deafy sat on a nail keg near the stove. He was sound asleep and snoring loudly.

Kim grinned. He had to admit that Deafy had more stamina than he did. But Kim could become more quickly rested. He removed the bacon from the stove and lay on his bunk. Deafy could sleep as long as he could sit on that nail keg! In a matter of moments Kim too was asleep.

In view of the probability that the relief men would leave for camp as soon as they received their pay on Saturday night, Kim and Deafy decided to go to town early Saturday morning to get supplies for the following week. The first thing that Kim did was to go to the drug store where he was able to purchase a lined tablet with an Indian head cover and a pencil. He then, very laboriously and meticulously, wrote his mother a long letter explaining that a business opportunity had developed that he felt that he could not ignore.

It pained him greatly to tell her less than the truth but he felt that less than the truth would be more comforting to her.

When he had finally finished the letter he had no idea how he could mail it. He put the return address of Box 61, Amarillo, Texas, on it and wished that he could see Wendy Terrell.

He went to Sal's place. She assured him that she would see that his letter was sent to Amarillo or Panhandle for posting at the earliest possible moment. Kim no longer questioned Sal. It was late afternoon when they returned to the rig. It was running smoothly, and they unloaded their supplies and prepared to cook a meal.

Kim was breaking eggs when he heard an unusual sound. It was the rolling sound of a horse snorting. For a moment, he thought he had imagined it; then it came again. He looked at Deafy, but Deafy had not heard. He was busy opening a can of chili. Kim walked to the door of the shack.

Two horsemen stopped near the rig, one fifteen feet behind the other. The rider nearest the rig was astride a blaze faced sorrel gelding. The other was riding a big, black stallion. Kim gasped. He fancied himself to be a judge of horseflesh, but he had never seen more magnificent animals. They were deep chested and had alert, intelligent heads and wide set eyes. The conformation of the horses indicated grace and balance.

The sorrel gelding was standing quietly, but the stallion was moving restlessly about.

Kim felt Deafy beside him and heard his exclamation. He turned. Deafy was staring. There was a sort of wonder in his wide open good eye. But Deafy wasn't looking at the horses; he was gaping at a handsome woman astride the black.

Kim looked again. He could see her face plainly, though neither rider had noticed them. Her face was gentle, and her dark eyes tranquil. A ruddy, healthy glow showed through the deep tan of her smooth cheeks. The heavy coat could not hide the mature woman contours, and the divided skirt made plainly evident her strong thighs and calves. Her feet were pushed far into the stirrups and her boots equipped with short-shanked, business-like spurs.

The woman might be thirty—or fifty, Kim decided. She looked as strong and graceful as the horse she rode.

She sat the restless horse with calm assurance. The animal tried repeatedly to turn away from the oil derrick, but each time the woman pulled his head firmly back and jabbed him gently with her spurs. Once, he turned to nip at her foot, and she smiled quickly, showing even, white teeth.

The rider of the other horse was a man, and that was all that either

Kim or Deafy noted at the moment. And he was in conversation with the fat driller. Only when the driller's voice rose in anger did they transfer their attention.

"Who says I cut your damned fence?" the driller asked belligerently.

The man on the sorrel gelding sat quietly. He was old, and his shoulders stooped.

"I didn't say you cut it," the old man replied. "I asked if you did."

"Whose business is it?"

"It's Beatenbow business," the old rider replied quietly.

"I don't know what the hell the Beatenbow is," the driller said in a loud voice. "And I don't give a damn. Now get that horse away from my rig."

He reached down and picked up a short piece of pipe and advanced threateningly.

The rider grabbed a pair of heavy fence piers from a scabbard on his saddle just as the pop-off valve opened, and white steam spurted from the side of the boiler. The gelding pricked up his little fox ears and looked at the steam curiously, but the stallion whirled and jumped several feet in one cat-like motion.

Kim took a step toward the frightened horse, then stopped. The woman rider had simply swayed with the horse's leap, and when he hit the ground she had his head pulled toward the rig. The powerful horse gathered his muscles and leaped again. This time, while he was in the air, the woman raked his sides hard with her spurs and again pulled his head toward the rig. Kim gasped in amazement. He had never seen such superb horsemanship.

The big black took two more leaps, and the woman spurred him. Then he squealed his anger and arched his full neck to one side. Kim winced as his long yellow teeth came together with a bone breaking click within an inch of the woman's foot. She brought her quirt down across his sensitive nostrils. The horse shook his head and squealed again, stamping his feet. Then he reached back in another attempt to get the leg of his rider between his powerful teeth. The woman pulled hard on the reins and hit him again across the muzzle with her quirt.

The big black pawed the ground in his anger. Then, without warning, he threw up his head and reared high in the air. Kim knew he intended to fall back and crush his rider. An involuntary cry came from his lips. But just as the horse reared, the woman deftly switched ends with her quirt, and before he had gone far enough back to fall, she raised up in her stirrups and brought the leather covered, lead-handled quirt down between his small ears.

Kim heard the blow distinctly. The woman had delivered it with all her strength which, Kim decided, was tremendous.

The stallion, having his aerial acrobatics so abruptly terminated, hit the ground hard on his dainty front feet. He stood for a moment with fore feet apart as if deciding what to do. The woman held her quirt poised. Kim saw her face clearly. There was no maliciousness in her face or eyes, only thoughtful watchfulness.

Suddenly, the big horse heaved a sigh, lowered his head, and started nibbling grass. The woman smiled and bent over to pat the horse on the shoulder. She talked to him in low, quiet tones.

Everyone had been watching the activity except the old man on the sorrell gelding. Neither man nor horse had turned his head. He picked up the conversation as though it had never been interrupted.

"That pasture up there," the old man nodded his head northward, "belongs to the Beatenbows. It's full of mares about to foal. Somebody cut our fence. I aim to find out who done it."

The fat driller reluctantly pulled his gaze from the rider behind the old man. He was still holding the piece of pipe.

"And I aim for you to get off of my lease, old man." The driller's voice was ugly. "You get off of that horse, and I'll—"

"What's the trouble, friend?" Deafy hurriedly walked between the driller and the rider.

The old man shifted his gaze toward Deafy. He didn't say anything for a minute. He simply sat on the sorrel gelding. Kim could not see his face plainly from the doorway where he was standing, but he could see the woman's face clearly.

Deafy and the rider stared at each other for a few seconds longer. Then, without a word, the rider replaced his fence pliers and dismounted. He was tall and stooped, and he tottered uncertainly on his high boot heels for a second.

"My name is Finch," he said and extended a horny hand to Deafy.

Deafy didn't hesitate. He met the outstretched hand. The two men had seen in each other a kindred spirit.

"My name is Deafy Jones," Deafy said.

"I run the Beatenbow horse ranch," the rider continued, "That is our foaling pasture just north of your outfit here. This morning somebody cut the fence and some mares got out. We trailed them and saw where they got a drink in that hogwaller over there. Now we got two dead mares."

"That ain't no hog-waller," the driller almost shouted, "it's a slush pit."

"I aim to find out who cut that fence," the man's voice was very quiet. He didn't look at the driller.

"Don't blame you," Deafy said, "I'll help."

"Well—dammit, Deafy," the fat driller said complainingly, "we needed some cable and me and the toolie just twisted some of that barbed wire together and—"

"Now you know who cut your fence, Mr. Finch," Deafy said. "How much do you figure he owes you?"

"Now wait a minute!" No one even looked at the protesting driller.

"I figure the mares was worth a couple of hundred a piece," Finch said to Deafy, "and our fence is still down."

"We will fix your fence," Deafy said, "and tonight this toolie and driller gets their pay. Between them they ought to have enough to pay for your horses. I'll see they do that."

"Like hell you will!" the fat driller yelled. His face was florid.

The tool dresser had taken no part in the argument until he heard Deafy make the statement about paying for the horses. Then he took a few steps forward, obviously intending to add his opinion.

"You boys better tend to your rig," Deafy said coldly as he turned to them. "We will talk about this later."

They started to protest but decided against it. They went back to the rig, muttering profanely.

"If you will tell me how to get to your place, I'll deliver the money tomorrow," Deafy said. "And your fence will be fixed before dark."

"We will appreciate that," Finch said. "Also tell your man that the next time he cuts a Beatenbow fence, I'll come after him with a saddle gun."

"He ain't my man," Deafy said. "But I'll tell him. And this rig will give you no more cause to pack a saddle gun."

The rider nodded. Then he gave Deafy directions to the Beatenbow ranch. It was across the river. Finch gave the directions briefly and adequately. Then he remounted the cat-footed sorrel gelding.

"See you tomorrow," he said as he rode away.

"You will," Deafy agreed.

The woman rider had not spoken a word except to the black horse since their arrival. Finch rode past her, and the black horse fidgeted to turn and follow. She held him steady for a moment longer while she stared at Deafy with thoughtful eyes. Suddenly she smiled.

"Thank you," she said and turned to follow the other horse.

Deafy didn't answer, but his adam's apple worked up and down spasmodically. He stared after them until they dipped into the ravine.

Oschner came out an hour later and brought the wages. Deafy took the money and informed the fat driller and the loud laughing tool dresser that they would have to run the rig on their own time until he and Kim repaired the fence.

Both men protested loudly and profanely, but Deafy was adamant. They finally agreed, however, for Deafy had their money.

It took Kim and Deafy almost two hours to untwist the barbed wire and replace it. Deafy was dissatisfied with the poor job but finally decided that it was the best they could do without tools and additional wire. He decided that it would do for the time being.

Deafy took his time getting back to the rig. The men were waiting.

"All right, Jones. We've worked two hours for nothing and missed a ride to camp," the fat driller said nastily. "Now pay up!"

Deafy said nothing but went to the shack and returned with a handful of bills. He handed each man a portion.

"What the hell is this?" the driller yelled furiously. "There ain't but a little over a hundred dollars here."

"I'm short, too!" the tool dresser said in a menacing voice.

"That's your wages," Deafy said flatly, "less four hundred dollars for them two horses."

"Why, you one-eyed old bastard!" the fat driller yelled. "There ain's no son-of-a-bitch that can short cut my wages." He started toward Deafy.

Deafy quickly backed up a couple of steps and grabbed a big Stillson wrench.

"I may be one-eyed," he said, "but I can see good enough to sink this Stillson wrench through your thick head."

Deafy started advancing on the man who quickly gave ground. It was the first time Kim had seen Deafy really angry, and it scared him. He knew Deafy was going to kill the man. The remark about his bad eye had been too much.

"Now you wait a minute, Jones." There was fear in the driller's voice.

"I'm just giving you and your loud mouthed friend one minute to get off this rig," Deafy said flatly.

"You're not giving me a damned thing, you old—"

The driller's fury was short-lived, for Deafy struck with the big wrench. It hit the man on the beefy part of the shoulder, but it was a hard blow, and the driller fell.

"Wait! Wait a minute, you damned fool!"

"One minute is all you got," Deafy said bitingly. "One minute to get out of here, or the next time this Stillson lands on your head." Deafy wasn't joking.

"All right," the man whined, rubbing his shoulder. "We'll go. But Wingate can take us into camp in the truck."

"He could," Deafy said, "but he ain't going to.—And about half of your minute is up."

The man started to reply but evidently thought better of it. He hurriedly got to his feet.

"Come on," he said to the tool dresser.

They started walking toward camp.

The next day Deafy took the WHITE truck and drove in the direction that the horseback riders had taken the day before. It was almost night time when he returned.

"Get the horses paid for?" Kim asked.

Deafy nodded.

New men came out on Monday. The following Saturday, Kim prepared to go to camp for supplies. Deafy wasn't going. Kim got in the truck, and Deafy cranked it.

"Kim," he said as he walked around to the cab to put the crank under the seat. "I wish you would buy me a toothbrush while you are in town."

Kim stared at Deafy in amazement. But Deafy didn't look at Kim. He started walking, stiff backed, toward the rig.

Then Kim remembered the smile that the handsome woman had given Deafy, and the way Deafy's adams apple had bobbed up and down.

Kim laughed aloud. He felt wonderful as he drove toward camp. He might even see Wendy Terrell—accidentally. And perhaps he might even have a return letter from his mother. The thought didn't improve his spirits.

CHAPTER VI

Kim was disappointed. He walked the length of the main street several times to no avail. In fact, he saw no one that he knew. He considered going to the Terrell house but decided against it. He wasn't at all sure what the custom in the oil camps would be. There was a possibility that he had a letter from his mother, which he badly wanted, but dreaded. He had, however, written her another letter explaining that the business venture he had entered with a friend was filled with promise and that he was feeling unusually well physically and mentally. He hoped that she would be reassured and that he would hear from her soon.

He did get Deafy's tooth brush, though. And he talked to several men who furnished him with news of the camp. And the news was bad. Eastern gangsters had moved into camp.

It had taken them little time to organize the camp and now every business house was assessed a "protection tax." Bootleggers paid for permission to operate. Gambling dens and houses of prostitution were assessed a percentage of their profits. None was exempt. Organized crime had arrived. The few stalwart individuals, who at first resisted, found their businesses burned out or blown to shambles by crude dynamite bombs.

Even Sal had to pay. She did not even try to resist for she had seen the same thing happen in other camps. She knew that it would not last. She had only to wait.

Blake Terrell watched without emotion as the crime organization wound its tentacles about the camp. People were fools to pay their money to a bunch of city hoodlums! If they didn't have the guts to hold out, they would get no sympathy from Blake.

As far as he was concerned, he would take care of his own. He wasn't paying Joe Shay a hundred dollars a day for nothing!

Blake was pleased with Joe. He was always at his side, and they were a formidable pair. Even the bootleggers did not accost them as they walked the board sidewalks of the camp.

Blake's attitude toward Joe was a strange one. Almost paternal. He demanded that Joe buy new clothes and get his hair cut. Joe complied, but he resented his employer's authoritative manner. It especially galled him to call Blake *Mr. Terrell.* Joe repeatedly thought of quitting the job, but he never did. He liked the excitement that Blake created. And he was intrigued by Maria, though he gave Wendy a wide berth.

Blake was aware of Wendy's dislike for Joe. Once in an east Texas field, Blake had hired Joe to do errands around the rig. Wendy was only twelve at the time, but Joe was big enough to do a man's work. Blake sent him to their house-truck for something. A few minutes later, Joe returned with his face red from scalding water. Blake would have killed another man who molested Wendy, but that incident seemed only to amuse him.

The next day, Deafy, who was with Blake at the time, gave Wendy a small, pearl handled pistol, and Wendy quite calmly told Blake that she would kill Joe Shay if he ever came to the house again.

Blake knew that Wendy wasn't joking, and he warned Joe not to go near her. But his warning was not needed. Since that time Joe had not gone near Wendy unless he was with Blake.

Blake knew he could handle Joe. Joe was like a tiger chained to his wrist. A word from Blake would unleash Joe's animal-like fury against anyone so unfortunate as to get in his way. It gave Blake a sense of power to have Joe always at his side. He could stand Wendy's disapproval.

Maria had at first disapproved of Joe, too. But after he bought some new clothes and cleaned himself up, her disapproval vanished. In fact, Blake had noted with a malicious sort of humor that his beautiful wife seemed to delight in teasing Joe. And Joe, like the animal he was, could not see that it was simply a form of amusement. Blake welcomed it, for it offered a sort of diversion for Maria. Her constant heckling for him to retire and move from the camp had become extremely irksome.

Even so, Blake would not countenance another man's interest in Maria. One night he invited Claude Butler to dinner when they had some business to discuss. Blake watched the lawyer's face carefully as he introduced him to Maria and Wendy. Butler's face showed no interest whatever in the women, and Blake watched with silent amusement, and relief, as his wife tried in vain to captivate the man.

What a cold fish of a man! But Blake was pleased that he was. Thereafter, he invited Butler to the house more often. Blake considered lawyers as little better than scavengers, and he had nothing but contempt for Butler, but the man's knowledge of law was a commodity that he could use. Blake was satisfied.

But all was not perfect with Blake. He had rigs going around the clock and several hundred acres of land under lease. Still, he had not been able to secure the Beatenbow land. And, to make things worse, he had heard that a local rancher was going into the oil business, and that the land would probably be leased to him. Old lady Beatenbow would be a fool to lease her land to that man, Blake thought. That place was big, and under it was a fortune. It needed Blake Terrell! If he could get it, he would be one of the biggest oil men in the country. And he intended to get that land. It was becoming an obsession with him.

Kim delivered the toothbrush to Deafy at the rig and told him the news of the camp. Thereafter news was brought to them by the succession of relief men that Oschner brought to the rig. It was a couple of weeks later that they learned that a man named Borger had bought the land on which the camp was located and had advertised business lots for sale. It was causing quite a stir in camp.

Soon after that news, Deafy and Kim heard that Blake Terrell was instigating a move for a special election that would move the court-house from Plemons to the new boom town as soon as it was incorporated.

Deafy and Kim welcomed the news of the camp for they had to be at the rig constantly. When they had to have supplies or equipment, one of them took the truck and drove into camp, returning as soon as possible. Through the long, tiring days and disrupted nights they toiled with their outmoded rig. Relentlessly, they pounded toward oil.

It was an endless thing, broken only by the arrival and departure of new relief men.

But there was one bright spot. Finch returned the week after he had first visited the rig. He was alone this time. Kim had not really looked at the man before.

Finch was well over six feet tall, and he was stooped and gaunt. He was very old, but when he shook hands with Kim, his grip was bony-hard and strong. He always wore a blue denim shirt, rough, high-heeled boots, enormous spurs, and worn leather leggings. On his head he wore an ancient, weather-beaten hat adorned with a leather band set with brass ornaments.

Once Finch stayed for lunch, and when he removed his hat in preparation to wash his face, Kim noted that he was completely bald. Where the hat had protected his head, the skin was startlingly white contrasted to the leathery texture of the rest of his face. His eyes were piercing and blue. His voice was slow and easy. He and Deafy talked for hours.

After his second visit, Finch returned often. Kim looked forward to his visits. He rode a different horse each time, and always they were splendid animals. Deafy and Finch sat and talked endlessly. They seemed to enjoy each other tremendously and developed a fast friendship. Finch had a quiet sort of humor and told fascinating stories of the plains. Deafy reciprocated with equally fascinating tales of the oil fields. Kim loved to listen to the men talk.

Deafy was almost worthless when Finch was around the rig, and Kim told him so. When an adjustment had to be made, it was Kim who did the work. It irked him that Deafy and Finch ignored him. Deafy paid not the least bit of attention!

One day Finch came to the rig, riding a beautiful horse, as usual, but he was leading the quiet natured, cat-footed sorrel that he had ridden the first time he came. The sorrel was saddled, and after a few minutes of conversation between Deafy and Finch, Deafy mounted the sorrel horse. Deafy looked so ill at ease and so out-of-place on the horse, that Kim laughed aloud. Deafy glared at Kim. A few minutes later, Finch and Deafy rode away from the rig together. Deafy bounced awkwardly on the sorrel.

They were gone all day, much to Kim's disgust. When they returned that night, Deafy was non-communicative, but he did more than enough work to make up for his absence. Thereafter, it was almost a weekly event for Finch to ride up to the rig leading the sorrel horse. Kim knew when he saw Finch that Deafy would be gone for the day. It was a bit puzzling to Kim, who had thought that nothing could move Deafy from the rig until they hit oil.

The handsome woman did not return again. Kim wanted to ask Deafy about her, but he did not. Deafy never explained his absences, and always when he returned, he would work harder than ever.

About the middle of April Deafy became surly and nervous. Kim was concerned for him. No man could continue the heartbreaking hours and not succumb to the strain. One windy day Kim brewed a pot of coffee and took a steaming cup to Deafy who was intently watching the cable rising and falling in the hole.

"Much obliged," Deafy growled as Kim handed it to him.

Kim didn't answer. He squatted on his heels beside Deafy and scratched a match on a piece of metal to light his cigarette.

"Don't *do* that!" Deafy almost yelped as he struck the match and cigarette from Kim's hand.

"Don't do what?" Kim asked in surprise and a bit of anger.

"Don't light that cigarette," Deafy said gloweringly.

"You're sure getting fussy, Deafy," Kim said crossly. "Worse than an old maid."

"You're right, Kim. I am." Deafy smiled weakly. "Reckon I'm just getting tired—or maybe old. We ain't supposed to be within a thousand feet of oil, but I got a feeling that we are closer. A lot closer!"

"You think it might blow?"

"I don't know what I think," Deafy said, still staring at the cable. "I just got a feeling—that's all. I don't think we ought to have any fire around the rig."

"All right," Kim said quietly.

"We're in a hell of a shape for it to blow," Deafy growled. "That damned Oschner ain't got a tank in a mile of this rig. If it's a gusher, we'll have oil all over this prairie."

Throughout the long afternoon they worked as usual about the rig. Deafy cursed Oschner for not bringing relief men. The engine ran smoothly, and the monotonous whine of the line as it ran through the shives was a comforting sound.

Then it happened!

Like a rumbling train, the crescendo built, and the oil gushed from the mouth of the well. Deafy and Kim ran to safety and turned to see the giant tower of oil, like a bending, black beacon, rise in the sky. It was visible in the camp two miles away, and men stopped to stare in awe.

The news spread quickly, and it was only a matter of minutes until hundreds of men and several women were on their way to the well. Even the lure of gambling tables and the smell of talcum powder could not keep the men from the sight of a gusher!

When the crowd arrived, they saw two men working frantically. They were drenched in oil, and the only color visible was the whites of their eyes. Men started lending assistance. Deafy shouted orders, and Kim followed them as best he could. Deafy had explained the procedure of capping the well, but like most of his explanations, this one had been inadequate.

Thousands of barrels of oil were being wasted. It literally rained oil, and tiny streams coursed through the grass and gathered into a big stream that flowed down the ravine near the well.

Kim paid little attention to the shouts of the crowd. He was much too busy trying to follow Deafy's instructions. The work was back-breaking. By nightfall several teams of mules and scrapers were busy damming up the ravine below the well. As the men and teams worked frantically, the oil flowed into the ravine, and a pool formed at the dam.

On into the night they worked. It was past midnight when Oschner and Blake Terrell appeared at the well, and Kim had a glance of Wendy and Maria as they sat in a car. But he had no time to speak to them. He wondered vaguely what they were doing there.

Oschner strutted about importantly and Blake shouted orders. It was almost daylight when they finally got it capped. The earthen tank formed by the dam was almost filled with oil.

Another ten thousand barrel well!

The wind shifted during the night, and when Kim and Deafy went to their shack to change clothing, they found everything oil-soaked and useless. Both were dead tired, but there was no possibility of getting sleep on the oily beds. Their food was also ruined. Luckily, the oil had not reached their money cached under a bed.

Deafy surveyed the mess glumly. "Well I guess we got a night in town coming anyway," he said.

"Suits me," Kim said heartily.

"We're through here, anyway," Deafy said. "She's capped, and as soon as Oschner gets some storage tanks up, he's got hisself a oil well."

"It's a big one isn't it, Deafy?" Kim asked proudly.

"Biggest one I ever seen," Deafy said without enthusiasm.

"What do we do now?"

"First thing is to get into camp and get us some clothes and grub," Deafy said. "Then we'll collect our money from Oschner. If he's got another rig ready, we can start drilling again. If he hasn't, we can get a job with somebody else I reckon. Suit you?"

"I guess so, Deafy," Kim said dubiously. "It's too late for me to go on out to California now anyway. I might as well work here until summer.

"What was you gonna do in California, Kim?" Deafy asked.

Kim realized that Deafy had never asked him before why he was on his way to California. Deafy just wasn't a question-asking man.

"I was on my way out there," Kim said casually, "to go to law school. But it's too late now to enter this semester. I'll have to wait until summer or fall."

"Well, I'll be damned!" Deafy said softly. "Now don't that beat all. Here, I been traipsin around with a lawyer and didn't know it."

Kim laughed. "Didn't hurt you a bit," he said.

They made arrangements to meet Oschner in camp and drove away in the *White* truck. Both of them were surprised at the growth of the camp in the days they had been absent. There were several new frame buildings, and just north of the *Double Six* there was a stack of red bricks.

They met Oschner at the designated place and collected their money. He wanted them to go out on another job. They agreed to go out the next day.

Their money was a sizable sum. Deafy peeled several bills off the roll and handed them to Kim, and then he separated the same amount and stuffed them in his own pocket. He placed the remainder inside his shirt with their other money.

A canvas tent had a clothing sign on it, and Kim and Deafy went in. They found, stacked neatly on the wooden floor, various sizes of overalls and khaki clothing and shoes, socks and underclothing. They purchased extras of everything.

They found a barbershop and, for two dollars each, were allowed to take a shower in a make-shift bath supplied by a barrel of muddy water. They both got haircuts and shaves.

Kim hadn't felt so good since he left home. When they walked out on the board sidewalk, he took a deep breath and grinned at Deafy.

"Let's find a steak, Deafy," he said, "I'm hungry as a bear."

"All right," Deafy agreed glumly.

"What's wrong, Deafy?" Kim asked. He knew that something was eating Deafy.

"Damned if I know," Deafy growled.

"Well *something* is," Kim said with conviction.

"I *know* something is," Deafy said with exasperation. "But I don't know *what* it is. I just can't help wondering what Blake was doing out at the well bossing everybody around."

Kim made no observation. He had been wondering the same thing. "Let's eat," he said.

They ate and bought groceries and bed clothing and stashed them in the truck.

"Deafy," Kim said, "Let's take tomorrow off and look around camp a bit. Oschner won't go broke if we miss a day."

"All right," Deafy agreed, "I reckon a man ought to take a day off every three months or so, anyway."

Kim was happy with Deafy's agreement. He didn't have any particular curiosity about the camp, but he felt that a full day there would almost certainly give him a chance to see Wendy.

They walked down one side of the street and back the other. It was almost a mile long and jammed with people. They passed the post office which was an unpretentious frame building. Kim was surprised and delighted that a post office had been opened in the oil camp. He entered and asked questions to find that it was only a sub-station and that mail that could not be delivered at Amarillo or Panhandle was being sent to the oil camp. He asked about mail for himself, but there was none. He wondered, if his mother did answer his letters, whether Sal or Wendy would have the reply.

In any case Kim determined to write his mother and explain as best he could what had happened and what was happening. Deafy had followed him into the makeshift post office. Kim turned to him.

"You going to write any letters, Deafy?"

"Not this time, I reckon." Deafy's tone was brisk and gruff. Kim was sorry that he had asked for he guessed that Deafy had no one to write.

They met a man that Deafy knew as they were leaving the post office. Deafy hailed him. They shook hands warmly.

"Heard you hit a big one, Deafy!" the man said.

"Kim," Deafy introduced, "this here is Lem Hotchkiss, an old toolie of mine. Got his own rig now."

"Pleased to meet you, Kim." Lem extended a huge hand. He was a big man and dressed in khaki clothing. His grip was stone hard, and he grinned a toothless grin.

"What do you hear around camp, Lem?" Deafy wanted to know.

"It's a big one," Lem said seriously. "But it's going to be worse than Spindle or Ranger as far as hell-raising is concerned. Last night, a bunch of hijackers slipped up on a rig and held up the crew. Took 'em down in a little canyon and held them while a truck hauled off the whole rig. Didn't leave nothing but the derrick."

"Well, I'll be damned," Deafy said in amazement. "I thought I'd seen everything, but that one beats me."

"It ain't as bad as it's going to get," Lem said. "A good rig right now is worth a million dollars—and everybody knows it!"

"Don't they have any law here at all?" Kim asked in wonder.

"Nothing but county law, since this ain't a town yet," Lem said. "They got a sheriff and two deputies, but they can't even ride herd on camp here. They arrested so many that they was spendin' all their time taking 'em to Plemons to jail. That's the county seat, and it's twelve miles from camp, and you have to cross the river to get there. The sheriff finally built hisself a trotline right here in camp."

"Now what in hell is a trotline, Lem?" Deafy asked in wonder.

"It ain't to catch cat-fish, Deafy." Lem showed his toothless grin again. "Come on. I'll show you. It ain't but about a hundred yards from here."

Kim and Deafy followed willingly. Just off the main street they came upon a frame building about sixty feet long. It was open at both ends and had no floor. Down the center of the building was a huge derrick timber, and at four foot intervals half inch bolts were set through the oak timber and the nut spot welded on the opposite side. A short chain was welded to each bolt, and on the other end of the chain was a leg iron. Attached to the leg irons were perhaps a dozen men. They sat dejectedly on the timber.

"There she is," Lem said with something bordering on pride.

"That is a jail?" Kim asked in wonder.

"Yep," Lem agreed. "Good 'un, too. The sheriff, he just hooks 'em on, and then they wait til somebody comes and bails 'em out."

"Well, I'll be damned," Deafy said again.

"Had one woman hooked on there," Lem said importantly. "She got arrested for peddling dope. Sheriff said he hated to hook a woman on, but he sure as hell wasn't going to let her peddle dope in Hutchinson County. All she did was send somebody down to her diggins to fetch ten thousand in cash to pay her bail."

"She paid ten thousand in cash bail?" Deafy squinted at Lem. There was doubt in his voice.

"She sure as hell did," Lem said emphatically.

"When will her trial come up?" Kim asked.

"Trial?" Lem asked in surprise. "Hell! They don't try nobody in this county unless it's for stealing a cow. They just set the bail high enough, and then nobody takes the trouble to bring 'em to trial. They ain't enough lawyers and judges in the county to try everybody, anyway."

"If they made a town out of the camp, they could have city police, couldn't they?" Kim asked.

"They could," agreed Lem. "And it looks like they are going to do just that. A couple of promoters from Oklahoma hit here about a month ago. Feller by the name of A. P. Borger and his partner, Martin. They bought 240 acres of land from a rancher down at Panhandle named Weatherly. They didn't get the oil rights of course, but they got the land, and they have cut it into lots and streets, and they're going to sell it off and make a town out of it. Camp sets on it right now. They call it the Borger Townsite Company. They start selling on the eighth of this month. That's tomorrow. You boys going to be around?"

"Hell, I don't know." Deafy shook his head dubiously. "Right now, I don't know nothing!"

"It's a wild one!" Lem said sympathetically. "I sent one of my boys to Amarillo today to get some guns." Then he added significantly, "I figure on keeping my rig."

"Didn't send for any extras, did you?" Deafy asked.

"I could spare you some, Deafy, if he gets as many as I told him to."

"I'd appreciate that, Lem," Deafy said. "I wouldn't want to lose a rig myself, even if it ain't mine."

"Who you working for, Deafy?"

"Oschner."

"Wouldn't want a job, would you?"

"Thanks, just the same, Lem," Deafy shook his head. "Kim and me will stay with what we got for a while, I reckon."

"I'll buy us a drink," Lem said. Deafy nodded absently.

They entered a frame building and sat at a rough wooden counter. Lem ordered a bottle of whiskey, and when he started to pay for it Deafy grabbed his hand.

"This drink is on Kim, Lem." Deafy grinned. "He owes me a drink for a doctorin' job I done for him on the train." Kim reached into his pocket and pulled out the roll that Deafy had given him. He handed the barkeep a twenty dollar bill and didn't get any change.

"That was a pretty expensive bandaging job, after all, Deafy," Kim said.

"I'm a pretty expensive doc," Deafy said jovially.

They sat for a few minutes, and Deafy and Lem drank the harsh whiskey. They talked. Kim listened.

Finally, Deafy moved to rise. "We got to be going, Lem. What time will your man be back with them guns?"

"Meet me here at sundown, Deafy, and I'll let you have the guns. My man ought to be back before then."

Deafy nodded.

They walked down the street. People washed past them. Everyone was hurrying. The day was sharp, the wind was cold for the time of year.

"Well, Kim?" Deafy asked wryly. "What do you think of it now?"

"I don't know, Deafy! I never have seen anything like it before."

"It ain't likely that you ever will again, either. Let's go put our money up before some feller takes it off of us."

"Where will we put it?" Kim had been wondering about that. He knew it would be dangerous to keep it on them.

"We'll get Sal to bank it for us."

Sal! Kim hadn't thought of his own money since they had gone out on the job.

"Will it be safe there, Deafy?"

"Safer than any place I can think of," Deafy said, "I ain't never heard of anybody hijacking a whore house."

Sal greeted them effusively. "Sal's glad to see you, Deafy Jones, and your young friend, too. Deafy, you haven't been working him *too* hard!"

Deafy grinned. "We ain't been working hardly atall," Deafy said and Kim moaned inwardly. "But we been makin money. Reckon you could bank it for us?"

"Sal can do anything you want her to, Deafy," Sal said with

conviction. "How much you got?"

"Five thousand, Sal, give or take a few hundred," Deafy said as he pulled the roll from his pocket and handed it to Sal.

"Whew!" Sal whistled in surprise. "Thought you said you hadn't been working, Deafy. Looks to me like you've taken up hijacking."

"We been making a hundred a tower, Sal—me and Kim both. And we're working around the clock, most of the time."

"Didn't know your friend was a driller, Deafy," Sal said in surprise.

"He is now."

"He *must* be! Who you drilling for?"

"Oschner."

"Oh!" There was a hint of disappointment in Sal's voice. She put the money in an envelope and sealed it. She didn't count it. "Well, you boys just come to Sal's when you want your money."

"We'll do that, Sal."

"You want a woman?"

"Not me, Sal," Deafy said. "I been working too hard."

"I'll get one for Kim," she said in a business-like manner.

Kim started to protest, but Sal was through the door before he said a word. He was surprised that she had remembered his name. He had supposed that he would simply remain "Deafy's friend" to Sal. He looked at Deafy and was embarrassed. But Deafy wasn't looking at Kim. He was leaning back in the rocking chair with his eyes closed.

Sal returned shortly followed by a dark-headed girl. "This here is Pat. Pat this is Kim," Sal introduced. "It was Pat's bed you slept in the first night you got to camp, Kim. You remember I told you she had got married. She just came back this morning."

Kim simply nodded. The whole thing was much too casual to suit him. The girl was pretty in a hard sort of way. She looked at Kim speculatively. Her eyes were dark and big, and Kim thought, they looked a little sad.

"Now you young folks run on back and have a good time," Sal said pleasantly. "I'm going to pour me and Deafy Jones a drink."

"Don't rush us, Sal," the girl said petulantly. "I ain't sure I want to take him to my room. I'm particular. You know that."

"I'm particular, too," snapped Sal. "You wouldn't be back here if the doc hadn't told me you was all right. And if I didn't know Kim was clean, I wouldn't of picked you for him."

It was time for him to assert himself, Kim decided. He didn't enjoy being talked about as though he were a prize bull. But Pat didn't wait. She flounced from the room.

"You know which room it is, Kim," Sal said complacently.

"I know," Kim said angrily. "But I don't have to have my women assigned to me, Sal. I can pick my own."

Sal looked at Kim in surprise, and Deafy opened his eye. Both of them knew that Kim was angry.

"Sal didn't mean nothing, Kim," Deafy mollified.

Kim glared at Sal, and then, to his consternation, he saw tears come into her large, blue eyes.

"You will excuse me, I hope, Kim," she said quietly. "I'm just a rough old woman. I been in the fields so long, I reckon I forget that there are still men who don't want to go to bed with a woman every time they come to town."

Sal averted her eyes while she was talking to Kim. Now, *she* was embarrassed, and Kim was sorry. That was the second time he had spoken sharply to her. And the first time she had given him a bed and taken care of his money for him. Kim knew that Sal wanted to be his friend.

"Would you like to have a drink with me and Deafy, Kim?" Sal asked as she poured a tumbler of whiskey.

"I'm sorry, Sal," Kim said feelingly. "I didn't mean to be rude to you. I'll go back and explain to Pat."

"All right," Sal said.

Kim left. It was an hour later that he rejoined Sal and Deafy.

Sal was obviously drunk and there was a strangeness about Deafy— a mellowness.

"Took you a awful long time to explain to Pat, Kim." Sal grinned at him. Kim grinned back.

"Kim's a good boy, Sal," Deafy said. His voice was low and gentle. Kim looked at him in surprise.

"Kim," Sal said. "You go and ask Pat to come up here and take care of the front. Then you and me and Deafy will go back to my room and drink."

Kim went after Pat. Five minutes later they were in Sal's room. It was bigger, and better furnished than Pat's room. There were several comfortable chairs. A picture of Calvin Coolidge hung on the wall, and a tintype of a man in a square hat was on the dresser. Sal bent over and pulled a large trunk from under her bed. She opened the lid, and Kim saw that it was almost half filled with currency. Kim gasped in astonishment. He was close enough to see the denomination of the bills. Most of them were ones and fives, but there were numerous fifties and hundreds. And he was almost sure that he had seen one thousand dollar bill.

Sal took the envelope in which she had put Kim and Deafy's money from the blouse of her dress. "I'll put it right here in this corner with Kim's money," she said.

They seated themselves, and Sal poured whiskey. Kim sipped his slowly and grimaced. It was harsh and strong.

"This here is mighty good whiskey, Sal," Deafy said. His voice was soft, almost melodious.

"Nothing too good for my friends, Deafy."

"Friends is a fine thing, Sal," Deafy said. "I ain't got many of 'em, but what I got, I appreciate."

Kim looked keenly at Deafy. Something was amiss. Gone were the harsh tones and brusque manner. Here was another man.

"You got lots of friends, Deafy," Sal consoled. "I reckon you got more friends than any other man in the fields."

"You're wrong, Sal! Wish you wasn't. But you are," Deafy said quietly. "I got lots of acquaintances, and they're mighty fine people. But I ain't got many friends."

Kim wanted to enter the conversation, but he couldn't find a way to do so. The whiskey was warming him.

"Well, *I'm* your friend, Deafy Jones!" Sal declared stoutly.

"I know you are, Sal," Deafy said. "And Kim is my friend too. And Wendy Terrell."

Kim looked closely at Deafy. But there was no jesting in Deafy's voice. Deafy meant what he was saying. He continued to talk.

"Three friends!" Deafy said softly and in wonderment. He looked at Kim and Sal lovingly. "I reckon I got the best friends of anybody. Here's to the friends of Deafy Jones." Deafy held up his glass and then drained it. Sal poured him another.

"Yessir!" Deafy said reminiscently. "Sal, you been my friend a long time. And Wendy, she was born my friend. Now comes Kim. He don't know he *is* my friend, Sal. But I do. I'll tell you something, Sal." Deafy leaned over and whispered conspiratorially, but in a manner that he knew Kim would hear. "I shanghaied Kim. I sure did. Brought him to camp with me, and he didn't even know he was coming. Know why I done that, Sal?"

"I know, Deafy," Sal said. Her voice choked a bit. "I knew the minute you two walked in that first day."

"Reminds you of him, don't he?" Deafy said with pride.

"He does, Deafy," Sal said. "The way he carries his head, and when he grins. And even when he gets mad."

"What are you two talking about?" Kim wanted to know. "Why don't you let me in on the secret?"

Deafy grinned at him affectionately. "Talking about you, Kim," he said. "And a boy that Sal and me knew a long time ago. A boy that got killed while he was fighting with General Bullard in the Argonne forest."

"Deafy's only son, Kim," Sal said softly. Kim felt a lump rise in his throat. He hadn't dreamed that Deafy was ever a family man. Sal kept talking. "Deafy raised the boy without a mother, Kim. His wife died when the boy was born."

Kim had been sitting looking at Deafy in wonder. He was trying to remember something that Deafy had said once. Suddenly, he did remember. It was the first day that they had gone to the rig, and Deafy was telling about himself, Blake and Wendy. And Deafy had said there was another *man* with them at the time. That man had been Deafy Jones' own son!

"I had dreams for that boy, Sal. You know that. Talked to you about 'em, didn't I?" Deafy's voice was getting even more mellow. "Was figuring on him marrying Wendy—and I was going to make 'em a million dollars and trot my grandkids on my knees. Was gonna eat Sunday dinner with 'em and buy the kids a Shetland pony." Deafy paused. "Didn't do it, though. Didn't get a chance. He never come home. Somehow, I knew he wasn't going to. I guess he didn't have a lot to come back to maybe. But I wanted my boy back, Sal." There was almost a pleading quality in Deafy's voice, and a tear showed in his good eye.

"We all did, Deafy."

"You know, Sal," Deafy said earnestly. "I'll bet that if he had come back and married Wendy, that even old Blake and me would have got along again."

"Wouldn't be surprised."

"Yessir! I'll bet we would," Deafy said almost in wonderment. "Blake ain't such a bad man, Sal. Folks don't understand him, maybe. But he thinks a lot of Wendy in his way."

Deafy must be awful drunk, Kim decided. They all were. He had often thought that some people were likely to be their real selves when they were drunk. Now he was sure of it. Deafy was actually a gentle, old man who thought that kindness was a sign of weakness. And Deafy was a man who would not let himself be weak. Kim was very glad that he was Deafy's friend.

And the conversation had answered so many questions that had been in Kim's mind when he hadn't been too tired to think at all. He had often wondered why Deafy had offered him his friendship. Now he knew, and he felt a response within himself toward Deafy. He replaced the son that Deafy had lost. And in turn Deafy filled some of the aching void left by the loss of his own father. At this moment, he not only had a feeling of respect and gratitude toward Deafy, he knew now that he really loved the old man. He hoped that he could ease some of the loneliness that he had seen in Deafy when his defenses were down.

Sal was pouring another drink. Kim didn't want another. His head was swimming.

"Do you suppose we ought to go, Deafy?" he asked anxiously. He wanted to see Wendy.

"Aw, let's not hurry, Kim," Deafy said. "And it ain't more than three o'clock now. Besides, we got to wait on them guns."

"Well," Kim said. "If you and Sal will excuse me, I think I will go get some coffee."

"You do that, Kim," Deafy agreed. "I'll meet you at the grocery store later."

"You come to Sal's place every time you are in town, Kim," Sal said as he rose.

"Why don't you go up and see Wendy, Kim?" Deafy said. "She'll be glad to see you."

"Do you think it would be all right?" Kim asked eagerly.

"Aw, sure, Kim, go on," Deafy encouraged. "Old Blake ain't got nothing against you. He probably won't be at home, anyway. Tell Wendy hello for me. Tell her I'll come to see her the next time I am in town. Would this time, but I'm sort of drunk."

Kim grinned. "Well, I might do that Deafy. I'll meet you at sundown."

The crisp air quickly cleared Kim's head. As he walked up the street he wondered how he could see Wendy. Just walk up to her house, he supposed. In Oklahoma, or California, there would be no problem. But a brawling Texas oil camp wasn't Oklahoma or California! He wondered what Wendy's father would say if he came calling. Probably make a scene. There was no doubt in Kim's mind that Blake Terrell disliked him intensely. What irked Kim even more, was that he was just a bit afraid of Wendy's father.

While mulling the problem over in his mind, Kim decided to eat something. He stopped at the Whitespot cafe where a tall, sad faced Negro man washed the dishes in greasy water behind the serving counter. Kim had been hungry when he went in, but the stale odors banished his appetite. He ordered a cup of coffee. He had drunk only half of it when he set it down with a decisive gesture and walked from the cafe.

It was only a ten minute walk to the house on the hill. Kim hoped that the liquor on his breath would not smell. There was only one car in front of the Terrell house. The grass had been beaten away by much traffic. Kim knocked on the door and waited, half apprehensively. He felt like a teen-age boy going on his first date.

The door opened, and a huge Negro woman stuck her head out. "What you want, mister?" Her voice was belligerent.

"Is Miss Terrell home?"

"No, she ain't," the Negress said firmly and started to shut the door when Kim heard Wendy's voice.

"Who is it, Rachael?"

"Some man," Rachael said, "asking for Miss Terrell."

The voice had sounded familiar to Wendy and she came to the door. Her face registered surprise and pleasure as she saw Kim standing on the step.

"Why, Kim!" she said. "It's nice to see you! Come in." Wendy extended her hand as she spoke and Kim felt a quickening of his pulse when she took it.

"You gonna let that man in man in dis house, Miss Wendy?" Rachael asked almost belligerently.

Wendy laughed. It was a musical sound. "It's all right, Rachael," Wendy assured the Negro woman. "Kim is a friend of mine. Besides—I have a letter for him—from his mother."

"Well—all right, Miss Wendy," the woman said dubiously. "But you know what Mr. Terrell said—for me not to let *no* man in dis house when he was gone."

"I know, Rachael," Wendy said, "and you are right not to do so. But *you* aren't letting Mr. Kim in. *I* am. Now you run along."

The Negro woman turned and walked toward the kitchen.

Kim grinned and removed his hat as he stepped inside. "She said you weren't at home."

Wendy smiled back at him. Her teeth were very white. "You asked for 'Miss Terrell' " Wendy explained. "Rachael thought you were asking for Maria. She calls her Miss Terrell. She calls me Miss Wendy."

"Oh," Kim said as he looked about the room. It was large and comfortable. A woman's touch was quite apparent. There was a rug on the floor and pictures on the wall. A green ivy bowl sat on a window sill and a shelf of books stood against one wall.

"Sit down, Kim," Wendy invited. "I'll get your letter for you. And then I want you to tell me what you have been doing." Then she added as she went to the hallway to get the letter, "It's good to see you."

Wendy handed Kim the letter and he hastily opened it but with foreboding that almost bordered on fear. Two minutes later he breathed a vast sigh and stuffed the letter in his pocket. His mother had not condemned him. In fact, she had alluded to his likeness to his father, whom she had loved, and whom Kim could never hope to emulate. Nevertheless the letter lifted his spirits immeasurably. He suddenly remembered that he had been ignoring Wendy and he turned to her.

"It must have been a very nice letter, Kim," she said. "I've been watching your face. Your mother must be a fine woman."

"She is," Kim said somberly, and Wendy sensed that he didn't want to talk more of her.

"What have you been doing?" Wendy asked absently.

"I've been working," Kim said in answer to her question. "Harder than I have ever worked in my life."

"I don't doubt it if you have been with Deafy!" She appraised him frankly, "But you have gained weight."

"I guess I have," Kim admitted ruefully, "but I don't see how! Deafy's cooking isn't the best I have ever tasted."

Wendy laughed. "I'll have Rachael fix us something to eat. I'm hungry, too."

"I wasn't hinting."

"I know you weren't," Wendy laughed again. "But I've eaten Deafy's cooking too."

"Well," Kim said a bit sheepishly. "It does sound good."

Wendy called Rachael and asked her to prepare some food. Rachael scowled her disapproval of the situation but walked back to the kitchen without saying anything.

"Where is Deafy?" Wendy asked brightly when Rachael had gone. "Did he send any message to me?"

"He's—in camp," Kim said hesitantly. "He said tell you that he would see you the next time he came in."

"Is he drinking?"

Kim felt that he should, somehow, keep Wendy from knowing, but he didn't see how he could do it. She was the most difficult person to lie to! He'd tried to a couple of times the first time he had seen her.

"Yes. He's drinking," Kim said.

"I thought he must be," Wendy said almost sadly, "or he would have sent word for me to meet him someplace." Then she added, "Deafy always comes to see me when he can do so without father's knowing about it. He likes to talk, but he doesn't like to see me when he is drinking."

"He's a strange man, when he's drinking, isn't he?"

"Yes. Deafy was once always like he is now when he is drinking," Wendy said. "That was before his son was killed, and he and father had their trouble. Since then he has grown a shell that only whiskey seems to melt."

Kim looked at Wendy in surprise that she knew of Deafy's son and then remembered that since she had known Deafy for so long, she certainly would have known about the boy.

"Bill Jones was wonderful to me. He was older than I was. But he played games with me and talked to me as if he were my own age. He and Deafy! When I was so lonely as a little girl, I don't know how I could have stood it if it hadn't been for them. They tried to help me, and I loved them both."

Kim could think of nothing appropriate to say. After a moment or two when Wendy sat thinking back over those days, she continued gravely.

"Bill went to the war. I remember how Deafy looked when he told me that Bill wasn't coming back. I couldn't help crying. Deafy was never the same after that. Then he and father broke up. Deafy grew that shell around himself."

"You know, Wendy," Kim said thoughtfully. "I get the strangest feeling about Deafy sometimes. Just the way he says something—or maybe the way he was talking tonight when he was drunk. I think he actually loves your father."

Tears suddenly filled Wendy's gray eyes. "He does," she said firmly. "I know he does. And father loves him. But father made a mistake once, and he is too stubborn to admit it. And Deafy is too stubborn to let anyone know how he feels. Once they would have done anything for each other. Now they think that they have to fight each other to keep from showing weakness."

"That's exactly what I was thinking tonight when Deafy and Sal were talking," Kim exclaimed, and then he could have bitten his tongue for mentioning Sal.

Wendy was amused by Kim's discomfiture when he mentioned Sal. "Obviously, you know little of the oil fields, Kim. Your life must have been rather sheltered," Wendy said. "Oil field kids know about houses of prostitution almost before they know their alphabet. They are as much a part of the oil fields as derricks and gathering lines. I am not at all shocked that Deafy was at Sal's place. In fact, I consider Sal more of a lady than many other women I know who are considered very respectable. At least, there is nothing hypocritical about Sal, and Deafy and Sal have been friends a long time," Wendy continued. "They enjoy talking and visiting."

"They sure do," Kim agreed heartily, remembering how they had excluded him from the conversation.

"We've talked enough about Deafy," Wendy suddenly changed the subject. She disliked the grim tone of their conversation and hoped to brighten it. "Now let's talk about you, Kim. How do you like the oil fields?"

"I don't know," Kim replied. "I sure don't like the camp, but I sort of enjoy working around the rig. It gets lonesome out there, though."

"I know," Wendy said sympathetically. "When I was a little girl, I used to think that oil fields were the lonesomest places in the world, and they always find them in the most desolate places. But they really aren't so bad when you get used to them."

"They will take a lot of getting used to," Kim observed a bit glumly.

"I suppose so," Wendy laughed. "But honestly, Kim, I was glad when I got father's wire to meet him here. I enjoy the excitement. And now I'm going to be sorry to leave again."

"What!" Kim's heart sank. "You aren't going to stay?"

"Not very long."

"But—but what will you do?"

"I'm not sure," Wendy said evasively. "Go back to New York for a while, I guess. Then I want to go to Paris. I'd like to study art there."

"Well, why don't you just stay here?" Kim said hopefully.

"Maria will be sorry she missed you, Kim," Wendy changed the subject abruptly. "She was quite smitten with you. She thinks you are very handsome."

"Where is she?" Kim asked. Wendy's remarks had not embarrassed him in the least, for there was no teasing in it.

"She and Father went to Amarillo early this morning."

"How does *she* like the oil fields?"

Maria is restless," Wendy admitted. "She—"

A knock on the door interrupted Wendy. Rachael appeared suddenly in the kitchen doorway.

"I'll get it, Rachael," Wendy said as she rose and walked to the door.

"Don't you let nobody else in this house, Miss Wendy." Rachael was taking her role as protector seriously. Wendy opened the door.

"Oh, hello, Mr. Butler." There was a trace of coolness in Wendy's voice.

"Good afternoon, Miss Terrell." Kim heard a suave, well cultivated voice. "I was near your home when it occurred to me that there was a bit of business that I needed to discuss with your father. Is he at home?"

"Father is in Amarillo, Mr. Butler," Wendy said crisply. "He won't be home until late, I'm afraid."

Kim sat and looked at the man as he stood just in the doorway. He was dressed in the finest clothes, and across his chest was a watch chain from which dangled a gold coin. Smooth fingers of one hand rubbed the coin gently. The other held an expensive hat.

"How unfortunate!" the man said, and Kim thought he detected a trace of humor in the voice. "However, it is just possible that Mrs. Terrell can give me the information I need. Would you mind asking her if she can see me?"

Wendy had not asked the man in, nor did she show any indication that she intended to do so. The man looked past Wendy into the room where Kim was sitting. His dark eyes rested on Kim for a moment, but not a trace of expression showed in them.

"Father's wife went to Amarillo with him," Wendy answered his question.

"Ah, yes. Well, perhaps another time, Miss Terrell." He shrugged his shoulders slightly. "I hope I did not—er—interrupt anything!"

Wendy did not say anything. She closed the door firmly as the man turned and left. She had not missed the innuendo, but chose to ignore it.

"Who was that!" Kim asked.

"His name is Butler," Wendy said as she walked toward Kim. "He is a lawyer who works for Father."

"You don't like him, do you?" Kim said quietly.

"He gives me the creeps!" Wendy shuddered delicately. Kim smiled at her expression, but realized it was probably an apt one.

"Does he come here often?"

"Yes. Father brought him home to dinner once when they had some business to discuss. He didn't even look at Maria, and that pleased Father, I think, but it infuriated her. I think he probably is the only man who ever ignored her. Since that time, Father has brought him here several times. And recently, Mr. Butler seems to be making it a point to drop by when Father is away."

"He certainly must be a cold-blooded man not to notice Maria," Kim said appreciatively. "Does he ignore you, too!"

"He doesn't ignore Maria, now," Wendy evaded Kim's question. "I wish he did. Those snake eyes of his light up when he looks at her."

"Well, why don't you—" Kim had been about to suggest that she tell her father when Wendy interrupted.

"I'm sorry, Kim," Wendy smiled again. "You probably think I'm foolish, but, well the man disturbs me."

"I can see why," Kim admitted.

"I'll see if Rachael has our food ready," Wendy said suddenly and walked rapidly toward the kitchen.

When Wendy left the room, Kim felt unaccountably depressed. He got up and paced restlessly. One of several pictures hanging on the wall intrigued him. He looked at it closely. It was a cottonwood tree, standing lonely and strong by a small ravine. The limbs were bare, but there was a stark beauty about it. In one corner, he saw a name. Looking closer, he could see that it was Wendy's. He was not particularly surprised, for she was a remarkable girl. And she was even prettier than he had remembered! Her skin seemed to glow, and her eyes were radiant. She seemed to sort of flow as she walked. He wished she weren't going away.

Just then, Wendy appeared in the doorway. "Let's eat," she said gaily.

"Sounds good," Kim said.

While they were eating, Kim, in answer to Wendy's frank and disarming questions, told her how he came to be in camp, how he had been on his way to Stanford to study law, and about his family.

Perhaps it was the good food and the quiet atmosphere. Whatever it was, before the meal was over, Wendy knew more about Kim than any other person had ever known, for Kim did not usually talk about himself. He even told her of his boyhood dream to become a doctor.

"Don't you think you might still become a doctor?" she asked softly.

"Nope!" Kim said matter of factly. "That was just a boyhood dream. I'll probably go on to school and get my law degree. Or I may just stay here and go into the oil business. Kim was surprised at his last statement—it was the first time he had admitted even to himself that he might stay there.

"But you can live on dreams, Kim," Wendy said earnestly. "At least, you can't live without dreams. I couldn't."

"What are your dreams, Wendy?" Kim asked abruptly.

Wendy smiled at him and then wrinkled her nose impishly. "I think I might tell you sometime, Kim," she said as she rose from the table. Then she changed the subject abruptly. "Maria and I were out at your well last night."

"I saw you," Kim said. He had been wondering if she would mention it.

"I saw you, too," Wendy said laughingly as they walked from the kitchen to the living room. "You and Deafy looked like two black ghosts. Father said your well was the biggest one since *Dixon Number 2.*"

"How is Blake—your father?" Kim didn't want to talk about the well. He didn't want to talk about Blake either, but it was the only way he could think of to change the subject.

"Impatient because Maria is making him miss a day in the fields,"

Wendy said. "Maria wants a new house and they are in Amarillo today talking to a building contractor."

"But—this one is new!"

"I know," Wendy answered, "but it *is* sort of—." She paused a moment and then went on deliberately, her gray eyes looking directly at Kim. "Father promised her a mansion the first ten thousand barrel well he brought in."

Kim could not miss the significance of the statement. Even here there weren't many ten thousand barrel wells.

"Our well?" he asked quietly. "Mine and Deafy's?"

"Yes."

"Blake owns it?"

Wendy simply nodded.

"Oschner works for him?"

"Only on that one lease," Wendy said. "Father knew that Deafy would never work for him, so he gave Oschner a percentage of the lease to hire Deafy and oversee the drilling."

"I had suspected something like that," Kim said. "So has Deafy. But we weren't sure."

"I've wanted to tell Deafy. But somehow I just can't," Wendy said.

"I'm glad you haven't," Kim said.

"I'm glad I told you," Wendy said. "Makes me feel better."

"I'm glad, too," Kim said slowly.

"Will you tell Deafy?"

"I don't know. We're supposed to go out on another job for him—for Oschner. I imagine it will be on the same lease. It seems a shame to spoil it now. Deafy is making a lot of money. So am I. I guess we're worth it. We brought in the well almost thirty days before they thought we could. I think we could do it again. Especially with good equipment."

"Good!" Wendy said enthusiastically. "It won't hurt to deceive Deafy a bit if it is for his own good." Then she added soberly, "Besides, I would like to have Deafy around where I can have an excuse to visit him occasionally. And you too."

"But—I thought you were going away!"

"I will, I suppose," Wendy said. "There just isn't much for me to do here, but Maria would be lonesome if I left, and—, oh, I just don't know! She wants me to stay. And I like her."

"*I* want you to stay, too," Kim said firmly.

"Do you, Kim?" a faint flush came to Wendy's face.

"Very much."

"I—I just don't know," Wendy said indecisively.

"When will Blake and Maria be back from Amarillo?" Kim asked. He was thinking that he had the day off tomorrow.

"They will be back tonight," Wendy said. "Father wants to be here for the sale of the townsite tomorrow."

"Deafy and I are staying too," Kim said.

"Good!" Wendy said. "You will enjoy it. There will be people here from all over the plains. The news has spread, and people are going to bring lunches and stay for the auction."

"What have *you* been doing, Wendy?" Kim wanted to get back to talking about something besides the camp.

"I've been to Amarillo twice with Maria. She likes to go shopping. Then I've been painting and exploring the river."

"The river?"

"Yes. It's a wonderful place. And I've made friends with a lovely family. The Beatenbows. Father went out there to try to lease their land, and I went with him. They have twelve thousand acres. They have lived here for ages. An old lady owns the place, and her widowed daughter lives with her. They have a huge old ranch house that sits under big cottonwood trees. It's the most peaceful place you ever saw. And Granny Beatenbow's granddaughter and her husband also live on the ranch. They're wonderful people. I've visited them several times."

Kim was so absorbed with Wendy's story that he did not connect the name with Finch, though he had heard it mentioned by him. "Did Blake get the lease?" he asked.

Wendy's laugh was a lovely sound. "No. And I don't think he will. He has met his match in Granny Beatenbow. She makes him act like a little boy trying to steal a piece of apple pie."

"She must be quite a person," Kim laughed as he thought of anyone quelling Blake Terrell.

Wendy's eyes twinkled. "The last time we were out there she told Father that she didn't think his oil derricks were nearly as pretty as red cattle on green grass."

"Blake didn't think much of that, I'll bet," Kim ventured.

"He didn't," Wendy agreed. "In fact, he finally got so mad, I thought he would have a stroke. Granny Beatenbow made him drink a glass of buttermilk before he left."

Kim laughed aloud. "I would very much like to have seen that."

The rest of the afternoon passed pleasantly and quickly. Wendy had a new phonograph, and she played some records for Kim. *Do-Do-Do* by Gershwin, the *Desert Song*, and *Trudy*, were the favorites. Kim enjoyed them immensely. And Wendy demonstrated some new dance steps. Kim could have watched her dance all afternoon. Her movements were fluid and graceful. Even the bumptious *Black Bottom* looked easy and smooth when she did it.

It was almost sundown when they heard a car drive up. Kim had no idea that so much time had passed.

"That's Father and Maria," Wendy said.

Kim didn't want to see Blake. He felt a bit guilty about being there. "I have to go," he said, too quickly.

"Stay for supper, Kim," Wendy invited.

"I really must go. I am supposed to meet Deafy at sundown." Kim picked up his hat just as the door opened.

Maria rushed into the room. Her arms were filled with bundles and she stopped short when she saw Kim. She recognized him immediately.

"Mr. Wingate!" she exclaimed in a pleased voice.

"Hello, Mrs. Terrell."

"This *is* a pleasure," her black eyes were dancing. Obviously she was in a festive mood. "Hello, Wendy."

"Hello, Maria," Wendy said. "Did you have a good trip?"

"A wonderful trip," Maria was excited. "But Blake didn't. He was impatient all day and he drove too fast, but—," she shrugged her pretty shoulders. "I bought the most wonderful dress, Wendy. And a hat—."

In the midst of depositing bundles in a chair, she stopped and looked from Wendy to Kim. Kim almost squirmed.

"You had a very nice day, too, I imagine." There was delight and approval in Maria's voice.

"We've been playing records," Wendy grinned at Maria. "And dancing."

"How ver-r-ry nice," Maria purred in obvious disbelief. "You must listen to records with me some time, Mr. Wingate—and dance with me too."

"Wendy is a good dancer," Kim said uncomfortably.

"Did you see the building contractor, Maria?" Wendy changed the subject.

"Oh, yes!" Maria was easily distracted. "And I saw *my* house in Amarillo! It is on a street named after one of the presidents, and it is tall—three stories high with turret windows. It's beautiful. I'm going to build one just like it."

"Did Father say he would?" Wendy asked excitedly.

"This afternoon, he says *no*. But tonight he will say *yes*," Maria said lightly. "We will begin it very soon. It will be the finest house in camp."

Just then, Blake came in the door. He was followed by Joe Shay. Kim felt a tremor, almost like fear. Blake glowered.

"Wendy," he roared without speaking to Kim, "What's this fellow doing in my house?"

"I invited him here, Father," Wendy said calmly. "He's been here all afternoon."

Blake's face flushed. "I told you not to let any man in this house when I'm gone."

"Kim is not just *any* man, Father; he's a friend of mine."

"I don't care whose friend he is," Blake shouted. "He has no right in this house."

"Say the word, and I'll throw the jelly-bean out, Mr. Terrell," Joe Shay leered maliciously.

Wendy's face turned white and freckles showed plainly across her nose. Her eyes sparked defiance. "You *couldn't* throw Mr. Wingate out of here, Joe Shay!" she said staunchly. "And Father wouldn't dare!"

"Say the word, Blake!" The look on Wendy's face had made Joe forget his manners.

"Shut up, Joe," Blake said shortly, "Now, Wendy—."

"Why don't *you* shut up, Blake?" Maria's musical voice interrupted. "Let's invite Mr. Wingate to have a drink. He is Wendy's friend."

Kim had been standing awkwardly during the exchange. He felt that he should say something, but he couldn't think of anything to say. And Wendy's assertion that Joe couldn't throw him out had given him a bad moment.

Blake started to retort to Maria, but apparently changed his mind. Evidently he knew when he was whipped.

"Be here at sunup as usual, Joe," he snapped and stalked out of the room.

Joe stood his ground a moment. Obviously he wanted to say or do something further. "I'll be seeing you, jelly-bean," he finally gritted and walked rapidly out the door.

"I'm sorry, Kim," Wendy said apologetically.

"It's all right, Wendy," Kim said. "It has been a wonderful afternoon. I haven't enjoyed one so much since I came to camp."

"I'm glad. Will you come back?"

"Yes. If you ask me."

"Will you have Sunday dinner with us?"

Kim hesitated. He certainly didn't want another scene with Blake.

"Perhaps your friend is afraid of your father," Maria said in a bantering voice.

"No, he isn't." Wendy said firmly.

"*Are* you afraid, Mr. Wingate?"

"I guess I am," Kim said truthfully. "But I'd like to come to dinner Sunday, Wendy. I'll be here at noon."

"Good!" Wendy said. "We'll be expecting you."

Kim walked back toward camp with mixed feelings. When Wendy had defied Joe Shay, Kim had felt that he could lick the world. Now, however, he wasn't at all sure and he kept a wary eye lest Joe Shay waylay him on the way back to camp. Actually Kim was not afraid of physical violence, but he still couldn't see why people wanted to hurt each other.

Resolutely he pushed unpleasant thoughts from his mind. It had been a good day. Maybe, the best day of his life. He hoped that Blake would continue to neglect Maria to the extent that Wendy would feel that she should stay here. That selfish thought didn't bother Kim's conscience in the least.

Deafy was not at the truck when he arrived, but Lem Hotchkiss appeared just at sundown, and Kim got the guns and ammunition and stashed them in the truck. He sat on the running board to wait. Again he pondered whether to tell Deafy that they were actually working for Blake Terrell. He was still debating the problem an hour later. Still Deafy had not shown up. Kim decided to walk about a bit. There was a new drug store that had been built since they were last in camp and he went in. He drank two malted milks then browsed about for a few minutes. On one counter was a new, single dial radio set. It was powered by a battery. Kim, thinking that it would be a lot of company at the rig, bought it. They could alternate batteries with the truck and keep one charged all the time.

From the drug store he went to an auto shop and bought a battery. He took his purchases back to the truck. Deafy still was not there. Kim waited another two hours and decided that Deafy must have been too drunk to leave Sal's place. He went there but was informed by Pat that Deafy had left before sundown. Sal was asleep.

Kim returned to the truck. Another hour and his anxiety gave way to irritation. Surely Deafy could take care of himself! He decided to look about camp.

A couple of blocks from the truck was a new movie house. *Ben Hur* with Ramon Navarro was showing. Kim decided to go in. Deafy could just wait for him a while!

The movie was packed and reeked of stale air and sweaty bodies. But it was warm and Kim finally found a seat in a back corner. It was good to sit down. He was dog tired and hadn't slept in almost thirty-six hours. Fifteen minutes later he was sound asleep.

Kim waked with a start and for a moment could not remember where he was. The show was still going and the place full of people, he noted with relief. He hadn't slept long! Hurriedly he made his way from the theatre to find Deafy who, by now, must be waiting.

To Kim's amazement the sun was shining when he stepped out on the sidewalk. He had slept all night! He had forgotten that the oil camp paid no attention to time. The show ran continuously, day and night!

Still, Deafy was not at the truck. Kim looked and, much to his relief, found that the guns, blankets and the new radio had not been disturbed, which was a near miracle! It had been foolish to leave them unwatched. But he had been irked with Deafy, and he had thought that Deafy would show up to take care of things.

Suddenly Kim was very concerned for Deafy and started looking for him. He saw dozens of people that knew Deafy, but none that had seen him that morning.

So absorbed did he become in his search for Deafy that he was unaware of the unusual influx of people into the camp. Wagons, cars, even a few buggies, clogged the street. There were children in some of the vehicles. They looked strange riding down the street of the camp.

Kim was making another weary round of the mile-long boardwalk when he came upon a large group of people gathered in front of the *Whiteway Dance Hall.* He hurried to join them, fearing as he did so, that he would see Deafy lying dead on the sidewalk. The men were laughing and cursing as he approached. There was, in fact, a carnival air about the group which added to Kim's fears. In the aftermath of violence, people in the camp seemed to react in that peculiar fashion.

"What's going on?" Kim asked anxiously as he edged into the crowd.

"Hell, man!" a big burly man said gaily, "We're going to live in a town now. These fellers have bought this land and now everybody has got to buy the lot they got their business on if they want to keep operating."

"Oh," Kim said with relief. He remembered what Deafy's old toolie had said about the new town being formed.

"Do you happen to know Deafy Jones?" he asked the man.

"One eyed old man? Chews tobacco all the time?"

"That's the one."

"I know him," the man said, "But I ain't seen him in camp. Last time I seen him was in Ranger."

"Thank you."

Kim worked his way toward the front of the crowd. A platform had been erected and on it were several people. They were equipped with pens, papers and legal-looking documents. Just then the auctioneer began his spiel.

He identified each lot by the business house that was located on it. The bidding began hurriedly and no time was wasted. Usually the lots were bought by the man owning the business establishment located on it.

Then the auctioneer came to the lot on which Sal's place was located. The description of the lot brought raucous laughs and jibes from the men. Kim was embarrassed for the women in the crowd. Especially those that had come from nearby towns and had brought their children with them.

A flurry of bidding answered the auctioneer's announcement of Sal's lot, however.

"Does everything on that lot go with the sale?" one man yelled.

"Everything goes—if you can take it," the auctioneer assured him.

"Then I'll bid five thousand dollars." The men roared with laughter.

It was then that Kim saw Sal. She was standing at the edge of the group, but when the five thousand dollar bid was made she started making her way to the platform. The men roared as she climbed up.

"Whatever these men bid, Mr. Auctioneer," Sal said, puffing from her exertion, "I'll bid higher."

"Ten thousand!" a man yelled, "provided the little chink girl goes with it."

The men howled again.

"I'll bid twenty thousand for my lot," Said said when the rabble had quieted, "and the man that bids more ain't never going to be welcome at Sal's place again."

The men quieted. Sal glared at them.

"It's yours, Sal," the auctioneer said.

"Good enough," Sal said grimly. Then she shouted at the throng of men, "As of right now the rates at Sal's is doubled."

A moan of protest went through the crowd. Then an angry man shouted, "Who in hell was running the price up anyway?"

"We was only joking, Sal," another yelled.

"Just the same," Sal said, her face flushed, "Your joke cost me twenty thousand. And I run a clean place for you boys."

The men yelled their approval.

"Let's pay it off, boys!" another yelled loudly, "Put it in the hat!"

Immediately hats started passing through the crowd. In a matter of five minutes the auctioneer, without counting the money, signed the deed for Sal's lot.

Sal was mollified.

"Prices just went down, boys!" she shouted from the platform, "Come to Sal's place anytime." With that she climbed from the platform.

Sal left the auction place, and Kim started to follow her when a man touched his arm.

"Wasn't you looking for Deafy Jones?"

"Yes," Kim said with apprehension, "Do you know where he is?"

"He's hooked on that damned trotline!"

"He's what!" Kim shouted in amazement. That was the only place in camp he hadn't looked.

"That's right," the man asserted. "I just got off a while ago myself. He's been there since last night."

"But—what on earth for!" Kim asked in amazement.

"Drunk and disorderly," the man said. "He fell down in the street last night. A dozen men have tried to bail him out, but he wouldn't let them. Said he had a partner that would come get him."

"Thank you," Kim hurried away.

Deafy must have been very drunk indeed, Kim thought bitterly. Otherwise, they wouldn't have had the nerve to hook him on that damned trotline. Kim was outraged.

Deafy was on the trotline all right. He was still drunk and talking to his fellow prisoners in a soft, melodious voice. He seemed to be doing his best to keep them from feeling ill toward the sheriff.

"Deafy!" Kim said sternly as he walked into the stinking building, "What on earth are you doing here?"

"Well, now Kimmy, me boy," Deafy said slowly and pleasantly, and Kim was only vaguely aware that Deafy had used the term that his father had used a thousand times. "That fine sheriff hooked me on this here trotline cause I was drunk and couldn't walk very good."

"That son-of-a-bitch!" Kim said feelingly.

"Now, Kim, you ort not to talk that a-way," Deafy said reprovingly. "It wasn't his fault. It was mine. Besides, he even let me keep my bottle."

"I'll get you out, Deafy," Kim said grimly.

"You do that, Kimmy me boy," Deafy approved. "But you don't use any more of them cuss words. That little building right over there is where you can pay my fine. I'd pay it myself, but I ain't got no money left," Deafy said apologetically. "I reckon I must of give it away to somebody."

Kim strode purposefully toward the small shack where he could pay Deafy's fine. But nobody was there. The Justice-of-the-Peace had gone to the sale. Kim went back to the trotline and told Deafy of the situation, which disturbed Deafy not at all.

Kim looked about for a minute and then made his way to an automobile garage a block down the street. A few minutes' search yielded a six pound sledge hammer. He grabbed it and walked back to the prison.

Deafy protested that Kim was breaking the law as Kim used the sledge to knock the ring loose from the bolt and freed Deafy. The other prisoners yelled encouragement as Kim pounded away.

Getting the chain loose from the derrick timber was fairly easy. The leg iron with the short chain attached, however, was still on Deafy's leg. Kim looked at it thoughtfully for a moment. Then he grabbed Deafy's arm and propelled him toward the auction place. Deafy protested as he dragged the chain behind him.

Kim left Deafy at the edge of the crowd and made his way to the platform and spoke to the auctioneer, who quickly announced that the jailer was needed. From his vantage point Kim saw a man hurriedly make his way from the crowd. Kim jumped down to intercept him. He caught the man just as he broke away.

Kim grabbed the man firmly by the arm. "You had a friend of mine on that trotline of yours," he said grimly. "I want you to unhook his leg iron."

"You got me away from that auction, just for that!" the man asked in amazement.

"I did," admitted Kim, "And you're not going back to it until you unhook him."

"That's what you—."

But the look on Kim's face stayed the jailer. "All right," he growled. "But you'll have to see the justice-of-the-peace to pay his fine."

"*You* see the justice-of-the-peace," Kim said grimly. "You can pay his fine just as well as I can."

"No I can't," the mailer said doggedly, "that man is in jail."

"No he isn't," Kim corrected the man. "He *was* in jail. I took him out. I just want you to unhook his leg iron." Kim pointed to Deafy standing contritely at the edge of the crowd, the leg iron around his ankle and the chain lying in the dusty street.

"Well, I'll be damned," the jailer gasped in amazement. "That's Deafy Jones. A dozen guys tried to bail him out this morning, but he wouldn't go. You must be Wingate."

"I am. What is the fine for being drunk?" Kim reached for the money.

"Hell! I dunno," the jailer scratched his head. "Didn't know it was a fine. But you will have to see the justice-of-the-peace."

"You can see him just as easily as I can," Kim said sternly as he handed the jailer a twenty dollar bill. "You just unhook that leg iron."

The jailer hesitated momentarily, then reached for the proffered bill.

"Might as well, I guess." He shrugged his shoulders. "A hell of a note to hook a man on just for being drunk anyway. Besides, the sheriff probably won't even remember him, so nobody will miss him."

The jailer pocketed the bill and unhooked Deafy's leg iron. Kim and Deafy didn't wait until the auction was over but headed for the lease.

It was almost sundown when the auction was over. The lots continued to sell at fabulous prices. A. P. Borger and his partner netted more than one hundred thousand dollars on the transactions.

Thus a town had been born. The Sodom of the Plains! The earth was its mother, the lust of men its father. And its name was Borger, Texas!

CHAPTER VII

A new rig was moved to the lease where Kim and Deafy hit their gusher, and it was a vast improvement over the first one. They were spared many of the tribulations they had suffered with the old, outmoded one. The shack in which they cooked and ate was also bigger and better.

As the hot summer months wore on, Oschner moved other rigs to the lease and built a bunkhouse and cook shack for the steady string of relief men coming out. Kim and Deafy assigned the men to the various tasks and alternated between the rigs, overseeing, repairing and managing. And, more and more, Kim had begun to take the initiative.

It was a fairly good arrangement except for the matter of paying the men. As yet there was no bank in Borger, and the oil companies had to transport vast amounts of currency from Amarillo, for no man would take a check. Transportation of the money was accomplished by caravans of automobiles carrying a complement of heavily armed and light triggered men. The cash was deposited in a central place in camp and tellers distributed the money to the various companies. The drillers then took the cash to the individual rigs. Always, the drillers were heavily armed. Oschner made arrangements with Kim and Deafy to pick up the money to pay the crews under their supervision. Deafy, unlike the other drillers who took their crews with them when they picked up the money, would let no one accompany him but Kim. He vowed that he and Kim would handle their own payroll without help. And they did. But Deafy insisted that Kim start carrying a gun. Reluctantly Kim agreed. It was bothersome at first, but finally he got used to the pistol in his belt and seldom thought of it.

But there were other problems involved in paying the men. It took a certain amount of bookkeeping, for which Deafy had not the least inclination. The job was turned over to Kim.

Everything progressed nicely. Kim and Deafy were busy, but they rarely had to work more than twelve hours at a shift except for supervising some repair or adjustment.

Nor did Kim tell Deafy that they were working for Blake Terrell. He knew that Deafy suspected it, but he had no absolute proof. The fact that Wendy began to visit the rig regularly contributed greatly to Kim's decision to leave things as they were. He enjoyed sharing the secret with her.

When she came to the rig, Wendy always brought food that was most welcome. Maria occasionally accompanied her, but Blake never came about. Kim supposed that he wanted to keep his connection with the lease secret as long as possible.

And Finch visited the rig regularly. Almost every week he would come, and Deafy would ride away with him. Kim still did not question Deafy about his absences.

Each Saturday, Kim and Deafy went in to pick up the payroll, returned to the rig, and paid the men. Then they would return to town. Deafy always got drunk, but never again was he hooked on the trotline. Deafy had a fine disregard for money. Both he and Kim always took a sum from their wages, and Sal banked the rest for them. Deafy's money vanished quickly. He bought whiskey for his friends, and he had many. He occasionally gambled, but he had absolutely no intention of winning and seemed irked if his money lasted too long.

Deafy never seemed to have any ill effects from his excessive drinking, and always was his old, crochety self after returning to the rig. He drank with Sal on Saturday nights. Kim went to see Wendy, and they occasionally went to see one of the three movies that were in town. Then Kim slept in the truck.

That first Sunday dinner at the Terrell's was not repeated. On that day, Maria had been scintillating. Wendy had tried to keep the conversation gay, but Blake had sat like an angry cloud, sullen and surly. Despite the efforts of Wendy and Maria, the meal had been strained, and Kim had felt ill at ease. Kim knew that Wendy would have liked to ask him again, but she would not subject him to her father's displeasure. Instead, she came to visit at the lease, and Kim visited her in town when he thought her father would not be present. They never mentioned it to each other, though both understood. They did not attempt to hide their visits from Blake. They simply arranged not to have them in his presence.

The *Hutchinson County Herald* had published its first edition in April and announced that the Santa Fe Railroad was beginning a line from Panhandle to Borger. No longer would the trucks and wagons have to freight supplies and equipment across the twenty-eight miles of prairie to the boom town. And the Borger Gas and Electric Company was furnishing gas to some of the business houses.

Thanks to a large number of carpenters and masons who were paid the very highest wages, the new Terrell house was finished in time to have the first telephone in Borger installed. From the small balconies on the third floor, Blake was able to see almost all the oil field. Blake knew that the tall, brick building was imposing, and he felt that it was nothing but proper that it should be his. He had drilled his own water well, and the house was equipped with four baths of which he was inordinately proud. The electric lights were kept burning day and night. Blake didn't like darkness. The many rooms were tastefully and expensively decorated under the supervision of Maria and Wendy. A circular concrete drive was built in front, and the yard was set with grass and trees.

Borger was growing. There were even those who had begun to talk of forming a school district and having regular school for the children of the oil field families. Businessmen had the streets oiled, and with the coming of electricity, the gas station men could charge batteries and operate air tanks. A regular hotel was opened.

Kim and Deafy worked on the day and night of the fourth of July simply because none of their crew would work, and they had to keep the rigs going. But on Saturday night, they went into town, and Deafy got drunk. Kim and Wendy played records and listened to the single dial radio set.

The next day, Wendy told Kim, the new Methodist church was going to hold its first service. Construction had been delayed because thieves had stolen the lumber for it. Kim and Wendy decided to attend, much to Blake's disgust and Maria's delight. Maria enjoyed seeing her husband's daughter defy him.

Kim bought some new clothing and a necktie. He felt garishly dressed, but it was the best he could buy.

The church service lasted almost an hour, and during that time, rocks were bounced off the side of the church, and loud and obscene language was hurled from the outside. The preacher studiously ignored the rabble and brought his message. It was like a cool wind on a parched desert. Kim felt immensely better when they left and was determined to bring Deafy with him the next time he came.

That afternoon, he and Wendy went for a long walk and then sat and talked for hours. It was a peaceful day.

The work on the school building progressed. It was a frame building, and there was much concern as to where teachers would be procured.

Their next well came in the day Rudolph Valentino died. It was not a gusher, but it was a good well. Oschner immediately had them move the rig a scant hundred yards away and begin drilling another.

That night, Kim went to see Wendy. She was unusually gay, and so was Maria. Blake was gone, and Kim danced with both Wendy and Maria to the jazz music of the record player. And he talked excitedly of their new well. He stayed until almost midnight.

After he had gone, Wendy and Maria sat in companionable silence for a few minutes.

"You're in love with Kim, aren't you, Wendy?" Maria's musical voice broke the silence.

Wendy was startled at Maria's question. She laughed uncertainly. "Don't be foolish, Maria!"

"Oh, but you are," Maria laughed. "I can see it plainly. You are always so happy after you have seen him."

"I am not in love," Wendy said firmly. "And I don't intend to be. Kim is a wonderful person. He's thoughtful and nice, but he is getting the oil fever, and I do not intend to fall in love with an oil man."

"Your heart will tell you, one day, that you *are* in love with him," Maria said complacently.

"Did *your* heart tell you that you were in love with Father!" Wendy flared. It was the first time she had ever spoken sharply to her father's wife.

"No," Maria admitted casually. "It didn't. But I do not have the heart of a woman. You do."

"I'm sorry, Maria," Wendy said contritely, "I didn't mean to say that. Please forgive me. You are so wonderful to Father and—I'm sorry!"

"Don't ever be sorry, Wendy," Maria said lightly. "Don't ever be sorry for anything."

A week later Maria came by the rig to tell Kim and Deafy that Wendy had left camp. The news shattered Kim.

"But why?" he asked desperately. "Why did she leave? She didn't say anything to me about it."

"She is running from someone," Maria said quietly.

"Who?" Kim asked belligerently. "If Joe Shay—."

"It isn't Joe Shay," Maria said calmly. "And it isn't Blake—or me. It's you Kim."

"Me?" Kim was incredulous. "Why, that's ridiculous. I have never—."

"I think it is ridiculous, too," Maria said. "But she is gone. And I promised not to tell you where she is."

Deafy had been listening intently to the conversation. At Maria's last statement his lips thinned and he squirted tobacco juice. Without a word he turned and slouched away toward the rig.

"Well, *somebody* has to tell me," Kim said desperately.

"Who? Blake?" Maria laughed. "He is the only other person who knows."

"*You* will," Kim said flatly.

"I might," Maria admitted. "Come to the house Saturday night. I'll make up my mind by then."

"I'll be there," Kim said grimly.

As soon as the men were paid on Saturday night, Kim hurried to the Terrell house. There were no cars there and Kim was afraid there would be nobody at home. He pounded on the door. Maria opened it almost immediately. Kim looked past her and saw no one.

"Blake isn't here," Maria laughed. "There isn't anyone here but me. Come in."

Cautiously Kim stepped inside, and Maria shut the door.

"Where is Blake?" Kim asked.

"He went to Amarillo," Maria said. "Joe went with him. And I gave Rachael the night off. Blake won't be back until tomorrow." She looked at him speculatively.

"Then I guess I'd better be going too," Kim said uncomfortably. "Why didn't you go too—I mean—,"

"I know what you mean, Kim," Maria said lightly. "You mean, why didn't I go too? I didn't want to. I had a date with you. Remember?"

"You said you would tell me where Wendy is," Kim said.

"I said I'd make up my mind about it," Maria corrected.

"Will you tell me?"

"Let me fix you a drink, Kim," Maria said pleasantly. "Let's not rush so much."

Maria turned and went to a cabinet. She took a bottle of whiskey and poured two drinks. She handed him one and she sipped the other.

"How long have you been in town?"

"I just got in," Kim gulped.

"I know. I've had a man watching for you since Blake and Joe left for Amarillo. Been to Sal's place yet?"

Kim started. His face got red and it irked him that it did. Maria laughed again.

"Men never quite understand, do they Kim, that all women are very much alike. What makes you think that if Sal knows men will come to her place, that I won't know it?"

Kim didn't answer. He sipped his drink and grimaced. He didn't like the stuff and was drinking only to kill time until Maria decided to talk.

Maria seemed to read his mind. "You don't have to drink that,
Kim," she said. "I need it. You don't. I've been drinking it since I
was sixteen. The first man I ever slept with got me drunk. Don't look
so aghast, Kim. It really wasn't that bad."

Kim didn't know what to say but he ventured, "I'm sorry."

"Don't be. I wanted him to."

Maria kept pacing the floor. She adjusted a picture on the wall and
seemed completely oblivious that the robe she wore was coming
apart in front. A long, slender, well-formed leg made its appearance
at every step. Kim wondered vaguely how he was managing to be so
objective about them.

"Are you going to tell me where Wendy is, Maria?" he asked. "I
shouldn't stay here, you know, with Blake gone."

"Don't worry about Blake," Maria said. "I told you that he
wouldn't be back until tomorrow. Besides, he would be tickled pink
to come home and find you in bed with me. It would relieve his
mind about you and Wendy, damn her pretty blue eyes. You're in
love with her, aren't you?"

"I—I don't know."

"I thought you were, but I wasn't sure until I saw that dreamy
look in your eyes when you were watching my legs just now. You
were thinking about Wendy's legs, weren't you?"

"Don't talk like that, Maria," Kim said weakly.

"Right though, wasn't I?" she said cryptically as she plopped
down in an overstuffed chair, her robe askew. One ivory breast, with
the strawberry nipple, was completely visible. Kim fidgeted.

"Relax, Kim" Maria soothed. "I'm not expecting anything now. I
wouldn't get it if I did. But I *am* going to get drunk. And I'll tell you
a little secret. Wendy's legs *are* prettier than mine. So are her breasts.
And don't be such a damned prude. Women see each other naked,
you know. I've seen Wendy without her clothes."

Maria's voice was conversational. And, though Kim felt that he
should be outraged, he wasn't. There was something very honest
about Maria. But he couldn't afford to stay any longer. Blake
Terrell's wife, or not, a man couldn't stand the pressure forever! He
started to rise.

"Sit down, Kim. I didn't mean anything bad about Wendy. Fact is,
I love the little bitch, even if she has got a more beautiful body than
mine. And I'm glad she's yours."

"She's not—."

"Yes she is. And you're hers. I don't give a damn whether you've
had her or not, though I think you have—that day when Blake and I
were gone to Amarillo and you were there when we got back—but I

don't care how many women you've had. You belong to Wendy. You know why? Because your minds fit. Wendy has a beautiful body, and a wonderful heart, and a mind as sharp as a newly filed drill bit. It adds up."

"If you'll excuse me, Maria—" Kim started again to rise.

"I won't," Maria said crossly. Her voice was losing its lilting quality. Evidently she had been drinking before Kim arrived. "Now sit still. I want to talk to you—. I'd rather go to bed with you, but you're—." She stopped and looked keenly at Kim. "You know, Kim. I'm only four years older than Wendy. When you marry her, that will make me your step-mother. How will you like that?"

"I—I don't know," he said lamely. "What I mean is, I don't know how I would like—. Where is she, Maria?"

"What will you give to know, Kim," Maria's smile was provocative and she stretched a slender leg toward Kim.

"You are just teasing, Maria," Kim said uncomfortably. "Besides, you husband—."

"Husband!" Maria spat contemptuously. "The only wife Blake needs, or wants, is an oil well."

"But, Maria," Kim said helplessly. "You surely—."

"Kim," Maria's voice was getting thicker, "remember I said you don't know women. You don't. Lots of things are important to them. Some women just want to be needed. Others want security— whatever that is. Some want money—others sex." She paused a moment and a bitter smile touched her pretty lips. "I'm a glutton, Kim. I married Blake Terrell for his money. But I learned to like sex a long time ago. I have had many good teachers. And now I want both. I pity women who never learned to enjoy their own bodies. I want money, too. If I have to choose—well—,"

Maria's voice had been getting sluggish as she talked, and her eyes had lost their brightness. Kim realized that she was very drunk. Without warning she dropped her glass on the floor and sank back in her chair. She was asleep before Kim reached her.

Kim lifted her and placed her on the divan. Then he mopped up the spilled liquor with his handkerchief and left the house. He locked the door after him.

Walking back toward the rig that night, Kim decided that he would leave the field as soon as this well came in. He had no intention of falling in love with anyone. He had been foolish to stay here in the first place! Deafy didn't really need him! And *Maria* was foolish to think Wendy was in love with him.

But both Kim's resolutions and convictions were shaky. The next few days he was grim and morose. Deafy sought, with good natured jibes, to bring him back to normal. But it was to no avail.

Saturday night Kim decided not to go into town with Deafy. Deafy's protests brought only grim refusals from Kim. The following week, Deafy didn't even ask Kim to accompany him, but he came back to the rig early. He was sober, but Kim did not even notice. He was much too busy making plans to leave the oil field.

By the middle of the third week after Wendy's departure, Deafy became so exasperated with Kim that he would hardly speak. He handed Kim a grease can and pointed silently to the crown block. Kim started to protest. They had other men that could do that, but one look at Deafy stayed his argument.

Kim had barely reached the top of the derrick when he heard Deafy yell. He turned to look and almost fell off the crown block. There, standing beside her Marmon coupe, was Wendy. She was a picture of loveliness as she stood in open-throated shirt and slim fitting trousers. Kim scampered back to the ground.

"We got company." Deafy's grin was wide.

"Hello, Kim," Wendy said and extended her hand as Kim approached.

"Hello, Wendy." Kim took her hand and looked at her with hungry eyes. Her hair was swept back just behind her ears, and her eyes seemed to glow and soften by turns.

"You two talk awhile, and I'll go see what that damned toolie is doing," Deafy said and walked away.

Kim continued to stare at Wendy.

"Do I pass inspection?" Wendy asked pertly and smiled.

"I'm sorry," Kim flushed and stammered a bit.

"Don't be, Kim. I like you to look at me." Then she added impishly, "Makes me feel sort of womanish."

"Where have you been?"

"To New York."

"Why did you leave, Wendy?" Kim asked meekly.

"Let's not talk about that now, Kim."

"All right," Kim agreed. "I'll get Deafy, and we will make some coffee in the shack."

"No, Kim," Wendy said quickly. "I didn't come to see Deafy. I came to see you."

"Why?" Kim asked and wished he hadn't.

"Because," Wendy laughed, "I wanted to. And I was afraid you might not come back to see me."

"You won't ever know how glad I am that you're back," Kim said candidly. "I wish you hadn't left."

"I'm sorry I did," Wendy said. "And I should have told you I was leaving."

"Why didn't you?" Kim asked.

"Sometime I will tell you why," she said seriously. Then in her direct manner she asked, "Will you go on a picnic with me tomorrow?"

"A picnic?" Kim asked incredulously.

"Yes. Meet me at sunup. At the creek by the house."

"I'll be there," Kim said enthusiastically.

"Good," Wendy said. Then she got in her car and drove away without looking back.

Kim stood staring after her until he heard Deafy yell. He looked to see Deafy standing precariously near the edge of the crown block platform trying to thread a cable through the block. Kim grinned and walked toward the rig, his resolve to leave the oil fields forgotten.

That night, after they had bathed and were ready for bed, Kim told Deafy that he was going to take the next day off. Deafy only grunted.

"You think I'm foolish, Deafy?"

"Foolish? Hell, I don't know what's foolish and what ain't," Deafy said grouchily.

"You think you and the boys can get along all right with the drilling if I go?"

"Got along all right a long time before I ever knowed you, Kim Wingate."

"I know, Deafy. But do you think the well might blow, or maybe I ought to stay and work? I know we need another hand."

"We need another hand, all right," Deafy agreed.

"Then, do you want me to stay, Deafy?" Kim almost shouted.

"Stay or go," Deafy shouted back. "I don't give a damn. I ain't telling you what to do or what not to do."

"All right, Deafy," Kim said apologetically. "I know it's probably foolish for me to take a day off at this time. I know I'm needed here. But I'm going anyway. I'm going to take the whole day off," Kim said with finality. Then he added almost defiantly, "I'm going to see Wendy. We're going on a picnic! Wendy Terrell and me!"

Kim looked at Deafy, fulling expecting wrath to be blazing from his one good eye. Instead, Deafy was bending over the kerosene lamp, and his leathery old face was creased with pleasure. Kim heard him blow gustily, and the light faded. Then he heard the springs of Deafy's bed creak as Deafy crawled in.

There was silence for a few moments.

"You know, Kim," Deafy said finally, "I was just about to think you didn't have no sense. But maybe you have. In fact, I was just about to decide that if Joe Shay didn't kill you, you was beginning to stand a good chance of getting old enough to turn out to be some boar-brained bastard like Blake hisself, or some old wore-out boomer like me. Then you wouldn't have nothing but work and money left. But you may turn out smarter than that."

Kim said nothing more. He knew that unpredictable, unselfish, old Deafy was pleased. And he was glad. The steam engine shut down, but from the very sound of it Kim knew that it was nothing serious. Kim simply lay and listened to the silence.

Then he heard Deafy chuckle.

"Picnic! Well, I'm a son-of-a-bitch!"

Kim smiled in the darkness and went to sleep.

————

Kim awakened long before daylight and almost stealthily donned his clothing. He debated a moment what to wear. Actually, he had very little choice. Finally he selected a new pair of denim trousers and a soft shirt.

He walked outside the shack. The air was brisk and refreshing. He decided to take the "ton-and-a-half." They might need it to run to town for repairs, but if they did they could use the *White*. Kim was in no mood for details. He wanted to see Wendy.

He had the truck started when he heard a roughneck yell.

"Hey—that's what I was going to town in for some new cable!"

Kim didn't pay any attention. He simply gunned the motor and drove away.

As he drove through the main street of Borger, the music blared from the gambling dens and dance halls. It was just getting light in the east, and people were scurrying about as usual with no regard to time. He parked the truck just north of the "Great White Way." It would be fairly safe there. People coming to and from the dance place would not be interested in the truck anyway. From there, he walked. It was not far to the creek where Wendy was to meet him—and where he had first seen her. The crescent moon in the west was almost down, and the sun was ready to show. He saw a jackrabbit scurry from beneath a sage brush bush. Then he was at the creek. He looked toward the Terrell house.

There was a light. He saw the door open and close. Then he saw Wendy coming toward the creek. She was wearing a slim, fitting skirt and a loose blouse. She walked with a firm, sure stride, carrying a package in her hand.

The rim of the sun pushed above the horizon. Its first rays struck Wendy's pushed-back hair and glinted in her eyes.

Neither spoke. They looked at each other for a moment, and Kim took the lunch package from her. Then they clasped hands and headed north toward the river.

There was still a cool, blue haze upon it.

They walked in silence for a few minutes. The sun, a great, orange ball in the east, rose rapidly. Near the edge of the river bottom the willows grew thick, and the sage was abundant. It was only a twenty minute walk from town, but when they entered the willows, it seemed like a curtain closing behind them. Even the sounds were muted. Kim followed Wendy down a dim trail. She walked with the grace of a deer. They came to a small clearing in the willows. Wendy stopped, and Kim came up beside her.

"Is this the place?"

"No. It is farther down the river. But this is the trail I always use. Look!" She pointed to the soft sand in the clearing. "You can see animal tracks. I always stop to see how many I can identify."

Kim looked but could ascertain nothing but ruffled sand.

"Here," Wendy said. "Here are the tracks of a doe and her fawn. Their tracks are always around the spring. And look, here are some fresh turkey tracks! You wouldn't think, would you, that there would be so much wild life here on the prairies, but it abounds here in the river breaks. I've seen coon and coyote tracks. And badgers and skunks—and oh, all sorts of animals. Here they have a great deal of shelter and food. Isn't it a wonderful place!"

Kim agreed. Certainly he hadn't suspected anything such as this so close to Borger.

"Come on," Wendy said eagerly. "Let's go on to my cottonwood and spring."

Wendy's enthusiasm was beginning to touch Kim. He followed her as she trotted down the dim trail. It was only a few minutes until they came to another big clearing that ran all the way to the river's edge. Where the river bank jutted downward, there stood a huge cottonwood tree that had somehow managed to withstand the flood-waters that occasionally rose in the river. Actually, the river channel was far from the sandy bank and was not more than a few yards wide and only ankle deep. The water tasted of alkali and was not fit for human consumption. It was good stock water, however, and a great boon to the ranchers through whose land it ran.

"Isn't it just as wonderful as I told you it was!" Wendy asked delightedly.

Kim looked at the huge, gnarled, old cottonwood. Some of its roots were exposed where the water had risen to it and washed away the soil. But beneath its great canopy the sand was smooth and cool. It was a restful place.

The morning passed quickly. They ate lunch under the cotton-wood and then walked east down the river. Kim suddenly realized they were probably just north of the rig.

"See that smoke!" Wendy exclaimed and pointed across the river. "That is the Beatenbow place—you remember, the ranch people I told you about."

"I didn't know we had come so far. I've heard of their ranch."

"Let's go over, Kim. I'd like you to meet them. They're very nice people."

"Do you think we should?" he asked dubiously.

"Of course, we should," Wendy said firmly. "You will love them. The whole Beatenbow clan lives on this river. There's the old grandmother whose husband homesteaded the place. And then there's Mandy who is Granny's daughter. She's a widow. Her husband was killed when he caught his foot in a rope, and his horse dragged him to death. Mandy is probably fifty years old."

"And there is Finch. He's the hired hand. Granny said that Finch has been with the Beatenbow family since her husband homesteaded the place. No one knows how old he is. He and Mandy operate a two thousand acre horse ranch. That is their foaling pasture that runs up to your lease."

"I know," Kim said. "I've met Finch. But I thought their ranch was much bigger."

"It is," Wendy said. "But there are only two thousand acres in the horse ranch. They furnish cow horses for nearly all the ranches in the Panhandle. They have ten thousand acres more. They raise cattle on that, and Mandy's daughter and her husband manage the cattle ranch. They live a mile farther down the river. They have two lovely children about seven and eight years old," Wendy said. "Where did you meet Finch?"

"He comes by the rig occasionally. He and Deafy are good friends."

"Well, I'll be darned," Wendy said in surprise. "And neither one of them has said a word to me about it."

Kim laughed.

"Come on, Kim," Wendy said. "Let's go over and see them."

They started walking across the sandy river bottom eagerly, as though some great new adventure awaited them just on the other bank. As indeed it did.

They didn't talk as they walked. Kim took Wendy's hand. The action was so casual and so natural that neither noticed. The sands were deep, and eventually they came to the channel of the river. The water was not more than ankle deep and only a few yards wide, but their shoes would be soaked if they walked across.

"Want me to carry you?" Kim asked.

"No. Let's pull our shoes off and wade," Wendy said. "It's so warm the cool water will feel good."

Kim agreed, and they sat and pulled off their shoes. Kim tied the strings of both pairs together and hung them around his neck. Wendy pulled up her skirt well above her knees, and they waded into the stream. The water was cool, and they loitered along the way. Wendy stopped to let her feet sink in the sand and watch the water flow over them. Kim kept moving his feet so that he would not sink as he watched Wendy. The sand was a mixture of irregular grains and the rounded quicksand so prevalent on the river. As Wendy stood and worked her feet, she sank deeper and deeper. Finally the sand was almost to her knees and the water well above them. As she had sunk, she kept lifting her skirt. She was completely oblivious of the fact that a great expanse of her strong, white thighs was made visible to Kim. No so Kim! He stared fascinated. He thought he had never seen anything lovelier. Then Wendy raised her eyes to him. They were radiantly alive, as though she has just discovered one of the great secrets of the universe.

"Isn't it wonderful!"

"What?" Kim asked vacantly.

"Just being alive!"

Kim grinned like an ecstatic half-wit and then suddenly noticed that Wendy was making no effort to free herself from the sand. He was startled.

"It sure is wonderful being alive," he said practically. "And you just keep on being that way by getting out of that quicksand."

He reached out and grasped Wendy's hand. They tugged for several seconds before she was freed.

"I've wanted to do that every time I have crossed here," Wendy panted. "But I never dared until today—when you were with me."

"Don't ever do it again," Kim said seriously. "That quicksand is treacherous."

"I won't unless you are with me," she said.

They sat for a few minutes until their feet and legs dried in the warm sun and then donned their shoes again. It was not more than half a mile to the Beatenbow house. As they approached, a lean, vicious-looking mongrel dog came rushing toward them.

"Come here, Gert!" Wendy cried. The big dog loped on and reared up on Wendy, licking her hands with a long red tongue.

"He is a vicious looking brute," Kim said. The dog had given him an anxious moment.

"Gert is not a he. She is a she," Wendy informed him. "And she's not at all vicious. Not with people. She is Finch's coyote dog. She has killed more than a hundred."

"I can believe that!" Kim said as he looked at the scarred face and torn ears of the dog.

Gert followed Wendy and Kim as they approached a long, low adobe house set under a huge cottonwood tree. There was a long gallery spanning the entire front, and barns and corrals were in back. Under the trees were droppings from the hundreds of wild turkeys that roosted there every night. It was a wild and lonely place. Kim and Wendy stopped at a small structure built of cottonwood logs from which flowed a stream of cool water.

"This is the well house," Wendy informed Kim. "Let's get a cool drink."

"Well house?"

"Yes, this little log house is built over a spring, and they keep milk in here so it will stay fresh and cool."

Wendy opened the door that was held in place with a cross bar. They entered the small house, and it was very damp and cool. As their eyes adjusted, Kim could see several crocks of milk placed so that the water ran by them constantly. In the center was a hole about three feet in diameter. It was lined with rocks. From it the stream sprang. A long-handled dipper hung from a wooden peg in one of the logs. Wendy removed the dipper and sank it deep into the spring. She handed it to Kim. He hesitated momentarily. He didn't relish the idea of drinking after someone else. Wendy noticed.

"It's a common drinking cup," she said. "But I doubt if a Beatenbow ever had a disease."

Kim took the dipper and drank deeply from it. The water was cold and sweet. He dipped it again and handed it to Wendy. Then they left the well house and walked toward the main house. They walked up on the gallery, and Wendy knocked.

"It ain't locked." The voice was rough and cracked, but it was feminine. Kim looked at Wendy questioningly.

"That's Granny Beatenbow!" she whispered and opened the door.

A small, wiry woman, obviously very old, sat in a huge rocking chair facing a large fireplace, back to the door. There was a knitted cap on her head and a shawl over her lap. Kim quickly took stock of the room in the moment they hesitated inside the door. It was large and comfortable. There were several chairs covered with cowhide on which the hair still remained. Over the fireplace there hung a long, muzzle-loading rifle. There was a line of pegs driven into the wall along one side of the room, and from the pegs hung various articles of clothing. Hooked rugs adorned the otherwise bare wooden floor. Two kerosene lamps sat on the mantle.

"Well, Wendy Terrell!" the old woman spoke almost harshly, without even looking around. "Are you just going to stand there! Come on in and let me take a look at your young man."

Wendy laughed again and went to the old woman. She bent and kissed the old woman on her wrinkled cheek. The old lady quickly wiped the kiss away.

"Now there you go, Wendy!" she said crossly. "Kissing a body whether they want to be kissed or not. You leave me be."

"I kissed you because *I* wanted to," Wendy said with mock severity. "I don't care whether you wanted me to or not. Anyway, how did you know it was me?"

The old lady grinned in toothless pleasure.

"How did I know it was you?" she said impishly. "I knowed it was you from the first step I heard. You couldn't fool me, young lady. Not for a second. I heard you come up on the gallery. Ain't heard nobody walk like you since my Mandy was young. You walk like a prancin' filly. Now—who is your young man? Bring him around and let me take a look at him."

Kim stepped forward almost reluctantly.

"Here he is, Granny. His name is Kimball Wingate."

"Humph," Granny said noncommitally as she glared at Kim. Her small, bright eyes were circled with wrinkled, leathery skin. Kim stood and shifted his weight uncomfortably. He felt that he had never undergone closer scrutiny. Wendy looked questioningly at Granny's face. There was almost complete silence for a few seconds as the old lady glared at Kim. Then, as if dismissing him, she turned to Wendy.

"Well?" Wendy questioned.

"Humph!" Granny said again. Then she began to rock slowly. The creak of the ancient rocker was a comfortable and ageless sound. "He ain't big enough!" she said firmly. "But I reckon he'll fill out."

Kim felt as though he should say something and looked at Wendy for a cue. But Wendy was looking at Granny.

"He one of them oil men?"

"Yes, Granny. He is." There was a slight note of defiance in Wendy's voice.

"Figured he was," Granny said with satisfaction. "I reckon you was bound to get yourself a oil man, Wendy."

"He isn't mine, Granny."

"Humph!" Granny snorted in disgust. Then she continued emphatically: "Mighty nigh got my fill of them oil men. They was one out here wanting to drill wells on our place again yesterday."

Granny began to rock faster. Obviously she was angry. "I know we got to let somebody drill a well on our place sooner or later. Times change. But I ain't going to be pushed."

"You won't be, Granny," Wendy consoled. "We didn't come to talk to you about leasing your land."

"I know you didn't, young lady," Granny Beatenbow cackled. "Now you leave me be. I'll talk about whatever I want to."

"You won't either," Wendy said just as emphatically. "Just because I came out here the first time with Father when he was wanting to lease your place doesn't mean I want to talk about it every time I come to see you. Lease your darned old ranch to anyone you like!"

"She's a dinger, ain't she son!" the old lady grinned at Kim. "You got your hands full. Talks back to Granny Beatenbow." She said it with satisfaction. "Ain't nobody done that since my Mandy was young—Mandy's my girl. Lives with me now since her man got drug to death by a horse most twenty years ago. Mandy's youngest and her husband live down the river a ways. They run the cattle, and Mandy and Finch run the horses. Mandy's a grandmother. That makes me a great grandmaw!"

"Where is Mandy?" Wendy was anxious to get the conversation on something besides oil.

"She went with Finch to drag some colts out of the river bog," Granny said. "Finch ain't so young as he oncet was, seems like. But Mandy helps out a lot. Mandy was mighty young to lose her man," the old lady said sadly shaking her head, "her only twenty-five when he got killed. She should have married again. But she never would. Now with me it was different. I was a old woman when Humphrey Beatenbow got hisself killed. Wonder he didn't do it when he started traipsin' all over the country with that young fool Billy Dixon, chasing Indians. But he waited and got run over by a bunch of four year old steers. That's his hat a hanging on that peg right over there." She nodded toward a big, stained hat hanging beside the fireplace. She wiped her eyes and then continued stoutly.

"Ain't much to have left of a man—but that's all I got. That and a lot of memories. I reckon that's more than some have. But, now with Mandy it was different. She should have married again—still ought."

"Where are the kids?" Wendy asked.

"They're out riding. They'll be here soon."

"And Tom and Phyllis?"

"Gone to Amarillo as usual!" Granny said with disgust. "Them two young 'uns don't seem to know they got a ranch to run. Their kids is spending the night with us."

"You're here alone!" Wendy said with concern.

"Not now. Was before you two come along. But you don't let that worry you, young lady! I been here alone lots of times. Something was to catch me they'd turn me loose when daylight come, anyway." Then she added defiantly, "Besides I ain't quite helpless yet."

"I know you aren't, Granny," Wendy said soothingly.

"Did your husband ride with Billy Dixon?" Kim asked eagerly. He had read much of the colorful Indian fighter.

"He did, young man," Granny said. "Almost got hisself killed several times."

"Those must have been exciting days," Kim said with a touch of envy in his voice.

"They was exciting all right," Granny admitted. Then she added, "When Humphrey and Finch came to this country back in '74, there wasn't nothing here but grass. He built this ranch with his bare hands."

"Your husband must have been quite a man, Mrs. Beatenbow," Kim said soberly.

"He was," Granny said stoutly. "They don't come no better than Humphrey Beatenbow was. And he took good care of his women folks too. Built a half dugout before he brought me out from Mobeetie. Furnished it good too. I bore him four sons and one daughter while he was living there," she said with pride.

"You have four sons?" Kim asked in surprise.

"Did have," Granny said. "I got only three now. My second boy got drowned when a headrise come down the river. Seems like the Beatenbows just can't seem to manage a natural death. Something always happening to us."

Kim said something else to Granny, and the old lady began another long answer. Both Kim and Granny were ignoring Wendy, though neither was aware of it. A smile of satisfaction touched Wendy's face, and she pulled a hooked rug beside the fireplace. With the grace of a cat she sat upon it and leaned against the wall. She watched and listened intently as Kim listened and the old woman talked. Occasionally, the conversation was almost incoherent, for Granny talked of the past, and it was hazy and dreamy to her.

It was almost an hour later when they heard activity outside the house. Granny was instantly alert.

"That's Mandy and Finch," she said to Kim.

Steps sounded on the gallery, and the door opened. Mandy stood in the doorway. She was the woman who had accompanied Finch to the rig the first time. She was tall and solidly built. Her face was tanned, and her eyes very dark and large, though they squinted a bit from the sun. She was built firmly but was womanly rounded. Her hands were large and strong, yet a gentleness was about her. She was still a handsome woman, and there were traces of former beauty that age or Texas sun and wind would never erase. She was wearing a man's shirt and a divided skirt. Her feet were encased in heavy boots, and in one hand she held a pair of leather gloves which she slapped gently against her thigh.

"We got company, Mandy," Granny said.

"I see we have. Hello, Wendy." Mandy walked toward them, and Wendy rose as did Kim.

"Hello, Mandy. It's good to see you," Wendy said. "This is Kim Wingate."

"Hello, Kim," Mandy extended her hand, and Kim felt the strong pressure of her grip but was surprised at the softness of her hand. "Deafy has told me about you."

Kim stifled an exclamation. He had vaguely thought that there was more than Finch responsible for Deafy's absences from the rig. But Kim said nothing.

"Mandy's my girl," Granny said with satisfaction. "Takes after her daddy. Got a girl of her own, too, and two grandkids. Her man got hisself killed by an outlaw horse." She paused a second. "Told you that though, didn't I."

"Your mother and I have been having a wonderful conversation," Kim said. "I could listen to her forever."

"Mama likes company," Mandy admitted and looked at Kim with friendly eyes.

"Where's Finch?" Granny demanded.

"He's unsaddling the horses. We had four colts in the quicksand today."

"Well, where are the kids?" Granny seemed intent on arguing about something.

"They're out riding, Mama. They'll be here soon. They will sleep here tonight. Tom and Phyllis won't be back from Amarillo until tomorrow."

"If they get back at all," Granny spat. "Finch runs that cow ranch more than them young 'uns do. Sometimes I think there ain't a speck of Beatenbow blood in that girl of yours, Mandy."

"She's young, Mama. She and Tom need to get away occasionally. I have to get some supper cooking," Mandy said matter of factly. "The children will be here soon—starved to death as usual. You and Kim will be here, won't you, Wendy?"

"We would love to, Mandy. But we really must go. We walked. I had no idea it was so late. We must have been talking to Granny for hours."

"Ain't been here but a few minutes," Granny stated flatly. "They'll stay, Mandy."

Kim started to protest and then changed his mind, and for once Wendy said nothing.

Mandy went to the kitchen, and they heard the bustle of pots and pans and the clang of an iron stove lid being dropped in place. Shortly there came the delicious smell of cooking through the house. The odor mixed with that of wood smoke, and Kim's mouth watered. Granny resumed her droning talk. Kim listened with fascination. A few minutes later there was the clatter in the yard, and the door burst open. Two children about seven and eight years old rushed through the door. Kim caught a glimpse of two small, bare-backed horses in the yard.

"Hi, Granny!" the youngest, the boy, yelled as he threw his hat at a peg on the wall. "We're going to stay with you tonight. When will supper be ready?" Then, spying Kim and Wendy, he stopped suddenly. "Who's that man?" He looked belligerently at Kim.

"That's Wendy's man," Granny said. "Now you behave yourself. Supper will be ready when your grandma gets it ready and not a mite before," she said sternly. Then to Kim: "These are my great grand-children. Phyllis's young 'uns. Don't know whether they got Beaten-bow blood or not. Can't tell yet. But they are a fright around the house. Keeps a body in a stew all the time."

The little girl had been looking with big eyes at Wendy and Kim. She had not said a word, but evidently the old lady's speech had not frightened her, for she walked in a sidling manner toward the old lady and leaned against her chair. Granny Beatenbow's gnarled, old hand lifted and softly caressed the child's fine, light hair.

"What is your name, young lady?" Kim asked.

The little girl simply continued to stare at Kim, but the little boy yelled.

"Her name is Peg. Mine is Humph—short for Humphrey. Named after my great grand daddy. That's his hat there on that peg."

"Now you hush up, Humph," Granny admonished. "Young 'uns are supposed to be seen and not heard."

"All right, Granny. I smell Mother Mandy's cooking, anyway." With that parting remark he rushed to the kitchen. He was gone only a few minutes when Mandy could be heard scolding him, and he immediately reappeared in the living room. He was holding a bit of dough in his hand.

"What you been into now, young spriggins?" Granny asked.

"Nothing. Just some dough. Mother Mandy is making biscuits."

"I can make biscuits!" it was the first time Peggy had spoken.

"Can you, Peggy?" Wendy asked.

"Course she can," Granny said harshly. "Lands alive! She's almost nine years old. Why shouldn't she make biscuits?"

The little girl started to walk toward Wendy, but her great grandmother's arm held her back. Humphrey was pulling the biscuit dough between his fingers and looking at it interestedly.

"Granny—I bet I know how God makes people."

The old woman looked at the young boy sharply. Kim and Wendy watched them both.

"Do you now! How is that done young spriggins?"

"He just makes 'em out of people-dough."

Kim and Wendy smiled. The old woman seemed to consider the statement for a moment.

"Humph!" she said. "That ain't far wrong, I reckon. Lots of folks ain't never thought about it one way or another."

Then Peggy, hungry for attention again, spoke as she looked with big eyes from Kim to Wendy.

"That ain't right, Granny," she said primly. "People breed each other just like cows and horses. I've seen 'em—lots of times. Cows and horses, I mean."

"You shut your mouth, young lady," the old woman said, but she grinned slightly. "Who's been telling you things like that, anyway!"

"Mother Mandy told me—and she knows."

"Well, you just march yourself into the kitchen and help Mother Mandy fix supper, young lady." Granny gave the little girl a spat on her backside as she trotted toward the kitchen.

"That young 'un may turn out to be a Beatenbow, yet," Granny said with pride.

It was only a few moments until Mandy came and called them to supper. It was still more than an hour before sunset. Kim, Wendy and Humph walked outside to a flat board set between two small trees near the well house. On the board was a pan, and hanging on a peg from one of the trees was a towel. Humph poured the water from a tin bucket and made a halfhearted dab at his face and wiped it with the towel.

Then Wendy and Kim washed their hands.

They were almost ready to return to the house when Finch walked toward them. Wendy's face lit up when she saw him.

"Hello, Finch," she said and extended her hand.

Finch merely nodded and offered his bony hand.

"You know Kim Wingate," Wendy said. "We are staying for supper."

Again Finch nodded and extended his hand to Kim.

"I'm glad to see you Finch." Kim said.

Still Finch only nodded. He removed his hat in preparation to wash his face. His head shone brightly in the sun. He calmly and deliberately went about his ablutions and then all of them walked to the house.

The food was set on a long table which was adorned with a red and white checked oil cloth. There were huge steaks, hot sourdough biscuits, brown beans, gravy, and hot, strong coffee. Wendy and the children drank cold milk.

There were no preliminaries. Everyone started eating. Finch sat at the head of the table. Mandy sat nearest the cookstove and occasionally rose from her chair to replenish a dish. Everyone ate quietly and with concentration. Kim thought he had never seen such a wonderful meal. He was astounded when the old lady asked for her third helping of gravy which she piled high on sourdough biscuits and then placed a big piece of yellow butter on top of it all. Kim supposed that she could not eat the meat because she had no teeth.

When the meal was finished, Finch leaned back and poured tobacco from a sack into a brown cigarette paper. He twirled the cigarette thoughtfully and stuck it in his mouth. Then he struck a match on his leather leggins and drew a lungful of smoke. Mandy refilled his cup with scalding coffee and Finch poured the coffee from the cup into a deep saucer. He held it up and blew on it gustily, then he drank with satisfaction. Kim watched in open-mouthed wonder and for a second was tempted to try it himself.

Finch's lighted cigarette seemed the signal for further conversation, and everyone started talking. Mandy and Finch talked of the ranch work, and Granny added a scathing comment occasionally which was ignored by everyone.

"Tom ought to move some more bulls into that north pasture," Finch ventured. "I rode over there today and he's got nearly four hundred cows up there now, and only eight bulls. If he ain't back by morning I'll take three or four up from the Gyp creek pasture."

"I can help tomorrow, Finch," Mandy offered.

"Maybe you better," Finch admitted glumly. "Them critters is hard to handle."

The conversation continued for a few minutes and then Finch rose. He left without a word to anyone. Mandy started gathering the dishes, and Wendy rose to help. Kim and the old lady retired to the living room and the children ran out into the yard.

As Kim and Granny Beatenbow seated themselves again, the old lady started telling of another Indian raid. It was something about a

Fort Elliott, but Kim listened only halfheartedly. He was drowsy after the big meal.

When Wendy and Mandy came from the kitchen, Wendy said, "We must go, Kim. It will be dark soon."

"I know it," Kim said. "I've enjoyed it so much here I hate to leave."

"So do I," Wendy admitted. "But we must."

They prepared to leave, and Mandy put her arm around Wendy. It occurred to Kim that there was something of a resemblance between the two women. He was at a loss to know what it was, though.

"I enjoyed talking to you, Mrs. Beatenbow," Kim said as he walked to the door.

"Come here, young man!" she demanded sternly. Kim walked back and stood before her. Again she looked at him keenly. This time it did not disconcert him.

"It may be," she said at last, "that Wendy picked herself a good man." She paused a moment and then continued. "And then again, maybe she didn't. Anyway, you might as well go ahead and call me Granny like the rest of the young whippersnappers around here do," she finished harshly.

Kim grinned and looked at Wendy who was smiling in sheer delight. They said goodbye again and started walking toward the river.

They didn't loiter on the way back. They pulled their shoes off and waded the water and headed for the cottonwood tree. The sun was almost down when they reached it. They sat for a few minutes and felt the heat from the warm sand rise around them. A three-quarter moon was pale in the east, but it would be bright when the sun went down.

"They're wonderful people aren't they, Kim?"

Kim nodded but said nothing. Wendy lay back and looked up at the tree above.

"What are you thinking, Kim?"

"Nothing, I guess. It's just that I—I—"

"What Kim?" Wendy said softly.

"Well—they're wonderful people, all right," Kim admitted. "But I wouldn't want to live like they do. They're almost isolated from everything out here on the river. Don't misunderstand me, Wendy—please. It's just that—well, I don't want to live like I'm living now either. I want something permanent, but I want it a little closer to—. Well, I guess I just want something sort of in between what they have and what I have now, and well—." Then he finished lamely, "I guess I like a little progress and permanency at the same time."

"I guess I do too," Wendy said. "But it took people like the Beatenbows and Finch to make this country a good place to live." Then Wendy added in a dreamy voice as she lay back on the sand and hooked her hands under her head, "There is something strong about this country, Kim. Strong and good. I can feel it."

"I've felt that, too," Kim said seriously.

"And I love the river. It's the wildest and the friendliest place I've ever known," Wendy said. She was so absorbed in her thoughts that she was not even aware that Kim had spoken. "I'd like to have a house by the spring. A house with walls a yard thick and foundations as deep as an oil well—and raise my children in one place and watch them grow and become a part of this country."

"Is that your dream, Wendy?"

"What, Kim?" Wendy said absently as she looked at him.

"You said once that you couldn't live without dreams. Is that your dream?"

"Part of it," Wendy admitted candidly.

"What is the rest of it?"

Wendy looked at Kim thoughtfully for a moment, and then the dreaminess in her eyes was replaced with a familiar twinkle. "Isn't that enough?" she asked impishly.

"You mean there isn't a man in your dreams?" he asked lightly.

"Oh, sure," Wendy admitted.

"What kind of man?"

"A very special kind of man. One that loves kids, and comes home every night. One that will love me more than a million oil wells."

"Wendy," Kim asked tentatively, "why did you come back here? I mean, well, there isn't much here for you."

"I don't know why I came back," Wendy evaded his eyes. "Maria said you came to see her once while I was gone."

"Yes. I did."

"What did you talk about?"

"I don't remember," Kim evaded. "I just wanted her to tell me where you were."

"Maria is a wonderful person when you get to know her," Wendy was looking closely at Kim.

"I'm sure she must be," Kim agreed. "Wendy—you're going to stay now, aren't you? You're not going away again without telling me?"

She was silent a moment. "I'm not sure, Kim. I may begin teaching at the school here in Borger. The building will be completed next month, and they have asked me if I would teach."

"Good!" Kim said enthusiastically.

"You think I will make a good teacher?"

"Well," Kim grinned. "You don't look like my teachers did. But I think you might do all right."

"I guess I don't look very school-teacherish at the moment," Wendy admitted as she stood up and brushed sand from her skirt. "But come on, I want to show you my cabin."

Kim agreed, and they walked up the trail, past the fork which led to the spring. Just over the hill there was a small adobe bunk house. Opening the door, Kim could see that the interior was neat and clean. The floor was of dirt, and there was a small pot-bellied stove and a kerosene lamp. There was one small window which was covered with celluloid and allowed only a dim bit of the fading light to come into the room. There was a bed, hand hewn, and covered with a tarpaulin.

Kim set about building a fire of the wood stacked behind the stove, while Wendy took from a shelf a coffee pot and a small sack of coffee. She went to the spring for water; by the time she returned the fire was roaring. Kim had lighted the kerosene lamp which cast a yellow light over the cabin. Darkness was rapidly settling, and the flare of the lamp looked cozy and warm.

"Brr—" Wendy said as she reentered the cabin. "It's getting cold. The haze is settling on the river, and that spring water is like ice."

"Come, warm by my fire," Kim invited as he set the coffee pot on the stove.

The coffee pot was soon boiling. They warmed themselves for a few minutes, and then looked about for something to sit on. There was only one chair, and a leg was broken on it. Wendy turned the tarpaulin back on the bed. Theere was a clean patched quilt on it. They sat. The springs were rusty and groaned, but held.

They looked at the fire for a few minutes, then Kim slipped his arm around Wendy. She leaned against him and turned her face to him. Kim kissed her then. It started gently but it didn't end that way. Kim felt a sharp explosion in the vicinity of his breast bone. Finally, he let her go, and Wendy leaned back in Kim's arms.

"I've wanted to do that since I first saw you," Kim said shakily.

"I guess Maria is smarter than I thought!" Wendy's breath was coming irregularly.

"What has *Maria* to do with it?" Kim asked.

"Nothing," Wendy smiled, as she thought of the time she had told Maria that she had never wanted a man physically. "Just something she told me once."

Kim started to turn Wendy's head to him again, but she rose and moved away. She stood looking at him a moment, her eyes were large and blue.

Suddenly Kim chuckled.

"What?" Wendy asked.

"I was thinking about Deafy," Kim said.

"And what has *he* got to do with it?" Wendy asked curiously.

"I was just thinking," Kim said, "He probably would crack my head with a stillson wrench if he knew that I took advantage of you tonight."

"He would probably crack your head because you *didn't.*" Wendy grinned. "Let's have some coffee."

Wendy sat, cross-legged on the bed, and sipped hers. Kim sat on the broken chair. Both were busy with their own thoughts. A coyote bark floating down the river was the only sound.

"Kim?" Wendy finally broke the silence.

"What, Wendy?"

"Will you go to Sal's place after you take me home tonight?"

Kim considered the question a moment. It seemed a perfectly logical question for her to ask. "No," he said quietly, "Not tonight."

"I'm glad, Kim." Then she added wistfully, "I wish it were possible—" Wendy flushed. "I mean—I wish you didn't even *want* to go."

"I don't."

"That isn't what I meant, Kim," Wendy said. "I meant that I wish you could—"

"I know what you mean, Wendy," Kim said.

"I guess I just don't belong to the lost generation," Wendy said seriously. "Right now, I wish I did."

"I'm glad you don't," Kim said firmly.

They walked toward the lights of Borger hand in hand in silence. Behind them the river haze settled on the Canadian. A hungry coyote howled, and Granny Beatenbow snored in her sleep. The worlds of the cowman and the oil man were still separate.

CHAPTER VIII

The week following Kim and Wendy's picnic on the river, the Santa Fe railroad line from Borger to Panhandle was completed. No longer was it necessary for the oil companies to transport their materials and supplies over the twenty-eight miles of prairie by truck and wagon. This made more vehicles available for the jobs in the fields, and Borger took another step toward its vague destination.

The school building was almost completed, and the families with children were heartened by the news. But Borger still had its problems. Organized crime tightened its grip. Murders were common. Drillers protected their equipment with shotguns and rifles. The honest and respectable people began discussing means of coping with the crime.

The county seat, being twelve miles away, also posed problems. People had to travel the rough roads and cross the treacherous Canadian river to record legal transactions. The only people who were pleased with the situation were those who made their money towing cars across the river. Business men began to grumble, and finally, Blake Terrell was successful in his movement to get an election called that would move the courthouse to Borger.

Blake thoroughly enjoyed playing the role of politician. He had become well known in the town and he even made several speeches that were well received. Blake felt that he was really becoming a big man.

There were, however, some things that did not please him. For one thing, Wendy was seeing entirely too much of Kim Wingate. Not that his daughter would ever become seriously interested in a namby-pamby like him, but—

And Claude Butler! The damned shyster had refused to aid Blake in his political endeavors. Blake should have fired him! He would have, too, except that the man was invaluable to him. But why had he refused to help Blake get the courthouse moved to Borger. Blake didn't like it! And he still had not got the Beatenbow lease!

Kim and Wendy visited the Beatenbows a few days prior to the election. They were enjoying Granny's caustic conversation, as usual.

"They'll have the school in Borger completed next month, Granny," Kim said during a conversational lull. "They have asked Wendy to teach."

Granny perked up. "And is she?"

"I think I may, Granny," Wendy answered. "They don't have any qualified teachers."

"And you're qualified, are you, young lady?" Granny's remark was scathing.

"Well, whe does have a college degree," Kim said defensively.

"Hmmm." Granny looked at Wendy keenly. "She never told me about that."

Kim was glad that he had been able to surprise the old lady. "She finished school back east," he continued.

"Well," harrumped Granny. "That don't mean she ain't got a lot of sense, anyway."

Wendy's laugh pealed through the huge old ranch house.

"But," continued Granny. "Wendy ain't got no business teaching school. She ought to be home having kids of her own."

Granny enjoyed hearing the news from the oil town. It was Wendy who casually mentioned the election to move the court house.

"What was that, young spriggins?" Granny cupped her hand behind her ear.

Wendy repeated the news. The old lady was perturbed.

"Going to move it from Plemons to Borger, be they?" she cackled.

"That is what they plan," Kim admitted. He was sorry the subject had come up.

"It'd make sense to move it to Stinnett," Granny said almost thoughtfully. "But they ain't got no business moving it to Borger."

Kim and Wendy were silent. Granny tapped her cane impatiently on the floor and rocked quietly back and forth in her chair.

"Wendy," Granny said in her cracked voice. "I don't mean nothin' about you and Kim—but them oil field people has done started meddlin'. Young spriggins," she looked sharply at Kim, "You go tell Finch to come here. He's out at the corrals with Mandy."

Kim dutifully left and found Finch shoeing a horse while Mandy held the animal's head.

"Granny wants to see you, Finch," Kim said.

Neither Mandy nor Finch showed the least bit of surprise. Finch let the horse's foot to the ground and silently followed Kim.

"Finch," Granny said as they entered. "Them oil field folks is trying to move our courthouse over to the oil town. You get on your horse and get word to every rancher in Hutchinson County that I want them to meet here next Monday night."

Finch rubbed his bald head thoughtfully, then nodded slightly and left the room without a word.

"Yessiree!" Granny said tapping her cane harder on the floor. "I reckon the time has come to show them oil field folks who it is that bores with the big auger in this county."

Both Kim and Wendy grinned at the old lady's descriptive language.

"Who is it that's doin' the agitatin' to move the courthouse?" Granny asked sharply.

Kim hesitated, and it was Wendy who answered. "Most of the business men in Borger are. But Father is the one who got the election called."

"Good," the old lady said with satisfaction. "I been hankerin' to take that Daddy of yours down a peg ever since I first saw him."

"A lot of people have," Wendy admitted with a smile. "But don't worry about it, Granny."

"I ain't worryin'," Granny assured them.

A few minutes later, Kim and Wendy were preparing to leave.

"Finch tells me that somebody is camping in our line shack acrost the river in the cottonwoods."

Kim and Wendy looked at each other guiltily. A twinkle appeared deep in Granny's small eyes.

"Yessir!" she continued. "They done cleaned the place up and stocked some food in there an everything."

"Granny—" Wendy began tentatively.

"You young spriggins might stop by it on the way back to town and see about it," Granny cut in sharply. "But you don't tarry long. Humphrey Beatenbow kept me there the first night we was married. Just nine months later my oldest boy, Tom, was born."

Kim and Wendy looked sheepishly at each other, and Granny cackled gleefully as they took their leave.

Blake made the most brilliant speech of the election campaign the night that the ranchers of Hutchinson County gathered at the Beatenbow ranch at the command of Granny Beatenbow. The ranchers listened attentively as Granny spoke in harsh tones. Many of them smiled covertly as she upbraided Blake Terrell and other oil men who sought to move the courthouse from Plemons to Borger. It should be moved, Granny said—to Stinnett. Then it would serve the cowmen better. The oil men were newcomers to the Texas plains, and they had no business trying to run things. It was up to the old timers to see that they didn't.

And, though the cowmen smiled as Granny held forth in caustic tones, they listened attentively. They respected her great wisdom and her knowledge of the plains and its people. She had lived a long time, and she loved her country the way it was.

Granny gave them their instructions. Several of the more substantial men were to see that the voters were given a choice of moving the courthouse to Stinnett—or Borger. And all of them were to see that the election was held according to the laws of Texas.

It was a thoughtful group of people that left the Beatenbow ranch that night. Less than a week later, it was officially announced that both Stinnett and Borger would appear on the election ballot as possible sites of the courthouse.

Blake Terrell laughed when he got the news. He knew that the ranchers were simply expressing their individuality. Stinnett was twelve miles north of Borger and across the river. There would be absolutely no point in moving the courthouse to that small town. Borger was the center of Hutchinson County now. It would continue to be. Blake intended to see that.

The oil men were solidly behind him. There weren't a hundred ranches in the county. And there were nearly seventy-five thousand people in the oil town now. The ranchers were fools to think they could pull such a trick. They didn't have a chance!

The day of the election broke warm and clear. Voting places were set up in Borger, Stinnett, and Plemons.

Blake Terrell rose early, as was his custom, and drove into town. Joe Shay accompanied him. The town was aswarm with people, as usual, but there was a holiday air about. Many of the men had not gone out on the job because of the election. The oil field men were prone to grasp any opportunity or excuse to stay in town.

The polls were to open at seven o'clock. By that time Blake had collected an imposing entourage of men. They were an arrogant, profane, and irresponsible group. Many of them were drinking. They marched triumphantly to the voting place.

Fifty yards away, a tall man wearing a wide, white hat stopped them. He wore a sheriff's badge on his chest.

"I'll check your credentials here," the man drawled.

"You'll what?" Blake asked belligerently.

"I'll check your credentials," the man said affably. "You have to be a property holder and also have a poll tax receipt to vote."

"Like hell you will!" Blake Terrell growled venomously. "What do you cow people think you are trying to pull anyway!"

"We ain't trying to pull anything," the sheriff said quietly. "We just aim to see that this election is held legal. That's all."

"The hell, you are!" Blake almost shouted. "You're trying to stack this election and you know it! Your job is sheriff—why don't you tend to it?"

The tall man's face hardened. "I aim to. I aim to. I'm one of the election judges of this here election, and I aim to see that nobody but qualified voters go to the polls. You show your credentials, Terrell, or you don't pass here. And your friends don't either."

Joe Shay had been taking in the exchange between his boss and the tall man in the big white hat. The group of men following Blake were quiet, obviously waiting for him to make a move.

"Say the word, Mr. Terrell, and we go in," Joe Shay said loudly.

The sheriff did not look at Joe. His narrowed eyes never left the face of Blake Terrell. Blake was thinking. Finally, he seemed to reach a conclusion.

"You say we have to own property and have a poll tax receipt to be qualified voters?" he asked.

"That is correct."

"If we voted, and if we were not qualified, then the election would be declared void—wouldn't it?"

"If you are not qualified, you are not going to vote," the sheriff said flatly. He had not raised his voice, but Blake Terrell got the meaning without difficulty.

"Who says we're not?" Joe Shay wanted to know.

"I say so." There was a steely glint in the eyes of the sheriff.

"You think you can keep us from it?" Joe's voice was nasty.

"I aim to try."

"Shut up, Joe," Blake said absently. He was still thinking. This was not at all as he had planned. "How do we know it isn't legal for us to vote?"

"You can take my word for it."

"What if we don't choose to do that?" Blake asked significantly.

"You don't have any choice," the man said flatly. "We figured you oil folks might argue the point, and so we deputized some of the boys to see that you didn't win the argument." The sheriff nodded his head over his shoulder.

Blake looked. So did Joe Shay and the group following Blake. To their utter surprise and chagrin they saw perhaps a dozen men suddenly materialize between them and the voting booth. The men were dressed in big hats and high heeled boots. They were carrying short saddle guns in their arms. They seemed to be paying no attention whatever to the discussion between the sheriff and Blake Terrell. They simply walked aimlessly in their awkward, cowboy fashion. Even Joe Shay's eyes widened.

"Those men are deputies," the sheriff said quietly. "They got their orders. Nobody enters the voting booth that I don't say is qualified."

Blake looked at the men for a moment thoughtfully. "I see what you mean," he said.

"We was hoping you would."

Blake and his entourage retreated from the polls.

Borger awaited the results of the election with apprehension. Not one of the boomers had thought to pay a poll tax even if he did own property. Not one in a thousand had anticipated remaining in the county as long as the six months required to establish residence.

The election results were brought from Plemons and Stinnett by automobile, and the news was announced by the election judge. A town of nearly seventy-five thousand people waited breathlessly as the results were read.

It was perhaps the only unanimous election ever held in a Texas county. The qualified voters had voted, to a man, to move the courthouse—to Stinnett.

And in that county of seventy-five thousand people, there were only seventy-two qualified voters!

Wendy definitely accepted a position as teacher in the new Borger school when a group of mothers called on her at the Terrell house. They promised that one of their husbands would accompany her to and from school each day to prevent any possible molestation.

Blake was furious when Wendy told him that night. "I'll not have a daughter of mine teaching a bunch of oil field brats," he said harshly.

"I was an oil field brat," Wendy reminded her father, much to Maria's delight. "Perhaps I still am."

"You were different," Blake said belligerently. "I gave you everything you needed."

"That is just what the parents of these children are trying to do," Wendy countered.

"I don't care if they are," Blake said doggedly. "I didn't ask anybody to help me give you things. I even built a house on a *White* truck so you could have a home. You remember that, don't you, Wendy?" Blake's voice had taken on a wheedling tone.

"I remember," Wendy said calmly. "And I remember learning to drive that big truck when I was ten years old. And I remember moving from camp to camp—and from school to school." Then Wendy's voice took on fire. "I also remember praying that the wheels of that big truck would come off in some cool spot beside a spring of water so that we could just stop forever, and not have to move again."

It took a moment for the impact of what Wendy had said to dawn on Blake. He hesitated, then stopped. Finally he said in a gruff voice, "All right, daughter. Sometimes you are as bull headed as I am. But if you're going to teach at the school, then I'm going to send Joe along with you every day to see that you get there and back safe."

"One of the children's parents will escort me to and from school after the first day," Wendy informed him.

"I'll take care of my own daughter," Blake said furiously. "I don't ask nobody to help me do that." He glared at her a moment, then added with suspicion in his voice, "Who's going to take you the first day?"

"Kim."

"Ah, hah!" Blake said with satisfaction. "I thought so. Wendy, I'm putting my foot down as far as that young man is concerned. He's nothing but a smart-alec young wildcatter. I don't like his friends—and I don't like him."

"You just don't like Wendy to like him, do you Blake?" It was the first time Maria had entered the conversation.

"It doesn't make any difference what I mean," Blake spat. "And you keep out of this, Maria. Kim Wingate has no more guts than a fly. He's not man enough for Wendy and never will be. I forbid him to come to this house again."

Wendy whirled and left the room without a backward glance.

"You're a cruel man, Blake!" Maria said when Wendy was gone.

"Cruel, hell!" Blake snarled. "That daughter of mine is just getting too big for her britches."

"Wendy is a woman," Maria said.

"Woman, hell! She's still just a kid."

"And Kim Wingate is a man," Maria continued.

"A man!" Blake whirled on his wife. "That bastard is nothing but a flunky for Deafy Jones. He'll never be a man."

"That may have been true when he first came to the fields, Blake," Maria said. "But he's a man now. You just haven't looked at him."

"Ha!" Blake snorted. "He would be afraid to even *look* at me. I've only put up with him as long as I have because you and Wendy put up such a fuss about him."

"You are wrong, Blake," Maria said. "He is not afraid of you. And he isn't any longer afraid of Joe Shay. I can tell by the way he looks at the two of you."

Blake looked sharply at Maria. There was surprise on his face.

"And if you won't let Kim Wingate come here," Maria said calmly, "then Wendy will go to him."

"Now that's a damn fool statement!" Blake shouted.

"Perhaps," Maria shrugged. "But she will. I know."

"Just *how* do you know?"

"A woman knows."

"A woman knows!" Blake said sarcastically. "You women think you know everything." He stalked from the room.

Kim pulled into the circular driveway an hour early the morning school opened. Wendy, alert and pretty, in a new dress and low-heeled shoes, greeted him at the door. Coffee was waiting, and they sat at a small table in the kitchen.

"Where are Maria and Blake?" Kim asked.

"Father left last night for Austin," Wendy said, "and Maria has the gas-eye."

"Gas-eye?"

"Yes. Almost everyone in the fields gets it sooner or later. I've had it twice. The fumes from the gas loosed by the wells infect the eyes, and they swell horribly and are very red and unsightly."

"I'm sorry," Kim said sympathetically. "Is there anything we can do to help?"

"Yes," Wendy said instantly. "Don't see her. She does look terrible, and you know how proud Maria is of her beauty."

"I know," agreed Kim. "What is Blake doing in Austin?"

"I don't know," Wendy answered. "He *said* that he was going down there to see about some insurance. You know that one of his wells over near Sanford came in last week, and it was poison gas. Several men were killed."

"We heard about that," Kim admitted. "Deafy said that there was an instance of that in Ranger back in 1917."

"How is Deafy?" Wendy asked eagerly. "Tell him to come to see me while Father is in Austin."

"How long will Blake be gone?" He was finding it more and more difficult to refer to him as Wendy's father.

"About a week." Wendy paused, and a tiny frown wrinkled her brow. "I've heard rumors that the Texas Rangers were going to be sent to Borger to help combat crime. I have a sort of intuition that Father's trip to Austin has something to do with that."

"Well," Kim said with conviction. "Someone certainly needs to help. Another man was murdered here last night and a business dynamited. Did Joe go with Blake?"

"Father gave Joe the week off. I wish he would fire Joe. He hangs around the house too much. And sometimes he and Maria—"

"They what?" Kim asked quickly.

"Never mind, Kim. We must hurry. I'll be late to school."

They took Wendy's Marmon and drove toward the school.

Wendy remarked about the huge crowd in town as she and Kim drove down the long main street.

"They are always here, night and day," Kim said. "But a lot of them came in last night to hear the fight on the radio."

"I suppose that's as good an excuse as any," Wendy offered. "Maria and I listened too."

Kim nodded. "Deafy and I heard the fight on our radio out at the rig. The darned battery went dead right after Dempsey knocked Tunney out."

"Dempsey didn't win," Wendy said, surprised.

"Yes he did," Kim said tolerantly. "We heard it."

Wendy laughed. "That wasn't the end of the fight. Tunney took the longest count in boxing history, but because of some sort of new rule—something about neutral corners—he wasn't disqualified. Then he won the fight."

"Well, I'll be darned!" Kim said in awe. "Old Deafy will have a fit when I tell him."

There was a mob of people at the school building when they arrived. Parents held their children's hands. The fathers looked grim and the mothers proud and determined. Since each child had to furnish his own desk, there were many orange crates and boxes in evidence. Each child carried his own lunch and a fruit jar filled with water.

But parents and children were not the only ones present. Kim saw dozens of men from the rigs. Most of them were drinking and evidently they considered the new school some sort of joke. They shouted and laughed though profanity was at a minimum. Perhaps the sight of mothers and their children restrained them a bit. Wendy and Kim pushed through the mob and entered the building. There were to be two teachers. Wendy was to have one end of the oblong structure and another teacher the other. The room was big and bare. Wendy looked about. No one was inside. Evidently they were waiting until the teacher took charge.

"What should I do?" Wendy asked Kim in a shaky voice.

"Darned if I know," Kim answered. "Let's find the other teacher."

The other teacher was a very red headed and determined looking older woman. She was sitting at a barren desk in her room at the other end of the building. She looked up questioningly when Wendy and Kim entered.

"I'm the other teacher," Wendy said uncertainly.

"You look more like a student than a teacher," the older woman said preemptorily. "Who is the young man?"

"He is a friend of mine, Mr. Wingate," Wendy answered. "He brought me to school."

"He'd better be here to take you home, too," the woman said. "These rooms were full of people two hours ago. I shooed them out and told them we would ring the bell when we were ready. My name is Miss McReedy."

They all shook hands, and Kim was very much relieved. Miss McReedy was short, squat, competent and alert. She gave the very definite impression that she would tolerate no nonsense.

"What should we do first?" Wendy asked.

"First, we will ring the bell." Miss McReedy reached under the desk and brought forth a brass bell with a black wooden handle. "Then we will register our students," Miss McReedy continued crisply. "That will take us most of the morning, and then we will have to assign them certain hours to come to school. We can't possibly get all of them in the building at one time. We will both work in this room today."

Miss McReedy thrust the bell at Wendy abruptly. Wendy unconsciously shrank from it.

"Ring it, young lady," Miss McReedy commanded. "And maybe you'd better tell me your name while you're doing it."

"I'm sorry, Miss McReedy," Wendy said apologetically. "I guess I'm a little excited. I've never taught school before. My name is Wendy Terrell."

"No one ever taught school before in a place like this," Miss McReedy said. "Ring the bell."

Wendy moved the bell tentatively, and as the clapper jangled she shook it violently. It was the first time Kim had ever seen her disconcerted.

Loud yells greeted the ringing bell, and people rushed through the doors. In a matter of minutes, Miss McReedy and Wendy had established an order of sorts. They took the names of the students down on a tablet and their ages and grades. Kim stood to one side and was surprised when he saw several of the younger dance hall girls sign up for school.

Things were going in an orderly fashion when Kim saw Joe Shay in the registration line. Behind him were perhaps half a dozen men of various ages and descriptions. Kim was startled for a moment and then decided that Joe probably had some message for Wendy from her father and was simply coming through the line to get to her. But Joe didn't go to Wendy's desk. He stopped in front of Miss McReedy.

"Do you have children of school age that you would like to register?" Miss McReedy inquired.

"Why—no ma'am," Joe replied innocently. "That is, not that I know of. I just thought that I might take up schooling myself since the teachers are so pretty." Joe looked over his shoulder and laughed for the benefit of those in line behind him. The men howled their approval.

Kim heard Wendy's sharp intake of breath. Joe was obviously drunk.

"Your remarks are not humorous, in the least, young man," Miss McReedy said icily. "Will you kindly step aside so that we may go on with our registration."

"Why—Miss schoolmarm!" Joe said. "I got as much right as most anybody to go to school. A feller as ignorant as I am needs schooling worse than anybody." Again Joe's cronies howled their approval.

Some of the men who had brought their children to school began to edge toward the desk. Kim was holding his breath. He was standing almost directly behind Miss McReedy.

"School would be a fine thing for you, young man. And I agree that you need it," Miss McReedy said calmly. "But your parents should have thought about that many years ago."

Kim could almost feel the anger rise in Joe when Miss McReedy made the remark. Joe's cronies howled their glee. But this time they were laughing at Joe.

"Why, you old bitch!" snarled Joe. "I got as much right to sign up as them dance hall sluts."

Kim stepped in front of Joe as he reached for the pencil in Miss McReedy's hand. It was a second before Joe recognized him. "Get out of my way, jelly-bean," Joe said venomously.

"Go away, Joe." Kim knew his voice shook and was ashamed that it did.

"Go away, he says!" jeered Joe and looked over his shoulder at the ruffians behind him. "Look here at the teacher's pet, boys!"

Joe's friends dutifully laughed again.

"Now boys!" Joe yelled. "You just watch Joe give the teacher's pet a spanking on his first day in school."

"Don't do it, Joe!" Kim pleaded, as Joe waved his arms to clear some room.

But Joe wasn't listening. Kim saw that it was no use, and, as Joe made elaborate movements for the benefit of his audience, Kim swung with all his might.

Kim felt his blow land and knew vaguely that he had cut his hand on Joe's teeth. Joe rushed, and after that everything was vague.

Dimly, he heard Miss McReedy's shouting commands for them to stop and the yelling of Joe's friends. Children were crying and women screaming. Kim fell to the rough wooden floor. Joe was on top of him, and he could smell the vile whiskey breath which was coming in hard, deep gasps. He placed his hands against Joe's chest to push him away when suddenly Joe wasn't on top of him anymore.

As Kim's vision cleared, he saw that several men had pulled Joe off of him. Joe was struggling and swearing violently.

"Go ahead and turn him loose," Kim said as he got to his feet.

"You will do no such thing," Miss McReedy's voice cut through the room. "Gentlemen!" she addressed the men holding Joe Shay. "If you will be kind enough to take that ruffian outside and clear the room, we will continue our registration."

"You son-of-a-bitch!" Joe spat at Kim. "That's the second time I been cheated out of your hide. I'll get it next time."

Kim didn't answer, and the men hustled Joe out of the room. His vile cursing could be heard even when they were out the door.

"And now," Miss McReedy continued briskly, "if all the parents will please step outside I shall ask some of the *gentlemen* present to stand guard at the door and admit only parents and their children. We will register one family at a time. As they leave, another will be admitted."

Those remaining in the room quickly voiced their approval and started leaving. Kim followed. He was almost to the door when he felt someone pull at his sleeve. It was Miss McReedy.

"You stay, young man," she commanded.

Kim turned. It was the first time he had looked at Wendy since the fight started. Her eyes were large and her face white. Her freckles shone like pennies on her face.

When everyone had left the room, Kim stood in front of Miss McReedy's desk. She had said nothing more to him, and there was a dead silence. Kim did not meet her eyes. She tapped a pencil on her desk. Wendy glanced at Miss McReedy with apprehension and at Kim with sympathy.

"Young man," Miss McReedy began.

"Yes ma'am?" Kim gulped.

"You realize that you disrupted the first day of school in Borger, Texas."

Kim nodded his head and fidgeted.

"Are you ashamed of yourself?" Miss McReedy asked sternly.

Kim considered momentarily. "No ma'am," he said and braced himself for a tongue lashing.

"Good!" Miss McReedy said approvingly.

Kim looked at her in surprise. Her blue eyes were very stern. "Men like you will make it possible for Miss Terrell and me to conduct a respectable school in Borger."

"Yes ma'am," Kim looked at Wendy with relief. Color was returning to her face.

"And now, young man," Miss McReedy continued, "since you are going to escort Miss Terrell home this afternoon, suppose you wash your face and make yourself useful the rest of the day."

Wendy hurriedly produced the thermos that was filled with water. She helped Kim bathe blood from his battered face. Miss McReedy supervised the operation.

A few minutes later Kim was fairly presentable except for a rapidly swelling and discoloring eye and a blood spattered shirt.

"And now, young man," Miss McReedy said, "if you will be kind enough to go to the door and ask the first family to come in, we will proceed with the registration."

Kim hastened to comply but Wendy's voice stopped him just before he reached the door.

"Kim!"

"What, Wendy?" Kim turned to her.

"You could have whipped him," she said staunchly.

"He quite probably could have, Miss Terrell," Miss McReedy's frosty voice cut in. "Particularly in view of the fact that you were ready to help with that little pearl handled pistol of yours when Mr. Wingate fell to the floor."

"Oh!" Wendy said in consternation, "I—I—"

"Never mind, Miss Terrell," the old teacher's voice was sharp, "A good teacher sees many things."

Then with a swift, bird-like movement of her wrinkled hand, Miss McReedy reached into a desk drawer and pulled out an enormous army pistol and laid it in front of her.

"If you had been alert, Miss Terrell, and not so absorbed in Mr. Wingate's welfare, you would have seen that I had the same thing in mind." She looked at Kim and smiled briefly.

Wendy opened her mouth in amazement. Kim stared a moment and then laughed aloud.

"Show our next students in please, Mr. Wingate," Miss McReedy said as she replaced the pistol.

Outside the school building Kim found that several of the fathers had armed themselves with shotguns and were patrolling the premises.

Registration went on throughout the day without further incident. Kim was a bit proud when several of the mothers voiced their approval of his actions when Joe Shay had attempted to interrupt registration.

It was almost dark when Kim returned to the rig that night. Deafy was in the shack and in a dark humor. He had already heard that Dempsey had lost his heavyweight title to Tunney.

"I ought to make kindling wood out of that damned radio." Deafy seemed to think it was the fault of the single dial set that his idol had fallen.

"It wasn't the radio's fault," Kim reminded him. "We forgot to take the battery in last week to get it charged."

"Just the same, I ain't going to listen to that damned contraption no more," Deafy said doggedly. And he didn't.

"A lot of kids registered at school today," Kim offered.

Deafy merely grunted. He was in no mood for conversation. Kim was disappointed. He wanted to tell Deafy about his fight with Joe Shay. There was a long silence. Deafy sipped his strong black coffee.

"I had a fight with Joe Shay." Kim could keep it no longer.

"Any damn fool could tell you been in a fight," Deafy said. "That eye is as black as the ace of spades."

"He didn't whip me," Kim said.

Deafy said nothing. Kim became irritated.

"I didn't whip him either. Some men pulled us apart."

Still Deafy said nothing.

"You're the aggravatingest man I ever saw, Deafy Jones!" Kim yelled furiously.

Still Deafy said nothing. Kim glared at the old man for a minute and then jumped up and grabbed his hat. "I'll check the rigs."

Deafy was calmly blowing his coffee when Kim reached the door. Kim stopped and turned.

"Well—darn it, Deafy," Kim said almost pleadingly. "I wasn't *afraid* of him."

A twinkle appeared deep in Deafy's good eye. "Didn't figure you was," Deafy said crossly. "Besides, I heard about it afore noon. Just wanted to see you get your dander up a little. Come have a cup of coffee. The rigs is alright. I just finished checking them."

Kim sighed and pitched his hat on his bunk. Deafy poured a cup of coffee.

"You're a regular old devil, Deafy," Kim said contentedly. He was glad to have a friend.

"You better get some sleep, Kim," Deafy said placidly. "You go on tower at midnight, and we got to pick up the payroll tomorrow."

That November Saturday morning broke raw and cold. A light, misty rain blew in from the north before Kim and Deafy finished checking their four rigs.

Just before noon, they went to the shack to change their oily clothing before going in to town to pick up the payroll. Kim wished Deafy would agree to take extra men with them, for robberies were occurring with alarming frequency. But Deafy steadfastly refused to do so.

While they were dressing, Kim brought up a subject that had become rather a sore one between him and Deafy. The Beatenbows had invited them to eat Thanksgiving dinner at their ranch. Kim and Wendy had been looking forward to it for weeks. Granny Beatenbow had insisted that they bring along their "folks."

Blake had agreed to go to the Thanksgiving dinner because he thought he might be able to lease the Beatenbow land. Maria had been delighted. But Deafy would hear nothing of it.

Kim badgered the old man unmercifully. Wendy cajoled to no avail. Usually Deafy would do anything Wendy asked.

"I ain't going to eat no Thanksgiving dinner with nobody," Deafy growled as he shook wrinkles out of a khaki shirt. "If I went, Blake would just say something that would make me mad and embarrass Wendy."

"No, he wouldn't," Kim said doggedly. "Blake can be all right when he wants to."

"All the same I ain't going!" Deafy replied emphatically. Kim dropped the subject but was determined to bring it up again before Thanksgiving.

They drove the *White* since they planned to bring some cable and casing on their return. They arrived in town just before noon. Patches of snow clung tenaciously in the lee of sage and mesquite. Alternate thawing and freezing had made the ground soft, and the streets of Borger were a veritable mire of mud and slush.

They sat in the truck and looked about for a few minutes. New buildings were still going up. In the cold north wind of that Saturday morning, Borger, like a seasoned old range bull, simply humped its back against the wind and continued business. It was payday, and although the drilling and hauling and gambling were incessant activities, there was always an extra flourish on Saturday nights.

The truck was loaded by two o'clock, and they pulled out into the street again. The big truck sank almost to its axles, but managed to keep moving. Finally they found a place to pull over a bit and dismounted. They were only a short distance from the shack that served as payroll headquarters for all the companies. They decided to eat lunch before picking up the money.

They had to wait a shorter time than usual to be served. Kim had steak that was tough, and fried potatoes and coffee. He was glad he wouldn't have to wash dishes. It was a luxurious feeling. Deafy ate two bowls of chili.

They finished their meal and emerged from the small cafe with a sense of well-being. They stopped for a moment on the board sidewalk and looked up and down the street. Their truck was unmolested, but another truck had stalled in the middle of the street. The drivers of mules pulling wagons loaded with equipment and trucks hauling heavy machinery cursed as they pulled through the mire around the stalled truck.

They made their way toward the payroll shack. There was a formidable ring of heavily armed men around the small building. The oil men were taking no chances. There were enough sawed off shotguns around the payroll building to stop an army of thugs. Deafy and Kim were challenged when they came within twenty feet.

"Whose men are you?" queried a big man with his coat collar turned up to protect his face from the cold wind. But the hands gripping the double-barreled gun were bare, and his fingers were on both triggers.

"We ain't nobody's men," Deafy said touchily. "We are Jones and Wingate. Running Oschner's rigs."

The man smiled briefly and relaxed his grip on the gun. He gestured with his head for them to approach.

Inside the shack, the air was full of tension. There were huge stacks of bills on a rough wooden table. Behind each stack of bills sat a man, and on the wall above each was a sign indicating the company for which he was paying. They approached the man seated under the *Oschner* sign. He was a new teller; Kim had not seen him before.

"Jones and Wingate," Deafy said shortly by way of explanation.

The man behind the stack of bills was small, and he wore a green celluloid eye shade. On his arms, covering his white shirt from wrist to elbow, were black dust-guards.

"Where is your identification?"

"What was that?" Deafy's bad ear had been toward the man.

"I asked for your identification," the small man said pleasantly.

Deafy considered the request briefly, and then thoughtfully shook his head.

"Ain't got none."

"I'm sorry, but I can't pay you without proper identification."

Deafy nodded again and spat tobacco juice. Kim started to speak, but Deafy silenced him with a brief shake of his head.

"Just as well," Deafy said pleasantly. "Don't care much about carrying that much money around anyway, with all them Oklahoma toughs I keep hearing about."

The teller became ill at ease. Obviously he had expected an argument and then the production of some sort of tangible identification. He couldn't afford to take a chance on giving the money to the wrong man. Oschner had been very specific about that. He wished Oschner were there—as he should have been. He had little doubt that the men were who they said they were. Their names were on the payroll as boss drillers. They didn't fit the description that Oschner had given him, however. They were supposed to be hardened oil men—especially Jones. A cantankerous, profane old man who was as dangerous as a rattlesnake and entertained opposition from no man—so Oschner had said. Here was a pleasant spoken old man and a tall, tired looking young man. Neither one appeared the least bit dangerous. Surely they couldn't be the boss drillers Oschner had spoken of so highly. Or could they? They did have a certain air of assurance and unconcern.

Deafy turned up his coat collar, and Kim pulled on his gloves. The teller stirred uneasily. He was hoping desperately that they would offer identification. Surely they could find someone who *knew* them, or they could produce some papers, or—something. Obviously, they had no such intention. In fact, they were leaving. Again the teller stirred uncomfortably.

"What—what—" he said uncertainly. "What shall I tell Mr. Oschner?"

Deafy spat again and considered the question.

"Tell him," Deafy said, "to have that payroll out to my rigs before sundown, or I'll shut 'em down." He turned to leave.

"You can't do that!" the teller protested.

Deafy turned again. This time his good eye gleamed for a second.

"Now mister!" Deafy said flatly. "You told me you couldn't pay me without I identified myself. That was all right. I ain't going to argue with you about that. You got to be careful and follow your orders." He paused and then continued, and his voice was harsh. "But now you go and tell me *I* can't do something—and they ain't no son-of-a-bitch going to tell Deafy Jones what he can and what he can't do. If Oschner can't get off his rump long enough to pay his men—then he can go to hell. Them rigs of his runs till sundown and not a minute longer unless he's out there with that money."

Deafy started stalking toward the door, his back stiff. The room had quieted, and everyone was staring.

"Wait a minute Mr. Jones." Kim heard the paymaster just before they opened the door. They turned, and the teller was smiling wanly.

"I guess you are Jones and Wingate, all right," he said a bit grimly. "Here is your money. Oschner said you were a crochety old bas—said you were emphatic."

Deafy's good eye twinkled for a second, and he walked back to the paytable. The small man started counting bills. He checked his book and counted out currency for each man in the crew. When he came to Kim and Deafy's account, he looked up in surprise and whistled softly.

"You must be a good driller, Mr. Jones," he said with a touch of wonder. "There isn't a driller in the fields drawing as much as you or Mr. Wingate. Is this just one week's wages?"

"One week's wages for us," Deafy admitted, "and one gusher for Oschner."

The man nodded his head unquestioningly.

"Guess you men are worth it."

"I guess we are," Deafy said.

The man finished counting the bills. Deafy signed the receipt for it and tucked the roll inside his shirt front under the big coat. They walked back to the truck.

Kim grabbed the crank and twisted mightily, but the motor only coughed and popped. Deafy choked it, but it just backfired again and refused to start. They discussed it briefly and had about decided that the magneto was not working properly. Deafy decided to check the gasoline line leading to the carburetor. He unscrewed it and found pieces of ice in it.

"Whole damned oil field full of gas, and we got some with water in it," he grumbled.

Kim was still panting slightly from the exertion of turning the big engine with the crank. Ordinarily, when a truck would not start, they jacked up a back wheel, put it in gear and turned the crank. But with the heavy load and the muddy street, it was impossible. Nor could they push or pull the vehicle. Cranking was the only way to start it.

"Well," Kim said philosophically and with the wisdom gained from nine months of wrestling with such problems. "There is only one thing to do. We will have to take the gas line loose from the tank and blow the ice out of it. Then if we prime the carburetor with good gasoline, maybe I can crank it."

"Maybe," agreed Deafy glumly. It always depressed him when machinery failed to function. "If we don't get this money back to the rigs by the time the day tower comes off, they will be looking for us with blood in their eyes."

Kim nodded grimly. He knew only too well how irate tool dressers and roustabouts could be if they weren't paid on time. He and Deafy had a good crew, but—

"You blow in this end of the gas line, Deafy, and I will crawl under and take the other end loose from the tank."

"I'll take it loose," Deafy said. "You been twisting that damned crank till you are puffing like a steam engine."

Before Kim could protest, Deafy had grabbed a small wrench and crawled under the truck. He sank deeply into the mud and grime but paid no attention to it. Kim heard Deafy grunt a couple of times and swear softly.

"All right. It's loose," he heard Deafy say a moment later.

Kim bent over the wide, square fender of the *White* and blew with all his might on the small copper tube. Nothing moved. He tried again with the same result. His ears started ringing. Deafy said nothing. He knew Kim was doing his best. There was nothing to say. Kim would know when the ice came out. Kim and Deafy had developed the sense of understanding each other and quite often would work together for long periods of time without speaking. Each knew what the other would do next.

Kim rested a moment and then sucked in a big lung full of air and closed his mouth around the tube. Just then he felt a hard object pressed against his back. He had never felt the muzzle of a gun before, but he knew instantly what it was. He let his breath out slowly, but did not otherwise move.

"Just hand over that payroll; don't turn around and don't ask questions," a voice said softly.

Hi-jacking in broad daylight on the main street of Borger was not a rare occurrence, but Kim had not expected any such thing. He thought for an instant of the .38 in his coat pocket but immediately discarded any nebulous idea of using it. The man had a gun in his back—and he would use it. Borger had not even learned the meaning of the word "bluff." Then Kim thought fleetingly of Deafy under the truck. Had Deafy heard? He wasn't making a sound.

"Hurry up!" the man said again, and jammed the gun harder against Kim's back."

"I haven't got a payroll," Kim said quite truthfully and a bit louder than necessary. It was still inside Deafy's shirt.

"You didn't eat it," the voice said menacingly. "I saw you and another guy come out of the payroll office not five minutes ago, and nobody goes in there for anything except money. Now you hand it over, or I'm going to slip a knife between your ribs. This gun would make a little noise, and even Borger might notice. But a knife is nice and quiet, and you will be just another drunk in the street. They may not even find out you are dead for several hours," he concluded venomously.

Kim considered the man's statement and knew it was true. Why
didn't Deafy say something. He knew Deafy could hear. But the
hi-jacker didn't even know Deafy was under the truck. What should
he do?

"Where is it, mister?" This time the voice was urgent, and Kim
knew he had to do something soon. "I'm going to give you until I
count three. One—"

"All right," Kim said resignedly. "Let me get off this fender and
turn around and I'll show you."

"Just tell me," the man said. "And keep your back to me."

"It's inside my coat," Kim said crossly. "I can't even get to it all
bent over like this."

"Straighten up, then," the man said cautiously. "But don't look
behind you, and don't bring anything out but money."

Kim straightened and felt the pressure of the gun in his back
lessen. The bandit had stepped back a pace to forestall any quick
movement by Kim that might knock the gun aside. Kim unbuckled
the flat metal buckle of his coat clumsily. His hands were cold and
numb. He was beginning to think the delay useless for Deafy still
hadn't made a sound. In a matter of seconds he was going to have to
betray Deafy's presence. The bandit was going to get money or
blood, and Kim was certain that it wasn't going to be his blood if he
could help it. His thoughts were racing as he fumbled at a coat
button.

"Hurry up!" the man threatened.

"All right. I'm—" But Kim never finished the sentence. From
under the truck came an explosion and from behind Kim came the
agonized scream of a man in great pain. Kim whirled.

The man who had been holding the gun at his back was now
grasping his side with his left hand, and his right arm was hanging
bloody and useless. Kim looked at the man's right hand. It was
completely mangled, and on the cold, muddy ground lay the forefinger and a bloody stump of the thumb. Kim stared aghast. The
finger lying disembodied, and the blood running together with the
muddy water and oil slick was a ghastly sight.

Deafy scrambled from under the truck shoving a fresh shell into
the chamber of his shotgun-pistol as he came. He pointed the big gun
at the bandit. Several men, seeing that the situation was under
control, crossed the muddy street to stare curiously at the trio. They
knew what had happened.

"Ought to have shot the son-of-a-bitch's head off," one man said
unsympathetically.

"All right, mister," Deafy said. "You sure ought to make good trot line bait. Let's go." Deafy waved the big gun.

"Please, mister," the bandit pleaded. "Take me to a doctor first. Some of those pellets went into my side, too."

Deafy considered the request a moment.

"All right. But I ought to just shoot you in the gut and leave you be."

The man said nothing, but groaned feebly.

"Kim, you go and get the sheriff. He will probably want to know what the shooting was about," Deafy said to Kim. "I'll take this bastard to Doc Bates' office."

Kim hurried toward the sheriff's office. Two men were there. One was the sheriff and the other a deputy. He told them what had happened. The sheriff sighed tiredly and followed Kim to the doctor's office. There the bandit had been stripped to the waist, and the doctor was looking at three holes in his side. Blood oozed from the perforations, and there was a bluish tinge around the periphery of each which showed darkly against the white skin. Kim wondered if Deafy and the sheriff would recognize each other. The sheriff was the same one that had hooked Deafy on the trotline. Evidently they did not.

"You are not injured badly here," the doctor said with professional unconcern. "We had better take care of that hand first."

The sheriff looked and showed no emotion.

"You shoot him?" he glanced at Deafy.

"Yep."

"How come?"

"Trying to hi-jack my payroll," Deafy said briefly. The sheriff nodded.

"That right, mister?" The question was directed at the bandit. For a second the bandit seemed about to deny the accusation, but a glance at Deafy changed his mind. He nodded his head affirmatively and then moaned as the doctor doused the mutilated hand with alcohol.

"I'll lock him up as soon as the Doc gets him bandaged," the sheriff said. "You will have to come down to the office to sign the complaint." There was resignation in his voice. There had been more than five thousand arrests in Borger in the short time he had been there. Policing Borger was a grueling task, and he and his deputies were a weary group of men.

"Ain't got no complaint," Deafy said shortly.

The sheriff's head jerked sharply. He looked in surprise at Deafy.

"You what?" he asked incredulously.

"Ain't got no complaint," Deafy said again. "And I got to get this payroll out to the rig before sundown."

"But—I thought he tried to hi-jack your payroll."

"He tried to," Deafy admitted. "But he didn't. If you want to hook him on the trot line for disturbing the peace, that's your business. I ain't got no complaint."

A tiny smile lit the eyes of the sheriff. He was of a tough breed of men and he admired it in others.

"Suit yourself," he said finally. "I can't lock a man up for more than twenty-four hours without a signed complaint." Then he looked at Kim. "You want to sign a complaint, young man?"

"No," Kim said briefly. He was staring at the bloody stump of the hand as the doctor dressed it. There was a tight white ring around his mouth, and his eyes were bright. The sheriff looked at him sympathetically.

"All right," the sheriff said. "I'll help you boys get out of town."

"We'd appreciate that," Deafy said.

"And you, mister." The sheriff looked at the would-be bandit through narrowed eyes. "You come to my office when the Doc gets through with you. You can't hide with that hand. I'm going to put you on the trot line for twenty-four hours just on general principles. If you aren't there when I get back, I'll find you and let you rot on that trot line."

"I'll be there," the man said quaveringly. Kim knew he would be.

They started to leave the doctor's office when Deafy spoke to the man he had shot.

"Just one other thing, mister!" Everyone except the doctor looked questioningly at Deafy. "You owe me twelve cents."

The man gasped in open mouthed amazement. Kim was stunned, and the sheriff looked surprised.

"Them shotgun shells cost me twelve cents apiece!" Deafy continued. "Now you pay up."

The man continued to stare a moment longer. Then he hurriedly started searching his pockets with his good hand. He found a half dollar and held it gingerly toward Deafy. Deafy took it and then carefully counted thirty-eight cents in change and handed it back to the man. The man shrank and for a second seemed about to protest, but the look in Deafy's eyes stayed him. He took the money without a word and put it in his pocket.

Kim looked at the sheriff, half expecting the man to interfere. Instead he saw a gleam of admiration cross the sheriff's face as he watched Deafy count the change.

On the way to the truck, Deafy and the sheriff engaged in casual conversation. The sheriff offered to buy a cup of coffee, but Deafy declined saying that they needed to get the truck started and get back to the rigs. The hold-up attempt was not mentioned.

It took only a short time to clear the gas line. They primed the carburetor, and then, with much encouragement and advice from both the sheriff and Deafy, Kim spun the crank. They seemed to be enjoying their association.

The truck finally sputtered and broke into a roar. Deafy and the sheriff looked at each other and nodded in satisfaction. Kim hurried around the side of the truck as it started, and his foot slipped. He fell on his hands and one knee. Then, directly below his eyes he saw, still lying in the mud, the lifeless fingers and coagulated blood of the bandit. He stared a moment and then regained his feet. He walked over and leaned on the truck and retched violently.

Neither Deafy nor the sheriff indicated that they noticed Kim, but he knew that both of them did and was grateful that they did not offer sympathy. He knew that the man would not die, and also that by the standard of Deafy and the sheriff, he had got off lightly. Nevertheless, it was an awesome thing and he could feel in his heart nothing but compassion for the man Deafy had shot.

Kim spat again and saw the water vendor coming down the street with his cart and barrel of water pulled by the mule. He hailed the vendor and rinsed his mouth with the muddy water. Then he drank another cup and reached in his pocket for money to pay the man. He felt nothing and was dismayed and disgusted. It seemed that he was forever being caught without money in Borger. But he was too sick to be embarrassed.

"I'll get some money from my friend." He nodded toward the truck where Deafy and the lawman were still talking.

"Never mind, son," the vendor said softly. "It's a hell of a place where a man has to buy drinking water, anyway."

He clucked to his mule, and Kim nodded his thanks as the cart pulled away.

"You all set to go, Kim?" Deafy asked cheerfully as Kim walked back to the truck. Kim nodded.

"Let us know if we can help you boys," the sheriff said jovially.

"We'll do that," Deafy agreed. "I'll drive, Kim."

Kim nodded again and climbed into the high cab of the truck.

Deafy pressed on the accelerator, and the idling motor of the truck roared. Deafy let out on the clutch too fast as he always did. But the truck responded, and with spinning wheels they moved down the street. Deafy waved out the side of the truck without taking his eyes off the road. The sheriff half saluted and grinned.

In less than five minutes they had reached the end of the long main street and struck off across the prairie. The grass tufts furnished support, and the truck was able to gain some speed. Deafy concentrated on his driving. Trucks were relatively new to Deafy, and it required all his attention. Kim felt strangely fatigued. He didn't even flinch when Deafy hit the cow trails full speed. It would be a wonder if the truck stayed in one piece until they got back to the rigs.

Deafy dodged mesquite and yucca with long, energetic turns of the wooden wheel. Kim was beginning to think they might possibly get back without mishap when they started down a long sloping hill about a mile from the rig. There were white rocks half buried in the grass tufts and a dry arroyo at the bottom of the slope. Deafy shifted his position uncomfortably as they picked up speed going down. Kim kept waiting for Deafy to brake the truck before they reached the bottom. But Deafy didn't brake. He simply spat a stream of tobacco juice between the spokes of the steering wheel with his one good eye staring straight ahead. Kim sat up in alarm. Then Deafy lifted both feet high off the floor board and pulled back with all his might on the steering wheel.

"Whoa!" Deafy yelled frantically just one split second before they hit the arroyo.

There was a crash as the truck hit and bucked its way across. Kim's hands were still deep in his pockets, and he got one glimpse of Deafy hanging grimly onto the wheel as he catapulted over the dashboard and onto the hood of the truck.

Then there was a minute of dead silence as the truck motor coughed and died. Kim felt a moment of gratefulness that the truck didn't have a windshield. He was lying across the square hood of the truck, but his momentum carried him no farther. As his vision cleared, he was looking directly into Deafy's face which was contorted in pain.

Kim hurriedly extracted his hands from his pockets and jumped to the ground and ran around beside the truck. Deafy was still sitting, staring straight ahead, when Kim reached his side.

"You hurt, Deafy?" Kim asked anxiously. But Deafy didn't answer. He simply stared blankly ahead. Panic seized Kim, and he reached up and grabbed Deafy by the shoulders and shook him violently. Deafy finally looked at Kim, but his one good eye had in it a look of disbelief and horror. His face was contorted in pain and almost white.

"Speak to me, Deafy!" Kim pleaded. "Where are you hurt? Speak to me Deafy!"

"Huh?" Deafy said blankly.

"Where are you hurt?" Kim shouted desperately. "I'll get you to a doctor. "I'll—"

"I swallowed my goddamn tobacco, Kim!" Deafy said in awe and consternation.

Kim's jaw dropped, and he looked in open mouthed amazement. Deafy's look was tragic. For almost a minute Kim stared; then relief and mirth flooded over him. He started laughing and could not control it. He whooped until the tears started rolling down his cheeks. He became weak and finally sat down on the damp ground and continued to laugh. Deafy just sat. It was perhaps two minutes before Kim regained control of himself. When he did, he felt better than he had in weeks.

Deafy failed to see the joke. He got out of the truck and walked, stiff backed, down the arroyo.

"Now Deafy's sick," Kim howled gleefully to himself. "I hope he's good and sick."

Kim had regained his composure when Deafy returned five minutes later. But there was a drawn and harried look on Deafy's face, and Kim thought it best not to pursue the subject.

It took them the better part of an hour to get the broken steering wheel repaired and the truck started. They reached the rigs thirty minutes before sundown. The men yelled their greeting, and Deafy permitted the day tower to quit work fifteen minutes early to come to the shack for their wages. He wouldn't pay the night tower until they finished their work after sun up.

The men grabbed their money, and with harsh and profane mirth suggested ways of spending it. Deafy permitted the night tower tool dresser to drive them to town in the ton-and-a-half. Then the night tower went on duty, grumbling. But they would draw their wages tomorrow. And Borger would be as wide open and inviting at sunup as it was at sundown! So what the hell!

After the men had left the shack, Kim and Deafy set about making supper. The hum of the engine told them that the rig was running smoothly, and there was a peace and quiet that they seldom enjoyed.

They fixed sardines and crackers, and Deafy had his inevitable two cups of strong black coffee. Kim diluted some "Pet" milk with water and warmed it over the coal stove. They didn't need much for they had had a good dinner in Borger. But Deafy was strangely quiet and Kim was a bit troubled by it. He hoped he hadn't hurt Deafy's feelings by laughing at him when he swallowed his tobacco.

They had finished eating, and Kim tidied up the place as best he could. But Deafy continued his silent mood. Kim kept glancing at him uneasily.

"Know what I'm going to do, Kim?"

"What?" Kim was immensely relieved that Deafy was talking again.

"I'm going to go to bed and sleep till twelve o'clock."

"Good!" Kim said with relief. "You need it. I'll watch the rigs."

"The boys can run the rigs," Deafy said. "They're running like a sewing machine. Listen to 'em!"

Kim listened and nodded in agreement. Then he waited, for he knew Deafy had more to say.

"Kim," Deafy began uncertainly. "I—"

"What, Deafy?"

"About that feller I shot today."

Kim hadn't thought of that since the incident at the arroyo. He wished Deafy hadn't reminded him of it.

"What about him?"

"Well—not about him exactly." Deafy was having trouble saying it. "About that twelve cents I made him pay me."

"Yes?" Kim was beginning to be more interested.

"Well," Deafy said almost desperately. "I didn't want his damned twelve cents. But word will get around about that. You can shoot a man in Borger, and nobody gives a damn. But if you make him pay for the shell you shoot him with, then folks pay it a bit of mind. That sheriff will spread the news, and them toughs will think twice before they fool with Jones and Wingate again."

Kim considered the logic of that a moment and decided that it was just macabre enough that it was probably true. He looked closely at Deafy and felt a bit of sympathy for him. He knew that Deafy felt no qualms whatever about shooting the bandit, but he was concerned that Kim might think him heartless.

"That's all right, Deafy. I was just killing time until you got that pistol of yours ready, anyway." Of course he had been waiting for Deafy! What else? That bandit certainly hadn't been planning to go away without the money!

"Hoped you would understand that," Deafy said and spat a stream of tobacco juice into the stove.

"I do," Kim said. And he did.

Kim was surprised that Deafy was as good as his word about getting some sleep. He wondered occasionally if Deafy ever did sleep. He was always up before Kim was and never in bed when he was. But tonight Deafy was in bed first. Kim blew out the kerosene lamp and crawled in between the covers. The sound of the engines running smoothly was a good sound.

Deafy was turning restlessly, and the springs of his bed creaked. Finally he cleared his throat tentatively.

"Kim?"

"Yeah, Deafy."

"Sorry about making you sick today when I shot that feller."

Kim sat bolt upright in surprise. What on earth had happened to Deafy! Kim was still trying to think of a suitable reply when Deafy continued.

"I'll go with you and Wendy to that dinner if you still want me to."

Good old Deafy! Trying to make amends for something that wasn't really his fault, and Kim knew it. Nevertheless, Kim also knew that he had Deafy trapped and he grinned in the darkness.

"That's fine, Deafy," he said. "I'll send word in to Wendy to-morrow."

Sending word to Wendy would eliminate any chance for Deafy to back out. Not that Deafy would have done so, for Deafy Jones kept his promises.

Kim lay back and smiled. He didn't know why he had so much wanted Deafy to go with them. But he had, and he felt not the least bit of remorse for having taken advantage of his friend. He was simply grateful that Deafy had given him the chance.

Deafy continued to toss and turn. Kim grinned again. Deafy was probably wondering how he would eat the turkey with a knife and fork.

"I just don't understand it!" Deafy mumbled under his breath.

"You don't understand what, Deafy?" Kim was a bit concerned. Perhaps his friend was having conscience pangs.

"First time I ever done that!" Deafy said incredulously.

"Forget it, Deafy," Kim said benevolently. "That man was asking for it. You did right in shooting him."

"Shooting him, hell!" Deafy growled. "It ain't that; I've shot men before.—But that is the first time I ever swallowed my tobacco."

There was a note of disgust in Deafy's voice. Kim chuckled and went to sleep.

CHAPTER XIX

The harassed Hutchinson county sheriff gratefully relinquished the task of maintaining the law and order in the oil camp when Borger was incorporated in November. The new police department was composed of eighteen men, and they went about their task with grim determination.

Their chore was not an easy one. Only two weeks ago, the police chief had been shot in the back as he came out of a drug store next to the *Midway Rooms*. Shortly after, another policeman was killed in a gun battle on Dixon Street.

These murders seemed a signal for lawlessness to flame with renewed vigor. The entire county rocked with violence and crime. City and county officials joined forces in their efforts to stem the tide. Through the roaring, flaming nights, the screams of human beings could be heard above the din of the holocaust. Bodies of murdered and robbed victims were found with increasing regularity in the small creeks and ravines near the camp.

A pall settled over the land. News of the corrupt and violent field spread across the nation. Women dared not venture out, and men carried guns and sought sanctuary of their homes like animals slinking to their dens. Outlaws Matthew Kimes and Ray Terrill were reported seen in Borger. Bonnie Parker, the vicious and deadly cigar smoking queen of crime was seen with her boyfriend, Clyde Barrow.

A bank in the city of Pampa, only twenty miles from Borger, was robbed in broad daylight. The bandits made off with thirty thousand dollars in cash. Two deputy sheriffs were found shot to death beside their car on a dusty road near town.

Stark, naked fear stalked the land. Law abiding citizens gathered in small, almost abject, groups to discuss ways of coping with the headlong orgy. It was rumored that the governor of the state had been asked to send the National Guard or the Texas Rangers to help establish law and order.

On Thanksgiving morning of 1927, thin grey snow clouds that had
hung over the oil field for a week were dissipated by a bright Texas
sun. A thin blanket of snow had fallen, and the wind had brushed it
into the lee of sage and mesquites, but by mid-morning, even those
patches were melted. The sun was shining brightly, and the air was
warm when Kim Wingate and Deafy Jones checked their rigs for the
last time before dressing to go to the Beatenbow ranch for Thanksgiving dinner.

They caught warm water from the pop-off valve to wash their
greasy hands and faces. Then they dressed in new clothing that they
had been able to find in camp.

Deafy was unusually quiet. Kim knew that he was looking forward
to the day with a great deal of apprehension, since Kim and Wendy
had made arrangements for Kim and Deafy to ride with her and her
father and Maria to the ranch. It would be the first time in many
years that Deafy had met Blake Terrell intentionally. Kim knew that
Deafy would have given a great deal to be out of the situation. But
he would go through with it.

Besides, Deafy would get to see Mandy and Finch.

Deafy put on a new, double-breasted, blue serge suit. His white
shirt was wrinkled, and one tip of the collar stuck up at an unattrac-
tive angle. He had trouble knotting his tie, and Kim helped. Kim had
never seen Deafy in a suit and tie before. He looked strange.

Then Deafy reached under his bunk and pulled out his shaving kit.
From it he took an oval shaped piece of black cloth to which was
attached a piece of elastic. He fitted the elastic over his head, and the
black patch covered his blind eye. Kim watched curiously, but made
no comment.

It was ten o'clock when their pickup truck pulled onto the circular
drive in front of the Terrell house. Deafy said gruffly that he would
wait outside. Kim did not argue with him, but bounded up the steps.
Rachael opened the door Blake and Claude Butler were standing in
the big room. Evidently, Butler was just leaving. Blake looked at Kim
and scowled slightly; then a look of forced geniality settled on his
face.

"Mr. Butler," he said formally, "this is Kim Wingate. Mr. Butler is
my lawyer."

There was no expression whatever in the man's phlegmatic eyes as
Kim extended his hand to acknowledge the introduction. The
lawyer's hand was as soft and smooth as Wendy's. Kim felt an almost
uncontrollable desire to wipe his hand on his pant leg when he
withdrew it.

Just at that moment, Wendy and Maria came into the room, and suddenly the atmosphere was transformed. Wendy was dressed in a simple blue dress that emphasized her eyes. Her shingle-bobbed hair was combed back. Maria's dress was black and deeply cut in the back. Her dark hair was gathered in a huge bun at the nape of her neck.

Maria greeted Kim effusively and seemed to ignore Butler. Wendy greeted Kim warmly. She looked at him with a saucy air of conspiracy. Kim grinned back knowingly. At last they had managed to get Deafy and Blake together.

Butler walked outside with them. Deafy was leaning against a fender of the pickup truck. Wendy and Maria greeted him warmly, and Blake nodded curtly.

Joe Shay drove their Stutz onto the driveway, and Kim opened the door to the back seat for Wendy. Blake walked around the car, and Butler opened the front door for Maria. There was a trace of a frosty smile on his face as he half bowed. As Maria sat in the seat, she seemed to lose her balance. As she leaned back her feet left the floor board, exposing much of her shapely, silken legs.

"But how clumsy of me!" Maria laughed as her dark eyes looked provocatively at Butler who had not closed the car door.

Butler quickly bowed again to hide the expression that he could not keep from his face and eyes. A slight smile plucked at Maria's lips, and a look of triumph leaped into her eyes as she looked at Butler.

Blake did not see the incident, for he was on the opposite side of the car. Nor had Wendy. But Kim did, and so did Joe Shay who was still sitting under the wheel. Joe glared murderously at Butler, and Maria turned to smile angelically at Joe.

"I won't need you today, Joe." Blake's voice was blunt.

"But, Mr. Terrell—" There was obvious disappointment in Joe's voice as he turned to Blake.

"You just be here when we get back," Blake said brusquely as he got under the wheel.

"But—you said—"

"Never mind what I said, Joe," Blake said harshly. "You do as you are told."

Kim saw the disappointment in Joe's eyes as they drove away, leaving him and Butler standing in the driveway.

On that same Thanksgiving morning, Granny Beatenbow and Mandy had risen even earlier than usual. Mandy helped Finch doctor a colt and then went back to the house to prepare for baking the three wild turkeys that Finch had killed the day before.

In the early morning sun, the animals about the Beatenbow horse ranch rollicked and played. The brood mares frisked about, and the few colts ran awkwardly and tossed their heads. The stallions pawed the ground and neighed defiance to the beautiful world. Chickens clucked in the yard, and a wild turkey called. The air was clear and clean, and the sounds carried far.

From inside the big ranch house, the delicious smells of roast turkey and dressing and baking bread wafted out to the giant cottonwood trees. Smoke curled from the chimney of the fireplace and of the cook stove.

Granny Beatenbow sat before her fireplace and waited for the Thanksgiving guests to arrive. She was wearing a new shawl, and her thin grey hair was pulled tight and straight over her small head. Her gnarled hands were wrapped about her cane which she occasionally tapped impatiently on the floor.

It would be a big day for Granny. The Beatenbows would be home. Her sons and their children, and their children's children. Granny had twelve grandchildren and eight great-grandchildren. She knew their birthdays and the year they were born. And, though she would make caustic comments about the fuss and bother, Granny thoroughly enjoyed the confusion and commotions of the Beatenbow family together.

And there would be friends there, too. Wendy Terrell and her folks were coming. And her young man and his friend.

Granny looked forward to Wendy's visit. That young lady had gumption. It didn't go to her head just because she was pretty. She know how to talk to a body. Granny liked to be scolded, and few people had the temerity to do that. Wendy did. And Granny liked it. Wendy could laugh, too. That young Kim Wingate wasn't half good enough for her. But then, mighty few men would be. But he would grow. Right now, he was sort of like a two year old colt. He would smooth out, though. She had noticed that he was getting bigger and hard the last few times they visited. He would make a man, all right.

Granny tapped her cane on the floor as she thought of Wendy's father. In some ways he was a lot like her Humphrey had been. It took men like him to whip something big. But there was something about Blake Terrell that made Granny impatient. He talked too much, for one thing. And he tried to push people. Granny didn't like to be pushed. She hoped that he would start some of his loud talking the way he had done when he tried to lease her land. It would take one of her boys just about a minute to straighten him out.

And that black-eyed wife of his! A body could see without half trying that she was a roving filly. But she was mighty pretty. The men folks would enjoy having her around for the day. Granny cackled softly to herself as she thought of that.

And there was young Kim Wingate's friend, Deafy Smith. There was something vaguely disconcerting about him. He had visited the ranch almost every week since the oil men had cut their fence, and two of their mares had drunk the bad water and died. He and Finch seemed to enjoy each other very much. Ordinarily, Finch's recommendation was enough for Granny, for she trusted Finch's judgment of horseflesh or people.

But Mandy seemed not to be herself when that man was around. Maybe, it was his eye that bothered Mandy. But that was foolishness! Mandy had doctored enough screw-worm calves and wire cut horses that the eye shouldn't bother her. Besides, the man always wore a black patch over his eye when he was at the ranch.

And Deafy Jones had refused to call her "Granny." He called her "Mrs. Beatenbow."

Granny was still thinking of the guests that would arrive in a few hours when Mandy came into the living room.

"Everything is about ready, Mama," she said. "I can put the bread in the oven when they get here, and it will be hot when we get ready to eat."

"You got plenty of turkey and dressing, Mandy?"

"Yes, Mamma," Mandy said pleasantly. "We have more than enough of everything. I'm going to dress now. Do you want anything?"

"If I want anything, I'll get it," Granny said grumpily.

"All right, Mamma."

Mandy left her mother and went to the southwest wing of the ranch house. There were three rooms there, and they were hers. No one but Mandy entered those rooms. Inside, the change was almost unbelievable. One large sitting room was furnished in comfortable, modern furniture. The bedroom was spacious, and a big, double window looked out over the river. It was feminine in every detail. The other room was small, and in it was a bath tub. An iron pipe ran from the wellhouse and was hooked to a coil of copper tubing in a small wood burning heating stove. The wellhouse was a few feet higher than the tub, and Mandy had only to turn a spigot to let fresh spring water run in. There was a neat pile of wood by the stove, and she laid a fire and lit it. In a few minutes the copper tubing would be hot, and when she turned the water in, it would heat as it flowed through the tubing. Her bath would be nice and warm.

While the wood fire was heating, Mandy went about laying out the clothing she would wear. She took some very frilly and sheer underthings from a bureau drawer and a freshly ironed gingham dress from

a hanger. She found some dark hose and high heeled shoes. Then she
tested the water and found it warm. She divested herself of the
divided skirt, rough boots, and coarse shirt.

The bath was good, and she loitered in it, soaking herself thoroughly. Then she dried vigorously on a coarse towel.

Mandy did not immediately don her clothing. Instead, she sat in
front of a big mirror in her bedroom and unpinned her long hair. She
brushed it with long, rhythmic strokes. As she did so, she looked at
her body. It was supple and strong. Her skin was dark and clear.
Mandy knew she had Indian blood in her, even though her mother
had never admitted it to her. And she had French and English too.

She looked at herself critically. Her body held no mysteries for
her, other than its refusal to grow old. She was almost fifty, but her
flesh was firm and her skin clear. Her eyes were bright and her face
serene.

Mandy would have been the last to agree that her life had been a
hard one. She had lived a good life. She had been one of the first
white children born in the Panhandle. Only the Goodnights and the
Kellys had been here before the Beatenbows. Then had come the
Ledricks and Lards and Walstads. It was a rough country, but, where
many women withered, Mandy had bloomed.

And there had even been Indians in the country when the Beatenbows came there in 1877. Her father homesteaded three sections of
land, and the Beatenbow family had lived and grown there until they
had one of the biggest and best ranches in the Panhandle. By the
time Mandy was fifteen, she could rope and ride with the best of the
men, and she had enjoyed every minute of it. Then, when she was
eighteen, Steve had begun working for her father.

He was a handsome, devil-may-care young man who had skinned
buffalo for Billy Dixon. He loved to laugh and drink and work. His
specialty was breaking mean horses. He was the only cowboy they
ever had who was unimpressed with Humphrey Beatenbow.

The day Steve and Mandy were married, Mandy's father stormed
and raved. Steve merely grinned and told Mandy to pack her things.
They moved to a half-dugout on a section of homesteaded land, and
Steve went gaily about building his own ranch.

It was a good three years for Mandy. Her husband was a man of
gargantuan appetites and animal-like inclinations. He drank when he
was thirsty, ate when he was hungry, rested when he was tired, and
made love to her when it pleased him to do so, which was often.
Mandy's appetites matched his own, and they were happy. Phyllis
was born in less than a year.

Then her father was killed in a stampede of steers he was gathering
for market. Less than two months later, Steve caught his foot in a

rope tied to the saddle of an outlaw horse and was dragged to death.

Mandy moved back to the ranch then, with her mother. Her brothers would have done so, she knew, but they had their own ranches by that time, and the Beatenbows believed in doing for themselves. It was their right. Then, for many years, Mandy and Finch ran the big cattle ranch, but when Phyllis grew up and married, they turned the cattle ranch over to her husband who was a good cowman. Mandy and Finch kept only the two thousand acres of land at the home place and the small horse pasture south of the river. Finch was getting old and could not work as he had once done, and Mandy felt that Phyllis's husband should have his chance, too.

Mandy accepted her lot philosophically and almost stoically. While Phyllis was growing up, her time was occupied with her child, and helping run the ranch. Since Phyllis had moved away, however, Mandy felt the return of the furies in her body that Steve had kindled so many years ago. Often, when she could not sleep at night, she quietly opened the double window of her bedroom and slipped out to walk along the river. She loved to listen to the bark of the coyote and the rustle of wild things. And she liked the smell of summer on the sand and water.

She had intended to marry again when a reasonable time had elapsed after Steve's death. Mandy was a woman who liked to be married. She had long since come to the conclusion that there was no one particular man just for one particular woman. Rather, it was a particular *kind* of man for a particular *kind* of woman.

But that kind of man had not shown himself. She had had suitors, of course. Dozens of them. And she had honestly wanted to be interested in them, but she hadn't been. Finally, she had resigned herself and had actually begun to hope that she would hurry and grow old.

And then she had ridden with Finch to the oil well the day their horses had drunk the poisoned water! When the man with the unsightly eye strode up, she had felt a stirring within her that had been dormant for years.

Steve had been the only man ever to do that to Mandy. There was little visible similarity between her Steve and the one-eyed man, but Mandy felt the strength and stamina of Deafy. Like an old range stallion, he was weathered and scarred, but nonetheless, a dauntless spirit emanated from him. Mandy felt it touch her. It was a thing she had yearned for, and now, when it came, it almost scared her.

Mandy signed almost inaudibly and finished brushing her hair. Then, with easy, slow motions, she dressed. She looked at the big clock on the wall and knew that the family would be arriving within the hour. Wendy and her folks, and Kim Wingate and Deafy would arrive soon after.

Mandy smiled into the mirror. She tucked a bit of stray hair behind her ear and walked toward the other part of the house. Her step was light.

The turkey was done to a turn and the dressing seasoned even to Granny's satisfaction when the first of the Beatenbow sons arrived. He was a rather small man, with a quiet smile and drawling voice. His wife was plump and pleasant. They, and their three children, had driven from Mobeetie since sunup in the Model-T Ford. Soon thereafter, the other two sons arrived with their families, which included several grandchildren. Granny and Mandy greeted each with obvious pleasure, but reserve. The Beatenbows were not a demonstrative family.

By eleven o'clock, several families from neighboring ranches had arrived. Kim and Wendy, along with Blake, Maria, and Deafy, were the last to arrive.

Mandy heard the car drive up and immediately came out to meet them. She shook hands with Blake and Maria and said hello to Kim and Wendy. Deafy was standing a bit behind the group, and Kim saw him surreptitiously spit out his cud of tobacco and rub a gnarled forefinger across his front teeth.

"Come," Mandy said. "I want you all to meet the Beatenbow family." She started toward a group of men standing under a cottonwood tree.

Everyone started walking toward the group except Deafy, who lagged behind. Kim knew that Deafy was trying to be as inconspicuous as possible. Mandy noticed Deafy waiting.

"Come on, Deafy," she said pleasantly and took him by the arm. "I want you to meet my brothers."

Blake opened his eyes in surprise. He hadn't even known that Deafy had met Mandy. Wendy looked at Kim questioningly, but Kim only grinned knowingly. Maria's delightful laugh caused the men under the cottonwood to look at them even more carefully. Deafy squared his shoulders and walked, almost belligerently, with Mandy toward the group.

Mandy introduced everyone to the group, presenting Deafy first each time, then Maria and Blake, and finally Wendy and Kim. Three of the men were Mandy's brothers, and others were neighbors and in-laws. Each acknowledged the introduction with awkward mumbles and strong handclasps. Kim noticed that Mandy's brothers were not physically big, but each had a certain air of distinction about him. They were browned by sun and wind and dressed in typical cowman fashion. Kim noticed that Finch was not in the group and wondered about it absently.

"Now," Mandy said when the introductions were completed, "Deafy, you and Kim and Mr. Terrell stay out here and talk to the men folks. Wendy and Maria and I will go in and help get dinner on the table."

Immediately after the women left the group, Blake started an animated conversation with one of the men. Deafy stood uncertainly and uncomfortably. Kim watched with interest.

"I've been out to visit your mother a couple of times before," Blake addressed himself to the older one of Granny's sons. "Told her I'd be willing to pay more than this land is worth just for a lease. I figure I could make you boys plenty of money. I have a big outfit. I could spud in a well on every section of your land within thirty days."

The man looked at Blake out of keen, squinted eyes. He was perhaps sixty years old.

"I haven't heard Mamma say what she was going to do," he said noncommittally.

"Well," Blake laughed deprecatingly, "I doubt if your mother really *knows* what she is going to do. She certainly is a fine lady—but she *is* old. I thought maybe you boys might be able to make her see the advantage of leasing to a big company like mine."

The conversation suddenly stopped. Everyone looked at Granny's son and Blake Terrell.

"Mamma *is* pretty old," the son said calmly. "But she still has her own mind. I expect that she will do with her land what she wants."

"But," expostulated Blake, "it belongs to you boys, too.—Or, it soon will. You have a right to—"

"Mister Terrell!" A muscle twitched in the jaw of Granny's son. "My daddy and mamma homesteaded this place here. I reckon there ain't no use to tell you what they went through to keep it. But they did. If Mamma wants to *give* the ranch away—that's her business. If she wants to lease it to you, then you get it. The only time us boys will interfere is to see that what she wants is done—and then only if she asks us. Us Beatenbows sort of lean toward letting other folks mind their own business."

Anger clouded Blake's face for a moment, for the man's meaning was painfully clear. Then, much to Kim's relief, he laughed.

"Well," Blake said in a rueful voice. "Your mother *did* show us oil men who owned Hutchinson county when they voted the courthouse to Stinnett."

A slight twinkle lit the eyes of Granny's son, and the muscle in his jaw relaxed. Then the group started laughing and talking again. It had been a bad moment.

A few minutes later, Finch came walking in his uncertain cowboy fashion, from the corrals. Deafy angled toward him. The men in the group talked with Finch for a few minutes. The conversation centered about cows and horses. It was quite evident that the men in the group respected Finch tremendously.

The morning wore on, and the sun grew warmer as it climbed higher. Children played about the yard and corrals. The men whittled and talked. Kim was ravenously hungry, and the food smells coming from the house made his mouth water. Finally, Mandy came to the gallery and told the men to come to dinner. As they walked toward the house, the children that had been playing in the yard swarmed toward Mandy.

"Now, you wait, children," Mandy said laughingly. "There won't be room for you at the first table. You will have to wait until the grown-ups are through."

"I *knew* it!" wailed one small boy. "We have to wait every time."

"Yeah," protested another. "And there ain't never nothing left but necks and wings when the grown-ups get through."

"Now you run along, children," Mandy said. "We will call you when it's time for you to eat."

"Well," one of the little girls ventured. "I hope Uncle Ed don't pray as long as he nearly always does."

The men in the group laughed, and Mandy bent over and picked the little girl from the ground and hugged her.

"We will eat real fast," Mandy assured her. Then she set the child back on the ground and swatted her. "Now you all run along and play."

Kim's heart went out to the children. He knew that it would be absolute torture for him to have to wait while the others were eating. But the youngsters were shouting and laughing again even before the adults got in the house.

The long table was decorated with a table cloth and more food than Kim had ever seen in one place. Three huge turkeys rested in the center of the table along with big bowls of dressing, pickles, wild plum jelly, and other assorted foods. It was a bountiful Thanksgiving dinner.

Mandy seated everyone. Finch was at the head of the table. Mandy sat on his left, closest to the stove. And, noted Kim, Mandy had seated Deafy next to her. Kim was on one side of Granny and Wendy on the other. The others were arranged about the table in various order. Kim counted twenty-two people. With the exception of Granny, they all stood at their places.

"Ed," Finch said, "will you offer the blessing?"

Ed was the son that had talked to Blake under the trees. His prayer was long and fervent. Kim sympathized with the youngsters in the yard playing.

The dinner was a huge success. Maria, for once, was content to sit and listen. They talked as they ate. Granny made caustic comments and enjoyed the dressing and gravy thoroughly. Blake made no further mention of the leases, but he extended himself to be nice to Granny Beatenbow.

Deafy ate prodigiously of the wild turkey and dressing. Mandy saw that his plate was always filled. The meal was perhaps half over when Granny became quiet. Even Wendy could get no more than an occasional grunt out of her. Her small, alert eyes were riveted on Deafy and Mandy seated across the table. When they got to the punpkin pie, Mandy put the biggest slice on Deafy's plate.

"Well, bless my soul!" Granny mumbled in amazement. "If that don't beat a hen-a-peckin'!" She was suddenly sure of Mandy's feeling for Deafy.

"What did you say, Granny?" Wendy asked.

"Mind your own business, young spriggins," Granny chuckled. "I reckon I ain't got the sense the good lord give a goose."

Wendy looked questioningly at Kim.

Kim had thought that they wouldn't make a dent on the huge food supply, but when the meal was over, he figured that the youngster who had made the comment about wings and necks was about right.

While the women washed dishes, the men went outside and lounged again under the trees. They talked of horses and cattle and oil. Kim loved to listen to the conversation, though he took little part in it. Later he and Wendy went for a walk on the river. It was a pleasant afternoon.

Deafy and Finch disappeared toward the corrals after lunch, and it was more than two hours before they returned. When they did come back, Deafy was talking to Finch in a low, melodious voice. Kim glared at him suspiciously. Perhaps Finch had a bottle stashed away somewhere. Kim made a mental note to give Deafy a good talking to when they got back to the rigs. He could at least have waited until Saturday night to do his drinking. Deafy paid not the slightest bit of attention to Kim. He and Finch finally went into the house to visit with Granny.

It had been a great day for Granny. Her boys had been home, and her friends had come to see her. She was feeling unusually chipper.

"Wendy," she cackled just as they were about to leave. "You bring that young man of yours in here a minute."

Wendy called to Kim who was standing in the front yard. He walked in and stood in front of the old lady. She poked the fireplace with her cane and then looked at Kim sternly.

"You ain't hardly spoke to me all day, young man," Granny said accusingly.

"I've been talking to everybody," Kim protested.

"You ain't even seen nobody but Wendy," Granny said. "But that ain't what I called you in for."

Kim waited.

"About that little horsepasture on the south side of the river—where you and Wendy got that cabin fixed up. Ain't much bigger than a corral, only got about a hundred acres in it."

Still Kim waited. No one rushed Granny Beatenbow.

"If you want to dig yourself a oil well on it—then go ahead. We don't use it in the winter time noway."

Kim was taken completely by surprise. He had never mentioned leases to Granny Beatenbow.

"Why, I'm not a driller, Granny—what I mean is, I don't have drilling equipment. I couldn't drill on that land. Besides, I doubt if I have enough money to pay for the lease."

"I didn't say nothing about money," Granny snapped, "If you want that horsepasture to dig a well on, it's yours. You probably are going to turn out to be a oil man anyway. You can pay when you get your well dug. I'll charge you interest from today on the lease money, like that banker did me when I had to borrow some money once."

Kim decided that he should pacify the old woman, though he knew he would never be able to drill on the land.

"All right, Granny," he said, "If I ever get enough money to buy a drilling rig, I will come out and we will sign the lease."

"Sign the lease!" Granny snorted. "You talk like Wendy's daddy. That lease is yours. You just dig the oil well when you get around to it and then bring me my money, young man!"

"But that wouldn't be—it wouldn't be legal," Kim protested.

"It would be legal all right," Kim heard a man's voice drawl. "If you want to drill on that horsepasture, go ahead." One of Granny's sons had entered the room quietly. "If Mamma says it's all right, it is. It's her land."

Kim gulped and looked at Granny's sons guiltily. "I didn't come out here to try to lease your mother's land," he said defensively.

"Nobody said you did," the man said quietly. "But you got the horse pasture anyway—if you want it. Mamma's saying so makes it as legal as signing a bunch of papers."

"I know—but—" Kim hesitated. "Well thanks a lot, Granny. If I drill on it, I'll bring you your money."

"You'll drill on it," Granny cackled complacently.

"If you have anybody make a question about it," Granny's son said quietly, "you send 'em to see me. I heard you and Mamma make the trade. I live down close to Mobeetie."

Kim shook his head slightly. That lease was worth a fortune if there was oil on it, and there probably was. And Granny had just sold it to him—on credit.

Blake gunned the Stutz as they left the ranch. A covey of quail flushed as they pulled out of the cottonwoods, and a flock of wild turkeys veered from their floating flight to the roosting trees. Blake was cordial on the way home, and Maria was her usual bubbling self. Even Deafy talked a bit. Wendy was quiet and Kim thoughtful.

It was a half hour before sundown when they reached the river. They had to wait until a team crossed from the south side to tow them back across. Maria was impatient at the delay.

"Couldn't we make it without the team, Blake?" she asked in her musical voice.

"We might, and we might not," Blake growled. "If we got halfway across and the quicksand got us, they would charge us twenty-five dollars to come and get us out. I saw two cars sink plumb out of sight out there last week."

Two cars were waiting behind them when the team finally arrived.

"What the hell took you so long?" Blake wanted to know as the teamster approached.

"You want towed—or not?" the teamster asked in a tired voice.

"We want towed," Blake affirmed.

The man hooked the team to the car and sat on the hood as they started pulling the car. It took perhaps five minutes to cross the river. At one point they could feel the car sinking, but the teamster slapped his lines, and the horses pulled faster. Another man was waiting as they reached the south bank.

"Anything doing?" the teamster asked anxiously.

"Not yet," the waiting man said grimly. "But this is about the right time."

They busied themselves unhooking the chain from the car. The sun had just gone down behind the horizon, but the red glow of it still lit the river.

The man who had ridden across on the hood came back to the car door.

"That will be five dollars, mister," he said.

Blake reached for his pocket. "You men got a pretty good thing here, haven't you? I'll bet you hope they don't ever build a bridge across this river."

"We make money," agreed the man. "But we haven't been able to—"

"Raise 'em, you mule skinnin' bastards!" a voice shouted.

Blake's hand stopped half way to his pocket. Deafy sat up in the seat, and Maria gasped. Wendy grabbed Kim's hand, and both teamsters lifted their arms above their heads. Kim knew they were back in the oil fields. It was like a dash of cold water after a warm bath.

"You're getting smart," another voice taunted, and Kim saw two men rise from some sage bushes perhaps thirty yards away. They started walking toward the car with guns leveled.

"That's what I started to say," the teamster resumed grimly to Blake. "We make money, but we can't keep it. They've hijacked us three times in the last week. Always wait 'til sundown when we have a lot of money on us."

Kim's pulse throbbed. He heard a low, ominous growl from Deafy and felt him stir. Kim quickly grabbed Deafy's arm.

The hijackers were within ten feet of the car when they stopped. The light was dim, but their features were clearly discernible. Kim had never seen either man before. The weapons they were carrying were repeating shotguns.

"That's right," one of the men approved gleefully. "You boys are getting smart. You lift 'em when you're told to. Now just hand over your money, and we'll be getting back to town as usual."

One of the teamsters started to say something, but a bandit halted him.

"No use talking," he said. "You know how we operate, and we know how much money you ought to have—and you'd damn well better have it. You, there in that car, pile out and lift your hands like everybody else."

Nobody moved for a second, and one of the hijackers moved up quickly and thrust a gun inside. It was only then that he noticed Wendy and Maria.

"Well! Well!" he shouted with satisfaction. "We got ladies tonight, too. What do you know about that!"

Kim felt that he should say or do something, but could think of nothing. It was Deafy who spoke.

"We'll get out, mister," he said. "But you leave the women folks alone."

"Who says so?"

"All of us says so," Deafy growled.

"And what if we don't?"

"Then you can just come in this car and get us," Deafy said flatly.

The bandit considered momentarily. "All right. The women can stay inside. But you men get out—right now."

Blake, Kim, and Deafy complied. They lined up beside the two teamsters and lifted their arms. Kim was grateful that Wendy and Maria were along; otherwise, he knew, the bandits would never have taken Deafy without a fight.

"Empty your pockets," they were ordered.

Blake started to say something and changed his mind. Kim had very little money, and he knew that Deafy had little. But Blake habitually carried large sums in cash.

The teamsters emptied their pockets, and the hijackers expressed satisfaction with their contribution. But they were displeased with the offering made by Kim, Deafy and Blake.

"Hell!" one man said in disgust. "They got more than that. Search 'em."

"No, you won't!" Blake almost screamed.

"Yes, we will," he was answered. "Either standin' up or layin' down. Which will it be?"

One of the men went about the search and found the big roll of money that Blake had neglected to produce. He expressed satisfaction by poking Blake in the ribs with his gun. Next came Kim. They found nothing. Then Deafy. The man moved his hands over Deafy's body. Kim held his breath; then he heard a stifled exclamation from the searcher. He had found Deafy's gun.

"Well, now just look at this!" the bandit said in mock consternation. "This fellow was packing a gun, and we didn't even know it." He pitched the gun to his companion.

Kim cut his eyes to look at Deafy. He could see Deafy's good eye glisten, and he distinctly saw Deafy pucker to spit. But Deafy didn't spit; he didn't have a cud of tobacco in his mouth.

"What kind of a gun is *this?*' the man who caught the gun asked, almost in awe.

"What's wrong with it?" the searcher wanted to know.

"Hell—it's a shotgun. Only it's got a pistol handle."

Deafy said nothing. The bandits were silent a moment. Finally, the one who had caught the gun asked, "You wouldn't be Deafy Jones, would you?"

"What difference does it make?" Deafy growled. "You got my money and my gun."

"It makes a lot of difference," the bandit answered. "I've heard about you. And I ain't taking your gun. I'll just take the shell out of it and give it back." And he hastily proceeded to do so.

"Suit yourself," Deafy said.

"Well," the bandit said defensively. "I don't aim to have you chasing me all over these oil fields just to get your damned cannon back. Come on, Blackie, let's go!"

They stuffed the money in their pockets and prepared to leave.

"Wait," Blackie said. "What are we going to do about that damned Stutz? It could catch us before we got half way to town in that Model-T."

"I already thought of that, Blackie. I'll take care of it."

With that the man turned and pointed his shotgun at one of the tires. The explosion was loud, and Maria screamed. Wendy gasped, and Blake started. Kim almost jumped out of his shoes, but Deafy didn't even blink his good eye. The man quickly pumped another shell into the firing chamber of the shotgun, as the car settled on the flat tire.

"Now," Blackie said with satisfaction. "We will just take these mule skinners' Model-T, as usual, and drive on back to town. You can find your car there tomorrow. We sure do want you to have transportation so you can come back out and make us some more money."

With that they moved to the car, which was parked by the corral. One of the men kept a gun pointed while the other cranked the Model-T. It started, and they jumped in and with a yell were off.

"Go get them!" Blake yelled.

"You just wait a minute, mister," one of the teamsters said grimly. "We were expecting them today. They always steal our car to make their getaway, so—we drained all the gas out of that Ford except what is in the carburetor. It won't run a hundred yards, and we got rifles stashed over there in them sage bushes."

"You folks just wait here," the other said quickly as both of them dashed to a clump of sage. They each grabbed a rifle and levered shells into the chamber just as Kim heard the motor of the Model-T sputter and die. It was just over a ridge, and Kim could not see it. The men ran toward the sound. In a matter of seconds, the rifles began spitting and were followed by shotgun blasts, yells, and a man's scream. Kim, Deafy and Blake started toward the shooting.

At the top of the rise, they stopped. There was absolute silence. Kim could see the Model-T about fifty yards ahead. One man was lying beside it, and another was sitting on the ground leaning against a wheel. The two teamsters were standing, pointing their rifles at the men.

They were puffing when they got there. Kim dreaded what he knew he was going to see. The man on the ground was obviously dead. One side of his face was blown away, and there was no movement in him. It was Blackie. Kim had never seen death by violence before, and was a little surprised that it did not shock him more. Now Blackie was only an inanimate object, even though blood still flowed from his face. But the other man was groaning in pain. He held his hand over his stomach, and Kim could see blood seeping between his fingers.

"Let's get our money back," one of the teamsters said. "And then we will haul them on into town. I doubt if a doc can do this one any good, but we might as well see."

"I know exactly how much I had," Blake said belligerently. "And I want every damned cent of it back."

"You'll get your money back, mister, less the five dollars you owe me," a teamster said.

One of the teamsters busied himself searching the dead man while the other started going through the wounded man's pockets. The man groaned and rolled on his stomach as the teamster searched him. Kim started to protest, but Deafy laid his hand on Kim's arm.

"You go on back to the car, Kim," Deafy said gruffly. "The women folks probably will be wanting to know what happened. Blake and me will help load these fellers in the car."

Kim knew that Deafy was trying to spare him the ordeal, but he made no protest. He wondered what Deafy and Blake would say to each other as they walked back together. Probably nothing. It would be an embarrassing situation for Deafy.

Maria was bursting with curiosity when Kim got back to the car. Wendy was quiet. Kim told them briefly what had happened and started jacking up the wheel in preparation to change the tire.

Blake and Deafy returned before Kim was finished. Both were silent.

It was after dark when they finally got back to town. Maria invited Kim and Deafy in for a drink. Deafy said that they had better be getting back to the rig, but Maria insisted, and Blake made no protest. Wendy squeezed Kim's hand, and Kim suggested that they might be able to stay a few minutes. Deafy silently acquiesced.

Maria enjoyed playing hostess in her beautiful new home, and she fixed the drinks herself. Rachael, the negress cook and housekeeper, was not in evidence.

Blake was in an expansive mood since recovering his money from the bandits. When Maria handed each a drink, Blake held his up and proposed a toast.

"To the Beatenbow lease and the Terrell Oil Company!" he said loudly.

Maria laughed and downed her drink. Kim sipped his, and Wendy, who did not like liquor, only made a motion with her glass. Deafy did not even raise his.

"Yes sir!" Blake said enthusiastically. "I'm going to get that Beatenbow lease if I have to turn this county upside down."

"Let me pour you another drink, my husband," Maria said in her musical voice. "And you must tell us how you propose to do that."

She poured Blake another drink, and Blake started talking in a loud, excited voice. He was addressing himself to Maria. He had not spoken directly to Deafy all day. Deafy sat dejectedly in a big chair.

Wendy motioned to Kim, and he followed her to the phonograph where they feigned selecting records.

"Isn't it wonderful about Deafy!" Wendy exclaimed delightedly.

"I'm going to hit him over the head with a Stillson wrench," Kim said belligerently.

"What on earth for?" Wendy asked. "He was perfect."

"He didn't have to drink when we were visiting the Beatenbows," Kim said doggedly. "Didn't you notice how he was talking after he and Finch came back from the corrals. I ought to break the old devil's neck."

Wendy's laugh floated through the room. "Kim, you idiot!" she said and squeezed his hand. "Deafy wasn't drunk. He was talking like that all day. It was Mandy."

"Huh?"

"It was Mandy," Wendy said delightedly. "Deafy is smitten with her. Didn't you notice that he spat out his chew of tobacco?"

"Well, I'll be darned!" Kim did remember.

A few minutes later they prepared to leave. Maria insisted that they have another drink, but Kim declined. The liquor was harsh, and he hadn't been able to finish the drink he had.

Deafy hadn't touched his. And Kim knew he wouldn't. He would ride to the Beatenbows with Blake Terrell to please Kim and Wendy. But he wouldn't drink Blake's liquor for any man.

CHAPTER X

A week after Thanksgiving, Granny Beatenbow was rocking contentedly by her fireplace when she heard a coyote howl on the river. It was broad daylight. She stopped rocking and listened intently. It came again and was followed by the mournful yapping of other coyotes. Granny hunched her bony shoulders in her shawl and poked the fire. She sensed trouble.

That afternoon, when Finch and Mandy came in, she hobbled slowly to the doorway of the ranch house and looked at their horses with shrewd, knowing eyes. The horses had unusually long, thick coats of hair. Even the chickens had put on extra feathers.

That night Granny instructed Finch to lay in extra wood for her fireplace and to haul more coal from Stinnett for the kitchen stove. She also sent word to Tom to buy extra hay and cake for the cattle ranch. She had lived far too long in the Panhandle to be unaware of the warning signs of nature. Only a fool would ignore them.

Granny's premonition proved correct, for scarcely a week later, a minute atmospheric disturbance began as a wispy swirl of snow on Point Barrow, gathering volume and momentum until it became a howling, raging blizzard that swept across Alaska and over the Yukon Territory of Canada. It pushed millions of tons of snow before it, hiding every obstacle in its path. Then, as it passed over North Dakota and South Dakota, it dropped much of its burden of snow on the lands of harassed cattlemen who fought desperately to provide food and shelter for their starving cattle.

Through Nebraska and Kansas it raged—and on into the Panhandle of Oklahoma and Northern Texas, a white, swirling, turbulent mass. The air, robbed of heat by the descending monster, was icy cold.

The blizzard rolled across the Canadian River and blew unabated for almost eighteen hours.

Kim Wingate knew that he would never spend another night and day half so miserable. Throughout the blizzard, he and Deafy kept the rigs going, though they had to do all the work themselves, for the men refused to go into the weather and remained in the bunkhouse playing poker and drinking. Deafy growled and went from derrick to derrick. Kim worked until he was ready to drop from cold and fatigue.

But the rigs ran.

During December and January, the erratic Texas weather plied itself with vigor. The cold, raw winds whipped, and the sun shone by intervals. Through it all, Kim and Deafy worked endlessly. But a change had come over Deafy.

After the Thanksgiving dinner at the Beatenbows, he found it necessary to leave the rig two or three nights a week, supposedly to go to town. At first Kim was apprehensive, lest Deafy drink too much as was his custom. But, strangely, Deafy never seemed drunk when he returned to the rig. And there was a mellowness about him. Kim discovered the reason when Finch visited the rig a couple of weeks later.

Finch dismounted from his horse and squatted to talk. Kim and Deafy sat on a rig timber.

"Why don't you go over and check that calf wheel on rig four, Kim?" Deafy was anxious to be rid of Kim.

"All right, Deafy," Kim said. He was content to let the old fellows enjoy their own company.

"Kim," Finch said as Kim started to leave, "Mandy said to tell you and Wendy to come out to eat dinner next Sunday when Deafy comes."

Kim looked at Deafy in astonishment, then grinned wickedly at him. Deafy looked quickly away.

"Perhaps we can, Finch," Kim said. "Thank Mandy for the invitation anyway."

Finch simply nodded.

"So that's where you have been going two or three nights a week," Kim said accusingly that night as he and Deafy sat on their bunks.

Deafy nodded sheepishly. Kim ribbed him for a few minutes before they blew out the kerosene lamp.

Deafy tossed and turned on his bunk after the shack was darkened. Kim knew that he had something to say, but he gleefully refrained from helping him say it.

"Kim," Deafy said tentatively.

"Yeah, Deafy?"

"Mandy sure is pretty, ain't she?"

"She sure is, Deafy," Kim said heartily.

As the icy fingers of winter wrapped themselves about the Panhandle plains, the relentless grip of crime and vice tightened on the oil town. Businesses, without exception, paid to operate. Murders were no longer newsworthy. Law enforcement officers who would not cooperate with the crime syndicate openly defied death. Across the nation, concern was growing. The attention of the Governor of Texas was repeatedly drawn to the boom town.

But through it all, elements of respectability clung tenaciously. Churches stayed open, and the school continued to operate. Each morning a parent, armed with a shotgun, called for Wendy Terrell and escorted her to school. In the afternoon, another escorted her home. Wendy liked the job and became absorbed in it. She enjoyed the children and felt that she was doing something worthwhile. They in turn loved her without restriction. It was a satisfying thing for her.

Wendy was restless, however. She had, quite unintentionally but completely, fallen in love with Kim Wingate. She kept fervently hoping that Kim would get his fill of the oil fields and go on with his school work. And Wendy, though she was a woman in love, was torn by her self-promised vow never to marry an oil man. It was a hectic, raw life, and Wendy had had her fill of it. She had long ago determined that her children would not have to endure the life she had lived. Nor had Kim ever declared his love for her.

She wondered if he did love her. If so, would he quit the fields if she asked him.

At one moment she was glad to learn she could be in love. At the next, she doubted if Kim loved her and was too proud to admit she loved without her love being returned. She was anxious to see him and disturbed when he left. But she hid all this very carefully under a cover of casual gaiety. Kim did not know how much tension he left within Wendy.

The days were long for Maria while Wendy was at school and Blake was in the fields. She became more and more bored with her lot. Occasionally she was able to coax Claude Butler to take her into camp while Blake was away.

The cat and mouse game she played with Butler was one of her few diversions. It had taken her weeks to light desire in those dead-pan eyes. But Mr. Butler, too, had proved to be only human. Now he had to hide his eyes from Blake Terrell when his wife was around. Maria was gratified. And when Butler was not available, she also delighted in provoking her husband's vicious, animal-like bodyguard, Joe Shay.

Blake, happily, was unaware of Maria's diversions. He had long since assumed that the inscrutable lawyer had no feeling for women. And Maria's attitude toward Joe only amused him.

The days passed swiftly for Blake. He went about his business of acquiring land for lease and in bringing more rigs to the fields.

Always at his heels was the evil shadow of Joe Shay. Occasionally Blake gave Joe a night off. When he did, Joe went into town and got hilariously drunk. Inevitably he got in a fight, and more often than not, he wound up his drunken orgies by going "nigger huntin.'' His hatred for Negroes was like a disease, and when he was drunk, he could not control his maniacal inclinations.

But Blake was not concerned with Joe's behavior.

Only two things galled him. He was unable to tell people that he actually owned the lease and the four rigs that Deafy Jones and Kim Wingate were running. He knew that if he did, Deafy would quit. He didn't want that, for that lease was making money, and good drillers were almost impossible to get. He had to content himself with having everyone think that Oschner really owned the lease.

And neither he, nor anyone else, had been able to acquire the Beatenbow ranch for drilling. Old Granny Beatenbow sat in her rocking chair in front of her fireplace and bided her time. Blake chafed, and there was absolutely nothing he could do. But he would get that lease! He had to! It had become a symbol of success to him. If legal means failed, he was prepared to resort to other means—and there were many.

Throughout the winter months, Finch visited Deafy regularly. Finch became almost talkative. He asked endless questions about the machinery, and Deafy was always glad to explain. They talked for long hours and drank coffee in the shack when the weather was cold, and Deafy continued to be absent from the rig two or three nights each week. He no longer even made a pretense of heading for town. And he bought some patent leather, low quarter shoes.

In March the winds suddenly switched from the north to the southwest and an occasional sunny, warm day brought welcome relief from the long, cold winter. In mid-March Finch came to the rig and offered the heartening news that Granny Beatenbow had predicted an early, wet spring. It would begin to rain before the month was out, she said, though the rains didn't usually come until mid-April.

Kim fervently hoped that she was right. He was tired of looking at the brown, barren land. It would mean, too, that he and Wendy could resume their picnics.

It had been a long winter for him. Countless cold, windy nights he had spent hours in the tarpaper bunkhouse watching the men play poker and listening to their vulgar jokes and raucous laughter. He half wished that Deafy would resume his sprees in town so they could go in together. Now, even carrying a gun, a man alone was not safe in Borger.

And Kim had time to think. Kim believed that at long last he was becoming a real man. He knew he was harder physically. He had learned to work hard and enjoy it. He took pleasure in doing a man's job and doing it well. And he felt that he was more able to handle whatever the future held in store for him.

The fact that he had been able to cope with the oil field had given him a confidence badly needed. He even toyed with the idea of succumbing to his old boyhood dream and studying medicine. But his thoughts were always inconclusive and, inevitably, he went to sleep thinking of Wendy Terrell.

The last week of March found Kim looking hopefully at the bleak, Texas sky in search of rain clouds. They began to appear about noon on Saturday, just before he and Deafy started in to pick up the payroll.

As they drove toward town, the rain clouds in the southwest darkened and moved closer. Lightning flashed, and thunder growled. Kim had intended to see Wendy while they were in town, but by the time they arrived, the rain was beginning to fall. They decided it best to pick up the payroll and get it back to the rigs.

The money was counted, and Deafy stuck it inside his shirt. The rain was falling in torrents as they emerged from the payroll shack. They hurried to their pick-up truck and drove down the muddy street. The knife-like tires cut deep in the grime, but as soon as they were on the grass tufts of the prairie, the pick-up gained speed. Still the rain increased in velocity, and it was difficult to see through the windshield. Kim was soaked by rain coming through the curtains.

They were perhaps two miles from the rigs when the motor of the truck began spitting, missed fire, and finally died. The water had soaked the wiring, and both Kim and Deafy knew that it was useless to try to start it again before it had a chance to dry out. That possibility was bleak, for the rain continued torrentially.

A half hour later, they decided to walk the rest of the way and deliver the money to the crews.

They dismounted from the truck and started sloshing through the rain and mud. Just before they came to Dixon creek, Kim heard a peculiar roaring sound. Then they topped a rise before it and stopped to stare in amazement. The usually dry creek was running bank full with muddy water. Cottonwood trees had been uprooted and swung down the swiftly moving current. The stream was thirty feet wide and moving with the speed of a locomotive.

"Now what?" Kim asked in awe.

Deafy didn't answer. He stood looking at the roaring creek. Then he turned and looked back toward town. The rain had almost stopped.

"I might be able to swim it," Kim ventured.

"You might," Deafy said. "But you ain't going to try. Look at them cottonwoods. You would land in the Canadian river before you even got started."

"But what are we going to do?" Kim asked.

"I dunno," Deafy admitted glumly. "Maybe it'll go down. We got to get this money to the crews. They'll want to gamble in the bunkhouse even if they can't come to town. And if we don't get the payroll to them, it will give a bunch of them an excuse to quit. We need every man. We got a well that's apt to blow, anytime."

Kim nodded, then added, "Well, I wish it would hurry and go down. I don't like to be standing around out here with all this money."

"I don't like it either," Deafy said. "But I don't know what we can do about it."

"Let's walk up and down a bit. Maybe we can find a real narrow place and jump across."

"This is as narrow as anyplace," Deafy said. "They ain't a bit of use to fret, Kim. We just got to wait. It's still an hour before sundown."

"Maybe we could—"

"There's Finch!" Deafy yelled suddenly. He started waving his hat.

Kim looked. Finch was riding down a ridge toward the creek. He was on the big, black stallion that Mandy had been riding the first time they came to the rig. Finch had seen them and was loping the horse toward them. As he neared the creek, his horse shied and pawed nervously. Finch spurred him to the opposite bank.

"What are you doin' out in this?" Deafy yelled to Finch. There was a broad grin on his face.

"Lookin' for strays," Finch ventured. "Looks like I found a couple."

"You sure have," Deafy yelled.

Kim thought that Deafy and Finch were acting like a couple of school kids as they bantered back and forth across the flooded creek. They had to yell to make themselves heard above the roar of the flood.

"Hey, Finch," Deafy yelled. "You couldn't come over here and tote me and Kim across, could you?"

"Too swift!" Finch yelled. "That creek would knock a horse down the minute he hit it but you can walk across by morning. The grass is short. It will run off in a hurry."

"Hey, Kim!" Deafy exclaimed suddenly. "I got a idea. Where is your pay book?"

"In the shack," Kim said, "on the table. Why?"

Deafy didn't answer Kim. Instead he yelled at Finch.

"Hey, Finch! Could you tie one of your saddle bags on your rope and throw it across the creek?"

"I could," Finch said. "But I won't try to pull you across. If you didn't drown, one of them trees floating down would kill you."

"I don't want to cross," Deafy said. "I just want you to take some money to the rigs and pay our crew. Kim's pay book is on the table, and it's got each man's name in it and how much he's got coming. Reckon you could do that?"

Finch considered a moment. "Reckon I could."

He began to loosen the lariat rope tied to the pommel of his saddle. Then he took one of his saddle bags and tied it to the end of the rope.

"Put your slicker in it and throw it, too," Deafy yelled. "Won't hurt you none to get yourself a bath while you are at it. I'll wrap the money in the slicker."

Finch grinned affably and said nothing, but he pulled off the slicker and stuffed it into the saddle bag.

It took two throws before Kim was able to grab the saddle bag. Then Deafy pulled the money from his shirt and wrapped it carefully in the slicker. He placed the slicker in the saddle bag and buckled the bag securely.

"Pull 'er across," he yelled.

Finch hauled on the rope. The horse shied as it snaked across the creek, but Finch held him firmly and drew the bag to him.

"They's ten thousand dollars in the bag, Finch," Deafy yelled zestfully. "You be careful of it and don't buy yourself nothing on the way to the rigs."

Finch merely grinned.

"Kim and me will be out as soon as this creek goes down enough to cross. You wait for us in the shack and have the coffee pot boiling. And don't pay nobody until he comes off his shift. It's marked on Kim's book."

Finch nodded and grinned again as he turned the big black and headed toward the rigs. The horse slipped and slid on the rocks and mud as he pulled himself up the red clay hill.

"Old Finch!" Deafy exclaimed affectionately. He was as delighted as a child that he had been able to ask his friend to do him a favor. And Finch had been equally pleased that he could do something for Deafy.

"Do you think he will be safe, Deafy?" Kim asked. He suddenly was having misgivings about Finch carrying so much money.

"Sure, he'll be all right," Deafy said with conviction. "They ain't a hi-jacker in Hutchinson County that could catch Finch on that black stud horse. Fact is, they wouldn't think about him having no money, anyhow."

"Well, I sure hope so," Kim said dubiously.

"No use worrying about old Finch!" Deafy said reassuringly. "He can take care of things. Let's go in and get us some supper."

"Do you think we should?"

"Oh, sure. This creek won't be down until near morning, Finch said. We'll go in and eat and then come back around midnight. Finch'll be in the shack."

It took them almost an hour to walk back to town. They went to the Whitespot cafe and ordered supper. The sad faced Negro that Kim had noticed so many times was washing dishes in the greasy water behind the counter. After they had finished eating, Deafy took a chew of tobacco. Kim had not seen Deafy so lighthearted since he had known him.

"You going to see Wendy, Kim?" Deafy asked.

"I don't think so, Deafy," Kim said. He didn't know why, but he had a feeling that he should stay with Deafy.

"Let's go gamble," Deafy said.

"All right."

Neither Kim nor Deafy had much money, and it took them less than three hours to lose most of it. Deafy did not take a drink, though he bought several for others. It was almost midnight when they came back to the Whitespot to have another cup of coffee before starting back to the rigs. It had been a pleasant evening for Kim though he would have much preferred spending it with Wendy. Still, he enjoyed the excitement and brawling of the town. He had seen little of it in the past months. They sat sipping silently on their coffee whem some men entered the cafe. They were muddy and water soaked.

"There they are!" one yelled accusingly.

Kim looked. The men were pointing toward him and Deafy. It took a second for him to recognize them as two of their crew.

"Where's our money?" one of them yelled.

"Cough up, or we're all quitting," the other added.

Deafy looked at the men in disbelief as they walked toward them threateningly.

"What happened, Deafy?" Kim whispered excitedly.

Deafy rose and met the men halfway. "You ain't got your money?" he asked in alarm.

"You know damned well we ain't," one of the men snarled. "I seen Oschner, and he said you and Wingate was bringing it out. He's looking for you, too."

"Come on, Kim!" Deafy headed for the door.

"Hold on!" one man snarled. "You ain't leaving here till we get our money."

"You'll get your damned money!" Deafy shouted and jerked the man's hand from his shoulder. "Come on, Kim. Something's happened to Finch!"

Kim had to run to keep up with Deafy as he went out the cafe door. Deafy didn't slow down as they started across the prairie toward the rigs. It was less than half an hour later that they arrived at the creek crossing where they had given Finch the money. The creek was lower, but it still looked dangerous to Kim. Deafy did not even hesitate. He sloshed in and started wading across. Kim hurried after him. They had to support each other as they neared the middle of the stream, for the current was still swift.

Frantically, they began scouring the area between the crossing and the rigs. The clouds had cleared, and a half moon furnished some light. In less than an hour they could see car lights coming from the town. Deafy paid not the least bit of attention. The cars came up to the crossing and stopped. Soon Kim could hear voices of men approaching. He yelled at them. Deafy continued walking.

The men arrived, and Kim was glad that Deafy had not waited, for they were Oschner and Blake Terrell accompanied by Joe Shay and Ralph.

Kim explained the situation briefly.

"Just like that damned Deafy Jones," Blake said angrily. "Thinks everybody is honest. That cowboy is half way to Amarillo by now. You'll never see that money again."

"No," Kim disagreed. "Something has happened to Finch. We've got to find him."

"Then you're looking in the wrong place," Blake said with disgust. "You'll find him with a woman, or in a gambling den."

"Well, I'm looking here until I know differently," Kim said and stalked away.

Kim was relieved to note that Oschner and Blake didn't leave. They needed all the help they could have to search the rough country. Soon other cars were pulling up to the crossing, and Kim heard other voices as men joined in the hunt. Kim found Deafy going down a rough arroyo and spoke to him.

"Others are helping, Deafy," he said encouragingly.

Deafy only nodded and continued his walking. His step was slower now, and Kim knew that he was tired. He started to accompany Deafy, but Deafy insisted that they stay apart so they could cover more country.

It was just beginning to break daylight when Kim found them. He first noted the torn ground above a small creek bank where a horse's hooves had slipped and pawed the ground. He rushed forward fearfully and looked over the bank. The big black horse lay on his side with his head twisted under him. Finch was still in the saddle, pinned under the horse. Kim yelled with all his might. He heard answering calls from the other searchers and hurried down the slippery bank.

In the bleak light of the breaking day. Finch looked like an emaciated elf. His hat was gone, and his bald head shone in the dim light. Mud caked his face, and his eyes were closed. Kim was sure he was dead, but he bent and spoke to Finch. Finch slowly opened his eyes. Kim breathed a sigh of relief just as he heard someone rush to the bank above. He looked to see Deafy, Oschner, and Blake Terrell.

"Did you find the money?" Blake yelled as Deafy slid down the clay bank. Kim didn't answer.

"Are you hurt bad, Finch?" Deafy croaked, for his breath was coming in gasps.

Finch grinned feebly as Deafy lifted his head from the mud. Deafy awkwardly brushed the mud away with his bare hand.

"Let's lift the horse off of him," Kim said hurriedly.

"Not just yet," Finch's voice was still soft, but it was weak. "I need a cigarette."

Kim hurriedly produced a cigarette and lit it. Finch took it in his mouth. It seemed to revive him a bit.

"You hurt bad, Finch?" Deafy asked again.

"I sure am, Deafy," Finch whispered. "Got a saddle horn in my belly and a leg busted. The stud boogered and fell. Told Mandy she ought not to ride him. Broke his neck. He was a good horse."

"We'll get you out from under him," Kim said again.

"What about the money?" Blake yelled from above. When he got no answer, he slid down the bank beside them. He did not so much as glance at Finch but hurriedly looked about for the saddle bag. He found it, and instantly he and Oschner started opening it.

"That fellow thought I stole the money, didn't he, Deafy?" Finch almost whispered and smiled feebly.

Deafy nodded his head in the affirmative.

"What you reckon he thought I'd do with ten thousand dollars!" Finch said almost in wonder.

"Deafy," Kim said desperately, "let's—"

But a glance from Deafy silenced Kim. "Let Finch finish his cigarette, Kim," he said quietly. He was still holding Finch's head in his hands.

Everything was quiet for a moment except for the rustling of Blake and Oschner pawing through the saddle bag. Then Finch groaned and let the cigarette fall from a big, rope calloused hand.

"Much obliged for the cigarette, Kim," he said in a low voice. "You fellows might as well try to lift this horse off of me, I reckon."

Kim hastened to get a hold of the saddle and started to lift with all his might. He heard another low groan from Finch. Deafy hadn't moved.

"It ain't no use, Kim," Deafy said in a choked voice.

Kim looked at Deafy. He knew the answer even before he looked at Finch again. Deafy let Finch's head down into the mud again. Finch was dead.

"Well, you're lucky ever to see that money again," Blake Terrell's voice was like a fingernail scratching on a rough surface.

Kim was almost hypnotized as he stared at Deafy Jones! Anger and pain were plain to see in the weatherbeaten old face. The hard, cold light of a breaking day glistened on a tear as it welled from Deafy's good eye and coursed down the crevassed cheek.

Suddenly, Deafy stood and glared at Blake Terrell. For a moment, neither said anything. Deafy raised a big, calloused hand as though to strike Blake. Then he slowly dropped it to his side.

"You goddamned fool!" he said chokingly. Then he turned and walked away. His shoulders drooped.

They buried Finch in the Beatenbow cemetery just above the ranch house. After the funeral Deafy worked harder than ever, and he had little to say to anyone. He did not mention Finch again. Kim wanted to say or do something that would ease the hurt in Deafy, but he knew there was nothing.

But Deafy continued his visits to the Beatenbow ranch. Kim no longer ribbed Deafy about being absent from the rigs so much. He was grateful that Deafy had some interest other than drinking and working.

They were going about their business of checking the rigs on the day of April first when a man drove up to the shack in a new *Reo Royale* roadster. The car was bright yellow in color. The man in it seemed unduly excited. He started toward Kim and Deafy in a trot. Deafy halted the man a few feet away and demanded his business.

"Oschner wants to see you in town," the man gasped. "Right now. Says it's important."

"You tell Oschner to go to hell!" Deafy growled. "I got to get the night shift started."

"He told me to bring you and Wingate into town," the man said tightly. "Didn't say what it was about, but I heard today that the Texas Rangers was coming in to clean up Borger."

The news caused Deafy to stop and ponder a moment.

"Maybe we'd better go in, Kim," Deafy said solemnly.

"Maybe we had," Kim said.

"Me and Kim will get the night shift started," Deafy told the man. "And then we'll come into town and eat. You meet us at the Whitespot cafe at dark."

"We ain't got time," the man said desperately. "Mr. Oschner told me to hurry."

"Well, we got time," Deafy said crossly. "Me and Kim ain't et since breakfast, and we ain't errand boys for Oschner. Tell him if he wants to see us sooner, then he can come out here."

The man evidently realized that it was useless to argue with Deafy, for he left hurriedly.

After checking in the night shift, Kim and Deafy bathed in the pop-off steam spout and went to the shack to don clean clothing. The steady grind of the rigs was audible in the twilight. A star in the west was beginning to show, and the lonely howl of a coyote was answered by another.

"What do you suppose Oschner is so anxious to see us about, Deafy? Do you know?"

"Ain't sure," Deafy said noncommittally.

"Must be pretty important for Oschner to pull both of us off the rigs."

"It's important, all right."

"Then you do know what it is about."

"I said I ain't sure," Deafy repeated. "But I been hearing for a month that the Rangers is coming in to clean up Borger. That means a lot of changes is going to take place."

"Do you think the Governor will really send the Rangers here?" Kim asked as he remembered what Wendy had said about her father's visit to Austin.

"That's what I hear," Deafy said.

"But—what has that got to do with us?"

"Maybe nothing. Maybe plenty," Deafy said without looking at Kim. Then he added enigmatically, "Mandy told me a month ago that her mother decided to let the Beatenbow lease go to a neighbor that has turned oil driller. Man named Patton."

Kim looked at Deafy with a puzzled frown. Deafy's mind occasionally ran in strange patterns. "I still don't see any connection,
Deafy."

"Blake and Oschner is hooked up some way," Deafy said with
conviction. "And if Blake has found out that old lady Beatenbow has
decided to give that lease to somebody else, then he's going to do
something about it. And he'll make his move quick, before the
Rangers come. Them Rangers is tough law men, so I hear."

Kim stirred uneasily. Deafy Jones was an extremely perceptive
person, and Kim wished heartily that he had told Deafy that they
were actually working for Blake through Oschner as soon as he had
found it out. It was too late now. He hoped that Deafy never would
find it out. If he did, Kim had no idea what his reaction might be.

"I don't see what the Rangers have to do with all this."

Deafy's only reply was an unintelligible grunt, and Kim knew that
it was useless to question him further. There was something strange
about Deafy tonight, and Kim had the very definite feeling that there
was soon to be some sort of culmination of things. It had been
building for a long time—ever since Wendy had told him that Oschner
was actually working for Blake. Kim wished fervently that he had
not deceived Deafy Jones!

They finished dressing and went outside to make a last check of
the rigs. Everything seemed in order. They got in the pickup and left
for town.

The man who had come to their rig earlier in the day was waiting
at the Whitespot cafe. Impatience was written all over him.

"You men ready to go?" he asked quickly as Deafy and Kim
walked in.

"We ain't et yet," Deafy said.

"You can eat after the meeting," the man said in exasperation. "It
won't last long."

"We'll eat now." Deafy did not even look at the man as he moved
toward two vacant stools at the counter. Kim and Deafy sat down.
There was not another vacant stool; so the man had to stand behind
them.

"All right," the man said crossly. "But hurry it up. Oschner give
me hell for not bringing you back this afternoon."

Neither Deafy nor Kim replied but gave their orders to the sad
faced Negro waiter behind the counter. The man behind them
fidgeted for fifteen minutes while Kim demolished a huge steak and
Deafy his usual two bowls of chili.

"All right," the man behind them gritted. "You've got your belly
full. Now let's go."

"Soon as we have another cup of coffee," Deafy said complacently and shoved his cup toward the waiter.

Suddenly the man behind them lost his patience. He reached and
grabbed Deafy by the shoulder and whirled him around. "Listen, you
old bastard," he said savagely, "Oschner sent me to bring you and
Wingate to that meeting, and I aim to bring you if I have to drag you
both."

Deafy's eye blazed, and he started to rise from the stool, but Kim
was ahead of him. He grabbed the man by the collar.

"You're not taking me and Deafy Jones any place that we don't
want to go," Kim said in a tense voice as he twisted the man's collar.
"And if you touch either one of us again, I'll break your jaw."

The belligerence went out of the man. "All right," he whined.
"But you guys are holding up a million dollar deal, and Oschner is
mad as hell. If you don't show up pretty soon, he's going to send a
bunch of his tough guys after you."

"Oschner won't send anyone after Deafy and me, unless he knows
we want to come," Kim said levelly. "Now you go over there and
stand by that door until we are ready to leave." Kim gave the man a
shove.

Deafy's one good eye had opened wide in surprise when Kim
grabbed the man. He stared for a moment, and then a gleam of pure
pleasure replaced the surprise, and his hard, old face softened.

Kim sat back down on the stool beside Deafy. Deafy's amazement
at his actions had been no greater than his own. But when the man
had grabbed Deafy, Kim felt as if a spring had suddenly been released
in him.

"This here sure is good coffee, ain't it, Kim?" Deafy said blandly,
as he poured some in his saucer and blew gustily.

"Sure is," Kim agreed. Then he and Deafy grinned at each other.

They finished their coffee and prepared to leave. The man was
waiting by the door.

"Follow me," the man said and walked out of the cafe. His car
was waiting.

Kim had wondered vaguely where the meeting was to be. They got
in the car, and the driver headed north, up Main street. Kim was
again surprised at the growth that had taken place. There were even
more cars and people than the last time he had been in camp, and the
street was longer. There were more gambling dens and dance halls
than ever.

Near the end of the street, the driver pulled over to the curb.
"That's the place." He nodded toward a long frame building.

A light showed dimly through the small, heavily curtained window in the front of the building. The driver of the car got out and walked hurriedly to the door. He knocked. He was a few steps ahead of Kim and Deafy, and he waited. The door hadn't opened when they walked up. It was several seconds before Kim heard a bolt slide.

"Come in," a voice called.

Deafy stepped back quickly and looked at the driver suspiciously. "How come you knocked, if they was expecting us?"

"I always knock," the driver said quickly.

"Like hell you do," Deafy growled. "And how come that door was locked, and it took them so long to open it?"

"How the hell should I know?" the driver said irritably. "I done what they told me to do." With that he hurried toward his car and drove away.

Deafy looked at the vanishing car and then again at the doorway. He seemed to be debating with himself. It was one of the few times Kim had seen him show indecision. Then, as was characteristic of him, he made up his mind with no words to explain or justify. His hand slipped inside his coat, and he spat a stream of tobacco juice noisily.

"All right, Kim," he said grimly. "Let's go."

Deafy opened the door quickly with his left hand and stepped into the room. Kim was only a step behind.

"Good evening, gentlemen," Claude Butler's smooth voice greeted them.

Kim looked quickly about. The room was long and narrow. A curtain partitioned the front from the back. Kim surmised, correctly, that the back part of the building was Butler's sleeping quarters and the front part his office. There was a long table with chairs lined on either side of it.

Butler was leafing through some papers. Next to him sat two men who were obviously thugs though they wore expensive clothing. One had an enormous diamond stick pin in a loud tie. Kim had seen him several times at the Double Six. Next to Oschner sat Ralph.

"Come in, Deafy," Oschner said. "We've been expecting you. How are you, Kim?"

Deafy and Kim only nodded to Oschner. They were looking at Butler.

"This is Mr. Butler," Oschner said. "He's a lawyer. These are the drillers I was telling you about, Mr. Butler. Name of Jones and Wingate." He made no pretense of introducing the others.

"I've had the pleasure of meeting these gentlemen before," Butler said suavely. "How do you do."

Deafy didn't acknowledge anything. Kim only nodded. The situation was not at all to his liking.

"Ain't you the lawyer that does Blake Terrell's paper work?" Deafy asked Butler abruptly.

"I have many interests, Mr. Jones," Butler admitted. "Won't you gentlemen be seated." He waved toward chairs.

Kim looked questioningly at Deafy. He had the distinct feeling that they had walked into a trap. Deafy's face showed no expression whatever. He was silent a moment, and then he slouched toward a chair and sat. Kim did likewise.

"I asked you men to come into town because I had some important business I wanted to talk over with you," Oschner said in what he intended to be a genial voice.

"We got that impression from the man you sent to bring us in," Deafy said noncommittally. His good eye was focused on Butler.

"Well," Oschner continued jovially, "I suppose we might as well get to it."

"Might as well," Deafy admitted.

"Gentlemen," Butler began in smooth tones. "Mr. Oschner has recently retained me to see after his business interests. Mr. Oschner plans to expand a great deal in the near future, and I have advised him to put all relations with employees on a business-like basis. I'm sure that you gentlemen will agree that such an arrangement can only be to the advantage of all concerned." He paused.

"Go on, Butler," Kim said quietly. It was obvious that they were dealing with Butler, not Oschner. Butler's eyes flicked to Kim, and there was a trace of annoyance in them. He had been concentrating on Deafy, and he did not welcome the distraction. But his eyes did not rest on Kim. They flashed back to Deafy almost immediately. Deafy sat immobile.

"When a man becomes er—substantial," Butler continued, "It then is increasingly important for him to conduct his affairs in a business-like way. It is to the mutual benefit of both employer and employee to have legal arrangements."

"I keep thinking you are trying to say something, Butler," Deafy said calmly.

"Perhaps I am putting it badly, Mr. Jones," Butler replied in a humble voice. "I know that you are a direct man. I, too, will be direct. Mr. Oschner and I have information, from an unimpeachable source, that the Texas Rangers will move into Borger within a week. That means that crime in this city will go underground, at least for a while. But it also means that the lawless element will range the fields more and more. The Rangers cannot possibly police the entire county, and a great many drillers have been so unfortunate as to have their drilling rigs stolen. In fact, Mr. Oschner has informed me that you and Mr. Wingate are among the few drillers in the field that have not been molested."

"We ain't been bothered," Deafy admitted.

"That means," Butler continued almost expansively, "that you are worth a great deal of money to Mr. Oschner. In view of that, I have convinced Mr. Oschner that you are worth more money than he is paying you. He has agreed to raise your wages and sign a contract to that effect."

"Well, now," Deafy said mildly. "That sure does sound like you have our interests at heart."

Kim looked at Deafy and tried to read his face. Was Deafy being deceived by such talk? Or was he simply playing a game of subterfuge with Butler? Kim wished he could be sure. He glanced uneasily at the curtained partition of the room. He had a feeling that Blake Terrell might be behind that curtain. Ralph saw Kim's uneasy glance and smiled thinly.

"I was sure that you would see it that way, Mr. Jones," Butler approved. "In fact, I was so confident that I already have the contract drawn up."

"Well, now, ain't that fine?" Deafy said as the lawyer handed him a piece of paper. He only glanced at the paper and handed it to Kim. "What does it say, Kim?"

Every eye in the room turned to Kim as he read the document. It was cleverly worded, but there was no question of what it said. Kim pitched it back on the lawyer's desk. "It says that Oschner will pay us a hundred and fifty dollars a tower to work for him as long as we are in the fields, Deafy," Kim said.

"Well, now ain't that fine," Deafy repeated again.

"There's more to it than that, Deafy," Kim said. "It also stipulates that we are to work for that sum so long as we operate in this county. And that as long as we are here, we can't work for anyone else. That means Oschner could drill for anybody, and we would have to work for him—or leave this county."

"Well, that sounds pretty good to me!" Deafy said. "I sort of doubt if anybody else would pay us that kind of money."

"But, Deafy!" Kim was suddenly irritated at Deafy. He had played the game long enough! "This sort of thing is ridiculous. Besides, I think it violates some law."

"I can assure you that it is a perfectly legal document, Mr. Wingate," Butler spat at Kim.

"I don't care if it is," Kim said. "It just isn't the thing to do."

"Why, Kim," Deafy said. "It sounds reasonable to me."

"All right, Deafy," Kim said resignedly. "I hadn't wanted to tell you—but Oschner is Blake Terrell's man. We've been working for Blake all along."

Oschner gasped audibly when Kim made his announcement, and the bodyguards stirred. Butler looked at Kim appraisingly. Kim could have sworn there was relief in Deafy's eye when he looked at him.

"Mr. Oschner," Claude Butler said softly, looking at Kim, "I think perhaps you and Mr. Terrell have made the mistake of under-estimating Mr. Wingate."

"Well, what the hell!" Oschner blustered after he had recovered from his surprise at Kim's statement. "What difference does it make who they're working for. They're making more money than any drillers in the field."

"And we're worth it," Kim shot back.

Deafy didn't say a word.

"I didn't say you wasn't worth it," Oschner almost shouted. "But if you have any sense, you will go along with this deal. Kincaid has quit Terrell, and he needs men bad. He's going to get that Beatenbow lease, and that means that you and Deafy will have a job for years. You'll get rich. All of us will!"

At the mention of the Beatenbow lease, Deafy perked up again.

"Terrell isn't going to get that Beatenbow lease," Kim said firmly. "A cowman named Patton is going to get it."

"You are sure of that, are you, Mr. Wingate?" Butler's eyes were faintly amused as he looked at Kim.

"I am," Kim stated flatly, but he looked at Deafy uncertainly.

"Information comes from one of them unimpeachable sources," Deafy agreed pleasantly.

"Gentlemen," Butler leaned back in his chair and started rubbing the gold coin gently. "It pains me a great deal to disillusion you. But Mr. Patton is not going to get that lease."

Deafy suddenly sat up straighter in his chair and leaned toward the lawyer. Gone was his air of unconcern. "Why is Patton not going to get that lease, Mr. Butler?"

Kim had never heard Deafy use the term mister before. It sent a cold chill along his neck, and suddenly the smoke in the room turned to icy fog. Evidently, the lawyer didn't feel the change—or didn't care. But the rest of the men in the room stirred uneasily. Kim looked grim. The bodyguards let their hands stray to coat pockets. Oschner frowned.

"Why, Mr. Butler?" Deafy repeated his question.

"Well, Mr. Jones," the lawyer blew a ring of cigar smoke toward the ceiling. "It seems that Mr. Patton—"

"Shut up, Butler!" Oschner shouted. "Don't tell them a damned thing. Terrell will raise hell. They already know more than they got any business knowing."

"Mr. Oschner," There was a hint of contempt in Butler's voice. "We have already underestimated these gentlemen once. I think that it would be unwise to do so again. Particularly in view of the fact that Mr. Wingate, at least, can read. The story will be in the *Hutchinson County Herald* tomorrow."

"I don't give a damn!" Oschner's face was red.

"You shut up, Oschner," Deafy growled ominously. "Go ahead, Butler."

"As you wish, Mr. Jones," Butler said with faint amusement as he leaned farther back in his chair. "It is a rather brief and sordid story. It seems that about two weeks ago, a gentleman from the east decided to go into the cattle business. He was fortunate enough to be able to purchase a section of land bordering that of Mr. Patton. He didn't get the oil rights, of course, but the land was rather cheap. He then stocked that land with some fine cattle. Those cattle suddenly began to disappear. Just yesterday, the county sheriff was led to Patton's barn where he discovered the fresh carcass of a beef and found the hide with the incriminating marking hidden under a stack of feed. Today Mr. Patton was charged with cattle stealing."

Butler paused for a moment; then he went on, "The concept of crime is a peculiar thing. And it is indeed unfortunate that such a man as Patton would stoop to it at his age. I have checked the criminal records of this county for the past year. Only one man has been sent to the penitentiary—and that was for stealing cows. So you see, Mr. Jones, I think it is safe to assume that Mr. Patton will not in the near future be interested in the Beatenbow lease."

Kim stared at Deafy, and his heart was sick. Surely Deafy must know that Patton had been the victim of a diabolical plot!

Deafy rolled his cud of tobacco about his cheek with his tongue. Then he looked at Butler. "You wouldn't happen to be the man that bought that section of land by Patton, would you, Butler?" Deafy asked quietly.

"Why, Mr. Jones," Butler said in mock surprise. "You are a very discerning man, indeed."

Deafy sat stone still for a moment. "You frog-eyed son-of-a-bitch!" Kim had never heard hatred in Deafy's voice before.

Anger flamed momentarily in Butler's dark eyes when Deafy hurled the epithet, and two hoodlums looked to him eagerly for a signal to exert their talents. But Butler didn't give the signal. With marvelous self control, he quickly veiled his eyes and smiled frostily.

"Your language is most expressive, Mr. Jones,'" he said icily.

"Just like folks to know what I'm thinking," volunteered Deafy. Kim grinned in spite of himself.

"That's enough of that," Oschner forced himself back into the conversation. "All we want from Jones and Wingate is their signature on this contract—and I aim to get it."

"Ah yes," Butler said. "We do seem to have strayed a bit from our primary objective. Perhaps we should get on with the business at hand."

Butler picked up the contract that Kim had tossed back on the desk, and the man with the diamond stickpin in his tie got up from his chair. Butler held the paper toward Deafy along with his gold-topped fountain pen.

"Let Kim sign first," Deafy said conversationally.

Kim looked at Deafy in amazement; then his amazement turned to anger. "I wouldn't sign that thing for all the oil in Borger!" he said furiously.

"I was just wondering!" Deafy said gently. "Let's go, Kim."

"Oh, no you don't!" Oschner yelled. "Not till you sign."

Deafy and Kim were almost to the door when the big thug with the diamond stickpin in his tie barred their way.

"You shut up Oschner," Deafy whirled on the man. "And move this goon to one side."

"The gentleman barring your way is my man, Mr. Jones," Butler said suavely. "And he will step aside when I tell him to."

Deafy's lips flattened against his teeth, and he spat tobacco juice on the floor. He looked like a lion at bay.

"Then tell him," Deafy said ominously.

"I shall be happy to when—"

But the lawyer never finished his sentence for Deafy Jones whirled and struck with one motion. Kim distinctly heard the blow and gathered his muscles to spring at Butler when Deafy's voice froze everyone in his tracks. Kim turned. The thug who had been barring the door was rolling on the floor with his face split open, and Deafy stood stolidly holding his shot-gun pistol.

"Any of the rest of you sons-of-bitches want some of the same thing, you just come and get it," invited Deafy.

Deafy's lightning fast movements had taken everyone by complete surprise, including Kim. Oschner's face was white, and his mouth hung open. Ralph's hand was still inside his coat. Butler had made no motion whatever. The sallow faced man who had been sitting beside him wore an expression of chagrin and anger.

"And I thought you were fast with a gun, Terrence!" Butler's well modulated tones expressed his amazement.

"But, Mr. Butler—!"

"Let's go, Kim," Deafy said disgustedly.

Deafy pointed the gun at the men as they stepped outside. They walked down the street without looking back.

"What do we do now, Deafy?" Kim asked.

"Right now, let's get a cup of coffee."

They walked in silence to the nearest cafe. The strains of "Baby Face" came from a record player in one of the dance halls and drifted over the prairie. The music was lost on Kim and Deafy.

They found a seat in the Whitespot and ordered coffee. The place was teeming with men, but Kim and Deafy were alone with their thoughts. They sipped for a few minutes in silence.

"Deafy," Kim said finally. "They're framing Patton, and we know it."

"Yep!" agreed Deafy. "And they're being damn smart about it. You can kill a man here and get away with it, but according to Finch, a Hutchinson County jury would send its grandma to the pen for stealing a cow."

"It's Blake Terrell's work," Kim said with conviction. "And I'm going to stop him."

Deafy looked at Kim with interest. "Just how do you figger on doing that, Kim?" he asked mildly.

"I don't know," Kim admitted. "But I'll do it if I have to figure out some way to frame *him.*"

"That wouldn't work, Kim," Deafy shook his head. "Blake would just send Joe Shay out to kill you. That Beatenbow lease has drove him plumb crazy. I knowed he was money hungry and mean, but I never did think he would send a man to the pen, or even kill one, just to get a lease. There's something about this place that's bringing out the worst in everybody, seems like."

"It sure does," Kim admitted feelingly. Then he added with finality, "But I don't intend to see an innocent man go to prison. It's ridiculous! Blake Terrell has to be stopped. If not for Patton's sake, then for Wendy's."

"I know how you feel, Kim," Deafy said wearily. "But it ain't your problem."

"It *is* my problem!" Kim said almost angrily. "If you think—"

"No, it ain't," Deafy interrupted Kim. "It's mine. I'll take care of it."

"But—but—" Kim sputtered. "You can't handle this by yourself!"

"Don't aim to," Deafy said. Then he added with a bit of pride in his voice, "Oil field folks may not be the best in the world, but they ain't all bad, either. I'll have help."

Kim felt both relieved and disturbed by Deafy's statement. He knew that he probably could not have aided Patton without help from someone. But he certainly didn't want to be left out, altogether.

"Well, I'm going to help, too," he said. "I'm an oil man the same as you are."

"No you ain't," Deafy said decisively. "It may be that I got to kill Blake. Hope not, but if I can't stop him the way I aim to, then he ought to be killed. Besides, you ain't a oil man. You didn't want to come to this camp in the first place. I almost wish you hadn't."

"Well, *I'm* not sorry," Kim said stoutly, "And I'm going to—."

"You're going to stay right here," Deafy said as he rose and pitched a coin on the counter. "I'll be back in an hour."

Before Kim could protest, Deafy had walked quickly from the cafe. Kim started to follow, but he knew it was no use. He sat heavily on a stool and ordered more coffee.

The slouch was gone from Deafy's step as he walked down the sidewalk. There was purpose and determination in his stride. He went directly to Sal's place. He was inside only a few minutes. When he emerged, Sal accompanied him. They got in the pickup truck and drove toward the Terrell house on the hill.

While Deafy was gone, Kim sat and drank the strong, black coffee. He didn't have a job now and he had no desire to get one. He was sick of the oil fields. As soon as Deafy returned he was going to Sal's and get his money. Then he was going to ask Wendy Terrell to go to California with him! There was no use putting it off any longer. She either loved him or she didn't! He should have done it long ago. Kim, in his rushing, turbulent thoughts failed to realize that Wendy might not know that he loved her. He would have assumed, if the question had ever occurred to him, that she knew it. There would have been no doubt about that in his mind.

He would miss Deafy! Anyone would miss the old reprobate! Deafy Jones had been a wonderful experience. But he couldn't hang onto Deafy's coat tail forever!

He was still making his plans when Deafy returned an hour later. Deafy's face was a pasty color beneath the dark brown stubble. His shoulders sagged and he looked sick.

"Deafy!" Kim exclaimed. "Did you kill him?" He dreaded Deafy's answer.

Deafy merely shook his head negatively. Kim breathed a sigh of relief.

"Did you—?"

"I'd just as lief not talk about it, Kim," Deafy said in a dull voice.

"I ain't proud of what I done. But I had to."

Kim had never seen Deafy look so tired and old. There was no fire left in him. He had no idea what Deafy had done to keep Blake from carrying out his nefarious scheme, but, Kim knew, he had accomplished his purpose.

Kim ordered fresh coffee. Deafy sat dejectedly. Kim wanted to do, or say, something that would erase some of the ache in his friend. But he could think of nothing.

"Whatever you did, Deafy," Kim said, "Blake Terrell had it coming to him. He is the most thoroughly wicked man I ever knew."

"No, he ain't, Kim," Deafy said almost sadly.

"He isn't what?" Kim asked in surprise.

"He ain't all bad. He's damned near it—but it ain't complete."

Kim was silent a moment as he considered Deafy's words.

"How long have you knowed we was working for him?"

"Since we brought in that first well. Wendy told me."

Deafy nodded. "I reckon I knowed it, too—but just wouldn't admit it. I reckon it ain't important."

They sat in silence for a few moments longer.

"What are we going to do now, Kim?" Deafy asked glumly.

Kim started to tell Deafy of his decision to leave, but he could not. Not right now.

"We will figure out something," Kim said, suddenly realizing that, like one shadow filtering through another, he had become the leader. It had been a subtle thing, but growing for weeks and months. Kim was no longer the boy and Deafy the man. Now the boy was a man—and the man was old. Deafy Jones needed Kim Wingate.

They sat in silence for a few minutes longer. The waiter asked them if they wanted whiskey. To Kim's surprise, Deafy shook his head negatively.

"How much money do we have now, Deafy?" Kim finally asked.

"Hell, Kim," Deafy said in surprise. "I don't know. Sal can tell us. She's still banking it."

Kim nodded. "Let's go into business, Deafy."

"What?" Deafy asked in surprise.

"You remember that little horse pasture Granny Beatenbow gave me the lease on?"

Deafy nodded and blew on his coffee.

"If I have it figured right, we have almost sixty thousand dollars cached with Sal. That's nearly enough to buy us a rig of our own."

"Damned if it ain't," Deafy admitted.

"Let's see if we can get together enough equipment to drill a well on it," Kim said enthusiastically.

Deafy considered the statement a moment. "Tell you what, Kim," he said finally. "I'll loan you my part of the money and work for you for nothing if you want to try it. We just might pull it off."

"Nope," Kim said emphatically, "it's full partners, or nothing."

"Then it's nothing," Deafy said flatly.

"But—why?" Kim asked with irritation. "You must have as much money as I do. More."

"It ain't that," Deafy said. "But if I went in partners, it ain't going to work out. I know that. It never has. But if I work for you, I figure it ought to be all right."

Kim looked at Deafy in astonishment. He knew that Deafy was thinking of his partnership with Blake Terrell.

"All right, Deafy," Kim said. "If you will lend me your money and work for nothing, I'll try it."

Suddenly Deafy grinned his brown toothed grin, "Well now, Kimmy me boy, you just hired yourself the best damned driller in Borger, Texas."

Kim laughed aloud and shook Deafy's hand. It was good to have Deafy himself again.

"One thing," Deafy said as they left the cafe.

"What's that?" Kim asked.

"You're the boss. Me—I'm just going to take orders."

"And I'll give plenty," Kim promised. He had forgotten his plans to leave Borger.

CHAPTER XI

The Texas Rangers, under order of Governor Dan Moody, moved into Borger early on the morning of April 4, 1927. They came by train. The town was expecting them. Reporters from the *Hutchinson County Herald* and from the Amarillo papers were on hand to meet them. Also on hand was a jeering mob of oil field ruffians who had not the perception to know that a reckoning was at hand.

The Rangers were comparatively few. The Captain spoke for a few minutes with some of the men who had made the trip to Austin seeking their help. But not another Ranger spoke to anyone. They were under orders, and they meant to carry them out. They were an impressive group of men, varying in size from very short to extremely tall. They were dressed in the traditional green uniforms, and their shirts bore the small badges designating their organization. Every man wore a gun plainly visible.

Quiet of eye and demeanor, they stood patiently while their Captain held conversation. They looked objectively at the group that had met them. The jeers of the riff raff, met by the cold, distant stares, turned to silence.

Upon completion of his conversation with the reception committee, the Captain turned to his men and in a quiet voice told them where their headquarters would be located. The Rangers silently gathered their gear and followed their Captain down the board sidewalks to the north. They looked neither right nor left. Their booted feet made strange, hollow sounds on the boards. To those who respected and obeyed the law, those footsteps were as reassuring as the sound of a mother's voice in a quiet, dark room. To the lawless, they were the harbingers of a fate long delayed.

The building that was to serve as their headquarters was a long, tar paper shack in which bunks had been installed. The men went silently into the shack and stored their gear. Then the captain closed the door, and they went into conference.

For five days, the Rangers emerged from their headquarters only to eat. They traveled in pairs, and they were uncommunicative. A local policeman acted as a messenger and escort for those with whom the Rangers wanted to talk. During those days, all the city officials were called to the Ranger headquarters. Having received the desired information from those men, the Rangers next interviewed many of the cowmen in the area, and also townsmen of known good repute.

Still the Rangers maintained their silence. The lawless looked and speculated. Uneasiness grew among them. A new and foreboding element had entered the boom town. The crime syndicate was non-plussed. They had not seen men like these before. Obviously, they were getting information about the town, but even when they emerged from their headquarters to eat, they seemed completely oblivious to the gambling, drinking, and other flagrant law violations about them.

The first two days, the criminals waited apprehensively. When no action was forthcoming, they grew irritable, restless, and finally belligerent. When the Rangers walked from the building to eat their meals, there was always a group of rowdies ready to hurl taunts and insults at them. The Rangers ignored them.

Early on the morning of the fifth day, the Rangers made their move. Every member of the Ranger force emerged from the head-quarters building early that morning. Each Ranger had a job to do, and he was authorized by the Governor of Texas to do it. There was no hurried or unnecessary activity. Each city official was called upon, and many of them were forced to resign immediately. The Rangers had men of their own selection available to fill the job.

By noon, the Rangers had rearranged the city administration to their satisfaction. Then they went to the gambling halls. All morning long, the rabble of the town had been watching the activities. Most did not believe that the relatively few Rangers would have the temerity to attempt to close down the violent town. Their optimism was short lived. The Rangers moved in. Slowly, surely, implacably. There was some resistance. The proprietor of one gambling establishment resorted to the only law that had been recognized before the Rangers' arrival. A steely eyed Ranger shot him through the heart before his shotgun had cleared the counter. Every other proprietor of gambling hall or bootlegging joint was put under arrest. A small group of men attacked two Rangers as they were taking one man to jail. In a matter of seconds, three of the hoodlums were lying in the street with bullet holes in them, though none was fatally shot.

By nightfall, the famous Borger "trotline" was filled with outraged and cursing men. They heaped vilification on the Rangers as they brought in more and more people. But the Rangers went stoically about their task. Additional chains and locks had to be installed. And still more and more arrests were made.

By sundown, it was evident that the epidemic of violence and crime had been halted. The tidal wave of raw emotions and unbridled human lust had finally run itself into the immovable obstacle of human goodness.

The Rangers ate in a group that night. They were a tired lot of men. They ate quietly and quickly. Then they went back to their headquarters. This day's work was done. Tomorrow was another day.

Throughout the night men gathered in small groups to talk in low voices. There was awe among them—and fear. What would come next? Bribery, threats and violence had failed against the Rangers. There must be a way.

But there was none. At sunrise the next morning, the Rangers appeared again. The Ranger Captain posted signs along the main street that every known violator of the law, bootleggers, dope peddlers, prostitutes, and gamblers must be out of town by sundown.

The evacuation edict brought new howls of protest. There was even some talk of open and concerted resistance. The Rangers began another day's work. Methodically and inexorably, they went about their business of enforcing the law. The relentless pressure made itself irresistible in a matter of hours. By noontime of the second day, every conceivable kind of vehicle was loaded with human beings of every description. The Rangers increased the pressure. A small crew of workmen, under the direction of the Rangers, started nailing boards across the doorways of the gambling dens.

The women offered the only resistance that the Rangers hesitated in meeting full force. The madams of the houses of prostitution screamed and raged, and finally begged. The Rangers consulted with their captain. That calm, quiet spoken man reiterated that no quarter would be given. The prostitutes would either leave Borger—or he would nail up the houses with the women inside.

Sal heard the news and started making preparations. She needed transportation, but she could find none. Not a man had entered her house since the Rangers had posted their signs, and Sal could not find anyone to send word to Deafy Jones. She waited. The Rangers got to her place just before noon. Sal offered no resistance. She gave her girls extra money, took her bag and walked into the street. People by the hundreds were scurrying by. None looked at Sal. Like a covey of quails fleeing from a hunter's gun, they were concerned only with their own safety. They had no time to help others.

With a sigh, Sal fell into the line of marching people. Most of them were headed southwest, toward Amarillo. That was as good a direction as any.

Wendy Terrell heard of the eviction notice during the lunch hour at school. The afternoon was interminably long. When her escort appeared to take her home that afternoon, she instructed him to take her by Sal's place. The house was closed, the windows and doors nailed tight.

Wendy was anxious about Sal. Wendy was only seven years old the first time she saw Sal. In a desolate and remote oil field camp, Wendy had been stricken with measles. The house keeper then employed by Blake to care for Wendy had refused to stay with her, and Blake brought Sal to their shack. Sal stayed with Wendy for almost a month, and during that time a strong friendship developed between them. Thereafter, Sal appeared at every oil camp the Terrells did. Wendy supposed that her business simply carried her to the various oil strikes that lured her father.

Blake even tried to get Sal to become their housekeeper on a permanent basis. But Sal refused. She had her own prosperous business, and she did not want to be dependent upon anyone. But she did arrange to be free during the daytime to be with Wendy. It was from Sal, one of the most famous of the oil field madams, that Wendy Terrell learned compassion and understanding.

Sal spent many hours with Wendy. They had been pleasant and wonderful hours for the lonely little girl. But, of course, such an arrangement could not last. When Blake felt that Wendy was old enough to understand Sal's business, he insisted that Sal not see Wendy any more. Sal left.

Actually, Blake had been a couple of years too late to serve his purpose of keeping Wendy from understanding Sal's business. Wendy already knew about Sal. She had never made any secret of it to Wendy, and Wendy was a precocious child. Sal usually maintained her establishments in the down-town areas of the fields. Frame buildings, or even tents, sufficed. And, unknown to Blake, Wendy had visited Sal's place several times.

Those trips had been wonderful, for they had filled a great vacant place in the hungry heart of a small girl. There were very beautiful ladies there, and they wore pretty clothes. They smelled wonderful. And they liked Wendy. She knew they did, for they had hugged and kissed her. Some of them even cried, and one gave her a bottle of perfume.

Once when she was there, her father came in. But one of the girls quickly hid Wendy, and soon her father left with another one of the ladies. He hadn't been looking for her anyway. But that was the last time Sal ever took her to her business house.

Wendy asked Sal about the pretty ladies, and Sal had explained. In the oil fields there just weren't enough ladies for all the men to have one, so a few of the women came to the oil fields, and the men took turns sleeping with them.

That had seemed like a very sensible arrangement to Wendy when she was seven. She didn't blame the men for wanting to sleep with those pretty ladies. They smelled so very good. Besides, she liked to sleep with Sal. Sal always held her close and made her feel warm, and safe, and wanted. She used to make believe that Sal was her own mother.

And now, at twenty-one, the thought of Sal always brought a twinkle to Wendy's eyes and a lump in her throat. She had learned many things from Sal. She had learned that some people were capable of many loves, and that some were capable of only one love. And she had learned that some unfortunates were not capable of loving anyone. Sal had said, too, that people did things that they really didn't want to do. She never could explain why, but Wendy had felt that she could understand. Once Sal had tried to explain to Wendy that people also needed things that they could not understand. If you were hungry, you knew what you needed, and food would satisfy you. If you were thirsty, you needed a drink, and that was easy to understand. But if a man needed a woman, the man didn't always understand that, but he needed her just the same.

"You mean, like me needing you, Sal?" Wendy had queried.

And Sal had laughed. Wendy loved to hear Sal laugh.

"What I really meant, honey, was like me needing *you.*"

Wendy couldn't believe that Sal needed anyone. She was so big, and so pretty, and so nice. And Sal liked people, and they liked her. The men who knew her seemed to almost respect her. And the girls who worked for her adored her. Incongruous and strange! Yet it was true.

And Sal had taught Wendy to respect honesty. She was an honest woman. Sal was an unusual woman! Wendy suspected, now, that prostitutes were among the most misunderstood women in the world. She knew that her father had never slept with Sal and for some reason was grateful to them both for it.

And now Wendy could understand that Sal's desertion of her business during the daytime just to be with her when she was small had been a real sacrifice. For even then prostitution flourished around the clock in the oil fields. Wendy also knew that many had condemned her for her friendship with Sal. But she was not concerned with what others thought; she was concerned that a person who had befriended her when she needed friendship was in trouble.

The night that Deafy and Kim decided to drill a well on the Beatenbow land, they went to Sal's place and got enough of their money to buy a small truck. Then they set out for the fields to try to find enough used equipment to assemble a rig. The trip proved a vacation for Deafy and a revelation to Kim. Deafy had many friends among the drillers, and they were of a caliber that Kim had not seen in the oil field before. They impressed him as being an honest, hard working lot of men. Kim began to realize that he had seen only the dregs in camp.

The men were glad to see Deafy. They talked for hours at each rig they visited, and they ate and slept with the crews. Deafy managed to bargain for used equipment at almost every rig. No money changed hands. They would pay when they got the equipment.

Only one thing marred the otherwise pleasant junket through the field. Both Kim and Deafy contracted gas eye as had many of the men they saw. The poisonous gas fumes, liberated from underground prisons by the drill bits, floated across the prairies. They infected the tender tissues of the eyes, causing them to swell and become very red and unsightly. They borrowed potatoes from cookshacks and made potato poultices to pack on their eyes at night. In two or three days the inflammation would subside, and no permanent damage would result. The infection was particularly painful for Deafy because his bad eye was also affected.

They had been scouring the field for nearly a week when they heard the news that the Rangers had arrived. But it was no concern of theirs, and they went on about their business of finding equipment. The day they found an engine that Deafy thought suitable, he announced that they had enough cast off equipment to construct a workable drilling rig. They headed back toward town in high spirits.

About a mile from town, Kim braked the truck to a stop and pointed. Deafy sat up straight in the seat beside Kim, and they stared in open mouthed amazement. A great mass of people was approaching. They came on foot, in trucks, cars, wagons—even on horseback. Kim started the truck and drove slowly toward the moving mass. When they were a few hundred yards away, Kim could recognize most of them as women. He drove closer and stopped the truck.

"What on earth is that, Deafy?" Kim asked.

Deafy spat tobacco juice. "I ain't got no idee, Kim," he said. "But it don't look like nothing I ever saw before."

As the mass of people approached, Kim and Deafy stared in astonishment and disbelief. There must be ten thousand people, Kim thought. As the leaders approached, Kim hailed one. He was a man on foot. His face was drawn and haggard, and he carried a cardboard suitcase.

"What on earth is this?" Kim asked in wonder.

The man stared vacantly for a moment. "You mean you ain't heard?"

"Heard what?" Kim asked sharply.

"The Rangers are in Borger," he said as if that explained everything.

"We heard about that," Kim said. "But what on earth is this?" He gestured toward the approaching mass of people.

"They're running all the gamblers and dope peddlers and whores out of town," the man grinned wanly. "There won't be enough people left in Borger by sundown to cook for them Rangers."

"Well, I'll be damned!" Deafy whispered in awe.

The man waved and started walking. Kim and Deafy sat in stunned silence. The mass exodus moved toward them. The people didn't look up as they passed the truck. Some of them Kim recognized. Their faces were drawn and haggard, and they carried every conceivable kind of baggage. Some of the girls carried only small bundles under their arms. By the hundreds they passed. There were gamblers, bootleggers, dope peddlers, prostitutes—a sorry conglomeration of humanity. Fear was on their faces.

Then Kim saw Pat, the girl in whose bed he had slept his first night in camp.

"Pat!" he yelled.

She looked up with vacant eyes. Then she recognized him and waved half-heartedly.

"Wait!" Kim shouted. "Here, Pat!" She walked toward the truck.

"What are you doing here?" Kim demanded almost belligerently.

"I'm trying to get out of Borger before sundown," Pat said tiredly. "The same as about ten thousand other people."

"But why?" Kim asked desperately.

"Because the Rangers said to," Pat answered. "They've been in Borger nearly a week. They relieved all the city officials and replaced them. The good, law abiding citizens are even talking of lynching."

"No!" Kim was aghast. Then he expostulated, "But why are *you* leaving?"

Pat smiled thinly. There was no makeup on her face, and she looked much younger and very tired. "I'm a whore, Kim. Remember?"

Kim shook his head as if to clear his vision.

"Where's Sal?" Deafy's harsh voice cleared Kim's mind.

"She'll be along," Pat said. "She had to leave just like the rest of us."

Kim sat in stunned silence. "How far behind you is she?" he finally asked.

"I don't know," Pat said. "Quite a ways, I imagine. She was carrying quite a lot of baggage. And Sal is fat."

Deafy chomped hard on his tobacco and spat.

"I'd better be going," Pat said. "The Rangers are behind us, and they don't want anyone to slow down."

Kim didn't even see Pat wave as she left. He sat and stared vacantly. The faces of the people passing were vague and indistinct. Suddenly he sat erect.

"She has our money, Deafy!" he almost shouted.

Deafy spat and nodded. "They didn't have no right to run Sal out of town," he said phlegmatically. "Sal ain't no whore." Kim knew that Deafy was angry.

"What will we do?"

"You just start the truck and drive real slow. We'll watch 'em as we pass."

Kim started the truck and drove ahead. He had a feeling that they were driving against tall, wind-blown grass. It was almost thirty minutes and after passing thousands of men and women that he heard Deafy's command to stop.

Kim braked the truck again and followed Deafy's gesture. It was Sal all right! She was walking, and she carried a big carpetbag over her shoulder. She stumbled over sage brush and through mesquite bushes, but she was looking ahead determinedly. She didn't look up as Deafy yelled. Deafy jumped from the truck and ran toward her. He finally had to grab her arm to stop her. It took Sal a moment to recognize Deafy. Her large eyes were bloodshot, and perspiration ran down her face even though the day was cool.

"Sal, you ain't got no business bein' out here!" Deafy said gruffly.

"Sal's glad to see you, Deafy Jones," Sal said tiredly. "I ain't walked so far since I was a kid."

"You get in the truck, Sal," Deafy said kindly. "Me and Kim will take you back to town."

"I'd like to get in the truck, Deafy," Sal said. "But I can't go back to town. The Rangers have run all the girls out. And the gamblers too."

"Get in anyway," Deafy said.

Sal climbed in between Kim and Deafy. They paid no attention to the curious stares of the others walking past.

"Drive toward town, Kim," Deafy said. "If we turn around and go back, they'll hop on the truck till we won't have a chance to get away. Circle sort of gradual, and we'll come in from the north."

Kim followed Deafy's instructions. As they circled nearer Borger, they saw long strings of people and vehicles crawling like ants from Borger, north toward Stinnett and southeast toward Pampa. They met a flatbed truck loaded with girls. One of them recognized Sal and yelled and waved. Sal looked at them mutely. Then suddenly she started crying. Great sobs shook her big body. Deafy spat and reached over and patted her on the knee. It was the comforting gesture of one friend to another.

"I got your money, Deafy," Sal said as she blew hard into her handkerchief.

"That's fine, Sal. That's sure fine," Deafy said absently. He hadn't even understood what Sal said. Kim breathed a sigh of relief and was a bit ashamed that he had been wondering about it.

"It's in my bag," Sal said, then added with something of her old fire, "The damned Rangers didn't get that!"

"What about your place?"

"They nailed it up," Sal said. "I don't know what the men are going to do now. There ain't a girl left in camp, at least not the kind of a girl that a boomer wants on Saturday night."

"What are we going to do now, Deafy?" Kim asked anxiously. They were nearing Borger as they circled, and Kim was afraid that they would meet some of the Rangers.

"Just work in toward town and pull down into that little creek behind Wendy's house," Deafy said.

Kim started to protest but decided against it. He knew Deafy had a plan in mind.

Finally they were able to get the truck down into the small, sandy creek near the Terrell house. They were perhaps three hundred yards away. Kim maneuvered close to an overhanging clay bank so that the truck was not visible from the direction of town. He cut the engine.

For a moment, the three of them sat in silence. Sal seemed content to let them do the thinking. She was very tired. Kim was at his wit's end. The move was up to Deafy. Kim was almost sure that even Deafy would not attempt to sneak Sal into the Terrell house.

"Kim!" Deafy spat tobacco juice. "You stay here with Sal. I'll be back pretty soon—I think. If I ain't, you sneak into town tonight and get some gasoline for the truck and then take Sal to Amarillo."

Kim nodded, and Deafy left without another word. Kim heard him grunt as he climbed out of the creek.

It was less than a half hour when Deafy reappeared. With him was Wendy. Wendy only nodded to Kim, and Kim nodded in return. Wendy went to Sal who was still sitting in the truck.

"Sal!" she admonished. "Why didn't you come on up to the house with Deafy?"

"I couldn't do that, Wendy," Sal protested tiredly.

"You could," Wendy said positively. "And you're going to. We have an extra room, and—"

"Now wait a minute, lass," Deafy said placatingly. "We knowed that Sal would be welcome as far as you was concerned. But that just ain't the thing to do. We need some help, alright—food and gasoline. But Blake would sure as hell throw a fit if you brought Sal home with you, and you know it."

Wendy whirled on Deafy. "I'm ashamed of you, Deafy Jones," she cried. "And you too, Kim Wingate." Kim felt as though a flashlight had been turned in his face when Wendy's eyes blazed at him. "You bring Sal up to the house this minute."

"Now Wendy," Deafy said reasonably. "That just wouldn't work, and you know it."

"Why wouldn't it?" Wendy wanted to know.

"Well for one thing," Deafy said hurriedly, "Blake—"

"Father!" Wendy said vehemently. "Are you and Kim both afraid of him like everyone else?"

Deafy started to answer, then closed his mouth hard. His jaw muscles bulged. The taunt had hurt. Sal looked at Wendy reproachfully. There was a long silence.

"I'm—I'm sorry, Deafy," Wendy gulped. "I didn't mean that, but—oh damn!" Tears suddenly welled in her eyes.

Kim had never heard Wendy swear before, and he knew that she was deeply moved. He walked to her.

"Now you just don't worry about nothing, Wendy," Deafy said. "We need some help from you. That's why I come up to get you. We just got to figure out—"

"Now what in hell is going on down there?" a voice yelled from the bank overhanging the creek. Everyone looked. Kim felt a chill as he saw a badge on the chests of the two men standing looking down.

Wendy started to speak, but said nothing. Deafy spat and fidgeted. Lawmen were something he didn't know how to cope with. Sal sat silently. It was Kim who answered.

"Who wants to know?" Kim racked his brain to try to think of a plausible explanation as to why four people would be standing in a dry creek bed arguing.

"The Texas Rangers want to know," the bigger of the two men answered stolidly.

"Oh." Kim paused.

"Well?" the man asked again. "What's going on down there?"

"Gentlemen," Kim sparred for time. "This is Mr. Jones, a driller, Mrs. Sal—" Kim mumbled for he didn't know her last name. "And this is Miss Terrell. Miss Terrell lives there on the hill." Kim gestured nonchalantly toward the imposing brick house. "My name is Kimball Wingate."

The men looked at them intently for a few seconds. "And what is your business, young man?"

"I'm a dirt moving contractor," Kim said in a flash of inspiration. "Miss Terrell wanted me to give her my opinion as to whether an earthen dam could be put across this creek to furnish irrigation water for her lawn and trees."

"Hmmmm—" The big Ranger looked dubious.

They waited. Finally the Ranger said, "Wait there a minute." He nodded to his partner to follow him.

The Rangers withdrew out of earshot. Their conversation would have been interesting to Kim and Deafy.

"What do you think?" the smaller man asked.

"Damned if I know," the other answered seriously. "That old woman isn't a whore. She'd starve to death even in an oil camp with her looks. And the old fellow with one eye isn't a gambler. His hands are too rough—but he's carrying a gun."

"What about the young girl and young man?"

The Ranger shook his head again. "That girl ain't a whore, either. If they looked like her, I'd be rounding them up and bringing them *back* to town! Besides, I've heard the Terrell name. He's a big oil operator. It's that smooth talking young man that I can't figure out."

"I can't either," admitted the other. "But he's lying. I'll bet on that."

"We might lie too, if we were in their places," the big Ranger said shortly.

They talked a few minutes longer.

"Folks," the big Ranger said as they returned. "The Texas Rangers have taken over law enforcement in Borger. We have asked several people to leave town. We aren't asking anyone to leave that has legitimate business here. If I were you folks, I would be careful to stay in for a couple of days." He nodded curtly, and they turned and left.

"Whew!" Kim sat suddenly on the sand.

"Kim," Wendy's eyes were twinkling as she looked at him. "You are a magnificent liar. I don't think I will ever believe you again."

"Well," Kim grinned ruefully. "Why on earth *would* four people be standing in a creek bed?"

Wendy laughed. "They would be hiding from Rangers!"

A twinkle appeared in Deafy's one eye, and Sal sat up a bit straighter.

"Anyway," Wendy said. "I know the answer to our problem."

Everyone looked at her hopefully.

"We will take her to our cabin."

"Your what?" Deafy asked.

"Wendy and I have a private cabin up on the river," Kim answered for her as they looked at each other conspiratorially. "It has a spring of fresh water and a cook stove and everything. It's in the Beatenbow foaling pasture where we are going to spud in our well."

"You kids sure ain't been very talkative about it," Deafy grumbled. He was beginning to return to normal.

"You and Deafy are going to drill your own well?" Wendy asked quickly.

"Kim is," Deafy said. "I ain't going to have nothing to do with it."

"Yes, you are, Deafy," Kim laughed. "You're going to do all the work. I'm going to be the jar head—and jar heads don't do nothing."

Deafy grinned, and Wendy's heart sank. Until now, she had hoped that Kim would be immune from the oil fever. Now there was no hope. She wondered bitterly what he would be when he was as old as her father!

CHAPTER XII

It took Kim and Deafy less than two weeks to assemble their nondescript equipment into a workable drilling rig. They spudded in on the small Beatenbow horse pasture. The well was located less than a quarter of a mile from the small cabin that Wendy had originally discovered and that she and Kim had visited so often. Now Sal was occupying the cabin.

Sal was grateful for her rescue, but she was far from content in the lonely cabin. The wild river country was not Sal's idea of a good place to live, and the coyotes howling at night frightened her. She was accustomed to having people around constantly and for two weeks she had seen no one but Deafy Jones and Kim Wingate.

Almost every day Sal came to the rig to watch Kim and Deafy work. More often than not, she stayed until late at night. Then she was afraid to walk back to the cabin alone. But Kim and Deafy paid little attention to Sal. They were much too busy trying to drill and oil well.

It was a memorable day when Kim started the engine and threw the lever that would start the cables moving.

"There goes *Wingate Number One!*" Deafy yelled.

Kim felt an immense satisfaction as he pushed the lever. Now he was an oil man!

The machinery worked perfectly, and just before sundown Deafy went to the shack. A few minutes later, he emerged. He was dressed in his blue serge suit and patent leather shoes. His tie was knotted badly.

"See you and Sal later, Kim," Deafy said and got in the truck. He drove north.

"Now where is *he* going?" Sal wanted to know.

Somehow, Kim was reluctant to tell Sal about Mandy. "He's probably going across the river and visit some friends of his that live on a ranch," Kim said evasively.

But Sal was suspicious. "Has he got a woman over there?"

"Well—" Kim hesitated.

"What's she like?" Sal wanted to know.

"I didn't say he had one," Kim protested.

"Yes you did," Sal replied emphatically. "Sal can tell. I knew that *something* was wrong with Deafy, but I didn't know what. Now tell Sal about her."

"Well," Kim considered his words carefully. "She's sort of—well—gentle. She's got big, friendly eyes, and she's not real big, not fat anyway, and she's—well Mandy's beautiful," Kim finished rather lamely.

"Figured she must be a hell of a woman," Sal said with satisfaction. "She'd have to be, to make Deafy Jones come courtin'."

"I think she's wonderful," Kim said. "So does Wendy. She's a widow. She's the daughter of the woman that owns the land I'm drilling on."

"Good!" Sal nodded her head. "I hope Deafy marries her. He needs a good woman. He hasn't looked at the same one twice since his wife died thirty years ago."

"You would like her," Kim said enthusiastically. He was immensely relieved. He had been a little uneasy that Sal might be jealous. "I'll take you over to meet her sometime."

"No, you won't!" Sal started as if Kim had stuck a pin in her.

"Why not? You're Deafy's friend, aren't you?"

"I sure am," Sal said staunchly. "Have been for thirty years. That's one reason I wouldn't go."

"But—"

"Kim," Sal said as though she were talking to a small boy. "You're not old enough to understand this maybe, but—well, a woman that's been in my business ain't never quite respectable again. With a man it's different. He can visit my place every Saturday night for ten years, and then turn respectable—even be respectable when he's doing it. It ain't that way with a woman. I don't know why it's that way, but it is. And it ought to be."

Kim tried to think of an answer and could find none. He knew that Sal was speaking the truth. He wished Sal would leave.

But Sal stayed. She wanted to talk, for she was lonely. They talked mostly of Deafy Jones. Kim learned, much to his surprise, that Deafy was only a couple of years older than Blake Terrell.

"Deafy just looks old," Sal said. "He has lived a hard life."

"Sal," Kim began tentatively. He had long wanted to ask Sal the question, and was almost afraid to do so. "Do you—?"

"Go ahead and ask, Kim," Sal said. "If I don't want to tell you, I won't."

"Well, do you remember a few weeks ago that a cowman named Patton was charged with stealing cattle?"

"I remember," Sal said, "It was in the paper."

"Then you know that the charge was dropped the following week," Kim went on. "Now I have reason to believe that Blake Terrell had something to do with that charge against Patton. I also have reason to believe that Deafy forced Blake to have the charge dropped. What I want to know is—well, how *could* Deafy stop Blake?"

Sal said nothing for a few minutes. The engine of the rig ran smoothly, and the stars shone brightly.

"Kim," Sal said finally, "Sal knew about Oschner calling you and Deafy into town and about Blake's lawyer trying to get you to sign a contract. I also knew that Deafy Jones kept Blake and his lawyer from framing that honest cowman."

"Deafy told you?" Kim asked in amazement.

"I went with Deafy that night to see Blake."

"You what?"

Sal only nodded.

"But, how—what—?"

"Kim," Sal said almost sadly. "Sal is going to tell you something tonight that only three people in this world know about: Deafy Jones and Blake Terrell—and me."

Kim waited.

"Maybe Sal talks too much," Sal said. "And maybe what I'm going to tell you tonight may make a difference in your feelings toward Wendy. If it does, you ain't fit for her anyway, so I am going to tell you how we stopped Blake Terrell. We didn't do it for the man he was framing, or for him. We did it for Wendy—and maybe for you."

"Go on." Kim had begun to feel the icy chill of fear steal up his back.

"It was just at the turn of the century, twenty-seven years ago," Sal continued. "Spindletop was booming. It was big. Bigger than Borger ever thought about being. Blake Terrell was a roughneck working for one of the big companies. He was young and good looking. I didn't have a house then; I was working in one. Blake came in pretty often. Then he quit coming. He had found him a private girl, one of them pretty little quadroons. He was living with her. She had a baby and died. Five years later, Blake married Wendy's mother."

"But what—how—" Kim stammered in perplexity.

"Blake's private girl's name was Crochet. She pronounced it Crow-

shay. Her son didn't like the name, so when he was twelve or fourteen years old, he just shortened the Crochet to—Shay. Joe Shay."

"You mean—"

"Joe Shay is Blake Terrell's bastard son."

"That's just simply not possible!" Kim said aghast.

"It is possible," Sal said. "And it's true. That's how we stopped Blake. We told him that if he went through with the deal that we would tell Joe that he was Blake's son, and that would mean that Joe would have an interest in the Terrell Oil Company. Blake thought we were bluffing, and we were. That is the only time I ever heard Deafy threaten to do something that I knew he wouldn't do. I think that Blake knew Deafy wouldn't do it on account of Wendy, but he wasn't sure about me. Anyway, he was afraid to take the chance."

Kim was speechless. His thoughts whirled.

"You know, Kim," Sal said musingly. "Deafy says that the real reason that Blake didn't go ahead with his plan was because he didn't want Wendy to find about Joe. Do you suppose it was?"

"Yes," Kim almost whispered. "I think it was."

Sal stayed a few minutes longer and asked Kim to walk her back to her cabin. Kim was glad to oblige and he wasted no time talking to her. He hurried back to the rig. He was glad to be alone, for he was troubled.

Kim went about his tasks automatically. Usually he looked forward to Deafy's return from the Beatenbow ranch, but tonight he rather dreaded it. He didn't want to talk—even to Deafy. Deafy was in high spirits when he did return, and he talked a great deal while helping Kim make adjustments about the derrick. Then they went to the shack for coffee. Deafy built the fire, and Kim gathered water from the pop-off valve. Deafy made the coffee, as usual. They sat drinking the coffee and listening to the hum of the rig.

Finally Deafy cleared his throat. "Kim," he began tentatively. "I guess I'll just go ahead and get it over with next Sunday."

"Get what over with?" Kim asked absently. He was preoccupied with his own thoughts.

"Me and Mandy," Deafy explained. "We are going to get married next Sunday."

"It took a minute for Deafy's announcement to make its impression on Kim.

"You are *what?*" Kim yelped and jumped from his chair as if a hot iron had touched him. His sudden movement spilled coffee on Deafy.

"What the matter with you, Kim?" Deafy said, half in anger and half in concern as he brushed hastily at the hot coffee spilled in his lap.

For a moment Kim said nothing. Then he started laughing and slapped Deafy on the back. "Nothing, Deafy!" Kim said delightedly. "I just couldn't believe that an ugly old devil like you could talk a beautiful woman like Mandy into marrying you—that's all. You ought to break news like that more gently."

Deafy grinned almost shyly. "Does seem sort of funny she would, don't it?" There was almost disbelief in his voice.

"No, it doesn't," Kim said stoutly. "Mandy could have looked a hundred years and done a lot worse. I think it is wonderful, Deafy. Congratulations."

"Kim," Deafy said earnestly, "Would you go with me?"

"Go with you? Where?"

"When—well, when me and Mandy gets married."

"Of course, I'll go with you, Deafy," Kim assured him. "In fact, you couldn't keep me away with that cannon of yours."

"Good," Deafy said with relief.

It was hours later that they finally went to bed, but even then neither of them went to sleep. Kim's feelings were torn between delight for the wonderful thing that had happened to Deafy Jones and the evil shadow of Joe Shay that hung over the Terrell family.

"Hey, Kim?" Deafy finally broke the silence.

"Yeah?"

"You remember that rancher, Patton, that was going to drill on the Beatenbow ranch?"

"What about him?"

"He's damned near famous," Deafy said with a chuckle. "He hit the first duster in Hutchinson county since the boom started."

"Are you joking?" Kim asked in disbelief as he sat up in bed. No one drilled a dry oil well near Borger.

"Nope," Deafy said. "Mandy told me about it tonight—and to make it worse, some hi-jackers held up his drilling crew and stole his string of tools. He up and quit the oil drilling business. Can't say as I blame him."

"I don't blame him either," Kim said feelingly as he thought of the horrible possibility that his own well might prove to be a dry one. "But what about the Beatenbow land? Isn't he going to drill on that?"

"Says he ain't. They never signed the lease, anyway."

"Who do you suppose will get it?"

"I dunno," Deafy said absently. "Ain't none of my business." He wasn't interested in oil wells at the moment.

Kim ran his hand through his hair and lay back in his bunk. The monotonous sound of the engine had always had a soporific effect

on Kim and he was tired. Finally his eyes closed, and he was almost
asleep when Deafy's voice again cut through the darkness.

"Hey, Kim!"

"What, Deafy?"

"Who you going to get to do your cooking for you after me and
Mandy gets married?" Deafy's voice was bantering. He wasn't even
sleepy.

Kim lay silent for a moment. "You will just have to bring Mandy
out and let her cook," Kim said in mock seriousness. "That would
sure be an improvement."

"Like hell I will!" Deafy chuckled. "I aim to move in with *her*.
You will have to find your own woman."

On Saturday before the wedding, Deafy took the day off. He
asked Kim to drive him into town. Kim wanted to know why Deafy
didn't take the pickup truck so he would have a way back, but Deafy
refused.

That evening, Deafy came back to the rig. He was driving an
almost new Model-T touring car. It was only then that Kim knew
why Deafy had not wanted to drive the truck. Kim felt a momentary
pang that he was using most of Deafy's money and that Deafy had
had to settle for a used Ford when he could easily have afforded a
new car if his money were not invested in the well.

The car was not the extent of Deafy's purchases. He also had
bought a new, blue serge suit and white shirt and a tie. He proudly
displayed his new wardrobe to Kim and then wrapped them carefully
in newspapers and placed them under his bunk. There was no place
in the small shack to hang them.

Sunday broke bright and clear. It was a beautiful spring day. Kim
shut the well down early. It was the first time since he had been
drilling that he had seen an oil well shut down voluntarily. But to
Kim, Deafy's marriage was much more important than any oil well in
the world, and they didn't have a crew to run it in their absence.

The ceremony was to be performed at the ranchhouse. Granny
was not physically able to go to a church, and she wanted her Mandy
to be married at home where she could see the wedding. Kim was to
be best man and Wendy bridesmaid.

Mandy's brothers and many of the Beatenbow neighbors were
present at the ranch when Deafy and Kim arrived. There were still
last minute arrangements to be made, and the men stood in the yard
and talked while the women went about their mysterious machina-
tions inside. While they were outside, someone noticed a group of
men walking across the river toward the ranch.

"Who can that be?" one of Mandy's brothers asked in a puzzled
voice.

Kim looked apprehensively. Surely a group of the town ruffians would not have the temerity to interrupt a wedding. He still remembered the bouncing of rocks on the side of the church the first time he and Wendy had attended. But the Rangers were supposed to have cleaned the rabble out of Borger! It was Deafy who had the explanation.

"Them is friends of mine," he said almost apologetically. "I asked them to come. Mandy told me it would be all right."

"We are glad they could come, Deafy. Your friends will always be welcome on the Beatenbow," Ed Beatenbow said.

Kim breathed a sign of relief. The men arrived, and Deafy introduced them. There were perhaps half a dozen. All were dressed in suits and ties, and Kim felt an unaccountable surge of pride. They were good men. Oil men!

Finally the preacher came to the door and informed them that everything was ready. They went inside. All but Kim and Deafy were instructed to remain in the big living room. They arranged themselves around the walls. Granny sat in her chair and glared ferociously about. Kim and Deafy were asked to go in the kitchen just off the living room and wait.

No one was in the kitchen. Deafy paced nervously about and continuously adjusted the black patch over his bad eye. It seemed to Kim that they waited for hours, though it was probably not more than a few minutes. Three times, he had to straighten the collar of Deafy's white shirt which persisted in sticking out at an almost horizontal angle. Kim thought Deafy looked fine in the new blue serge suit.

Then Mandy entered by the outside door of the kitchen. She was accompanied by several women—including Wendy.

Mandy's dark eyes were shining, and her cheeks flushed. She wore a long, blue dress, and her hair was combed almost straight back and knotted in a bun at the nape of her neck. Kim thought he had never seen a lovelier woman.

The other women exclaimed their admiration as they fussed about in woman fashion. Mandy stood while they made last minute, unnecessary adjustments. There was a half-smile on her lips.

Then Mandy looked at Deafy. His obstreperous shirt collar was again askew, and his eye patch had slipped a bit. But Deafy was no longer aware of his own predicament. He could only stare at the beautiful woman that he was about to marry.

Suddenly Mandy smiled at Deafy and crossed the room to him. She straightened his collar, and then with calm assurance and purpose she swiftly removed the black patch from Deafy's eye and tossed it in the kindling box beside the stove.

Deafy started when Mandy removed the patch, and then a flash of fear crossed his face. But Mandy did not seem to notice. She reached up and took Deafy's face between her hands. Then she kissed him full on the lips.

Kim knew that he never would again see such absolute joy so plainly written on a human face as he saw on Deafy Jones at that moment. Kim looked at Wendy. Her face was radiant.

Deafy and Mandy stood in front of the big fireplace as the preacher read the marriage vows. Mandy stood proud, straight and lovely. She looked, thought Kim, like a queen revived from a thousand years ago. Deafy stood with squared shoulders.

After the ceremony, there was a general celebration. A huge meal had been prepared by neighbor women, and they served the guests in the big kitchen. Deafy Jones sat at the head of the table.

Soon after lunch, Deafy and Mandy boarded Deafy's new car. The entire group gathered to see them off and wish them good luck. They planned to go to Amarillo and return the next day. Kim grinned and waved as the Ford pulled away. But Deafy did not see Kim; he was much too absorbed in maneuvering the Ford along the narrow road through the cottonwoods.

Deafy's friends took their leave immediately after Deafy and Mandy left. Soon after, Kim and Wendy drove back to town together. Neither Maria nor Blake had been at the wedding.

As soon as the "company" had left, Granny Beatenbow called her three sons in to see her. She had something to say to them. They gathered in the living room in front of Granny's fireplace. No one else was allowed in the room—not even the in-laws.

A half hour later, when the sons emerged, they were sober faced and quiet. Ed surreptitiously wiped a tear from his eye. Not a person asked the purpose of the conference. It would have been useless anyway. It was a Beatenbow talk.

The children made preparations to leave. It was Ed's wife who asked who was going to stay with Granny until Mandy returned.

"Nobody," Ed said curtly.

His wife looked at him in surprise. Ed was not one to speak in a sharp tone.

She protested stoutly. Granny was entirely too old to be left alone at the ranch. The other women agreed. One of them would stay.

"Mamma knows what she wants," Ed said. "Us boys asked her about it when we was talking to her. She says she can eat left-overs from the dinner at supper time, and Mandy and Deafy will be back tomorrow."

"I don't care what she says," Ed's wife rejoined. "You're not going to leave that poor old lady here by herself. I'll stay here, and you can come get me next week."

"You'll do nothing of the kind, wife," Ed said in a tone that his wife had heard very few times in their thirty years of marriage. She made no further comment.

Granny's goodbyes were short and cryptic. She had already had her say to her sons. When they all had gone, she poked her wood fire and rocked slowly in front of the fireplace. The only event that Granny Beatenbow had longed for, and thought she would never live to see, had taken place that day. Her Mandy had her a man. A good man. Granny nodded her head in satisfaction and pulled her shawl closer about her thin shoulders.

Night fell on the river. It was calm and peaceful. Granny listened to the river sounds as she rocked slowly. Hers had been a good life—a long life. Her sons were strong, good men. They had their families. Good families. Now, Mandy had hers, too.

The Beatenbows had done their part in conquering a strong and resistant land. Changes were coming. But changes had come before. And strong people were not afraid of change. The future held no fear for Granny. The Beatenbow name would live, and men would respect it for a long time to come.

Slower and slower Granny rocked. The fire dwindled, but she did not poke it with her cane. Finally the ancient sound of the creaking rocker stopped altogether, and the fire died out.

A coyote howl floated down the river, and a covey of quail hovered closer together. A half grown eagle peered over the side of his nest, and the wide, bright eyes of a great horned owl peered into the darkness.

Kim drove Wendy straight home after the wedding and returned to his rig. Sal was waiting and full of questions about the wedding. Kim talked to her as he worked. He had to get the rig running as soon as possible. He could run it that night and the following day and night. He had worked more than thirty-six hours at a stretch many times before, and he could do it again. Now he was working for himself. And Deafy would be back again on Tuesday morning.

By nightfall, the rig was running smoothly. Sal made coffee, and Kim told her everything he could remember about the wedding while they sat in the shack. Sal walked back to her cabin alone that night.

The machinery was operating remarkably well considering that it had been fashioned out of cast off equipment, and Kim was able to get snatches of sleep during the next day and the next night. But by sunup Tuesday morning, he was looking forward to Deafy's return. He was very tired.

But Deafy did not return on Tuesday morning, nor Tuesday at noon, nor Tuesday night. Sal sat on a rig timber and watched Kim work. The second day she cooked Kim's meals and kept the coffee hot. She was glad to be able to help. It gave her something to do. The boiler developed a leak, and Kim was forced to watch it continuously. That night he did not get to sleep at all. And Sal did not return to her cabin. She cooked supper for Kim and slept on Deafy's bunk. The next day and night passed in a sort of a dream for Kim. He was staggering as he went about his work. Sal tried, to no avail, to get him to rest. Kim merely shook his head and kept stubbornly at his task. Deafy or not, he was going to keep that rig running.

Kim was still on his feet Thursday morning, but he was performing his tasks automatically. For four days and nights he had kept the rig running without help. He no longer had any concept of time, and Sal had to force him to drink the strong, black coffee.

It was almost noon of that day when Deafy rode up to the rig on the gentle, blaze faced sorrel that had been Finch's favorite horse. Kim looked at him vacantly and without recognition.

"What's the matter with you, Kim?" Deafy asked anxiously as he dismounted awkwardly.

"Got to keep the boiler going," Kim said dazedly.

Just at that moment, Sal came from the cabin and hailed Deafy.

"What's the matter with Kim?" Deafy asked sternly.

"He's been working four days and nights without sleep," Sal said defensively. "And he won't stop. I've tried to get him to, and he won't do it."

"You get in that shack, Kim," Deafy said sternly. "I reckon I can run a while now."

"Got to keep the boiler going," Kim mumbled and started staggering toward the derrick.

Deafy grabbed Kim's arm and led him toward the shack. Kim struggled feebly for a moment, and Sal took his other arm.

Inside the shack, Deafy gently forced him to lie on the bunk. Kim mumbled something unintelligible and sighed. He was asleep before his legs straightened out.

Kim awakened to the smell of boiling coffee and frying bacon. He opened his eyes slowly and stretched tentatively. He groaned as his sore muscles flexed. It was almost dark outside, and he could hear someone moving quietly about the cabin. Kim raised up and set his feet on the floor.

"Ohhh—," he moaned and pulled his ear gently. "I could have slept all night too, Deafy."

"You *have* slept all night, and all day too."

Kim jumped as if a gun had gone off at his feet. Mandy's laugh floated from the shack into the dusk.

"Mandy! What on earth are you doing here?"

"I came to get my husband. I thought you were never going to let him come home," Mandy said lightly. "And now, since you are finally awake, I'll light the lamp."

"Where is Deafy?" Kim asked as Mandy touched a match to the kerosene lamp wick. The yellow lamp cast a touch of gold to her face, and Kim thought he had never seen her look lovelier.

"He's working on the rig. He got the boiler fixed."

"How long have I been sleeping, Mandy?" Kim asked apprehensively.

"About thirty hours, according to Sal."

"Oh, Mandy!" Kim said in consternation. "I'm terribly sorry! Why didn't you wake me?"

"Deafy wouldn't let me. I wouldn't have, anyway," Mandy said calmly. "Now, you go wash, and I'll have you something to eat."

"Well, I can sure eat!" Kim said with vigor. "That smells wonderful, Mandy. I'm half starved. Has Deafy been running the rig ever since I've been asleep?"

"Yes."

"He shouldn't have done that!" Kim said heatedly. "He should have shut the well down and gone on home."

Mandy laughed. "Marriage hasn't changed Deafy *that* much, Kim."

"I guess not," Kim grinned. "How is he?"

"Fine," Mandy said softly. "He is a wonderful man, Kim."

"He certainly is, Mandy," Kim said enthusiastically. "And he's a lucky man, too."

"Thank you, Kim."

"And Mandy," Kim began uncertainly, "About Sal—it was I who moved her into the cabin. Deafy didn't even know—"

Mandy's delighted laugh interrupted Kim. "You're wonderful, Kim!" she said. "No wonder Deafy thinks so much of you. I know all about Sal. She told me herself how you and Wendy and Deafy rescued her from the Rangers. I would have been disappointed if you had done anything else."

"Whew!" Kim grinned and pulled his ear.

"Did you think I would be jealous of Sal, Kim?" Mandy's eyes twinkled.

"I don't know what I thought," he admitted.

"I think Sal thought the same thing," Mandy said. "She left the rig as soon as I came this morning, and she hasn't been back. I had to go to the cabin to see her. She has been Deafy's friend for a long time. I wouldn't want Deafy to ever fail a friend."

"He never would," Kim said stoutly.

"He has been worried about you, Kim," Mandy said solemnly. "But it wasn't his fault that he was gone so long."

"Of course not, Mandy," Kim said quickly. "I knew that you were just—" Kim stammered and stopped. He felt the blood rush to his face.

"It wasn't that, Kim," she said as a tiny smile played about her face and then faded. "Mamma died."

"What!" Kim almost yelped.

"She died the night Deafy and I were married."

"Oh, *no!*" Kim whispered hoarsely. "Granny—dead! I—I just can't believe that!"

"A neighbor found her Monday morning," Mandy said calmly. "She was sitting in her rocker in front of the fireplace. She hadn't even gone to bed."

"That's—that's terrible!"

"No, Kim," Mandy said as though she were talking to a child. "It isn't terrible. Mamma was ninety years old. She knew she was going to die. She told my brothers after Deafy and I left after the wedding. That is why she wanted to be alone at the ranch that night."

"But why—why would she want to be alone," Kim asked incredulously.

"Mamma had a lot of Indian blood in her, Kim," Mandy said as though that explained everything.

Neither Kim nor Mandy said anything for a few moments. The light of the kerosene lamp flickered, and the sound of the engine chugged dully.

"When is the—when are you—?"

"We had the funeral Wednesday."

Kim looked at Mandy a moment, and then tears welled in his eyes. "And Deafy didn't even tell me!" he said accusingly.

"Don't blame Deafy, Kim. Please!" Mandy said quietly. "He wanted to, but I asked him not to tell you. We didn't tell Wendy, either. Mamma loved both of you very much. I hope you knew that. But I heard her say many times that young folks shouldn't be made to look at the dead. Mamma was a great believer in living. I think she would have wanted it the way it was."

"She was the grandest old lady I have ever known," Kim whispered.

"Yes," Mandy said matter-of-factly. "Now you go wash and tell Deafy to come to supper."

"I—I'm just not hungry, Mandy," Kim said weakly.

"Yes, you are, Kim," Mandy replied. "And so is Deafy. Hurry now, before it gets cold."

The cold water revived Kim somewhat, and when he and Deafy re-entered the shack, the cooking smelled good again. The supper consisted of beans, thick bacon slices, canned tomatoes and bread.

The conversation was light and happy. Granny's death was not mentioned, and Kim knew that Mandy had, with a woman's wisdom, put it behind her. Kim ate ravenously.

"Your larder needs replenishing, Kim," Mandy said smilingly as she passed him the beans for the third time.

"What!" Kim said with fine disdain. "This sumptuous banquet came from my larder, Mandy? No king ever had a finer meal!"

Mandy and Deafy smiled at each other, and Kim beamed at them like a proud parent.

"Mandy," Kim said. "I told Deafy that if he married you, he would just have to bring you out here and let you do my cooking for me. Now, you see, he has already done it."

Deafy grinned happily.

As Deafy and Mandy prepared to leave an hour later, Deafy informed Kim that he would return at sunup. Kim protested stoutly, but Deafy gave him to understand in no uncertain terms that he wasn't going to quit work just because he was married. Kim grinned and waved to them as they rode away.

After meeting Mandy, Sal seemed to be lonelier and more disconsolate than ever. She showed up at the rig every night as soon as Deafy left for the ranch, and she usually stayed until almost morning.

"This here wilderness life just ain't for Sal," she said almost desperately. "Them howling wolves makes me shiver at night, and I hear all kinds of sounds about the cabin. I wish you would take me to Amarillo."

"All right, Sal," Kim said. "I will. Just as soon as I can hire an extra hand so I won't have to shut down the well again."

But before Kim had a chance to keep his promise to Sal, three men came to the rig early one morning. Deafy knew one of them.

"How is it going, Deafy?" the man asked.

"Fine!" admitted Deafy. "We're keeping busy. What's new in town."

"Quite a bit," one of the men grinned. "The Rangers have shut everything down. They dumped five thousand gallons of whiskey in that little draw out west of town. Slim here swears he saw jackrabbits chasing coyotes the day after they dumped it."

"Guess they mean business, all right," Deafy said. "I hear them Rangers is tough."

"They're tough, all right," the man said with a touch of admiration in his voice. "No tougher law men in the world. But they can't plumb clean up a oil camp. You can buy whiskey now, but you have to pay twice what you did before they come to town. And you have to slip around to get it. There's a dozen men that's got mash barrels hid under the floor of their shacks. Most of the business houses has got a hollow partition loaded with bottles of whiskey."

"Didn't see hardly how they could keep drinking out," Deafy said seriously.

"There is still gambling in the shacks," the man continued his report. "So we got about everything we need, except women. That's what we come to see you about."

Deafy glared at the men suspiciously. "What'd you come to see me for?"

"We thought you might tell us where we could find Sal," the man said. "A bunch of the boys has got a house that she could live in and maybe bring a few of the girls back to town. Slim, here, is willing to make out like she is his wife."

Slim grinned self-consciously. "I drawed the low card," he explained.

Deafy spat and considered the news briefly. "I might be able to find Sal," Deafy finally said. "I'll tell her you boys' proposition."

"You do that, Deafy. The boys will appreciate it."

The men left soon after, and Deafy went to tell Sal the news. Sal moved back to town the next day.

CHAPTER XIII

In the days following Sal's return to Borger, it became apparent to Kim that they would have to have additional help in order to keep the rig going around the clock. He was almost exhausted. Deafy spent many nights working when, Kim thought, he should have been at home. He broached the subject to Deafy and was pleased when Deafy agreed to accompany him to town to find relief men. They shut the rig down Saturday at noon to go on their mission.

Kim had been to town once since the arrival of the Rangers, and then had stayed only long enough to get groceries and return to the rig. Deafy hadn't been in since he was married.

The changes in Borger were obvious. There was an almost sedate atmosphere. They drove down the long main street and saw relatively few people on the sidewalks. The gambling dens still had boards nailed across the doorways. Two Rangers and one policeman were patrolling the street. Borger lay as quietly as a shackled lion. But crime had not been stamped out! It had only been driven underground. Sal was back in business. So were bootleggers. Where, before, they had hawked their wares openly, they now slipped about and whispered. Where, three weeks previously, every business on Main street had profited by the unbridled spending, now only relatively few were enjoying prosperity. One man informed Kim and Deafy that property values in the town had dropped fifty percent since the arrival of the Rangers. A few who had screamed loudest for law enforcement were now grumbling because of lack of business.

Kim and Deafy bought supplies and a few needed materials. Then they set about trying to find some men who would work on the rig. They asked everywhere to no avail. Kim was becoming very discouraged when, late in the afternoon, Deafy spied two bedraggled looking men walking down the street. He straightway asked them if they were looking for work. They were.

Since it was almost sundown, they decided to eat supper before leaving town. The news was joyfully received by the two men that Deafy had hired. They were obviously broke, and just as obviously, hungry.

They went to the Whitespot cafe and found only a few men inside. Almost the only familiar thing about the place was the sad faced Negro man washing dishes behind the counter. They ordered supper, and the men began eating ravenously. The food seemed to lift their spirits, and they began talking loudly and boisterously. One of them had particularly unsightly teeth. It was evident that they had another pair of riffraff, who would stay just long enough to earn a week's pay and be off again. It was disheartening. Kim wondered how the two men came to be in Borger. Either the Rangers had overlooked them, or they had returned since the undesirables had been driven out.

Deafy and the men walked out of the cafe. Kim was at the counter paying for the meal when a man came up to him.

"Your name Wingate?" he asked.

"That's right."

"You are wanted up at the Terrell house," the man said brusquely and turned to walk swiftly from the cafe before Kim could question him.

Kim wrinkled his brow in thought. Wendy had told him the week before that she was going to Amarillo to shop today. He hadn't expected to see her. He walked out on the sidewalk where Deafy and the men were waiting.

"Deafy," he said, "I have to stay in town a while. You and the men go on out in the truck. I'll walk out later. There are some cots in the engine room for them to sleep on."

"All right, Kim," Deafy said as he looked keenly at Kim. "Did that feller that just come out of there bring you a message?"

"Yes."

"You want me to stay in town with you?"

"No."

"All right. I'll take these fellers on out and get them started."

"No, Deafy," Kim said. "You just take them out. I'll fire up when I get there. You go on home. Mandy will be expecting you."

Deafy hesitated a second. "All right, Kim. But you be careful in town tonight."

"Sure as hell wisht I had some money," the bigger of the two men said wistfully. "I'd stay in town with you. There's still plenty of women, if you just know how to find them."

Kim did not answer. He started walking rapidly toward the Terrell house. The light was burning on the porch when he arrived. Kim had never seen that light extinguished, day or night. Blake had given Rachael strict instructions that it should always be kept burning. Blake hated darkness.

The metal knocker sounded loud in the twilight. Kim waited a second and then lifted it a second time. Maria opened the door.

"I came to see Wendy," Kim said.

"Wendy isn't here," Maria said crisply. "I sent for you. Come on in."

"No, sir!" Kim said emphatically, remembering the last time he had been to the Terrell house when Maria was alone. "Where is Blake?"

"Blake is in Amarillo," Maria said with a trace of irritation in her voice. "And don't just stand there like an idiot. Come on in. I'm not going to rape you."

"What *do* you want?" Kim asked as he stepped inside the door.

"I want to ask you a question."

"What is it?" Kim said brusquely.

"I want to know about Joe Shay."

"Joe Shay?" Kim said incredulously.

"Yes. What do you know about him?"

"What on earth do you mean, Maria?" Kim asked in a troubled voice.

"Just what I said," Maria asserted firmly. "There is something strange about Joe. Blake treats him like no other man. He condones everything Joe does or says. The damned animal makes me feel as if I'm walking naked in front of him every time he looks at me. I don't really mind that, for I like men to look at me. But when I mentioned it to Blake, it only amused him. Blake would kill another man that did the same thing. I want to know why."

"You're just imagining things, Maria."

"No. I'm not."

"Well," Kim said desperately, "I don't know any more about Joe Shay than you do."

"I don't *know* anything," Maria said. "But I have a very strong suspicion. But I need to be sure. You have lived with Deafy Jones for a year. He has known Blake and Joe for a long time. He has talked to you."

"No," Kim said truthfully. "Deafy has not told me anything about them."

"You're a damned liar!" Maria spat at him.

"Deafy has not said anything about them," Kim reasserted.

"Then he *would*. If you asked him."

"No," Kim said firmly. "He wouldn't. And if he did, I wouldn't tell you."

"Why not?"

"Because I wouldn't betray a confidence. Besides, I am sure there is nothing to know, anyway."

"I think there is," Maria said with conviction. "And if I'm right, it would be a wonderful opportunity for you to get even with Blake."

"For what?" Kim asked in amazement. "Blake hasn't done anything to me."

"He will! He hates you, Kim," Maria said. "He'll kill you. Or make Joe Shay do it, just to keep you from getting Wendy."

"Shut up, Maria," Kim almost shouted. "And I've talked enough."

Kim grabbed his hat and rushed out into the night. The clean, cool air stilled some of the tumult in him. There was not the least doubt that Maria suspected that Joe was Blake's illegitimate son. The implications of that were appalling. With proof of her suspicions, she could make a plaything out of Blake Terrell. And she would!

But she could never be sure! Because only four people in all the world knew that to be true. Kim would have bet his life that none of the four would ever tell the secret. But Maria was a shrewd and brilliant woman! And Blake Terrell, with his neglect and domineering, had stirred hatred in her.

What if Maria questioned Wendy? What if she planted a seed of suspicion? Kim shuddered.

He walked very fast toward the rig. He made the distance in less than an hour. A couple of hundred yards away, he stopped and shouted. It was dangerous to approach any rig at night without identifying oneself, and it was doubly dangerous to approach Deafy.

Finally he heard Deafy shout for him to come on in. He knew that one of the men must have told Deafy that he was out there, for Deafy couldn't hear well around the machinery. Deafy should have been home with Mandy, Kim thought, as he walked into the light of the rig. But Deafy and the man with the unsightly teeth were busy threading a pipe.

"You're home early," the man said with an attempt at humor. "Thought it'd take you all night to get caught up on eating and Sal's place."

Kim didn't answer. Deafy looked at him sharply.

"Wasn't there, huh?" Deafy said.

For a moment, Kim feigned ignorance, but under the directness of Deafy's steady gaze, he immediately shed the hypocrisy.

"Nope."

"What the hell!" exploded the man. "Don't tell me Sal's up and left Borger, again!"

"Sal's still in town," Deafy said complacently. "It wasn't Sal's place that Kim was going to."

"Then he's a damn fool!" the man said flatly. "There ain't no line girls that can beat Sal's women—and I don't care what big eastern town they come from."

Deafy merely squirted tobacco juice. Kim smiled bleakly. Suddenly he felt very tired and lonely. Deafy seemed to sense Kim's fatigue and frustration.

"You go to the shack and sleep about ten hours, Kim," he said gruffly. "You look more like you was forty years old than twenty-three, and I don't want a tired man on the job. Liable to get somebody killed."

"You go on home, Deafy," Kim said. "Mandy will be expecting you. I'll change clothes and take over."

"I ain't tired nor sleepy," Deafy said. "Besides Mandy won't be expecting me. Likely she knows I'm old enough to look out for myself. You're tuckered, and I don't want no damn fool dropping a Stillson off the tower on somebody's head. Men is hard to find. Now you do like I said."

Kim opened his mouth to reply but closed it again without saying a word. He went to the shack and felt Deafy's one good eye on his back all the way.

Inside the shack, he lit the kerosene lamps and looked at his face in the cracked mirror. He *was* beginning to look old. Little white lines converged on the outside corners of his eyes. The sun glare and wind made him squint. In the protected crevices, his skin was still white while on the exposed surface the sun and wind had whipped it to a leathery brown.

He rummaged through the grub box and found some sardines and crackers. The walk had made him hungry again. He ate and then brushed his teeth. He looked at his bunk and the oily clothing he had discarded before going to town. In the morning the oily clothing, almost stiff from sweat and grease, would feel good against the wind. And they would feel clean. There was a rare cleanliness that accompanied fresh perspiration. He had come to enjoy sweating. It was a cleansing thing—not the stale putrefaction prevalent in the Double Six. At the moment he felt stale and filthy. Swiftly he removed his clothing and wrapped a towel about him. He walked from the shack toward the rig. The pop-off valve was spewing white steam, and he walked into it. He could remember the first time he had seen Deafy do that. He smiled bleakly as he thought of it.

"Thought you said you didn't go to Sal's place," he heard one of the new men yell. "Don't see why you want to wash off that good talcum smell. Hell, if you got the claps, you might as well enjoy it while you can."

"You shut your goddamned mouth and get up on that crown block with a oil can," Kim heard Deafy growl.

Kim heard no more from the men, and when he finished his bath, he stepped out of the steam to dry his body. The wind was cold and felt good to his body and cleared his mind. He rubbed hard with the towel and walked back to the shack. He blew out the lamp and crawled in his bunk. He crossed his hands and locked his fingers under his head. He stared at the dark ceiling.

He didn't want to think of what Maria had said to him, but he could not help himself. What if Maria or Butler—? And Wendy? No wonder Deafy had said that he would kill Blake Terrell if he could not stop him another way. A man who would subject his daughter to such, should be killed.

Kim ran his hand through his hair and rolled in his bunk. Even when he had first come to Borger, he had not been as lonely as he was now. And he was frightened—frightened of the things he couldn't change, of things he didn't know. He was frightened for Wendy. He thought of her clear, blue eyes that were sometimes dove-grey, and how her small gold flecked nose crinkled when she grinned.

He pulled the soiled covers about him and went to sleep listening to the monotonous sound of the drilling rig near the shack. He dreamed of taking Wendy to California and lying in the sun, and laughing and playing where people did not seek shadows like friendless animals.

CHAPTER XIV

The day after Maria had summoned him to the Terrell house, Kim suffered the torture of unruly thoughts. Suppose Wendy found out that Joe Shay was Blake's illegitimate son! The very thought of it made Kim sick. What if Maria made an effort to trace Joe's birth?

And suppose his well turned out to be a duster? It probably would, Kim thought with fine pessimism.

He wished Deafy were at the rig. But Deafy had left at daylight and wouldn't be back until the next day. In the meantime, Kim had to watch the two men. They were sorry help and he was short and cross with them.

The day was agonizingly long. Kim didn't eat lunch and drank only a cup of coffee for supper. He was staying close to the rig. It was almost daylight when a cable broke and the men went leisurely about fixing it. Kim was impatient.

"Now you just take it easy, young feller," the man with the bad teeth said lazily. "We'll get it fixed after a while."

"I want it fixed right now," Kim flared and threw down his wrench. He straightened up suddenly and barked his head on a derrick timber. His frayed temper snapped. "And my name is not *young feller*. It's Mr. Wingate."

"Well pardon *me!*" one of the men said with elaborate sarcasm.

Kim started to say something more, but closed his mouth hard. He turned and stamped away. He was disgusted with himself. Another year, he thought, and I'll be as bad as Blake Terrell!

He started toward the shack, intent on getting some food. But halfway there, he changed his mind and walked to the pickup truck instead. He cranked it quickly and heard the men yell as he drove away. He couldn't understand what they said, but he could probably guess anyway. They could fix the rig—or shut it down! At the moment he didn't care.

The pickup bounced over the grass tufts and rocks, but Kim was unaware of them. He skidded into the Terrell driveway just at sunup. The truck had not come to a complete stop when he jumped out. The porch light was on, as usual, and he could see a light in the kitchen window. He banged the big, brass door knocker noisily.

He waited a minute and then raised the big, metal knocker again. Just then, the door opened a crack.

"Who's dere?" a suspicious voice asked.

"It is I, Rachael, Kim Wingate."

"What you want dis time o' de mornin', Mr. Kim?" Rachael asked as she opened the door.

"I want to see Miss Wendy," Kim said as he stepped inside.

"Laws a me! Mr. Kim, is you drunk?" Rachael asked, wide-eyed, as she took in his greasy clothing.

"No, Rachael," Kim said firmly. "I'm not drunk. Now, where is Miss Wendy?"

"She's in de bed, where she ought to be dis time o' de mornin'. Now you scoot right on out of here, Mr Kim," Rachael said sternly.

"No, I'm not going to leave. I want to see Wendy. Now go tell her I'm here."

"But, Mr. Kim," Rachael said dubiously, "I don't 'spec Mr. Terrell gonna like that. He just et his breakfast and left a few minutes ago.— Him and that Joe Shay. 'Sides, Miss Wendy cain't see nobody. She got de gas eye.'

"I don't care if she has hydrophobia," Kim almost yelled. "I want to see her."

"Please, Mr. Kim," Rachael pleaded. "You gonna wake Miss Terrell. What you want to see Miss Wendy for, anyhow?"

"I want to ask her to marry me!" Kim yelled.

"Laws a me!" Rachael's eyes grew wide in astonishment, and then her black face split in an enormous smile. "Laws a me! You just wait a second, Mr. Kim. I'll go tell Miss Wendy you wants to see her. Now don't you go away!"

Rachael was chuckling and mumbling to herself as she hurried toward the stairway. Her fat body jiggled as she ascended. In less than five seconds she reappeared at the head of the stairs.

"Miss Wendy say for you to come right on up, Mr. Kim," Rachael beamed down at him.

Kim bounded up the stairs.

"Mr. Kim," Rachael said conspiratorially as he reached the top, "You stays jus' as long as you wants. I gonna be right smack at the bottom of these stairs, and they ain't nobody gonna innerupt yo. Not even Miss Terrell."

"Where is her room, Rachael?" Kim asked.

"That third door down the hall, Mr. Kim," Rachael said breathlessly. "On de lef'."

Kim knocked.

"Kim? Is that you?" Wendy's voice sounded sleepy.

"Yes. Wendy, may I come in?"

"Of course not, Kim," he heard her laugh. "It wouldn't be proper, and besides I have the gas eye. I look terrible. What on earth do you want?"

"I want you to marry me," Kim said loudly to the blank door.

For a moment there was complete silence. Then Kim heard the dull thud of Wendy's bare feet hitting the floor. And a second later, the door opened just a crack.

"What did you say, Kim?" Wendy's whisper floated softly to him.

"Wendy," Kim's voice carried the urgency he felt. "I want to marry you. Please, Wendy, will you marry me?"

Again the complete silence greeted Kim. His heart was churning like a drill bit. Still she didn't answer.

"Wendy!" he said desperately. "Did you hear me? I love you. Will you marry me?"

"I heard you, darling!" Wendy's voice was faint.

"Well, will you?"

"Yes, Kim! Yes! Yes! Yes!"

"When?"

"Whenever you want, darling," Wendy said softly.

"As soon as my well comes in?" Kim asked eagerly.

"Kim," Wendy's voice was lilting. "I don't care if your well never comes in."

"Wendy," Kim said. "May I kiss you?" He was beginning to feel a little silly talking to the closed door.

"Oh, Kim!" Wendy's voice whispered regretfully. "I would like so very much to be kissed right now, but I don't want you to see me with my eyes all swollen and watery. I'll make it up to you a million times!" she promised. Then she opened the door a bit wider and reached through.

Kim grabbed her hand and squeezed it hard. "I love you, Wendy. I've got to get back to the rig."

Wendy laughed happily as she heard him pound down the stairs. He could be an oil man, if he wanted! Or a lawyer—or anything else. But he would always be Kim Wingate! And she loved him. Her heart sang as she waltzed around the room and whirled onto the bed.

She laughed again as she thought of the strange spectacle they must have presented with Kim at the door shouting his love. She hoped Maria had heard! She wanted the whole world to hear! She longed to feel his arms around her, squeezing tight, and to feel his lips!

But there was time! A lifetime!

Kim heard Wendy laugh as he started down the stairway. Rachael was still posted at the bottom step. Kim went down three at a time.

"Whoopee!" he yelled jubilantly as he hit bottom. "She's going to do it, Rachael! She said she *would!*"

"I knowed that, Mr. Kim," Rachael said happily.

Kim grabbed the big negress and started whirling her about the room. He was acting idiotic, he knew. But he didn't care.

"That was a very nice proposal, Mr. Wingate," Maria's musical voice interrupted their dance.

"Huh?" Kim looked at Maria stupidly.

Maria laughed. She was sitting on the divan. She was wearing a robe, decorously closed, and her usually well done hair was a bit askew. She looked as though she had been up only a few minutes.

"I said, you propose very well, Kim," Maria repeated.

"Oh!" Kim came back to earth. "I guess it was pretty bad," he said lamely.

"I think it was very wonderful, Kim." There was no jest in Maria's voice. "I wish I had heard one just like that a long time ago."

Kim looked at her suspiciously. He half expected her to laugh. But she didn't laugh. And there was no derision or mockery on her face. Instead, she looked serene, and a little sad.

"I'm sorry, Maria," Kim said soberly.

"Don't be, Kim," she said. "Don't ever be sorry for anything."

"I didn't mean about Wendy and me," Kim hastily explained, thinking Maria had misunderstood.

"I know you didn't," Maria said softly. "You meant you were sorry for me!"

"I—I guess I'd better be going."

"Goodbye, Kim," Maria said tenderly as she took his hand. "I think it is wonderful! I hope both of you are so very happy!"

There was a sort of finality about the way Maria offered her good wishes. Almost like a farewell!

Triumph rode high in Kim as he sped back toward the rig. He was the luckiest man in the world! Now, if his well was a good one! And it would be. It had to be! With his luck, he couldn't hit a dry hole now. He might even get the Beatenbow lease since Patton had quit the oil business. He'd bet that Granny would have wanted him to have it. And when this well came in, he would have enough money to become a big oil operator! Maybe even bigger than Blake Terrell!

At the moment he was even glad he had met Joe Shay. Had it not been for Joe, he probably would never have seen Deafy Jones, or Borger—or Wendy. Kim's thoughts were as bright as the morning sun shining in his face. It was a wonderful day!

Kim bounced up to the rig and jumped out of the truck. The rig was running. Deafy must be back. He was. Kim saw him looking at the cable that had broken just before he left for town.

"Hey Deafy!" he yelled. "Come into the shack. I have something to tell you!"

Deafy looked up and started slouching toward the shack. "Them hands ain't worth a damn, Kim," Deafy grumbled as he entered. "The rig was shut down when I got here an hour ago."

"You old devil!" Kim said affectionately. "You thought you were pretty smart, didn't you—talking poor Mandy into marrying you! Well, let me tell you something, Deafy Jones. You're not the only one that's pretty smart. Wendy's going to marry me."

Deafy looked at Kim for a moment, surprise clearly written on his face. Then the surprise was replaced by an expression of delight. "Now don't that beat all!" he said mildly and sat on a bunk.

"I just asked her a while ago," Kim bubbled. "And she said she would."

"Is that where you was gone when I got here?" Deafy asked.

"Yes. I got her out of bed to ask her. She said she would," Kim repeated again as if he still couldn't believe it, and perhaps saying it would make it really so.

"I just *knowed* it!" Deafy said. "I just knowed you two kids would do that!" His voice betrayed his emotion.

"I guess we are about two of the luckiest men in the world, Deafy, don't you?"

"I guess we are," Deafy agreed. "I sure would like to have seen Wendy's face."

"Me too," Kim said.

Deafy looked at him in surprise. "I thought you said you asked her to marry you, Kim. Are you ribbing me again?"

"Nope," denied Kim. "But she had the gas eye and wouldn't let me in. I proposed to her through a crack in the door."

Deafy sat for a minute as if stunned. Then suddenly he started laughing. His roar shook the shack. Kim looked at him in astonishment. Deafy's laugh was a rare thing. He usually expressed his mirth with a grin.

"Sounds kind of funny, I guess," Kim said when Deafy's laughter had subsided. "But it worked."

"That's the important thing about it," Deafy agreed. "When you getting married?"

"As soon as that well blows."

Deafy considered a moment. "What if you hit a duster?"

"I'm not going to," Kim said confidently. "In another thirty or forty days, it's coming in. And then I'm going to get the Beatenbow lease. You wait and see!"

Kim's reference to the Beatenbow lease caused Deafy to sober. For a moment, he shifted about uncomfortably. Kim noticed.

"What's the matter, Deafy?"

"About that Beatenbow lease, Kim," Deafy said. "You ain't going to get it."

"Why not?"

Deafy was silent.

"Oh!" Comprehension dawned on Kim. "*You're* going to get it. Good! I was just talking anyway, Deafy. I didn't really want it."

"Not me," Deafy said. "Blake Terrell."

"What?" Kim gasped his astonishment.

"That's right."

"But—but," Kim stammered. "If Granny didn't want him to have it, I don't think the children—."

"It was Mrs. Beatenbow that let him have the lease," Deafy interrupted.

"But—I hadn't even heard about it, Deafy," Kim said lamely. "I'm sorry."

"Blake ain't heard about it hisself, yet," Deafy said. "The day me and Mandy got married, Mrs. Beatenbow called in the boys—right after we left. Mandy says that she knowed she wasn't going to live much longer. Anyway, she told the boys that she wanted Mandy to have the horse ranch. That's just a couple of thousand acres that her Daddy homesteaded when he come to this country. Then, she said that the ten thousand acres in the cow ranch ought to be leased for oil. She was disappointed that Patton quit the oil business, for she had wanted it to go to a local man. She wanted the Beatenbow to be just as big and important in oil as it had been in cattle and horses. She figured the lease ought to go to a man that was big enough to hold it and take everything from under it. She knew Blake was that man. The boys will likely tell him about it pretty soon."

"Oh!" Kim could not keep the disappointment from his voice.

"Sort of hit me too," admitted Deafy. "But when you get right down to it, that old lady was smart, Kim. You couldn't find a man that will get more oil, and faster, than Blake will. And a duster wouldn't make him quit. She made the right choice, all right, even if it does gall us."

"I suppose so," Kim said glumly.

"Course, they'll have to watch Blake. He'd steal the whole thing if he could. But them Beatenbow boys ain't no fools. They're different from Blake, but they're just as tough. Tougher, maybe. They won't let him get away with anything."

"Well, anyway," Kim said brightening, "We have an oil well to drill. And boy! Am I going to drill it in a hurry."

"Don't blame you," Deafy said feelingly. "Let's get at it."

During the first two months of the Rangers' occupation of Borger, the attitude of the business men had softened considerably toward the lawless element. Their business continued to slump. A real depression was making itself felt. Grumbling increased to outright criticism of the Rangers. Business men were seriously considering petitioning the governor to remove them. It was becoming more and more apparent that they wanted justice—tempered with prosperity.

But the Rangers went about their business imperturbably. If the governor wanted them removed, he would issue the order. In the meantime, they would enforce the law. A certain amount of friction was developing between them and the local police, which bothered the Rangers not at all. They took orders only from the Governor of Texas, and their captain. Local politics was no concern of theirs.

But the local police, abetted and supported by the business men, and perhaps inspired by jealousy, began more strenuous opposition. It had begun with small differences and grown to vast proportions. Finally, one of the local policemen made the mistake of attempting to strike a Ranger during an argument over an arrest. The Ranger shot the policeman, superficially wounding him. The incident was a signal for rebellion against the Rangers. The Ranger was charged with attempted murder, and a group of business men, including lawyers, real estate men, hotel operators, and many others, met to draft a request to Governor Dan Moody to remove the Rangers from Borger. The local police could handle the situation.

Governor Moody received the request to remove the Rangers at the same time that he heard one of his Rangers had been indicted for attempted murder. Moody contended, with much valid basis, that if one of his Rangers had intended to kill a man, he certainly would not have only wounded him superficially. He steadfastly refused to even entertain any thought of removing the Rangers so long as a cloud was hovering over that organization.

Thus, the incident that had served as an excuse for the business men to request the withdrawal of the Rangers had backfired. The local citizenry went quickly about bringing the Ranger to trial and straightway cleared him on the grounds of self-defense. Then they petitioned the governor again.

Kim heard news of the rift from the men he employed to help at the rig, but Kim was not concerned with the Ranger situation. He concentrated all his energy on keeping his machinery running as if the very intensity of his desire would make it drill faster. He hadn't even been in to see Wendy again since she had promised to marry him. And she had not visited the rig, much to Kim's disappointment.

The crashing of derrick timbers awakened Kim one afternoon late in July. He jumped from his bunk and ran to the door of the shack. Pieces of the derrick were still settling to the ground after having been heaved into the sky by the powerful force of oil and gas escaping as the bit had made its final plunge that opened a channel of escape to the surface of the earth.

Kim stood a moment, fascinated by the sight of his well. From the corner of his eye, he saw Deafy and the two men running away from the crashing timbers and flying oil. A hundred yards away, they stopped and turned to look. A cry of triumph rose in Kim's throat.

Then, as suddenly as a lightning flash, the tower of black oil changed to a giant yellow and gold torch. Flames lashed futilely at the sky, and the well roared as it belched an endless supply of the volatile fuel into the holocaust.

Kim's cry of triumph changed to a groan of despair. Somewhere in that tangle of wreckage two pieces of metal had banged together, or a pebble had bounced from the casing, causing the spark that could turn an oil man's dream into a nightmare. With no thought of what he would do, Kim ran toward the burning well. Fifty yards away, the waves of heat emanating from it drove him back. He retreated slowly, protecting his face with his hands as he did so.

Deafy and the two men came to Kim. Deafy took Kim's arm, and they withdrew from the heat of the flames.

"What do we do now, Deafy?" Kim asked desperately.

"First thing," Deafy said grimly. "You better go get your clothes on."

Kim looked down at his bare feet and legs in amazement. He was still in his underwear. He was much too discouraged to be embarrassed or amused. Neither Deafy nor the men said a word as he turned and walked away in silence.

Kim dressed in a daze. An hour ago, he was on the verge of riches. Now he had no idea what was in store for him. And to make his situation much more desperate, almost all of his and Deafy's money was gone. He had not mentioned the fact to Deafy, for he had had great faith in his well. Somehow he had just *known* that it would come in. Well, it had come in, all right!

The flames from the well were rising almost two hundred feet into the air and were visible for miles around. Throughout the fields, men stopped in their work to stare and then shake their heads sadly as they returned to their jobs. Many, who could leave their work, or who were not working when they saw the fire, headed toward it. An oil well fire was an awe inspiring and fascinating sight.

By the time Kim was dressed, a small crowd had already arrived and were gathered about Deafy. They were talking in subdued tones as Kim walked up to them.

"Is the well ruined, Deafy?" Kim asked. He paid no attention to the others, many of whom were looking at him sympathetically.

"I don't know, Kim," Deafy said. "This is the first well that ever fired on me, and I been drilling for nearly thirty years."

"But can't we put out the fire some way?" Kim asked doggedly.

"We can get somebody to shoot it," admitted Deafy. "And the way I understand it is that if the well is strong enough, it will keep the hole open and the oil coming out after the TNT goes off and puts out the fire."

"That's right," offered a red headed man standing near Kim and Deafy.

Kim looked briefly at the man but returned his attention to Deafy quickly. Deafy was looking keenly at the red headed man.

"Ain't you Kincaid?" Deafy asked the man.

"That's right."

"Used to be Terrell's super, didn't you?" Deafy asked.

"I used to be. I quit."

"Heard about that," Deafy said and spat tobacco juice. "What do you know about fires?"

"I've had a couple of—"

Suddenly the wind changed and drove the heat from the fire toward the group, and they had to retreat several yards. More people were quickly gathering. Deafy grabbed Kincaid's arm and nodded to Kim. They withdrew from the group.

"What was that you was saying?" Deafy asked Kincaid.

"I've had a couple of wells fire when they came in," Kincaid said. "They're about as close to hell as I care to get, but they can be handled."

"How?" Kim asked eagerly.

"Well," Kincaid said with conviction. "You got to shoot the well. That's a cinch. Otherwise it would just set there and burn till all the gas was gone and the oil too, probably. That means you got to hire somebody to tie a real heavy weight onto about ten pounds of TNT and tote it up to that well and drop it down into the mouth of it. If the pressure is strong enough to blow the TNT back out, then it blows up half the country along with the man. If it goes down the hole, then it explodes and puts out the fire—cuts off the air from it, so they tell me."

"But what about the well?" Kim asked almost frantically.

"Well," said Kincaid. "It it's got enough pressure, it just starts flowing again after the explosion stops it for a second. It'll push out a lot of gravel and dirt. Some of 'em even fire a second time—but it isn't likely. Then you cap it, and you got yourself an oil well."

"What if there isn't enough pressure to push the debris out of the hole after the explosion?" Kim wanted to know.

"Then you just have to drill again," Kincaid said flatly. "One of the wells that fired on me was strong enough to keep flowing after it was shot. The other one didn't."

"What do you think about this one?" Kim asked eagerly. "Do you think it would keep flowing?"

"Well," Kincaid looked thoughtfully at the flaming well. "It isn't the strongest well I've seen in this field, but it's got a lot of power."

Both Kim and Deafy were looking at Kincaid expectantly.

"I'm no authority on the subject," Kincaid said almost defensively. "But I'd say you have an even chance."

"That's good enough for me," Kim said grimly. "Who can I get to shoot it—do you know?"

"There's a man in Amarillo named Tex Thornton that is plenty good, so I hear," Kincaid said. "Terrell used him once. He comes pretty high, but there aren't many people with nerve enough to walk up to a burning well with enough TNT in his arms to blow up an acre of land."

"How much does he charge?" Kim asked apprehensively.

"Terrell paid him five thousand dollars," Kincaid said.

"Well!" Kim said resignedly as he suddenly sat on the ground. "That does it! We haven't *got* five thousand dollars."

Deafy looked at Kim in surprise. He had taken little part in the conversation since Kim and Kincaid had begun talking of shooting the well. Kim didn't meet Deafy's glance.

"Well," Kincaid's face softened into a good natured Irish grin. "If you get him to shoot it, and he does a good job, your well is worth plenty of money. If he doesn't do a good job—then there isn't anyone to pay."

"I can see that," Kim said glumly. "But suppose he got the fire out, and then it didn't have pressure enough to flow. I'd owe him five thousand dollars—and I wouldn't have a well either."

"That's just a chance you got to take, Kim," Deafy said earnestly.

Perhaps for the first time since their association, Kim paid no attention to Deafy. He looked at Kincaid.

"You have seen wells shot?" he asked.

Kincaid nodded.

"Could you explain to me how it is done?"

"Well," Kincaid said. "It takes three men. They wear asbestos suits. Two of them walk along with the man carrying the TNT and carry hoses hooked onto a tank truck and keep shooting a stream of water on the man carrying the explosive. He goes right up to the well and then drops the TNT down with a heavy weight on it. Then—well that's about all there is to it, I guess."

"Do you know where I could get asbestos suits?"

"Sure—"

"Whoa!" Deafy yelped in alarm. "Now you wait just a minute, Kim. You ain't fixing to do no such damn fool thing as—"

"Wait, Deafy," Kim said. "Let Kincaid tell me."

Kincaid looked uncertainly from Kim to Deafy. "Well, I know where you could find some suits, all right. And there's a water truck in town. Nearly all the rigs have some TNT about. You could find rigging all right. But I sure wouldn't recommend that anyone try to shoot a well that didn't have experience."

"Neither would I!" Deafy said feelingly. "Kim was just talking. We'll get Thornton."

"Thornton didn't have any experience the first time he shot one!" Kim said almost belligerently. "And I don't have five thousand dollars to pay him."

"I don't give a damn if you ain't!" Deafy growled. "You ain't going to shoot no oil well with TNT!"

Deafy stalked away. His back was stiff as he marched toward a group of spectators. The grass around the well was dry, and little tongues of flame ate at it. Men stamped them out and looked in awe at the tower of flame.

Kim talked a few minutes longer with Kincaid and then got into the pickup truck and drove toward town. Kincaid joined Deafy.

The rest of the day and night, Kim went about his errands in town. His face was grim and drawn. It was almost sun up when he returned to the fire. Even at that hour, there were more people present than there had been the day before. Kim looked at them without interest. In the seat beside him were two roustabouts who still were not quite sober. In the back of the pickup were three asbestos suits, ten pounds of TNT and a piece of anvil iron from which the base had been cut with an acetelyne torch. It would go down the hole. An hour after noon, the tank truck filled with water and equipped with hoses would report to the fire.

Kim cut the motor and dismounted from the truck. The two men with him sat for a moment. Their faces were taut and drawn. It was beginning to dawn on them that they had hired out to do a terrifying job. The sight of the towering flames and the roar of the well were beginning to melt their whiskey courage.

Kim went about removing the gear from the truck. Curious on-lookers came to stare. They had heard that Tex Thornton was going to shoot the well. When Kim gingerly removed the wax covered TNT, exclamations of surprise and alarm rippled through the crowd. They quickly withdrew.

Kim paid no attention to them. He went about readying the gear as Kincaid had told him it should be. The two men that he had hired to help him shoot the well helped unenthusiastically.

Deafy and Kincaid arrived a few minutes later.

"Kim," Deafy began brusquely. "I been doin' a little figuring. Kincaid and me went to Amarillo last night. Tex Thornton is in Dallas, but he'll be back day after tomorrow, and I left word that you wanted him to shoot the well. He ought to be here in a few days."

"I'm going to shoot the well myself, Deafy," Kim said without looking at him. "I hired these two men to help me."

"Now, Kim," Deafy said harshly. "I ain't going to let you do no such a damn fool thing."

"Yes, you are," Kim said flatly. "Kincaid, I sure will appreciate it if you will help me with this gear. The water truck will be here right after noon.

Deafy's jaw muscles worked, and he spat a stream of tobacco juice. Then he turned and started walking away. He had gone only a few steps when he faltered and stopped. His step was slow as he walked back to Kim.

"Fix it as good as you can, Kincaid," Deafy said tiredly.

Kim and Kincaid went about fixing the weight to the TNT. Deafy stood uncertainly. Finally he gave up and started helping. They checked and rechecked. It was a tedious job, and they took their time. But by the time the water truck arrived, Kim was ready to don the asbestos suit. It was a fairly simple procedure, and Deafy helped Kim with the cumbersome garment. Kim noticed that Deafy's hands were trembling. Kim looked at Deafy and grinned with reassurance that he did not feel.

Kincaid started helping the two men who were to keep the water hoses on Kim. The first man had one foot in the asbestos suit when he suddenly stepped out of it. Kincaid looked at him in surprise, as did Kim and Deafy.

"Look, Wingate," the man said almost humbly. "I just ain't got the guts for it. I was drunk when I hired out to you, and I had never seen a well fire before. Didn't sound so bad when you told me how it was done. But I ain't drunk now—and I reckon I'll just have to ask you to take me off your payroll."

"Me too," the other man said quickly. "You can't hold a man to what he agreed to when he was drunk anyway!"

Kim stared at the men, and their gaze shifted. Suddenly they both started walking rapidly away.

Kim sat dejectedly on the running board of the truck. There was little he could say and nothing he could do. He pulled at his ear and looked about. To his surprise, there was a ring of cars almost surrounding the fire at about a quarter of a mile distance. The roar of the fire was the only sound.

As the two men walked away, Deafy and Kincaid looked at Kim. Then they looked at each other. Their gaze held for almost half a minute.

Then their eyes broke contact—and each reached for an asbestos suit.

It was then that Kim looked at them. Deafy's face was set in hard lines, and Kincaid's usually florid face was white.

"What are you doing?" Kim demanded.

"Being a damn fool—as usual," Deafy's hard lips pressed flat against his teeth in a feeble grin as he pulled on the suit.

"Oh, no you're not," Kim protested. "You and Kincaid aren't going to do any such thing!"

"Yep, Kimmy, me boy, we are," Deafy said. "We done talked it over."

"And I say you are not!" Kim said hotly. "It is my well, and you and Kincaid don't have anything to do with it."

"Like Deafy said, Wingate," Kincaid interrupted. "We have already talked it over. Get ready."

"No!"

"Lost your nerve, Wingate?" Kincaid taunted.

A hot reply was almost on Kim's lips before the grim look on Kincaid's face stopped him. He looked from the face of one man to the other. Fear was plainly written on each. But there was no indecision there.

Kim felt a surge of pride and humility. A lump rose in his throat as he looked at Deafy. He had never seen Deafy afraid before. Then he remembered once having heard Deafy say that a man who never did get scared was just a plain, damned fool.

Kim wished that he could say something that would make both of them understand how proud he was that he had been allowed to know them. But he knew that this was one of the times when words could not say what he felt. Kim looked away quickly and started adjusting his suit.

Ten minutes later, each man had his suit on. The head gear was a sort of helmet with a glass front, much like a welder's hat. Deafy was the first to put his on. Kim was adjusting it when he heard an exclamation, and Deafy started tearing the gear from his head.

"What's the matter, Deafy?" Kim asked apprehensively.

Deafy didn't answer. Instead he held the hat toward Kim and rubbed at his eyes. The glass front of the hat was covered with brown liquid. Deafy had forgotten and spat tobacco juice. There was no place for it to go, and it had covered the glass front of the helmet and bounced back into his eye.

Both Kim and Kincaid laughed as Deafy spat out his cud of tobacco and wiped the spittle from the helmet. Deafy grinned ruefully.

Fifteen minutes later the truck had been driven as close to the fire as possible, and the three men, clad in the asbestos suits stood for a moment looking at the fire. The engine of the truck furnished the power to propel the water and was left running.

Kim gathered the heavy weight to which the TNT was attached into his arms. He held it gingerly. Then he started walking slowly toward the fire. He felt the water from the hoses manned by Deafy and Kincaid play on him. The stream was intermittently interrupted as Deafy and Kincaid sprayed each other.

Closer and closer, Kim approached. There was complete silence except for the roar of the fire. The thousands of people, well out of the danger zone, looked in awe as the three cumbersome figures approached closer and closer to the burning well. The tension mounted, and men held their breath. One woman quietly fainted and was noticed by no one.

Inside the asbestos suit, Kin Wingate felt as though he were being broiled alive. Sweat rolled into his eyes. He stared in sheer fascination at that small base of the fire where he must deposit his deadly cargo. The water from one hose played on him constantly now, and he knew that Deafy and Kincaid were taking turns spraying each other while keeping one on him at all times.

When he was within twenty-five feet of the well, Kim was positive that he could never make it. The heat was like a giant hand squeezing the very life out of him.

Grimly, he stalked forward. He felt no fear—only a remoteness. The terrifying heat waves were hotter and hotter. Then he was ten feet away, and he stumbled. A gasp went up among the spectators. But Kim regained his feet and kept going forward. The heavy anvil had become almost too heavy to carry further.

Then he was there! Slowly he sank to his knees and inched forward. The heat was too much! The water sprays were turning to steam as they struck him and his vision was not clear. On his stomach, he inched forward.

Then, with the mightiest effort of his life, Kim Wingate moved the heavy weight of the anvil forward and pushed it into the spewing flame that shot from the ground. He felt it fall and then jerk the TNT from his arm. Then he rolled backward and lay flat on the ground. Two seconds later, the well emitted a giant burp, and for a moment nothing came from the well. Then a column of greenish-black oil replaced the yellow tower of flame in the sky.

Cows grazing on the brown grass nearby raised their heads and stared with bovine curiosity as cheers from the thousands of people who had watched the drama unfold floated across the prairies. Then the cows complacently returned to their never ending task of maintaining a full belly.

CHAPTER XV

Blake Terrell, freshly barbered and impeccably clad, parked his Stutz in front of Claude Butler's office and stepped to the sidewalk. He stood for a moment looking to the northwest. The flame and smoke from Kim Wingate's well was clearly visible. Blake chuckled. He'd bet the Beatenbows were sorry that the old lady had let Kim have that horse pasture lease.

Thought of the Beatenbows brought Blake back to his present, happy situation. Unless something unexpected happened, he would be one of the biggest independent oil men in Texas before sundown, for he was to meet the Beatenbows in Stinnett at four o'clock to sign a lease on ten thousand acres of the Beatenbow ranch. It would be one of the biggest deals ever made in Hutchinson county!

Blake looked again at the smoke and flame pouring from the burning well. He smiled and strode purposefully into Butler's law office.

Butler looked up as Blake entered. He was as handsomely dressed as Blake, and his dark eyes showed no expression whatever as Blake spoke to him. He leaned back in his chair and crossed his small, almost feminine, hands over his expensive vest.

"Good afternoon, Mr. Terrell," he said suavely.

"Where were you this morning?" Blake asked bluntly.

"Since you inquire so courteously, Mr. Terrell," the lawyer said frostily, "I was out of town—looking at a burning oil well."

"Half the fools in town were out there," Blake said touchily. "But you could have waited. That well will burn until Tex Thornton gets back from Dallas. I know."

"You know a great deal about the oil fields, don't you, Mr. Terrell?" Blake missed the mockery in Butler's voice. "Isn't it possible that someone else might have intelligence enough to drop a few pounds of TNT into a hole?"

"A lot of men have *sense* enough," Blake conceded. "But there isn't a man in a thousand that has *guts* enough. Handling TNT is a lot different from handling that fancy fountain pen of yours, Butler!"

"Perhaps it is." Butler took the gold topped fountain pen from his vest pocket and turned it slowly in his fingers as if considering the wisdom of Blake's statement.

"Well, quit that damned fiddling!" Blake said irritably. "We're due in Stinnett at four o'clock. I want to get there early so you can check those lease papers again before I sign."

"I checked the Beatenbow lease papers yesterday," the lawyer said almost absently. "They are in order."

"They'd better be," Blake growled. "But I want you to check them again today just to be sure."

"Sorry, Mr. Terrell," Butler smiled thinly. "I will not be able to accompany you today."

"The hell you won't," Blake glared at the lawyer in surprise. "I pay you to do what I say—and I say you go with me."

"I've earned your handsome retainers many times over, Mr. Terrell," Butler smiled urbanely. "And it just happens that I have some personal business that I must attend today. I shall be unable to accompany you."

"Damn your personal business!" Blake snarled. "Every oil man in Texas has been after that Beatenbow lease ever since this field opened—and I got it. We sign at four o'clock, and you're going with me to see that everything is legal."

"Everything *is* legal," Butler assured Blake. "I told you that I checked those papers yesterday."

"You checked them *yesterday!*" Blake spat; then he continued sarcastically, "I guess it hadn't occurred to you that they could have changed those leases since then!"

"They haven't," Butler said calmly. "One of the Beatenbow men and their lawyer were there when we examined the papers. And, Mr. Terrell, though it may be difficult for men like you and me to understand, there *are* people who believe in *right*—rather than legality. They wouldn't change those papers without your knowledge and consent."

Damn the man, anyway! He was right, of course, but he irritated Blake. Always fingering that gold coin on his watch chain with those pretty hands. Probably never had done an honest day's work in his life. But Blake wanted Butler with him when those papers were signed!

"Now look, Butler," Blake said in placating tones, "I'll need someone to go with me anyway. I might get held up, or—"

"Take Joe Shay with you."

"I gave him the day off."

"I think you action may have been ill timed, Mr. Terrell," Butler said almost whimsically, "particularly in view of the fact that Governor Moody has just ordered the Rangers out of Borger."

"What?" Blake almost yelled his surprise.

"You mean you didn't know?" Butler's voice was mocking.

"I—I—No," Blake said belligerently. "And I don't think you do either. Where did you hear that, anyway?"

"The wire came in about fifteen minutes ago. They are to leave within twenty-four hours. At noon tomorrow, the law in Borger will be back in the hands of local police."

"Why wasn't I told about this?" Blake demanded.

"Why, Mr. Terrell," Butler purred. "I should think that a man of your status, with all your connections in Austin, would be the first to know."

"That'll be enough out of you, Butler!" Blake's face was getting red. He didn't have to take that sort of talk from any lawyer! "And you can just forget about that personal business of yours for the day. You're going with me!"

"Mr. Terrell," Butler said conversationally, ignoring Blake's anger, "you just do not seem to understand. I told you that I had personal business to attend today. I have absolutely no intention of accompanying you to Stinnett."

"All right, damn you!" Blake's hand came down hard on the lawyer's desk. "But if there is a flaw in that lease, I'll have your hide! In the meantime, you're fired!"

"As you say, Mr. Terrell," Butler's voice was equable, but a tiny malicious gleam appeared in his usually expressionless eyes. "I assure you, however, that I have as much interest in the legality of that lease as you do."

Blake stared at the lawyer and a muscle twitched his jaw. Without another word he turned and stalked from the lawyer's office.

Again on the sidewalk, he stopped and looked scowlingly about. He was very angry. He was aware that Butler had been deliberately taunting him. But why? It worried Blake.

Briefly Blake considered the possibility of finding another lawyer to accompany him. But that would take too much time. Besides, a new lawyer would have to go over the papers thoroughly and ask a million questions. That wouldn't do. The Beatenbows said they would be ready to sign at four o'clock.

Blake brushed his moustache rapidly with a bent forefinger and looked up and down the street. He wished that he had not given Joe the day off. He had a feeling that he was going to need him. But there was no point in looking for him now. He would already be drunk.

Blake pulled his hat a bit firmer on his head and stalked purposefully toward his car. He was just opening the door when he felt a slight tremor in the earth, followed by a low, booming sound. Blake stopped. It was only a second before the significance of the shock and sound registered. He looked quickly toward Kim Wingate's well. A long, black tail of smoke was drifting away. It was unattached to any base.

The fire was out! Blake stared in disbelief. It couldn't be. Thornton wouldn't be back from Dallas for a week! But it was!

A feeling of urgency gripped Blake. Quickly he jumped in his car and headed toward Stinnett.

Blake arrived early and was pacing up and down in front of the courthouse when the Beatenbow family finally arrived. Blake hurried toward the cars. He cursed his haste, but he could not help himself. He was half way down the walk by the time Ed Beatenbow had his car door open.

"You're on time, Mr. Terrell," Ed greeted him. The three Beatenbow men and their wives were in the front car.

"Yes sir!" Blake said and knew that he was being too cordial. "I'm always on time for business appointments."

Blake gallantly removed his hat and opened the car doors for the Beatenbow women. He shook hands warmly with all the men.

"Well, I reckon everybody made it," Ed Beatenbow said as he glanced at the car behind.

Blake looked. Mandy and Deafy Jones were getting out of the other car. Blake swore under his breath. He had known Mandy would have to sign the lease, but there was no reason why Deafy had to come too! Blake's jaws clamped, then he forced a smile.

"Glad to see you, Mrs. Jones," Blake said to Mandy.

"It is nice to see you Mr. Terrell."

"Hello, Deafy." Blake didn't extend his hand, but he made the greeting as cordial as possible. Until that lease was signed, he would be polite to the devil himself. "Glad to see you got your fire out. You certainly were lucky to get Thornton as soon as you did!"

There was a grim light in Deafy's good eye when he looked at Blake. His grimy face was lined with weariness. He pressed his hard lips flat and spat tobacco juice.

"We didn't get Thornton," he said bleakly.

"You didn't!" Blake surprise was evident to all. "Then who—?"

"Wingate shot it," Deafy said. There was quiet pride in his voice.

"Wingate!" Blake was incredulous.

"Wingate," Deafy reiterated.

"Well—I—. Glad to hear it," Blake said lamely. He would not have been more astonished if Deafy had said the wind had blown it out.

"I expect Mama had Kim figured right," Ed Beatenbow said calmly. "She always said he would make a man."

"I guess she did." Blake simply could think of nothing else to say.

"Well," Ed continued in his unhurried way, "I reckon we might as well get the lease signing over with since everybody is here. Our lawyer is already in the clerk's office."

"Fine, fine!" Blake was recovering quickly. "No use wasting time. I didn't bring a lawyer with me, but I knew that you boys would fix the lease up all right anyway. No use in *me* bringing a lawyer."

"Your lawyer was over here all day yesterday," Ed said firmly. "So was ours. I was here, too. They tell me the lease is all right. Let's sign it."

Ed and Blake led the way to the county clerk's office. The Beatenbow's lawyer had a table cleared of everything but the lease papers. He greeted the group cordially as they entered.

"Well," the lawyer said after greetings had been exchanged. "The papers are all ready for signature, if you are ready to make payment, Mr. Terrell."

"I'm ready," Blake said importantly.

"Then sign here, please." The lawyer indicated the places for him to sign.

Blake signed his name with a flourish.

"Now for the family," the lawyer said expansively. This meant a fat fee for him.

Each of the Beatenbow men signed. They wrote slowly and carefully.

"And now, Mrs. Jones." The lawyer held the pen to Mandy.

Mandy signed and laid the pen on the table. The lawyer picked it up and held it toward Deafy.

"And now, Mr. Jones."

Deafy jumped as if the lawyer had suddenly pointed a gun at him. "I ain't supposed to sign that thing!" he said in alarm.

"Oh, yes, Mr. Jones," the lawyer laughed.

"You mean—*he* has to sign it?" Blake asked in disbelief.

"Yes, Mr. Terrell, he does," the lawyer said, raising his eyebrows. "The laws of the state of Texas do not allow a woman to dispose of her separate property without her husband's joinder. You could not possibly have this lease without Mr. Jones' signature."

Blake's grey eyes filled with the defiance and anger of a trapped animal. He looked apprehensively at Deafy Jones.

But Deafy did not look at Blake. He swallowed hard, and his jaw muscles bulged. He hesitated a second. Then he took the pen in his big, calloused hand and slowly and laboriously fixed his signature to the documents.

Blake Terrell slowly let out a long breath.

"Fine. Fine," the lawyer approved. "And now, everything is in perfect order. You have ten days in which to begin drilling operations, Mr. Terrell."

Blake nodded.

During the signing of the lease, Blake had had to curb an urge to shout at the men to hurry. Suddenly, when the thing was done, he felt a strange reluctance to take his copy of the lease when the lawyer proffered it to him. He folded it slowly and put it in his pocket. Then he looked at Deafy Jones. Deafy was leaning tiredly against the wall with his attention focused on his greasy shoes.

The group filed out of the clerk's office.

"Well," Blake's boisterousness returned once they were outside the clerk's office. "This is going to be a fine thing for all of us. It will be a big operation, but I can certainly handle it."

"Mama figured you could," Ed Beatenbow said quietly.

Courteous farewells were made. Blake got in his car and drove toward Borger. Strangely enough, he was almost reluctant to return. The signing of the Beatenbow lease had not afforded him the satisfaction he had anticipated. It was that damned Deafy!

On the way back to town Blake had to go within a mile of Kim Wingate's well. He decided to drive by. He got there just in time to see Kim Wingate direct the last of the capping operation and get into a truck and drive toward town. Kim didn't see Blake.

Blake watched a few minutes longer and then he too drove toward town. He had been amazed that Kim had shot the well, and he was further surprised at the authority he had displayed in directing the men in capping the well. Blake admired tough men, and for a moment he was almost sorry that Joe Shay hated Kim Wingate so much. If it weren't for Kim's interest in Wendy, Blake decided, he could almost like the man.

But Joe and Kim would fight. They had to. A year ago, Joe would have killed the greenhorn in two minutes. Now Blake wasn't sure that Joe would find Wingate so easy to handle. It would be a fight worth seeing!

Blake's thoughts turned to Maria. She would be pleased that he had got the lease. In his mellow mood, Blake even thought of taking her to New York, or around the world, as he had promised. But that could wait until he had his rigs pumping oil from the Beatenbow!

But Maria would wait! She had no choice. As long as he held the purse strings, he held her. He intended to keep it that way.

Now that the Rangers were gone, Joe Shay would earn his salt again, too. He wouldn't like it, for Joe was getting used to easy living. But he would work! Blake's money held him like a chain. If he could just get control of Kim Wingate's lease, Blake decided, he would be a happy man. He would like to get that young man under his thumb. Maybe he could! If there was a possible way, Butler could find it!

Damn Butler, anyway! Blake rankled at the thought of the man. Well, he would come around soon enough. It wouldn't take him long to find out that others didn't pay like Blake Terrell! And this time Blake would call the tune!

Blake stopped at two of his wells on the way to town and chatted amicably with the drillers, much to their surprise. For some reason that he could not fathom, Blake was reluctant to return home. Nevertheless, he was whistling as he pulled into his driveway. The porch light was on, and Blake's step was jaunty as he trotted up the steps and opened the door.

"Hello, Father." Wendy was just coming into the room. She was wearing a light blue dress that emphasized her sparkling eyes. The color was high in her cheeks, and there was a radiance about her.

"You expecting company, Wendy?" Blake could feel the expectancy in his daughter.

"Yes, Father," Wendy said happily. "Did you get your lease signed, all right?"

"Humph!" Blake said grouchily. "Where's Maria?"

"Why, Father," Wendy said in surprise, "She went to Amarillo with Mr. Butler just after you left today. I thought you knew."

"I knew no such thing," Blake shouted. "And she has no business in Amarillo!"

"Well, don't worry about her," Wendy said lightly as she rearranged a small bouquet of black-eyed daisies and plumed thistle in a vase. "She will be all right. Oh! I forgot. She left a note for you."

Wendy picked up a small envelope from the table and handed it to Blake. It was sealed. Blake glared at Wendy and tore the paper angrily.

Blake read the note, and Wendy heard his quick intake of breath. She looked at Blake. His face was white, and the hand holding the paper trembled.

"What's the matter, Father?" Wendy asked with concern. "Is something wrong?"

"Did she tell you?" Blake asked, suddenly sitting on a chair.

"Tell me what?"

"No!" said Blake, looking keenly at his daughter. "She wouldn't."

"Wouldn't what?" Wendy said imploringly. "Father, what's happened?"

"She's left me, that's what!" Blake shouted as the blood returned to his face. "Tells me to see her lawyer—Butler!" Blake smashed the letter with his fist.

"Oh, No!" Wendy said in a frightened voice. "Maria wouldn't do that!"

"She wouldn't, huh?" Blake threw the letter across the room. "Well she has. The scheming bitch!"

"Father, stop it!" Wendy said angrily. "I won't let you talk about her that way."

"They'll never get a nickel of my money." Blake hadn't even heard Wendy. "I'll get that damned Butler first and her later. Where's Joe Shay."

"I don't know where Joe Shay is." The freckles were showing plainly across Wendy's nose. "And I don't care. I hope I never see him again."

"Never mind!" Blake yelled and grabbed his hat.

Kim's mind raced as he drove to town. His fire was out, the well capped, and Kincaid had agreed to oversee his lease while he was away. He felt wonderful.

Driving down the newly graveled and oiled main street, Kim was surprised to see couples entering and exiting from dance halls and gambling dens that had been closed for almost three months. There was a general air of celebration in the town.

Kim parked his pickup truck near the new brick hotel and got out. He stopped the first man who passed.

"What's going on?" Kim asked, nodding in the general direction of the dance halls.

"Hell, man, ain't you heard?" the man said gleefully. "The governor's ordered the Rangers out. They're already packing. They leave tomorrow."

Kim whistled under his breath. Then he turned and walked toward the new hotel. There wasn't one chance in a thousand that he could get a room there, but with his luck, anything could happen.

Kim felt very conspicuous in his grease stained clothing as he walked across the quiet, well lighted lobby. But, with determination and a feeling that his luck was still with him, he approached the clerk.

"I would like a room, if you have one," he said.

"Yes, sir," the clerk answered politely. "With or without a bath?"

"*With* a bath," Kim said feelingly.

"You are lucky," the clerk smiled politely. "One was vacated less than half a hour ago. Just sign here, please."

Kim signed his name.

"Do you have luggage, Mr. Wingate?" the clerk asked as he looked at Kim's signature.

"No," Kim replied. "But I will have just as soon as I can go out and buy some clothes. I wanted to find a room first."

"I understand." The clerk nodded his head wisely. "You will not want your key until you return then?"

"I'll be back in an hour," Kim said as he pulled a small roll of bills from his pocket.

"Never mind, Mr. Wingate," the clerk smiled professionally. "Your room will be waiting. You may settle your account when you leave. How long do you plan to be with us?"

"I—I'm not sure," Kim was a bit distracted. He was remembering the first time he and Deafy had tried to find a room in Borger and how shocked he had been when Deafy kicked the non-cooperative clerk from his cane bottomed chair. He grinned a bit ruefully at the thought.

"Borger certainly has changed, hasn't it?" he ventured.

"It certainly has," the clerk agreed. "And it will change more."

An hour later Kim returned, carrying three bags. A porter grabbed them as Kim entered the lobby, and Kim felt a bit silly as he followed the Negro to the desk. The clerk gave the porter a key.

"Just ring if you need anything, Mr. Wingate," the clerk said with pride in his voice. "We have telephones in every room."

"I sure will," Kim grinned.

Two minutes later he was in his room on the third floor. He tipped the porter lavishly and looked about. The room was new and clean, though cigar smoke still lingered from its previous occupancy. A rug covered the floor, and the bed looked soft and inviting.

Kim picked up the telephone and somewhat to his surprise the operator answered immediately. Kim gave her the telephone number of his home in Oklahoma. On the third ring he heard his mother's voice. They talked for several minutes. Kim told her of all that had happened, including his new oil well. He was much relieved when his mother indicated no displeasure and was delighted that he was able to detect some pride in her voice.

"I'm going to California," Kim told her. "Then I'm coming home to see you. When I do—I'll have a wife with me!"

"That's wonderful, Kim," his mother said hesitantly. "Is she—I mean—."

"I couldn't describe her in a month," Kim said. "You'll just have to wait until you see her!"

Finally they said their goodbyes and Kim leaned back in the big overstuffed chair.

Memories suddenly flooded through Kim. He remembered the first night he spent in Borger. He'd slept in Sal's place. Kim laughed. He'd bet that this bed wouldn't be a bit nicer than that one had been.

Then Kim opened the door to the bathroom. The white porcelain tub looked almost too good to be true. It was clean and gleaming, and the water was steaming hot. Quickly he divested himself of his oil stained clothing and hopped in. It was a wonderful feeling. Only then, did it occur to him that he had not bathed in anything but a pop-off steam valve in more than a year.

The night was warm. Kim dressed carefully. His new clothing fit fairly well, and he looked at himself with satisfaction. He knotted his tie carefully. The glow of the electric light illuminated his face. There were lines that had not been there a year ago. The youthful softness had given way to a lean hardness. His skin was browned by the Texas wind and sun, and it contrasted sharply with the white shirt and his blue eyes.

He still could hardly believe his good fortune. He had never expected to remain in the oil camp more than a few days, or weeks at most. Now it had become a part of him. He hoped that Wendy would approve his new plan for the future. It was as fantastic as his decision to remain in the camp had been. But here, anything could happen! And Borger was going to grow. It would, one day, be a place where people would be proud to live!

Kim thought briefly of Deafy and Mandy. Who would have thought that crochety, profane, soft-hearted old Deafy Jones and gentle, lovely Mandy would ever find anything in common! It was like the meeting of two worlds!

And Finch! Kim thought of him with little sadness and no regret. Finch had died, but he had died as he wanted to die. Doing what he wanted to do. Few men did that.

And old Granny Beatenbow!

Kim thought of them all and felt a knot in his throat. They were all a part of him now. But the past was past. He was looking to the future. Next week he and Wendy would be in California. There they wouldn't have to stalk about like animals evading predators. They could laugh and talk and walk in the sunlight or moonlight with no fear that death lurked in the shadow of a tar paper shack or a canvas tent.

Paradoxically, Borger had come to symbolize both life and death to Kim. He had thought many times that he had never really lived before he came to the oil camp. But he had become sensitive to the feel of death there, too. It seemed that he could smell the imminence of it.

And that troubled Kim at the moment—for he had a vague feeling of foreboding. Of uneasiness.

Oh, well! He supposed that every man who was about to tell a prospective father-in-law that he was going to marry his daughter, had premonitory feelings. Especially if that man was Blake Terrell.

Kim grinned at himself in the mirror. Then he headed toward the Terrell house.

Five minutes later, he pulled into the driveway. Both Blake's and Wendy's cars were there. Kim jumped out of his pickup truck and bounded up the steps. He was just reaching for the knocker when the door burst open.

"Get out of my way!" Blake Terrell shouted and brushed Kim aside. Kim stood in startled surprise as Blake jumped in his car and drove away.

Kim looked through the door. Wendy was standing in the middle of the floor. Her hands were clenched at her sides, and her eyes were big. She looked frightened and very alone. Kim rushed to her.

"What's the matter with him?" Kim asked in astonishment as he hurried to her.

"Maria's gone," Wendy said tremulously. "She has left Father."

"I'm sorry," Kim said lamely, for he could think of nothing else to say. He took Wendy by the arms.

"It wasn't her fault." Wendy leaned back and looked up into Kim's face. Then she added almost defiantly, "I don't blame her."

"I don't blame her, either, Wendy," Kim said gently.

Suddenly Wendy's blue eyes filled with tears, and Kim felt as if a crown block had fallen on him.

"Kim—p-p-please kiss me."

Kim grabbed Wendy to him. He held her for several seconds and then very quietly and very thoroughly kissed her. Then Wendy, with a small sigh, laid her head on Kim's chest again. Kim held her tightly.

"Kim?" Wendy asked in a small voice. "Do you know how I feel right now?"

"No, Wendy," Kim said hoarsely. "How do you feel?"

"With your arms around me, I feel like I'm all safe and warm in a good strong house, and a storm is blowing outside. And I feel like I'll never be lonely again."

Her voice was muffled in his coat, but Kim heard every word Wendy said.

"You never will be lonely again, Wendy," Kim vowed and kissed the top of her head. "We're going to get married. Right now. Tonight."

"Oh, Kim," Wendy almost wailed. "We can't, not tonight."

"Tomorrow then," Kim said stoutly. "I'll find the preacher tonight, and we can go to Stinnett in the morning for our license, and—"

"Oh, Kim," Wendy said breathlessly, "I want to more than anything in the world. I've had my wedding dress for two weeks. Maria helped me make it. But we couldn't now, not when Father is having so much trouble and—"

"Yes, we can," Kim said firmly. "And we're going to. Blake's had three wives, and he'll probably have a dozen more. I'm just going to have one wife—and I want her now."

"Darling," Wendy blinked back tears. "I know you don't like Father, but I wish you could understand him. Oil is his whole life. He dreams oil, and he lives oil. It's a disease. A lot of men are afflicted with it. Father has the disease. So does Deafy. It just affects men differently. Father wants the power and money it represents. Deafy just wants to be around it."

"Oh," Kim said almost blankly, "I forgot."

"What, darling?"

"My well! It came in. I forgot to tell you."

Wendy stared at him a moment in wonder, then she threw her arms around his neck.

"I know about it. Everyone in Borger knows about it—and how you shot it with TNT. Kim, you might have been killed!"

"Deafy helped. So did Kincaid," Kim said. "And Kincaid is going to run the lease for us while we are gone."

Kim continued eagerly. "We can be married tomorrow in time to catch the train to Panhandle. It makes connection with the one going to California. We'll have a long honeymoon. And then, Wendy, would you mind—. I mean," Kim was almost stammering, "Oh, Wendy, I would like almost more than anything to go on to college. Not to study law—but medicine. I used to dream of it, but I didn't seriously consider it, because I didn't think I was man enough to do it. But now—I *can* do it! I know I can. It would mean several more years but—."

"Kim," Wendy said ecstatically, "I think that is the most wonderful thing that could happen! You'll make a wonderful doctor, and—."

"And we'll come back here and build us a house by our cottonwood and spring—."

"And raise a dozen kids, and—."

Both Kim and Wendy were laughing and talking at the same time. Their hearts were singing with love and hope.

"I'll go find the preacher!" Kim shouted his exhiliration.

"But, Kim," Wendy protested feebly. "I've always dreamed of a church wedding, and flowers and friends—."

"You'll have them all," Kim assured her. "I'll get word to Deafy and Mandy. The Beatenbows can be here by tomorrow afternoon, and the church will be filled with people! You just wait and see!"

"Oh, Kim," Wendy's eyes glowed and she brushed away a tear of happiness. "I'll be waiting for you. Tomorrow is going to be the most wonderful day in the world!"

"It sure is." Kim grinned and kissed her again. "You be ready to go after our license in the morning. I'll get the preacher and tell Blake tonight."

"Kim," Wendy looked crestfallen. "I—I think I'd rather you didn't tell Father. I want everything to be perfect tomorrow, and—"

"Oh," Kim said, suddenly remembering. "I'd forgotten about Maria's being gone. You can't stay here alone tonight."

"Rachael's here," Wendy said. "Besides, I *want* to be alone. I want to be lonelier than I have ever been in my life, just tonight. I want to dream a million dreams. I'll be waiting for you in the morning, darling, and then I'll never be lonely again as long as I live."

"You never will be," Kim said, and kissed her hungrily.

"I'll love you forever, Kim," she whispered. "And I'm going to be the only wife you will ever want."

Kim kissed her again and walked out into the warm night air. On the porch, he stopped a moment and looked at the lights of Borger. They seemed soft and friendly.

Kim found the Methodist minister just as Blake Terrell stamped into Claude Butler's office.

"I've been expecting you, Mr. Terrell," the suave lawyer said calmly. His dark eyes were expressionless. "You are late."

"You'd damned well better be expecting me," Blake said furiously. "I'm going to wring your scrawny neck."

"No, Mr. Terrell," Butler replied calmly. "You are not going to do anything. I had anticipated that you might deviate from your usual custom, and be tempted to do something illegal. So I took necessary precautions against such an eventuality."

The lawyer nodded his head toward two men standing behind Blake. Blake turned. He recognized the man with the long, jagged scar down his cheek. The other he had never seen before. They were holding guns pointed directly at him. Blake turned to the lawyer again.

"You son-of-a-bitch!" he spat venomously. "Where's Maria?"

"Mrs. Terrell is on her way to New Orleans," Butler said almost languidly. "I shall be glad to communicate any message that you wish to send her."

"I'll do my own communicating!" Blake yelled. "You just tell me where to find her."

"I'm afraid you will have to communicate through me, Mr. Terrell," Butler said *"Your wife is my client now."

"Why, you—." Blake made a move toward the lawyer.

"Don't forget yourself, Mr. Terrell," Butler smiled thinly. "My friends are just behind you."

Blake stopped his advance. Butler wasn't bluffing.

"All right, Butler," he said with controlled rage. "Tell your client that I never want to see her again. And tell her not to come whining back to me for money. She'll never get another cent from me!"

"Mr. Terrell," Butler said conversationally as he leaned back in his chair and started fingering the gold coin on his watch chain. "I wish you would be seated. I have something to tell you about Texas law."

"You'll tell me nothing, Butler!" Blake shouted. "And—."

"You want him to set, Mr. Butler?" one of the men behind Blake asked ominously.

"No, Terence," Butler said. "Let Mr. Terrell stand if he wishes. I was merely being polite."

"Then, all right," the man growled. "But you go ahead and talk. He'll listen."

"Thank you, Terence," Butler said politely. "As I was saying, Mr. Terrell, I wish to enlighten you concerning some Texas law. In the first place, your wife will not ask you for money. She has plenty of her own."

"She hasn't got a damned cent," Blake yelled. "And she never did have! I got her out of a New Orleans night club where she was dancing for—."

"I'm not concerned with your wife's *past*, Mr. Terrell. I'm concerned only with her *future*. You see, Mr. Terrell, the state of Texas has a community property law. One half of everything you have acquired since you married belongs to your wife. And you, being the astute business man you are, have acquired a great deal since coming to Borger—including the Beatenbow lease!"

"That's a lie!" Blake's face drained of color. "It's a damned lie. Nothing I own belongs to that bitch, I don't care who says so."

"The *law* says it does, Mr. Terrell," Butler smiled maliciously at Blake.

"She'll get nothing from me," Blake raged. "She left me. I didn't leave her."

"The law is not concerned with the circumstances. The law does not care why she left you, nor where she goes, nor how long she stays. Half of everything you own in Borger is legally hers. I intend to see that she gets it!"

"You—you—" Blake's rage choked him. "So *that's* why you were so interested in that Beatenbow lease being good!"

"Precisely," admitted Butler. Then he added significantly, "In fact, Mr. Terrell, I have been unusually meticulous in caring for your business for the past six months."

"You low down son-of-a-bitch," Blake gritted. "You're a crooked, damned traitor! I'll send Joe Shay after you."

Suddenly the lawyer lost his poise. Anger suffused his usually expressionless face. He stood and thrust his face within inches of Blake's. His black eyes gleamed.

"That's right, Terrell," he said grittingly. "I'm a crook. A *legal* crook. So are you. That's why we understand each other so perfectly. As for Joe Shay—I hope you *do* send him after me. I can think of nothing I would enjoy more than having Terence put a bullet in that damned animal of yours."

"I'll kill you myself!" Blake screamed and reached toward Butler's throat. His hands had almost closed on their mark when he felt the hard metal of a gun barrel ram into his back.

"Terence," Butler said without taking his eyes from Blake's face. "If Mr. Terrell moves one inch closer to me, will you please shoot him."

"Any time you say, Mr. Butler," Terence agreed.

Blake let his hands fall to his sides. Then with a deep breath, he turned and walked toward the door.

"By the way, Mr. Terrell," Butler's taunting tones stopped Blake. "I'll deliver your message to my client in person. I'm leaving for New Orleans myself tomorrow."

Blake stumbled into the night with Butler's mocking laugh ringing in his ears.

Kim left his pickup near the hotel and walked down one side of the long main street. He looked in every business establishment where he thought Blake might possibly be. Many of the buildings were now made of lumber, and there were a few of brick. Borger was beginning to achieve a look of permanence. The boomers said it wouldn't last. That it would fade away when the oil was gone. But that was not true. Kim knew it wasn't. One day people would be proud of this town. There was still plenty of oil and no sign of depletion. Only the wild speculation had slowed, chiefly because leases were rapidly being cornered by the big companies.

But the new Borger lay ahead! Tonight the boom town was coming alive again. For the first time in almost three months canvas covered gambling dens and dance halls were open. Even the notorious *Double-Six*, enclosed only by the high wooden fence, was again doing a booming business. Kim approached the place and listened to the raucous laughter meshing with the charleston and blackbottom tunes.

He paused at the entrance and wished that Deafy Jones were with him. He was almost tempted to pass the place. But Blake was as likely to be there as anywhere else. He went in.

Quickly Kim looked about. He did not see Blake, but the enclosure was big and it was entirely possible that he was there. Kim started making his way through the gambling tables which circled the cleared place in the center that was reserved for dancing. The dancing couples Kim passed over quickly, knowing that Blake would not be among them. They were a nondescript group. The men were dressed in coarse work clothing and the women, with painted faces and deep V dresses, seemed determined to thwart whatever curves and lines nature had given them.

Wendy could never have achieved such an effect, even if she tried! Kim thought proudly. She was much too luxuriously endowed.

But enough of that! He had to find Blake Terrell. Kim was fervently hoping that Joe Shay would not be with him. What if he were! Kim had lost his fear of Joe, but since he had learned that Joe was Blake's illegitimate son, and by biological circumstance, Wendy's half-brother, Kim had resolved not to fight him, if it were possible to avoid it. If they fought, Kim knew, somebody would almost surely be killed. It was not a pleasant thought.

Kim breathed a sigh of relief when he left the *Double-Six*. If he could not find Blake, his conscience would be clear. Blake might be in Amarillo, for all he knew!

Just as he was harboring that comforting thought, he saw Blake striding down the street. He was a block away, but the big shoulders and the arrogant carriage of white Stetson was unmistakable. Even at that distance Kim could read anger in his bearing.

Kim steeled himself. This job of telling Blake that he was going to marry Wendy was a fearsome one at best. With Blake in the mood he was in tonight, it was terrifying. But Kim strode after him.

Blake was peering into every building he passed. Obviously he was searching for someone. When he came abreast of the *Whitespot* cafe, he stopped. Kim was not more than thirty feet away but Blake did not see him. He entered the cafe. Kim followed.

The cafe was filled with men. Two Rangers sat on stools at the counter. Blake was making his way toward the rear.

Then Kim saw the object of Blake's search. Joe Shay was sitting alone at one of the tables and Blake was making his way toward him. Joe was happily harassing the sad-faced negro waiter. Obviously, Joe was very drunk and he had a bottle of whiskey in front of him.

Kim looked questioningly at the Rangers. They were paying no attention to Joe. Their job in Borger was done. The governor had ordered them out. Tomorrow they would be leaving.

The Rangers knew that the town would erupt like a volcano as soon as they were gone. In the meantime, they were not going to concern themselves with a drunken oil field ruffian. They concentrated on their food.

Kim returned his attention to Blake who walked within a few feet of Joe's table and stopped to watch as Joe berated the hapless negro. The waiter wiped coffee and whiskey from Joe's table with a soggy rag.

"Nigger," said Joe evilly, "I'm giving you just five minutes to bring me my bacon and eggs, and if you ain't back by then—" Joe reached into his pocket and pulled out his big knife. He snapped open the switch blade and waved it menacingly at the frightened Negro.

"Yes suh!" the poor Negro answered hurriedly. "Yes suh! I sho will bring you food in a hurry."

The Negro turned quickly to leave. As he did, Joe stuck out a big foot and tripped him. He fell on his face.

Joe laughed uproariously. It was a fiendish sound. He was joined by other men in the cafe who laughed and shouted their approval of Joe's action. They were enjoying the plight of the hapless Negro. The Rangers did not even look toward Joe.

Blake stood for a moment looking down at the Negro who was getting back to his feet.

"Just bring him coffee, waiter," Blake said. "Black and strong. A pot full." Blake's voice cut through the din in the room.

A silence followed Blake's order. Joe Shay and the Negro looked at Blake Terrell, as did every other man in the room.

"Yassuh!" There was obvious relief in the Negro's voice as he scampered away. He was grateful that Joe's attention had been diverted from him.

"Well, well," sneered Joe as he looked at Blake. "If it ain't Blake Terrell! Set down, Blake, and have a drink."

Joe was obviously angry at Blake for having interrupted his fun. He was just as obviously drunk; otherwise, he would never have called Blake by his first name."

"I don't want a drink, Joe," Blake said. And then he added in an authoritative tone, "Neither do you. We have work to do tonight."

"Oh, no, Blake," Joe said drunkenly. "You're wrong. I do want a drink. I want a lot of drinks. Besides, you give me the day off—remember?"

Joe leered at Blake and lifted the bottle to his lips. Blake stepped forward and grabbed the bottle.

"What the hell?" Joe yelled in anger and surprise.

"I said you don't want a drink, Joe," Blake said levelly. There were subdued laughs from the men in the cafe.

"And I say I do!" Joe shouted. "I'm not a damned kid anymore, Terrell. And I'm not working for you tonight!"

"You're not a tool dresser now either, Joe," Blake said significantly. "But you're working for me tonight—or you're not working for me at all."

It took a moment for the meaning of Blake's words to penetrate Joe's alcohol-fogged brain. When he understood, his eyes filled with fury. Blake wasn't bluffing, Joe knew, and he hated Blake Terrell's guts. He would kill the bastard one day. But he couldn't afford to do it now. He had no desire to become a tool dresser again. He liked the easy living that went with working for Blake.

With an effort, Joe controlled his anger. His day would come!

"All right, Mr. Terrell," he said sullenly. "What's the job?"

"That's better, Joe," Blake approved and pulled a chair back and sat across from Joe. "We're going to call on my lawyer."

"That son-of-a-bitch!" Joe spat. Then he shouted, "Where's that damned nigger? I want some coffee."

Blake's eyes reflected his approval of Joe's opinion of the lawyer. Then he looked at the Negro waiter who was standing by the counter holding a pot of coffee and two cups. The soppy rag that he used for mopping tables was thrown across his shoulders. He had been waiting for the exchange between Joe and Blake to cease.

"Bring Joe's coffee," Blake snapped his fingers.

"Yassuh!" The negro hurried toward the table and set the pot of coffee between the two men. Then he reached over to place a cup in front of Joe. In doing so, he knocked over the whiskey bottle, and its contents poured into Joe's lap.

"You black bastard!" Joe snarled as he vented the pent up fury that Blake had created on the hapless negro. "I ought to cut your throat."

Joe grabbed his big knife that was still lying on the table and swiped it at the terrified negro. The man squealed and jumped backward. With an instinctive gesture to defend himself, he pulled the sopping rag from his shoulder and flung it at Joe.

The wet rag flattened as it sailed through the air. It hit Joe full in the face, blinding him for a second. He jerked the rag from his face to expose eyes filled with maniacal anger. With an animal-like yell he flung himself at the Negro.

The Negro was half-way to the door when Joe caught him. The knife flashed and the Negro screamed. Both men fell to the floor.

Kim Wingate, still standing just inside the door, sprang to pull Joe away. But he was too late. Someone was ahead of him. One of the Rangers who had been seated at the counter grabbed Joe's arm to pull him off the fallen Negro.

"Get out of my way!" Joe panted, flinging the Ranger aside. He didn't even look at the man who had interfered. His eyes, filled with hatred and viciousness, had never left the Negro.

"Let up, mister," the Ranger said grimly as he stepped between Joe and his victim. "You just stabbed a man."

"I'm going to kill the black bastard!" Joe yelled and veered around the Ranger toward the Negro.

The Ranger was obviously no match for Joe's strength, and he knew it. In a movement almost too quick for the eye to follow, he jerked his gun from its holster and struck Joe on the side of the head.

The blow knocked Joe against the cafe counter, but it did not even stun him. He looked, for the first time, at the man who had interrupted him. Joe started after the man. His black eyes glittered with reptilian malevolence and murderous intent. He did not even recognize the man as a Ranger.

"He's insane!" Kim thought desperately. "Nothing can stop him now."

Like a snake after a bird, Joe advanced toward the Ranger. He was holding his big knife in front of him.

"Don't do it, mister!" the Ranger said tensely.

No expression, save hate, crossed Joe's face. Suddenly, he lunghed. The Ranger stepped back quickly and Kim heard his gun boom.

Joe Shay stopped in mid-stride. Then he seemed to grow smaller as he sank slowly to the floor. He fell almost at the Ranger's feet.

The sound of the gun was followed by a moment of complete silence. Blake Terrell was the first man to move. He ran to Joe and raised his head from the floor. He looked at Joe a second and let his head fall back to the floor. Then he rose to confront the Ranger who had shot him.

"You killed him!" Blake shouted almost in the Ranger's face.

"I sure did, mister," the Ranger said grimly.

"I'll have your hide for this!" Blake screamed in rage. "I know the governor, you murdering son-of-a-bitch! I'll—"

"You'll do nothing, mister!" The other Ranger grabbed Blake's

arm and swung him around. "The sergeant was acting under orders—
Ranger orders. Until noon tomorrow, we are the law in Borger. Just
one more word out of you, and you go on the trotline!"

Blake glared at the Ranger a moment, and suddenly the starch
went out of him. His shoulders slumped, and he turned to kneel
beside Joe again. Blake ran his hand through Joe's long, black hair,
and Kim heard him sob. A part of Blake Terrell had just died.

"Somebody ought to get a doc for that nigger!"

"You'd think Shay was Terrell's brother, the way he's taking on!"

Kim heard the remarks as he stumbled blindly from the cafe and
into the clean, cool air of the night.

CHAPTER XVI

The Methodist minister and his wife lay in their bed talking in the quiet, low tones of companionable people who had done well their day's work. Their year in Borger had been a hard one. But a good one. Bringing the word of God to a lawless town was not a job for the fainthearted. Their church had been stoned, their congregation small, and their ministerial efforts ignored for months.

But there were rewards. Abundant rewards! Things were changing. Gradually, from the merciless, brawling town, there was emerging the hard core of goodness. Congregations were growing, and people recognized the minister on the streets occasionally.

And tomorrow, in their church, there would be a wedding! The first church wedding in Borger. And such a lovely young couple! The minister smiled in the darkness as he listened patiently to his wife talk of how they would decorate the church. The alter would be surrounded by wild flowers and sage, and—.

A heavy knock startled them. They listened in silence a moment. The knock was repeated. The minister rose and donned a robe. The knock came again as he turned on the light in the living room. He made his way to the door, opened it just a crack and peered out into the darkness.

"Who is it?" he asked cautiously.

"My name is Blake Terrell." The voice was gruff.

"Oh, yes, Mr. Terrell," he opened the door. "Come in."

The minister noted with approval the big bulk, the distinguished features and authoritative air of Blake Terrell. He was indeed a handsome man. It was the first time the minister had ever seen Blake, though Wendy had long been one of the faithful of his congregation.

"Was there something about the wedding, Mr. Terrell?" he asked courteously.

"About a funeral," Blake said, looking directly at the minister for the first time.

"Oh!" There was a slight pause. "I'm afraid I mistook you for someone else, Mr. Terrell. I'm sorry. I'll be of help if I can."

"You can," Blake said as he took a deep breath. "A—a man got killed tonight. I want to have a funeral for him in a church."

"I see." The minister nodded his head slowly and looked at Blake questioningly. "A relative?"

"He—he worked for me."

"I see," the minister said again. "When was he killed?"

"About two hours ago."

"And when do you plan to have the funeral?"

"Tomorrow!"

"Tomorrow?"

"Yes. Tomorrow."

"But, Mr. Terrell," the minister protested. "I'm afraid that's hardly possible—I mean—"

"That's what churches are for, isn't it?" Blake said harshly.

"It is," agreed the minister. "Among other things. But—"

"I'll pay for the funeral."

"It isn't that, Mr. Terrell," the minister said protestingly. "It's just that I—"

"You what?"

"Well," said the minister almost desperately. "Tomorrow will hardly give you time to notify the man's relatives and friends. And certainly they would not have time to come to the funeral."

"This man didn't have any relatives," Blake said bitterly. "And he didn't have any friends."

For a moment Blake and the minister stood facing each other. It was the minister who finally broke the silence.

"I'm sorry," he said in a compassionate voice. "Of course, I shall conduct the funeral for him. Won't you please have a chair while I get a pencil and paper. I will need some information from you."

Blake made no move toward the chair that the minister indicated. He stood stolidly. He had not removed his hat.

The minister secured a piece of paper and a pencil.

"What was the man's name?"

"Joe Shay."

"At about what time did the accident occur, Mr. Terrell?"

"It wasn't an accident."

"What?" The minister looked up in surprise.

"It wasn't an accident. He was shot."

"Shot?" the minister said in horror. Then his tone became very business-like. "Mr. Terrell, I cannot conduct a funeral for a man who was shot—not until the authorities have investigated and—"

"There will be no investigation," Blake said grimly. "It was the law that killed him."

"Mr-r. Terrell." The minister lost some of his composure. "I'm afraid that I am a bit upset. I-I want to do the thing that should be done. But I'm just not myself at the moment. And, you see—well—the church had been reserved for a wedding tomorrow. I thought that was what you had come to see me about."

"No."

"Mr. Terrell," the minister said abruptly, looking squarely at Blake. "Do you have a daughter?"

"Yes. Why?"

"Is her name Victoria?"

"That's her name. We call her Wendy."

"Do you know a young man named Kimball Wingate?"

"I know him," Blake said sharply. "What are you driving at, preacher?"

"Your daughter is to be married in my church tomorrow, Mr. Terrell," he said calmly. "Didn't you know?"

"I—I—no. I didn't know." Blake reeled as though he had been struck.

"Won't you have a seat, Mr. Terrell," the minister said kindly. "I'll get you a glass of water."

The minister pushed a chair toward Blake. Blake sat in it. He removed his hat and rubbed a big hand over his face. Then he brushed slowly at his moustache with a bent forefinger. He stared at the floor with unseeing eyes for a moment; then his bent forefinger brushed more rapidly at his moustache. He raised his face to the minister, and his eyes were blazing.

"My daughter is not getting married in your church tomorrow, preacher," he said in an impassioned voice. "Because I'm her father —and I won't let her."

"I'm afraid you will have nothing to say about the matter, Mr. Terrell." There was a steely quality in the minister's voice. "Unless Mr. Wingate misrepresented their ages, which I doubt very much, they are both legally of age. It is not necessary for them to have your consent, though I'm sure they would want it."

Blake half rose as the minister spoke. His big hands gripped the arms of the chair, and veins stood out like small ropes across his face. He glared beligerently for a moment. The minister did not move. Suddenly Blake collapsed in the chair as though the strength had left his body.

For more than a minute, the two men sat in complete silence. Outside a puff of wind pushed, and the house creaked. Finally, Blake looked at the minister again. There was agony in his eyes, and the heart of the man of God went out to him.

"What—what time did they plan to have their wedding?" Blake asked haltingly.

"At three tomorrow afternoon. They want to catch the four o'clock train."

Blake nodded his head and sat for another moment in silence.

"If—if we had the funeral at sunup," he asked haltingly, "Do you think that it would interfere with their wedding?"

"I'm sure it wouldn't." The minister's voice was gentle. "The women would have plenty of time to decorate the church."

"All right, then," Blake said. "You be at the church at sunup. I'll pay you well."

"That won't be necessary, Mr. Terrell."

Blake pulled his hat on his head and walked slowly to the door. His hand was on the knob when he half turned again.

"About the wedding, preacher—?" he asked haltingly. "It'll be a nice one, won't it?"

"The nicest Borger has ever seen," the minister smiled faintly. "Your daughter is a lovely person, and she is marrying a fine young man."

"I mean—" Blake was groping. "There will be flowers and every-thing, won't there?"

"The women of the church are going to decorate."

"Preacher," Blake turned full to the minister, "Would you do something for me?"

"Yes. If I can."

Blake pulled a big roll of bills from his pocket. He made no pretense of counting them, but held them out to the minister.

"Would you buy the flowers for my daughter's wedding for me?"

The minister looked at Blake questioningly, then flicked through the roll of bills. He gasped in astonishment at the denominations.

"But, Mr. Terrell," he protested, "this is enough money to fill the church with flowers."

"Then fill it! Use what is left over for anything you want. Just don't let anyone know I bought them."

"You don't want your *daughter* to know you sent flowers?" The minister's eyes were puzzled and troubled.

"No."

"But, why—?"

"Never mind why!" Blake said grimly. "Will you do it?"

"All right, Mr. Terrell," the minister said. "I'll have to send a car to Amarillo for them."

"There is enough money there to hire a car."

"More than enough, Mr. Terrell," the minister said quietly. "Would you like for me to get flowers for the funeral too?"

Blake's face turned pasty.

"No!" he said hoarsely. "And don't put any of those flowers in that church tomorrow until we are through with the funeral."

The minister quickly agreed. He was afraid Blake was going to be sick. "I will take care of everything," he said. "And tomorrow you will see your daughter married in the most beautiful church in the world!"

"I won't see her," Blake said in a cracked voice. "I won't even be there."

"But, of course you will," the minister said. "You have to give the bride away."

"I guess I gave her away a long time ago, preacher," Blake's voice trembled. He walked hurriedly from the house.

The clang of metal on metal traveled loud and clear on the summer air as dawn broke behind a dark bank of clouds in the east. The wind, like a capricious colt, skittered about, kicking up puffs of dust, as though trying to decide whether to break for a long, hard run, or to scamper about for a while and then settle down to a lazy day.

In the church, the minister waited apprehensively. He turned the lights on, and then turned them off again. It seemed that the church was not bright either way. He wished there were some flowers.

He was pacing nervously when he heard a car approaching. He went to the door and saw the black hearse coming up to the church. Two cars followed it. He watched as the hearse made a wide turn and backed up to the door. Two men got out. The minister looked vainly for the others. There were none.

"I don't know how we are going to get him inside," one of the men said. "He'll weigh two hundred pounds without the casket, and we've got to lift him up them steps."

The minister looked about desperately. Blake Terrell was in the car immediately behind the hearse. He was alone. In the other car sat two men and a woman. The men got out of the car and came forward. One was Kim Wingate. The minister did not know the other. He had only one eye.

"We'll help," the older man said.

"Thank you," the minister said gratefully. "If you will, I think we can manage."

With much effort, they were able to get the casket up the steps and into the narrow door. The undertakers rolled it down the aisle.

The minister looked at his audience. Blake Terrell sat on the front seat. He looked at no one. His face was white and drawn. On the seat behind Blake, sat young Wingate, the one-eyed man, and the woman.

The minister read the 23rd Psalm and from a compassionate heart brought forth words that he prayed were adequate. Never in his career as a minister had he found himself in a situation so perplexing and so frustrating. He felt that something sinister was present in his church. His eyes were drawn again and again, without his will, to the closed casket in front of him.

Fifteen minutes later, the minister stood in front of his church, panting from the exertion of lifting the casket down the steps and back into the hearse. He saw the one-eyed man walk, stiff backed, to his car without either speaking or looking at Blake Terrell. The woman followed him. Then young Kim Wingate walked up to Blake. The minister could not hear what was said, but he saw Blake nod his head slowly in the affirmative. Then Kim joined his companions.

The hearse drove away toward the cemetery. The two cars drove back toward town.

The minister shook his head and took a deep breath. Then he looked about his church. And he smiled. Today was the wedding! The sun had come from behind the cloud bank, and the church was brighter now. The minister opened both side doors. The fresh prairie breeze blew in.

By noon the sun was shining brightly, and the clouds had disappeared. The wind shifted from southwest to east and brought the clean, washed breezes from the rains dropped by the clouds.

People began arriving early at the church. There were exclamations of delight and surprise as they looked, with eyes that were hungry for beauty, at the flower bedecked church. There were subdued whispers and conversations that precede a solemn and happy occasion.

The Beatenbow family filled the entire front row. Mandy sat beside her brother Ed and his wife. Far back in the church, shrinking as if it would make her inconspicuous, was Sal. At three o'clock, there was the hushed expectancy preceding the appearance of the bride and groom.

At a given signal from the minister, the small choir burst forth in song. When the song ended, Kim Wingate and Deafy Jones emerged from a small waiting room and stood before the minister. Kim was pale. Deafy was dressed in his blue serge, and his shirt collar somehow had managed almost to obscure his tie.

Mendelssohn's ' Wedding March" clanked from the piano. No one

knew, or cared, that it was badly out of tune. The minister breathed
a silent prayer of thanksgiving as he listened to the most beautiful
music he had ever heard.

Every head turned to the door, and a sigh wafted through the
church as Wendy, in flowing white dress and veil, walked proudly as
a queen, down the aisle. She was leaning on the arm of Blake Terrell.

Kim looked at Wendy and gulped. It seemed an age before she
stood beside him.

The ceremony was short and simple. Kim's heart pounded inside
him. When the minister asked who gave the bride away, Kim held his
breath.

But there was no hesitation in Blake's voice, and Wendy flashed
him a grateful look. Deafy grinned happily, and Mandy's soft eyes
misted. Sal blew loudly in her handkerchief.

Immediately after the ceremony, Wendy and Kim left for the
Terrell house. They barely had time for Wendy to change to her
travelling dress before the train departed.

Almost all who had attended the wedding were waiting when they
arrived at the depot. Someone had managed old shoes and rice.
Wendy was radiant, and her happy laugh sounded like a rippling
stream as the rice fell on her. Kim grinned self-consciously.

All interest was focused on Kim and Wendy. No one noticed the
small band of Rangers who were quietly and efficiently loading their
gear on the same train. They were leaving as inconspicuously as they
had come.

The train gave a short whistle. The crowd shouted and talked
excitedly, and Wendy looked about almost frantically until she spied
her father. He was standing alone, and a bit apart from the crowd.
Wendy made her way to him. Kim followed.

Wendy threw her arms around Blake who bent and hugged his
daughter to him, and his white Stetson fell to the ground.

"Thank you, Father," she said tremulously. "Thank you for
helping to make this the happiest day of my life."

"I had nothing to do with it," Blake said gruffly.

"Wish me happiness, Father!" Wendy pleaded. "Make it perfect!"

Blake's face was hidden in Wendy's hair as he held her to him. His
eyes shut tight and he swallowed hard.

"I want your happiness more than anything in the world,
daughter." His voice was husky.

"Thank you, Father," Wendy said rapturously. "Thank you with
all my heart."

Blake pushed Wendy away and held her at arm's length. Then he
turned to Kim.

"You make her happy, Wingate," Blake said fiercely, "or I'll have your hide."

"I'll make her happy," Kim said eagerly and grasped Blake's hand. "I'll make her happy as a woman can be!"

The train whistled again, and Wendy reached up to kiss Blake. Her eyes twinkled as she whispered in his ear.

"The flowers were lovely, Dad," she said. Then she grabbed Kim's hand and they ran for the train.

Blake's face showed his surprise as he looked after his daughter and her husband hurrying to the train.

"Can't even trust a preacher!" he grumbled to himself. "He said he wouldn't tell her." But there was no rancor in his words.

Kim and Wendy stood on the rear platform and waved happily as the train pulled away. Deafy Jones wiped surreptitiously at his good eye with a coat sleeve.

Two minutes later the crowd had dispersed. The Beatenbows gathered in a small family group to talk. Mandy and Deafy joined them. Blake stood alone watching the train in the distance.

Suddenly, Blake straightened his shoulders and turned from the depot. His white Stetson was still lying in the dust and he picked it up and slapped it against his leg a couple of times. Then he set it firmly on his head. He looked toward the Beatenbow family, and Deafy Jones.

"Deafy!" Blake's loud, harsh voice was easily heard. "I want to see you a minute."

Deafy looked at Blake, and disappointment clouded his good eye. Deafy had heard that tone too many times not to know that Blake was ready for action. But the disappointment in Deafy gave way to grim acceptance. He had never in his life backed away from any man—and he wouldn't start now. Blake was standing perhaps forty feet away. Deafy started toward him, walking stiff backed. Blake met him half way.

"Deafy," Blake said gruffly as they met. "I never had much use for fancy language—so I never learned how to use it. What I got to say will have to be plain talk."

"Say what you got to say, Blake," Deafy's eye blazed and he spat on the ground. "I reckon I can understand it."

"I've been wrong." Blake's voice was bitter and harsh. "I've been a damn fool—and as wrong as a man *can* be. I—I'm sorry!"

It took a moment for the import of Blake's words to penetrate Deafy's brain. Then they did—and the blaze in his good eye gave way to a look of incredulity, and finally sheer joy. The hard lines of the weatherbeaten old face softened, and his shoulders straightened. He looked twenty years younger.

"Hell, Blake," he said gently, "men fall out once in a while—
especially in the oil fields. Ain't nothing to worry about."

"I'd like to make it up to Wendy," Blake said; his voice was
gentler now. "And you, too, Deafy—if you'll let me."

Deafy started to speak and then checked himself. He spat on the
ground.

"Thanks just the same, Blake," he shook his head. "But you don't
owe me nothing. Besides, I reckon I got everything I ever wanted."

Blake nodded his head. They stood for a moment in the embarrassed silence.

"Tell you what, Blake," Deafy finally said.

"What?" Blake asked eagerly.

"Well—I'd like to shake with you, Blake," Deafy thrust out his
calloused hand.

Blake grasped it quickly and the tensions and hatreds of the years
melted away.

"Well, Deafy," Blake said with some of the old ring in his voice, "I
guess I'd better be going. I've got just nine days left to spud in on the
Beatenbow and—."

Just then, as if heralding the departure of the Rangers, a shot rang
out on main street. It was followed quickly by another, and then the
scream of a man in pain. Mandy hurried over and took Deafy's arm.
They all looked for a moment in the direction from which the shots
had come.

"As I was saying, Deafy," Blake resumed the conversation. "I
guess I'd better be going. With the Rangers gone, Borger is going to
be a hell camp again—and I've got to move rigs and crews to the
Beatenbow."

"Crews won't be easy to get in Borger now, Blake," Deafy said.
"The lid is off—with them Rangers gone."

"I know," Blake agreed. "But I'll find 'em." He turned and walked
purposefully to his car.

"He'll do it, too!" Deafy said almost in a whisper. "If he has to
shanghai men and spud in with a post hole digger—he'll do it! But it's
going to be a hell of a job—and he ain't got the help he did have!"

Mandy looked at Deafy's face as he stared after Blake's car. In her
eyes were sympathy and understanding thatonly very wise and very
good women ever know.

"Wouldn't you like to help him, Deafy?" she asked gently.

Deafy started. He looked away a moment and then back to
Mandy.

"I ain't got much sense, Mandy," Deafy admitted ruefully. "I
reckon I would."

Mandy squeezed his arm. "I'll ride home with Ed," she said softly. "Will you be home for supper?"

"I sure will, Mandy," Deafy grinned happily. "And maybe you better set an extra plate—just in case Blake comes with me!"

Mandy's dark eyes twinkled as she watched Deafy's Model-T bounce after Blake's Stutz.